WAYWARD
SON

Walt Disney Pictures
"Morning Light"

A 2008 film based on an
original idea by Thomas J. Pollack

WAYWARD
SON

TOM POLLACK
WITH JIM ALVES AND JOHN LOFTUS

Cascada Productions, 2901 West Coast Highway, Suite 200
Newport Beach, CA 92663 • info@waywardsonnovel.com

For my loving father,
Thomas C. Pollack,
who passed away in 2010.

Acknowledgments

We extend our recognition and sincere thanks to the dear people in our loyal "reader posse," numbering nearly one hundred, who devoured the various versions of the manuscript and offered their thoughtful suggestions for creating a better novel. Their names are listed below. Jim Madden—you win the patience award for the most reads!

Also, we wish to thank Don Jacobson and Jason Myhre of D. C. Jacobson & Associates for their encouragement and expert guidance as we took the decision to launch Cascada Productions and publish this novel ourselves.

We also owe a huge debt of gratitude to our talented editors, David Jacobsen and Steffany Woolsey.

And of course, we honor our lovely wives, Jennifer Pollack, Jackie Alves, and Lori Loftus for their encouragement and support. We simply don't know how you put up with the three of us as we forsook your company for one another's during this endeavor. We promise you some wonderful vacations before we try anything like this again!

Tom, in particular, has some additional thanks to express.

Muchas gracias to H. M. Juan Carlos, the King of Spain, for inviting me to Europe in 2004, where we collaborated in helping to establish a professional grand prix sailboat racing circuit called the Audi Medcup. This venture allowed me to spend free time near ancient ruins in Rome, Herculaneum, Athens, and other exotic locations, where the core ideas for this novel germinated and were then researched.

Thank you, Betty Pollack, my amazing and loving mother, for encouraging me to travel the world in search of adventure. I found it!

To my buddy Jim Demetraides, with whom I spent enormous amounts of "spare" time at Loyola Marymount engaging in strategy/role-playing games and creating fascinating characters.

My eternal love and respect for Jennifer and our fabulous children, Lance and Fallon, for patiently listening to me think out loud about the novel in the car, at home, on vacation, etc., etc.

And finally, my dear friend Roy Disney, a terrific, down-to-earth guy who loved his *New York Times* crossword puzzles and taught me more than a few lessons about storytelling later in life. I miss you.

THE READER POSSE:

Adam Alves	Eric Grasmeyer	Ross Pake
Michael Alves	Jim Grasmeyer	Tony Petruzzi
Michael Badran	John Grasmeyer	Betty Pollack
Michael Baynes	Ken Grasmeyer	Dave Pollack
Edward Bonlarron	Jenny Green	Debra Pollack
Jamie Bott	Steven Hornyak	Fallon Pollack
Kari Bretschger	Richard Jacobsen	Kate Pollack
Jim Burke	Andrew Johnson	Lance Pollack
Brenda Clauss	Terry Kerr	Lisa Pollack
Peter Clayton	Paul Kim	Sam Pollack
James Cocara	Marjorie Koss	Steve Pollack
Lynn Coleman	Becky LaForge	Thomas C. Pollack
Carol Dalton	Pastor Pete Lasutschinkow	Fr. Michael Pontarelli
Cornell Dascalu	Peggy Lobdell	Jan Potter
Margaret Dascalu	Jason Loftus	Keri Jo Raz
Kim Delaney	Lori Loftus	Kent Riley
Jim Demetriades	Heather Madden	Marisa Rudder
Nancy Demetriades	Jim Madden	Ann Scanzaroli
Janet Demetriou	Patsy Marshall	James Scanzaroli
Pete Demetriou	Albert Mason	Peter Smrechek
Linda Dillon	Fran Messenger	Val Smrechek
Erin Doe	Helene Mochedlover	Kendall Souza
Warren Duffy	Gina Moish	Laura Steil
Mark Eisele	Betty Mulford	Tim Timmons, Sr.
Catherine Faddis	Dave Mulford	Judith Toor
Debbie Farquhar	George Munz	Dr. Jean Traux
William Fecia	Erin Nagle	Ed Underwood
Erich Friedman	Rob Nagle	Susan Valera
Kari Garrett	Anne Najar	Jerry Walker
Tom Garrett	Richard Najar	Alex Wasilewski
Ken Giacommuzzi	Mike Nash	Jim West
Danni Good	Kristin Orloff	Clarence Yoshikane

"Choose this day whom you will serve..."

JOSHUA 24:15, NLT

North Shore, Oahu, Hawaii

Amanda knew this was the moment of decision.

Hurtling down the steep curl of the biggest wave yet, she trailed her hand along its glassy face to slow her descent and stay slotted inside the iridescent green tube. She'd never been in the barrel this long before, and her instincts were to kick out, but the rush was incredible. Maybe just a little longer…

This morning's waves at the Banzai Pipeline were beyond belief. Gorgeously shaped double overheads broke some two hundred yards farther out than normal. She'd already ridden several monsters that barreled and re-formed two or three times.

Now, as she savored the precarious balance between gravity and speed, Amanda heard the faint, rhythmic sound of gongs pealing from the shore.

"Bells?" she thought. "That old church is miles from here."

The distraction proved costly.

Her board slid upward, and the wave pitched her over the falls, slamming down on her with a thunderous roar and plunging her under the water. Amanda was caught in a powerful washing-machine surge that left her with no sense of up or down.

She knew from experience to stay calm and wait it out, but the undercurrent was relentless, seemingly eternal. Even worse, she felt a wrenching tug on her ankle as her tether snagged in the coral beneath. Amanda began to struggle, but the Pacific was too powerful an adversary.

Then the bells sounded once again.

CHAPTER 1

Malibu, California

Rolling over onto her side, she opened her eyes, reached to the night-stand, and fumbled for her iPhone. The insistent bell tower ringtone indicated an unknown caller, and the display read Blocked. Breathing a deep sigh of relief, she drowsily answered the phone and brought it to her ear. Who could be calling at 4:07 in the morning?

"Amanda?" The voice was tentative, yet startlingly familiar.

"Juan Carlos!" She blinked hard and shook her head slightly.

"Did I wake you up?"

"Actually, I'm glad you did. Are you in LA?"

"No, I'm in Ercolano helping with the new excavations."

"You're in Italy? What about Real Madrid?"

"Oh, soccer is history now. I tore up my knee last season and had to quit. I moved here in the fall. I've been here almost a year now. My grandfather Silvio got me the job."

"So you're back to archaeology." From their days in college together at UCLA, Amanda knew it was his first love. She pictured Juan Carlos in Erco-lano—ancient Herculaneum, the Roman resort town on the Bay of Naples in the shadow of Mt. Vesuvius. The volcano's catastrophic eruption had buried the town, together with neighboring Pompeii, in the first century AD. It was an archaeologist's dream.

His voice pulled her back. "Yes, yes, but we can catch up on all that later. I'm sorry to call you so early, but it's really urgent that we talk about the *nuovi scavi*."

"*Digame*, Johnny." Spanish to his Italian, accompanied by the pet name only she was allowed to use.

"You read about the earthquake last month?"

"Everyone did. It was so weird. August 24. The exact anniversary of Vesuvius in 79 AD."

"Right! Well, our team is exploring a site near the Villa dei Papiri. Up to now, no one rated it as very interesting. But the earthquake opened up a narrow crack in a wall of rock, only half a meter wide at its entrance but very deep. We sent in a robot with a fiber-optic camera, but even its path was partially blocked by fallen rocks."

"And...?" The romance of archaeology was one of the links that had brought them together.

"*And* we have distant pictures of a half-obscured bronze door—perhaps the entrance to a large underground chamber. But it's what's inscribed *on* the door that's amazing. Latin and Greek, of course. But we can also make out Aramaic, Hebrew, and Chinese!"

Amanda nearly dropped her phone. "Aramaic? Chinese?"

"*Incredibile, ma vero*. You must see the pictures. I would e-mail a few, but this find is highly confidential at the moment. But that's not really why I'm calling. No one here has the language skills to handle this. Plus we need someone with field experience and a slim figure who can navigate the long crevice. I want you to come to Italy..."

"But Johnny, I can't just pick up and leave my job for—"

"Amanda," Juan Carlos cut in with an urgent tone, "Silvio has reason to believe that this could be bigger than the Dead Sea Scrolls. Maybe even than the Rosetta Stone. We need you. You can fit through that crack easily, brush away the dust, and decipher the rest of the words. If we can get the door open, no one is as qualified as you to make a survey of the chamber. And time is of the essence!"

"How do you think I'll get permission from the Getty so fast?" Ever since her graduation from UCLA, the Getty had supported Amanda's PhD in papyrology. Now she was full time on the staff of the Getty Museum's Villa location in Malibu.

"No problem. Silvio spoke to Dr. Walker late yesterday. Arrangements are being made. You know that the Getty and Silvio's employer are partners with the Italian authorities. I guarantee that Walker will let you come over. I think they may even pay for your airline ticket."

Amanda wavered. She couldn't just leave everything and jet over to Italy, could she? But what if it was bigger than the Rosetta Stone? Juan Carlos had always had a level head. And Silvio, his grandfather, was a world-renowned archaeologist, the head of the Museo Archeologico Nazionale for the past thirty years.

"When would I come?"

"Immediately. We don't know how long we can keep the discovery under wraps. I already looked at flight schedules and..."

"Are you talking about today?"

"Absolutely. You can catch a British Airways flight from LAX tonight at 11:00. You'll be at Fiumicino Airport in Rome tomorrow night at 11:30 our time. I'll meet you there outside the baggage claim and we'll drive a few hours to Ercolano."

Amanda smiled. "You seem to have thought of everything. But I still have to talk to Walker. And I'll need to make arrangements for Plato." She looked down to the foot of the bed where her seal point Siamese lay curled up like a question mark.

"Plato? Who's Plato?"

Was that jealousy in his voice? "Only the cat I got last year at the shelter."

"Oh, of course. Can you call me back later today?"

"Right after I see Walker. What time is it there now?"

"Lunchtime. Just after one o'clock."

"I'll call you before you eat dinner."

"It'll be great to see you again."

Amanda paused. "Before dinner, then. And Johnny, one last question."

"Yes?"

"How did you find my cell number?"

"*O chica mia*, I never lost it. Ciao."

As the line went dead, she could hear him smile.

❧

Amanda slid her custom surfboard into the back of her Jeep. The yellow Wrangler had been a twenty-first birthday present from her dad, and although it was now seven years old, she couldn't think of parting with it. The Jeep symbolized the special bond between Amanda and her father, forged after her mom's early death from cancer. For almost ten years he had been her only parent. Then, at the end of her senior year at UCLA, he died tragically. A product engineer for Pacific Oil & Gas and an ex-Marine, he had tried to save a group of trapped workers in a refinery fire in Nigeria. He saved them all, but paid with his life.

Since Roger James's death, his only child had found solace in the ocean. Although bothered since her early teens by an occasional bad dream that, like this morning's, usually involved drowning, Amanda was not one to give fear any reign in her life. As for many surfers, the waves helped to keep her centered. Amanda surfed in the early morning near the Getty Villa in Malibu whenever conditions were right. She had met some good buddies, but it was the sport's solitude that appealed to her above all else—that and the moment of release that came with carving the face of the perfect wave.

Amanda knew from yesterday's wave report that an offshore Santa Ana wind would combine with swells from a storm off the coast of Mexico to produce impressive waves on California's south-facing beaches. And after the phone call from Juan Carlos Bribon, she needed some time to mull things over. Amanda did some of her best thinking on her board. At 5:15, as the morning light was barely a glimmer, she cruised through the residential streets of Malibu and picked up the main artery, the Pacific Coast Highway—PCH in local lingo—and headed north to Point Dume.

Amanda's favorite break lay at the base of hundred-foot-tall sandstone cliffs that offered some of the most stunning ocean vistas in southern California. The mansions at Point Dume were the trophies of business tycoons rather than Hollywood stars. Amanda, who had lived all over the world because of her father's job assignments, sometimes amused herself by conjuring up comparisons to Point Dume. There was Acapulco in Mexico, of course, with its countless red-tiled haciendas overlooking the azure waters of the Pacific; and Ercolano, playground for the elite of the early Roman Empire. The estates of Cap d'Antibes in the south of France were similar, as was Victoria Harbor as seen from the Peak in Hong Kong—anywhere that human materialism clung to natural beauty like a barnacle.

As was typical in September, mist shrouded the coastline when Amanda parked her jeep on an inconspicuous turnoff on PCH. Jogging across the highway with her board under her arm, she followed a nearly hidden path between two large properties. In a dark wetsuit, her figure was barely noticeable in the half-light.

It had taken her months of trial and error to find the narrow path. The estates on each side were lavishly, and almost impenetrably, landscaped with sprawling, ground-level bougainvillea and tall hedges of gorse, with its distinctive fragrance of vanilla and almond. Using thorns and spines—albeit tastefully—the wealthy owners had made every effort to choke off access to the ocean in order to maintain their precious privacy. Amanda smiled slightly as she threaded her way between the bushes. "Surfers are sometimes more resourceful than billionaires," she thought wryly. The public still owned everything below the mean high-water mark, at least according to the California Coastal Commission.

Reaching the cliff's edge, Amanda carefully negotiated the steep steps that led to the beach. Even in the semidarkness, she could see that the text message from SoCal Surfwatch had been right on. The swells stretched in perfect lines that reached to the horizon. Long, slow curls punctuated the break in even sets, shoulder high for the most part with a few overheads.

As she attached her leash just above the small, ancient scroll tattooed on the inside of her right ankle, Amanda noted with satisfaction that she was in sole possession of the break. Taking a deep breath and clearing her mind, she positioned her five-foot-ten frame along the center of her board and began to paddle out. In half an hour, the sun would be up.

She paddled and caught, paddled and thought. It was a biorhythm by now. As she listened to the surf, the colors diffused through the thinning mist. "Why is this dawn special?" she wondered. Somehow one telephone call had lifted a weight from her shoulders. A longer interval between sets arrived and, with characteristic discipline, she made a mental inventory.

On the one hand, Juan Carlos had made an offer that was hard to refuse. Her job had begun to weigh on her. Dr. Walker never really criticized her, but neither did he seem likely to promote her. Exploring a major find in the nuovi scavi ruins might have a professional payoff. She had been to Ercolano a few times before, when she worked on papyri for the Philodemus Project for her PhD at UCLA. The Bay of Naples wasn't hard to look at, even after Point Dume!

But there were questions in her mind, most of them about Juan Carlos. Was he aiming to rekindle the romance they had shared as undergraduates? Did she want him to? He had been her lifeguard when her dad died—a save that neither of them would ever forget. She'd been on the floor in her bathroom, with several Vicodin in her stomach and a fifth of vodka clutched in her hand. She vaguely recalled a breakneck ride to Cedars-Sinai Hospital, where they pumped her stomach. Although her religious life had seen its ups and downs, Amanda thought she had found a guardian angel. But how did that square with their drifting apart after graduation?

They had met eight years earlier, as juniors at UCLA, after he scored the winning goal in the conference championship game. The memory of Juan Carlos throwing his jersey in the air, displaying his impeccably chiseled torso to thousands of cheering fans, was etched in Amanda's brain. She almost blushed while waiting for the next set of swells to form.

"What would Dad want me to do?" She was pretty sure of the answer. An ex-Marine, Roger James had always aimed for the jugular. Though not a classicist like his daughter, he would often quote the Roman poet Horace's maxim, Carpe diem! By urging Amanda to "seize the day," Roger let her know that, in his mind, anything was possible for a young woman growing into the twenty-first century.

Now the sun was up. Bits of mist still clung to the coastline in a golden halo shimmering around the palaces of Point Dume. As she rode her final wave, Amanda's gaze fell on the largest mansion. This was, in fact, one of the properties bisected by the border path that led to the beach.

It had been completed only recently. From a segment on *Entertainment Tonight*, she'd learned that it belonged to Luc Renard, a tabloid billionaire with business interests around the globe. The property was about fifty acres, and the main house—as distinguished from numerous outbuildings—dwarfed all of the neighboring mansions. Renard had christened it with a distinctive name: Villa Colosseum.

"How odd," thought Amanda absently. The Roman Colosseum was an arena of blood sports and death, so why would anyone name his house that way? But that thought drifted from her mind as her board glided lazily through the shore wash. It was time to go back to the apartment and get ready for work.

After jogging across the short stretch of beach with her board and climbing toward the path, Amanda recalled a tabloid story she had seen about an all-night party at Villa Colosseum. She found herself thinking about the mansion again. What did such a place look like on the inside? she wondered. Who made it onto the invitation list, and how?

Soon Amanda had forgotten all about Renard's villa as she warmed up inside the Wrangler. The upbeat, mellow sounds of Jack Johnson's acoustic guitar rang from her speakers, the perfect accompaniment to the brightening day. By seven thirty, she was back in the apartment, smiling at Plato's usual noisy greeting at the door.

"I really have to hustle," she thought. She realized that the surf session had done its work—she had already made an unconscious decision.

She would go to Ercolano. But Juan Carlos wanted her on a flight from LAX tonight. She stepped into the shower, grabbed a razor, and tried to shampoo her hair and shave her long, well-muscled legs in record time. While the steamy water engulfed her body, she wondered what Juan Carlos would think about her newly toned shape. When they dated in college, she had not yet taken up surfing.

Amanda lived in a small one-bedroom apartment—all she could afford in the high-rent district of Malibu—but at least it had decent closet space. How long would her trip last? Since there was no way of knowing, she decided to play the odds and pack outfits that could be recycled every three or four days. Within twenty minutes, she'd slotted a basic wardrobe into her mother's well-worn Louis Vuitton waterproof canvas. It held not only Amanda's clothing, but also the memories from their many travels together during her childhood.

On an impulse, she grabbed her copy of *The Town of Hercules* for the fifteen-hour flight and stuffed it, along with a *New York Times* Saturday crossword puzzle collection, into her backpack, which she would use as a carry-on.

Now to arrange for Plato. They had never been separated, and she worried a bit about how he would adjust. There was no way she would put him in a kennel. It was way too expensive, and besides, there wasn't time to find one.

Amanda called Laura Mendez, her sorority sister and billiards club buddy. The two of them played in tournaments together. Besides surfing, billiards was Amanda's favorite pastime. Laura ran a grooming center for dogs in Pacific Palisades.

"Hello, Laura? I hope I'm not waking you up. It's Amanda."

"Of course I know who it is. You forget caller ID?"

"Yeah, well, I just wanted to know if you could take care of Plato for a week or two."

"You going away? Eloping, perhaps?" Laura secretly hoped that her friend would find Mr. Right and ease up on the twelve-hour workdays.

"I have an offer to take a look at some excavations in Italy. I'm going to try to leave tonight."

"*Buenas vacaciones.* Don't worry, I'll look after him."

"You still have the spare key, right?"

"Yep. Now pack your bags and have a great time."

"Thanks, Laura. You're the best! Plato's food is in the kitchen cabinet. *Arrivederci*...oh, by the way, I'll say hi to Juan Carlos for you."

"Juan Carlos! Amanda, what..."

"Sorry, Laura! Gotta run!"

CHAPTER 2

Getty Villa Museum, Malibu, California

A manda's commute was brief. The magnificent Getty Villa was only a fifteen-minute drive from her apartment. Everything about the Villa had been meticulously planned. The access road from PCH, for example, was not just a long and winding driveway—it was paved with many-sided flagstones, just like the ones used in Herculaneum and throughout the Roman Empire in the first century AD. She never failed to relish the groves of sycamore, eucalyptus, pine, and coast redwood flanking the drive. And then the two-story south façade of the Villa would appear, the stuccoed and painted upper level spanning the canyon with its stately Corinthian colonnade. "I can't believe I get to work here," she thought for the hundredth time.

Amanda's office was in the Spanish-style Ranch House. The building had been J. Paul Getty's original residence in the canyon. Along with the Villa and the other outlying buildings, the Ranch House had undergone a nine-year, multi-million-dollar renovation, during which the museum was closed to the public. She had been in college and grad school back then, but since her doctoral work was supported by a scholarship from the Getty Trust, she visited the Villa regularly. Those were exciting years, with her grasp of conservation growing exponentially—not only because of the Getty's commitment to antiquities, but also from her day-to-day involvement with the Villa renovation project.

The Ranch House was one of the buildings surrounding Conservation Court. Others included the conservation training laboratory, the nerve center for a UCLA masters program on the conservation of ethnographic and archaeological materials, as well as an office building for Getty staff. Staffers seldom used the court's official name, calling it Monkey Court instead after a central fountain with three cast primates. Amanda punched in her employee code on the keypad and entered the building, all the while under the watchful scrutiny of security cameras and muscled guards dressed in stylish blue blazers. They wore electronic earpieces to ensure constant contact as they protected a collection of ancient art worth billions.

Like almost everything else at the Getty, her small office was sleek and stylish. After switching on the lights, she sat down at her desk, opened her laptop, and checked her e-mail. No surprise—since last night there had been four messages from her boss, Dr. Walker.

Archibald Walker was a museum pro. In his early sixties, he had the style exactly right. Tweeds in cooler weather, seersucker in warmer, and always ready with an ingratiating smile. Svelte, baritone-voiced, and trust-fund wealthy, he had been an undergraduate at Dartmouth, then studied for his doctorate at the New York Institute of Fine Arts. As a newly minted PhD, he did a turn at the American School in Athens. From there, it was on to the American Academy in Rome for a year.

Classical archaeology was in his blood, and the field needed people like Walker. He raised money effortlessly but brooked resistance with impatience, as if all those aristocratic bones in his body verged on the brittle. To cross Dr. Walker was virtually unthinkable.

He had been at the Getty since the Villa first opened in 1974. Amanda ruefully compared him to a skilled surfer. He had negotiated every tricky wave that came his way—the scandal of the Greek kouros forgery, the repatriation debates, the budget slashes, the departure of the Trust's CEO under a cloud. Walker dodged the wipeouts and always seemed to catch the good rides. When serious doubts were raised about the authenticity of the kouros, Walker privately let it be known that he had harbored reservations about the archaic Greek sculpture in the Getty collection for years.

E-mail was one of Walker's Achilles' heels, however. In the early 1990s he had been a skeptic, but then he plunged into cyberspace with the zeal of the converted. E-mail afforded him the chance to calibrate what he disclosed or concealed to colleagues far more efficiently than face-to-face encounters. It was the key to a perfect poker face, he thought. But the tool he wielded to make himself inscrutable only resulted in making him seem authoritarian.

The gin bottle was Walker's second failing. All the schmoozing to raise funds, perhaps, had contributed. It was not a glaring flaw, but still something that caught the staff's attention. Yet Walker owed his position to the powerful Curator of Antiquities, who was enthralled with his fundraising prowess. It seemed unlikely that even a deluge of cocktails would dislodge him.

As Amanda scanned her in-box, she breathed a sigh of resignation while she made her way through the spam grams, as she had nicknamed them. The first was a department-wide "alert," advising all members that the annual picnic at the Beach Club in Santa Monica had been suspended because of the slow economy. The second was addressed specifically to her: Walker wanted a briefing on the restoration of the antikythera device, a precious handheld relic of ancient engineering that had been dropped in the Getty's lap six months ago. In the third message, Walker inquired if she could share with him her column for the upcoming issue of the Getty Conservation Institute Bulletin. Perhaps the next column might include something about the antikythera? he wondered.

Finally, there was a cryptic note: "Command appearance this evening at Point Dume. Please report to my office at 10 a.m. sharp."

"Report?" Amanda thought with annoyance. "Does he think he's running a police precinct or a museum department?" She shook her head and tried to focus on what needed to happen before her flight.

During the early morning, she busied herself with the antikythera, since Walker would be sure to ask about it at their conference. Often billed as the first mechanical computer, the antikythera mechanism was first scooped from the sea near the island of Crete in 1901. Now displayed in the bronze collection of the National Archaeological Museum in Athens, almost everything about it—function, origins, and purpose—had been the subject of lively debate.

About the only thing agreed on by experts was that the antikythera was one of the world's earliest known geared devices.

The recent receipt by the Getty of a second antikythera, however, might break the stalemate. The mechanism came to the museum from the Vatican. Although its origin was murky, the device itself was not. Virtually all seventy-two of its gears, with equilateral triangular teeth, were intact. And the two-thousand-character "instruction manual" on the first antikythera was dwarfed by the five thousand characters on the mechanism the Vatican had sent—not to mention the fact that this more sophisticated version could be dated to about 250 BC, at least a century before the one in Athens.

Was the antikythera built primarily for navigation? For calendar making? For astrological forecasts? For predicting celestial events or pinning down the dates of festivals like the Olympic Games? The Getty conservators, led by Amanda James, figured that their priceless bronze bauble might well yield the answer.

With the speed she had cultivated to neutralize spam grams, she zapped her current column to her boss, then typed a detailed report on the antikythera team's progress to date. She attached a memo indicating that she felt there would be sufficient material for an update to the Vatican. Particularly interesting, she wrote, were the results from the ESEM (Environmental Scanning Electron Microscope) exams, which revealed most of the five thousand characters with stunning clarity. Then, as insurance, she prepared a bulleted list of talking points on the latest batch of Herculaneum papyri she had been restoring.

Amanda had been fascinated by papyri since her undergraduate days. The papyrus plant's widespread distribution in tropical Africa and its adaptability into sheets and strips made it an ideal medium for writing in the ancient world, beginning as early as 3000 BC. There were alternatives, of course, notably ostraca, or potsherds, as well as leather. But for availability and price, no material bested papyrus.

After the earliest excavations of the Villa dei Papiri in Herculaneum began in the 1750s, a trove of nearly eighteen hundred papyrus rolls came to light, thus giving the Villa its name. The rolls were carbonized by the volcanic eruption of Mt. Vesuvius that buried the town in AD 79, and unrolling and reading them proved especially challenging. Two and a half centuries after the discovery, UCLA and the Getty were still busy with the task. By that time, it was clear that the Villa dei Papiri—by many accounts the most luxurious in either ancient Herculaneum or Pompeii—had been the repository for written works of exceptional interest. For the Getty, participation was natural—the Villa dei Papiri was the principal model on which Mr. Getty's Malibu museum was based architecturally.

The Villa's original owner, Lucius Calpurnius Piso, had a taste for philosophy. As the father-in-law of Julius Caesar, Piso's wealth meant that he could indulge his leanings, and he commissioned Philodemus, a philosopher with roots in Syria, to shape the library collection. Not surprisingly, the collection came to include many of Philodemus's own works, which focused on ethics, rhetoric, government, and music, as well as the history of philosophy.

Prior to the excavations of the 1750s, none of Philodemus's prose works had been known. So Amanda's deepening involvement in the UCLA/Getty's Philodemus Project had a twofold cachet: she was part of a team that was carefully bringing an important ancient author to light, and the team was also advancing their technical know-how as they delved ever deeper into the only surviving private library from the ancient world.

By nine forty-five, Amanda felt ready for her meeting down the hall. She suddenly remembered her promise to confirm with Juan Carlos, yet she needed to raise the issue with Walker, who had clearly been brought into the loop. She wondered how much Johnny's grandfather, Silvio, director of the nuovi scavi, had told her boss. She decided to carefully tease out the extent of Walker's knowledge.

At the stroke of ten, Amanda knocked on his door. A resonant voice welcomed her inside the office. Archibald Walker's digs were more than a shade snappier than hers. The department head presided from behind a Louis XV desk with ormolu mounts and marquetry inlay, placed so that a view of the Villa's exquisite gardens could inspire executive decisions via floor-to-ceiling windows. Courtly as always, Walker rose to greet her, motioning her to the polished conference table near the desk.

"My dear Amanda," he intoned. "How good of you to be prompt. We have a busy agenda this morning, so I am glad to see you looking so fresh!"

"Well, I guess surfing has some job benefits after all," she thought, keeping her face neutral.

"Let me give this to you right away," she replied, placing the printout of her antikythera report on the table. He gave it a cursory glance.

"Splendid, splendid. You'd be able, then, to compile a detailed report for our clients in Rome ahead of schedule?" Walker passed a hand through his swept-back white hair.

"Absolutely. I think we're far enough along now to report some very exciting findings."

"Yes, I agree entirely. Good show!" Walker beamed broadly.

"He's got me right where he wants me," thought Amanda. "I wonder if he'll bring up the papyri." She carefully arranged the list of talking points in front of her.

"But now," said Walker, shifting gears with a businesslike tone, "it has come to my attention that they want you over in Italy. I mean, of course, at the freshly discovered site near the nuovi scavi in Ercolano. I had a phone call late yesterday afternoon from Dr. Silvio Sforza, the site director."

Amanda acknowledged the new tack in the conversation with a neutral smile as she shifted slightly in her chair, recrossing her legs under her white lab coat.

"Of course, I don't see how we can deny Silvio your services. It is, as one might say, *la forza del destino*. We are all in this together, as I am sure you will appreciate. It's very much a last-minute thing, but I have told him that the Getty will be delighted to have you participate. He wasn't specific about the actual site, but he praised your linguistic and conservation talents highly. So I was delighted to assure him that we will pick up your airfare..."

Walker's sonorous voice trailed off for a moment, as he rose to extract an envelope from a drawer of the antique desk. Returning to the conference table, he placed it in front of Amanda.

"*Auguri,*" he smiled, wishing her good luck. "*E buon viaggio a Roma.*"

Opening the itinerary, Amanda saw that it was for the same British Airways flight that Juan Carlos had mentioned. She realized that thanks were in order.

"That's very nice of the Getty," she replied. "And…of you, Dr. Walker."

She never called him by his first name. He hadn't invited her to.

"Don't mention it," Walker said with a casual wave of his hand. A purple signet ring on his pinky caught a ray from the recessed halogen overhead.

"There is something else, though," he continued. "I imagine you are pressed with making arrangements. But late yesterday another call came through, from Villa Colosseum in Point Dume."

"Oh?" Amanda suppressed her curiosity, even as she thought back to her musings on the beach this morning.

"You are aware, of course, that Luc Renard is one of our most generous benefactors?"

"Actually, I didn't know that."

The department head clucked genially. "Oh, yes, he has been extremely forthcoming, not just with pledges, but with the real thing—if you catch my drift. Mr. Renard asked his assistant to call. He is particularly eager that you should be present at the unveiling ceremony this evening."

"Unveiling ceremony?" Suppressing a giggle, Amanda had a split-second mental image of a bride on her wedding day.

"Yes, he is hosting a generous benefit for the museum. The occasion is the first public exhibition of the murals he has commissioned from a relatively unknown artist named Giovanni Genoa. I, of course, received an invitation some weeks ago. But the caller was emphatic about Mr. Renard's desire that you would also be in attendance."

Amanda thought that Walker's stress on this last point sounded forced. But she forged onward.

"Will I have enough time to catch my flight?"

"Not to worry." Walker rose and walked over to his desk again. He picked

up an embossed invitation in a heavy linen envelope and passed it ceremoniously to her.

"They will be starting at six. I have advised Mr. Renard that you will need
to leave for LAX no later than eight fifteen."

"Thank you, Dr. Walker. Of course, I will be there."

"It will be a very long day for you, but we need to keep our patrons happy,
don't we?" Walker inclined his head, as if to indicate that the audience was over.

Amanda rose to her feet, collected the itinerary and the invitation, and
made what she judged to be a dignified exit. Back at her office, she hurriedly
dialed the country code 39 for Italy, and then the number in her iPhone for
Juan Carlos.

"It's on," she said. "British Airways Flight 268, leaving tonight."

"Fantastic!" came the voice from across the ocean. "I will meet you at
Fiumicino. *A domani sera*, Amanda. And have a safe flight."

☙❦☙

Fifteen miles to the west in Point Dume, as Archibald Walker and Amanda James
were conferring at the Getty, the monogrammed, twenty-foot-tall iron gates of
Villa Colosseum swung open to admit an approaching vehicle. An impossibly
stretched limousine glided through. The gates shut with a discreet click.

Several minutes later, the limo disgorged its passenger in front of the
villa's broad esplanade. The driver politely ignored the man's grimace as he
rose to his feet. He was tall, lithe, and sandy-haired, rounding forty, dressed
casually in golf slacks and a monogrammed shirt. Wraparound sunglasses only
slightly softened his angular, sharply grooved features.

Exiting from the house to meet Luc Renard was a white-jacketed Filipino
butler. Simultaneously, a furious barking broke out. Three full-grown Dober-
mans and a pair of muscular Rottweilers raced around the far corner of the
mansion, baring their fangs to greet their master. Delighted, Luc allowed
them to approach and lick his outstretched hand, then snapped his fingers

for them to sit at attention. The diminutive butler Polberto winced but held his ground.

"Good morning, sir, and welcome back. I trust you had an enjoyable flight from Tokyo?"

"Interminable, Polberto," he groaned. "It's good to be home. Let's go inside. It's too bright out here."

Luc strode toward the bronze, double-story doors, which opened at a keystroke on Polberto's remote.

"Would you like something to drink, sir?" the butler inquired.

"No, nothing. Listen, I'm eager to know if everything's ready for tonight. The invitations said Regrets Only, I recall. Have there been any regrets?"

"Not a single one, sir. The *Los Angeles Times* is calling it the 'A list' party of the season."

"Well, that's a surprise. Anytime I get an assist from a competitor I have to be grateful."

"Arnold Schwarzenegger's social secretary phoned to say that he might be a little late, but no more than half an hour."

"That figures. Now that he's back on the movie set, James Cameron runs the Terminator's schedule," Luc chuckled with a hint of disdain. "Let me know if he hasn't arrived in time for the unveiling, I'll do it myself if necessary."

"Yes, sir. Mr. Genoa asked me to inform you that Miss Meier phoned Dr. Walker at the Getty. She was assured that Ms. Amanda James will be at the party."

"Excellent. Make sure she's well taken care of—the full VIP treatment. We have plans for her."

"Very good, sir. Will there be anything further at the moment?"

"Yes, please tell Maestro Genoa to meet me in the conservatory in half an hour. We have some last-minute details to cover."

Polberto bowed obediently and withdrew.

CHAPTER 3

Villa Colosseum, Point Dume, California

A s the sinking sun painted the Pacific far below, Luc Renard stood on the balcony of Villa Colosseum with his muralist in residence. Giovanni Genoa was no taller than Polberto, reaching only to Luc's shoulder. His balding pate was crowned with long white hair that bushed out at the sides. Flared eyebrows and a grizzled beard, also white, gave Genoa a grandfatherly look. Yet the effect was far from serene. No one would have mistaken the painter for Father Christmas. Instead, his muscled upper body and habitual forward-leaning stance suggested the power and restlessness of a being long accustomed to hunting for a living.

Both men were dressed for the party, Luc in a maroon Armani silk jacket and Giovanni in a dazzling white tuxedo, jauntily garnished with a maroon cummerbund. Both wore Bruno Magli loafers and looked like a matched pair.

"You are pleased with the murals, signore?"

Luc guffawed. "*Pleased* is not the word, Giovanni. I am delighted… ecstatic in fact! What you've accomplished in three years Michelangelo couldn't have done in ten. The murals are stunning, truly extraordinary."

"That is most kind of you, signore." The painter bowed graciously to acknowledge the praise he had sought.

"Your murals make Diego Rivera and Orozco look like street artists, graffiti boys. The guests will be enamored of your creations. They will open their arms to embrace you. And they will open their wallets to support the Getty." Luc clapped his hands gleefully.

"But, signore," Giovanni Genoa interposed. "Ever since you commissioned the murals, I have felt that you...perhaps—how shall I put this?—wondered why I have presented the theme of violence so graphically?"

"No, you're on the wrong track there," replied Luc. "I *wanted* you to highlight human passion in all its intensity. Violence, warfare, rivalry, lust—it is strife that marks the human condition. History is a chronicle of devastation, Giovanni."

The painter received this gnomic utterance thoughtfully.

"Some philosophers speak of progress, rather than decline," he responded. "Think of the Enlightenment, for example—"

Luc cut the older man short. "Progress is rubbish. The illustrious leaders of the Enlightenment, Diderot, Voltaire, Locke, Hume and Montesquieu, and all the rest, didn't have to live through the twentieth century. Mass murder is rampant, Giovanni. Every bone in my body tells me it will become even more so."

Luc glanced at his watch. "A quarter to six. They'll be here soon. I think I should review the prepared remarks for the ceremony. Shall we go inside? Let's convene in the library."

Luc put his arm around the painter's shoulders. "I am glad I found you."

Giovanni Genoa bowed a second time in assent and fell into step beside his patron. "And I, you," he said softly.

As they made their way to the library, Luc was reassured to see dozens of uniformed staffers attending to last-minute details. Now that the black satin drapes were in place to conceal the murals in the great hall, a team was hastily dismantling the scaffolding and spiriting it away for storage. In the foyer, artists were putting the finishing touches on two massive ice sculptures, each depicting a heavily armed, battle-ready Roman gladiator. Ornamental bronze basins below the plinths would catch the melting runoff while multicolored lasers from above would captivate the guests as they entered the foyer.

The mansion resounded with a cacophony of tuning instruments from the dual hundred-piece orchestras situated inside and outside the villa. In the center of the great hall, a stone dais constructed of large blocks of snowflake obsidian would serve as the focus for the unveiling ceremony. Technicians buzzed over the lighting, the microphone, the podium, and the seating arrangements for dignitaries.

Dozens of waitstaff in black-and-white jackets clustered around their supervisors in a final drill. In their late teens and early twenties, attractive and graceful, many of these young women and men anticipated the moment of discovery—their own, that is, by an influential mogul in entertainment, sports, or another celebrity field. The guest list tonight would be full of such power brokers.

☙❧

It was 4:45 p.m. when Amanda pulled the yellow Jeep Wrangler into the garage of her apartment building. She had barely an hour to shower, change, and repack. If she was going straight from Villa Colosseum to LAX, she would have to change at the airport. Dr. Walker had used his pull to get her admitted to the business class lounge, which offered convenient changing rooms. As for the Wrangler, she would use the airport's long-term parking. Expensive, but there was no other option with such sudden arrangements.

Plato, of course, was delighted to see her, despite the long, affectionate good-bye she had given him that very morning. But he was not finicky. Amanda's unanticipated reentry meant some extra bites of savory food. He rubbed against her legs as she hastily opened a can and spooned his meal into a dish.

Out of the shower, Amanda chose a black cocktail dress belted with an aqua sash. She scooped a pair of three-inch pumps off the shelf. She debated whether to wear her hair down or use the tortoiseshell combs her mother had given her when they lived in Japan. She decided in favor of the combs. For jewelry, she selected a favorite pair of aquamarine earrings and a simple gold locket on a chain. Once upon a time, it had held a picture of Juan Carlos. Now that they had drifted apart, however, the locket held only her mom's photo. She kept telling herself that another picture would take Johnny's place when the time was right.

Almost ready, she checked her answering machine. Most of her friends used her cell number, but some callers continued to use the landline. Pressing the speakerphone button, she found she had two messages. The first was from Dr. Walker.

"Just an *aide-mémoire*, Amanda. You have to leave the party early, so please try to arrive no later than six fifteen. I'll wait for you outside the library. The staff will inform you where it is." *Beeeeeep.*

"Well, how about that," she murmured to herself. The voice equivalent of a spam gram.

The second message was from British Airways, reminding her that check-in for her flight to Rome was a minimum of two hours before the scheduled flight time. If she didn't meet the deadline, her reservation might well not be honored.

"Time to split," Amanda thought. Grabbing the Louis Vuitton and her backpack, she blew a kiss to Plato, let herself out, and double-locked the door.

Arriving at the front gates of Villa Colosseum thirty minutes later, she found a traffic jam. Limos were stacked up on PCH the way the vehicles of lesser mortals clogged the I-5 freeway on weekday mornings. As she maneuvered the Wrangler into the procession, Amanda thought how incongruous her vehicle looked in this parade. She showed her invitation to one of the four armed guards at the main gate and was waved forward.

After a ten-minute crawl, she reached the esplanade in front of the mansion's main entrance. Several athletic, raven-haired valets who looked like clones jockeyed for her attention. The tallest one issued her a claim check and took custody of her car keys.

"My bags will be okay?" she asked him.

"No worries, Miss. Mr. Renard's garage is totally secure. I'm Rob, if you need anything," he added amiably. She caught him admiring her emerald green eyes and her well-proportioned body as she stepped out of the car and onto the paving stones.

Amanda nodded, and the Wrangler swiftly disappeared around the drive and into an underground garage. She noted with satisfaction that it was only 6:10 p.m. Dr. Walker would not be kept waiting.

Amanda took her first proper look at the villa, and it nearly overwhelmed her. "Wow!" Amanda thought. "Europe's largest cathedrals have nothing on these doors." She gazed as the great bronze portals swung open wide to admit the partygoers. They must have been thirty feet tall. Directly inside, an elegantly coiffed, middle-aged woman smiled a greeting and stepped through the crowd right in front of her.

"Ms. Amanda James?" as she slid a small picture of Amanda back into a jacket pocket.

"Yes, I'm Amanda."

"Welcome to Villa Colosseum. I'm Sandra Meier, Mr. Renard's executive assistant. Mr. Renard is especially pleased that you were free to attend tonight."

"I'm glad to be here. It's quite a house. Perhaps you could assist me, Ms. Meier. I need to meet up with Dr. Walker. He said he'd be outside the library. Can you please point out the way?"

"Yes, indeed," the assistant assured. "We're now in the Palatine foyer. Walk straight ahead to the great hall, which you will see on your left. Then continue a little farther toward the balcony. The second door on your right leads to the master library."

"Thank you, Ms. Meier. Perhaps we'll run into each other again a bit later on."

"You're welcome. I'd love to chat with you about your work at the Getty. By the way, the unveiling ceremony is scheduled for seven o'clock sharp."

It did not escape Amanda's notice that her new acquaintance was the niece of architect Richard Meier, who had scored a sensation with his design for the Getty Center in Brentwood a dozen years ago.

While still in the foyer, she paused to inspect the gladiator ice sculptures. The Colosseum theme was plain, but to what purpose? Amanda's curiosity was piqued.

She made her way to the master library and could see Dr. Walker exiting from it through beautifully carved double doors. Before they closed, she could make out detailed ancient maps mounted on one of the room's walls.

Dr. Walker slid the old-world retaining bar across both doors, as though to say that only he was important enough for admittance to that room.

"That rat, he must have slipped in there for a quick look for himself," she thought, "just so he could have an opening gambit with Luc Renard."

"Right on time!" Dr. Walker beamed. "And you're looking lovely, Amanda. Let's track down our quarry. I'll do the introductions."

Amanda fell dutifully into step alongside her boss. They retraced half the route to the foyer, and then turned right to enter the great hall.

This was a cavernous space on the scale of Louis XIV's Versailles. The length of half a football field, the room was sixty feet wide and forty feet high, with a barreled vault ceiling and a patterned granite floor. Although drapes still hid the murals, she quickly calculated how much manual labor—let alone imaginative design—would be required to decorate such a space. Even the wealthy bankers of Renaissance Florence, the Medici, might have paused before they offered patronage for this project.

Dr. Walker's purposeful stride soon led them to Luc Renard, who stood at the ceremonial dais, surrounded by technicians. After a brief pause, he broke free and extended his hand.

"Dr. Walker! Welcome to Villa Colosseum."

"It is a privilege to be here on such a momentous occasion, Mr. Renard. May I present one of our brightest stars at the Getty, Ms. Amanda James?"

Luc Renard turned to Amanda. He stared at her eye to eye in her high heels, which lofted her several inches above Walker. For several seconds Luc admired her stunning good looks, then flashed a precise, gleaming smile and extended his hand.

"What a pleasure, *Doctor* James! I am so glad you were able to join us."

Amanda returned the smile. Inwardly, she was gratified at Renard's obvious mention of her credential in front of her superior. Luc's grip was warm and confident.

"I have often seen your beautiful house, Mr. Renard. But never the inside. I surf about half a mile down the coast near Little Dume Beach."

"Indeed? I hear it's a popular break."

"Well, maybe a little *too* popular. That's why I go there very early in the morning."

Cocktail chitchat, thought Amanda somewhat impatiently. Although she did wonder what it would be like to be the lady of this house and married to a man as powerful as Luc Renard. His appearance was a bit unsettling, though. Why was he wearing dark sunglasses indoors? "Never trust a man who doesn't show you his eyes," her mother had often said. Did Luc want her here as just another Getty sycophant like Walker?

"Dr. Walker," Luc turned and looked down at the department head. "I wonder if you would excuse us? I have some matters I would like to discuss with Dr. James in private."

Archibald Walker's jaw dropped. He was being dismissed, there was no doubt, but to protest would have been futile. Was Renard going to put the moves on Amanda? What could these "matters" be? She had never met Renard, as far as Walker knew. However, he now remembered that Amanda *had* given a Getty Villa tour to some of the tycoon's top Japanese executives a year ago. They must have been impressed enough to tell Renard about her.

A practiced smile, blending complicity with flattery, creased Walker's lips.

"Of course. I will hope to see you after the unveiling." Dr. Walker disappeared into the crowd, but not before replacing his empty martini glass with a fresh one from a steward's gleaming silver tray.

Luc turned his full attention to his beautiful guest. "Amanda, permit me to address you by your first name. I have heard so much about you. It is especially serendipitous you are here tonight for the unveiling. Are you familiar with the works of Giovanni Genoa?"

"No, Mr. Renard, I can't say that I am."

"Please, call me Luc. I first met Giovanni several years ago at an art show in Rome. I found his work so compelling that I asked him if he would consent to create a series of large-scale murals for Villa Colosseum. Happily, he accepted. Mr. Genoa is comparatively unknown in the art world, but tonight you will see what a brilliant discovery I have made."

"The scale of the paintings is exceptional. I can't wait to see them," she said.

"That, of course, will be the evening's pièce de résistance. But there is another reason that your presence here tonight is so gratifying. I have just returned from a brief trip to Tokyo."

"How did you like Japan?"

"I've been there many times. Renard Enterprises has publishing and entertainment interests all over the world. I must say, though, that Japan is one of the more agreeable destinations on my travel docket."

With a gesture, Luc ushered Amanda away from the podium and toward the end of the great hall that led to the balcony.

"Let's have a look at the sunset. Here at Point Dume it rivals sundown on the Bay of Naples."

With a start, Amanda thought of Juan Carlos and the nuovi scavi.

Out on the balcony, one of the orchestras was in the middle of a Cole Porter medley. Luc gestured to the conductor to reduce the volume a bit. Polberto approached to take drink orders. They both requested Chardonnay.

"Try the Kistler Sonoma 2006," suggested Luc. "It's rather fine. Gains velocity on the finish, as they say."

"Excellent choice," she agreed as Polberto hurried away.

Luc continued. "I should tell you why I went to Japan, Amanda. A week ago, one of the company's most talented—and I may say most valuable—employees suffered a stroke. For fifteen years, Foster Benedict has hosted one of our most popular TV shows, _Exposed_. It's a celebrity thing. Has had a lot of support in Asia and Europe. Also from the _estancias_ crowd in countries like Argentina. Viewership is growing steadily."

"I am not familiar with it," admitted Amanda.

"It doesn't matter. The premise is simple—like a televised _People_ magazine. Japanese people want to hear about, and look at, American celebrities. It's an escape from their daily routine."

"So now what will you do to replace Mr. Benedict?"

"That's where I think you can help. Last year, my Tokyo publishing executives were at the Getty Villa on a reward trip to L.A. They told me that you spoke Japanese fluently when you gave them a private tour. Apparently, there were no Japanese-speaking docents available that day, and you were graciously volunteered by Dr. Walker to show the group around."

Amanda recalled the brusque phone call from Walker ordering her to drop everything and head over to the Villa's main entrance.

Luc continued, "I must also admit to having snuck into a lecture you gave last fall. It was the same night as a Getty Trust board meeting, when I presented them with a $25 million matching-donor check. I briefly listened to you speak about the library at the Villa dei Papiri. The lecture was in the Getty Center auditorium, you remember? You had every man's attention in that room, as well as the jealousy of most of the women!"

Luc chuckled flirtatiously, while Amanda wondered how to acknowledge his praise.

"Since then, I have inquired about your background. Dr. Walker has shared your credentials with me and told me a great deal about your foreign language skills. You lived in Japan?"

"Yes, I graduated from high school in Tokyo. We lived there for two years."

"How's your Japanese these days?"

"Better than average for an American, I suppose," Amanda smiled.

"You are too modest. I'm sure you could thrill our Japanese viewers."

"Are you suggesting…?"

"Yes, I want you to go to Japan. Your looks, your poise—and above all, your intelligence—make you ideally suited to replace Benedict as host of the show. Of course, Walker has no idea of what I have in mind. You would have to leave the Getty. But think of the opportunities opening up for you with your own TV show!"

While Luc spoke, Amanda's thoughts flashed back to her teenage years. She had to admit that she'd admired the celebrity lifestyle, and even fantasized about living it one day. As Luc's soothing words flowed on, she daydreamed about his offer until Polberto returned with the wine.

"The formula is easy to master. I predict you'll catch on within a week. Walker says you're a quick study for every assignment you've ever had at the Getty."

"Aren't there other qualified candidates for this position?"

"Yes, frankly, there are. But I don't want them. I want *you*. It's our chance to reinvigorate the show, give it a beautiful host who speaks our audience's language, and expand that audience even more. It's all about ratings."

"I'm flattered that you think I have the potential, Mr. Renard…er, Luc. I can't believe this, though. I'm supposed to be going to Italy tonight," she stuttered.

"Ah, yes, Walker mentioned that. Something archaeological?" Luc inquired whimsically as he sipped his Chardonnay and continued to admire her from behind his designer sunglasses.

A muffled warning rang in Amanda's mind, and she decided to downplay the matter. "Yes. It's no big deal, but I've got an old friend over there who thinks I can help him with a small project."

The sun now kissed the horizon in a blaze of color. Luc smiled broadly and removed the sunglasses to reveal his hazel eyes that sparkled in the evening glow. Amanda thought him quite handsome now that she could see his face, although she still could not quite place his accent.

"Amanda, you've heard the old expression 'fish or cut bait'? Respectfully, I am pointing out to you that this is a fork in the road. I can't offer you the job straight out, but I can say that our senior people in Tokyo, many of whom you have already met, will interview you with the deck stacked in your favor. How much would you make five years from now if you stuck with the Getty? Eighty or a hundred grand? This position has a signing bonus of $150,000, plus a starting salary of $350,000 for year one and up to half a million in year two, depending on the ratings. The opportunities for growth are limitless. We *need* you."

Luc moved slightly closer to her. "And I know you can do it."

Amanda had no idea how to reply. She sipped her wine and made a show of looking out at the sunset. "This is very unexpected, Luc. I am flattered, as I said, but you will have to give me some time to think about it."

"My dear, time is one thing we have very little of. Can we meet here on the balcony in an hour, after the unveiling ceremony? Let's say seven forty-five. We'll discuss it more then."

Although taken aback, Amanda didn't want to refuse. "Perfect," she said.

"And by the way," Luc added before departing, "I believe I've seen you surfing the break." He motioned to a telescope mounted on the balcony railing. "I know you'll miss that in Tokyo, but during your eight paid vacation weeks I'll make sure you have opportunities to get to some of the greatest breaks in the world." Luc pointed to the surf below. "Think Fiji, Indonesia, Phuket!"

He winked conspiratorially, and then he was gone, with a silent Polberto in tow.

Amanda lingered on the balcony. How bizarre life could be! For the second time in a single day, she had been urgently entreated to leave home for foreign ports. What could be made of Luc Renard's offer? She had no obvious media qualifications for the job. Up to now, Amanda had lived in a highly credentialed world. The BA led smoothly to her doctoral program. The PhD was the driver's license of academia. Was it possible that Renard was steering her to Tokyo based primarily on her looks and foreign language ability? And how much did he really know about her, anyway? Perhaps Luc just needed an attractive blonde who spoke fluent Japanese—rare, yes, but not impossible with his resources, Amanda considered.

She strolled over to the telescope he had pointed out. There was still enough light to see the break plainly, and she could make out the figures of several sundown surfers catching their last waves of the day. Curious about the scope's power, Amanda stared through the eyepiece.

The vista was a blur. The lens was cracked. She looked up again at the surfers and determined there was no way a person could make out anyone's face from this distance. "How did he know it was me down there?" she asked herself.

It was ten minutes to seven. She could kill some time by celebrity watching in the great hall, which was filling up with hundreds of guests, or she could take a peek at the rest of the grounds. She decided to check out the inlaid pool, which was visible from the balcony, with its candles and delicate flowers floating in small, colorful containers.

Amanda descended a curved flight of marble stairs. She smiled at an elderly couple holding hands as they climbed in the opposite direction. She thought how lucky those two were to have each other and grow older together. Would her life ever take that path?

For such a large mansion, the pool was surprisingly intimate—roughly the size of a standard lap pool, she guessed. The party was so well attended that many of the guests had spilled out of the villa and sought more open space in the pool area. Waiters circulated with trays of drinks and hors d'oeuvres. Laughter and lively conversation filled the air.

Oddly enough, it was often at parties that Amanda felt most remote and disconnected. Since graduation from college, she had been no stranger to loneliness, and it was starting to take its toll.

CHAPTER 4

Villa Colosseum

At five minutes to seven, the orchestras fell silent. After a short pause, three differently pitched gongs reverberated throughout the great hall, signaling that the unveiling ceremony was imminent. Amanda found herself standing next to Dr. Giorgio De Luca, former director of the Cotsen Institute of Archaeology at UCLA. Amanda had known him from her grad school days. This year, she'd read he had been given the Trowel Award, the Institute's highest honor. He greeted her warmly, and accepted her congratulations.

But they had no time for shoptalk, as a final series of even more resonant gong notes rang out. Striding to the center of the dais, Luc Renard grasped the microphone.

"Ladies and gentlemen, it is my great pleasure to welcome you to Villa Colosseum. As I look around the room, I am overwhelmed by the number of distinguished guests who have united here this evening to grace me with your presence and to support the Getty. Please forgive me if time precludes the individual recognition of so many luminaries. But I cannot overlook two gentlemen whose leadership has been invaluable in the effort to ensure that the Getty remains one of our most vital cultural institutions."

Luc gestured to the row of chairs installed behind the podium.

"Please join me in saluting Dr. Richard Hamilton, the president and chief executive officer of the J. Paul Getty Trust."

A scattered wave of applause swept the room.

"And we also welcome Dr. Michael Winslow, the esteemed director of the J. Paul Getty Museum."

Another scattered wave.

"This evening's benefit marks a very special milestone in my life. Several years ago in Rome, I had the privilege of meeting a remarkable painter, Giovanni Genoa. Such an artist, I am convinced, comes along only once in a century, perhaps in an epoch. I knew at once that his towering talent was the lens through which I needed to project my vision of humanity, in all its power and glory. Please join me in saluting Signor Giovanni Genoa."

Slowly and smoothly, Giovanni Genoa rose from his seat as the great hall resounded with applause.

"It is now my privilege," Luc continued, "to introduce a man who needs no introduction. He has graciously consented to carry out the unveiling of the Villa Colosseum murals painted by Signor Giovanni Genoa this evening. Ladies and gentlemen, I give you the Honorable Arnold Schwarzenegger, former governor of the Golden State of California!"

As the Governator took the microphone, the applause grew more robust. Whatever unpredictable political winds blew in California, it was impossible not to admire this Austrian native's tenacity and poise.

"Good evening, friends! I am honored to be invited to this assemblage. As the National Endowment likes to say in Washington DC, 'A great nation deserves great art.' Well, so do a great state and a great city! The Getty, which we are supporting tonight, is truly a jewel in the crown of Los Angeles. And our host, Luc Renard, has worked tirelessly to keep it so. Mr. Renard's vigor in industry is matched only by his dynamism as one of our region's most effective patrons of the arts. It is therefore with the greatest pleasure that I will now throw the switch that will reveal the murals in this great hall to public view for the very first time."

He held up a silver oblong box, perhaps three times the size of a TV remote. The gongs sounded once more. Then, all around the room, the satin drapes plunged to the polished granite floor. After a second or two of silence, the intake of breath was palpable.

"*Funtaahstic!*" echoed off the walls in the great hall, Schwarzenegger's pet phrase filling the void as the crowd braced itself. Then, a torrent of applause.

This was, after all, what they had all come for. The TV cameras and paparazzi photographers quickly captured the moment of awe for the evening news, blogs, and tabloids.

The ancient world was Giovanni Genoa's theme. But his murals did not exactly evoke Edgar Allan Poe's homage to "the glory that was Greece / And the grandeur that was Rome." Instead, the painter's focus was on man's bestial nature.

Next to Amanda, Dr. De Luca let out an audible gasp as he gazed at perfectly rendered soldiers and slaves splattered in gore. He clasped the cross around his neck and whispered a prayer in Italian that Amanda recognized.

"An object lesson, or a pandering to our baser instincts?" Amanda wondered as she spent the next half hour circling the great hall. There, thrusting upward from the floor to the vaulted ceiling, image after image testified to cruelty and bloodlust. "This stuff makes waterboarding seem like child's play," she thought.

As she moved from scene to scene, however, she had to acknowledge the technical facility of Giovanni Genoa. Color, form, composition, scale, perspective, decorum: there was not a point she could fault. However unknown the diminutive painter may have been to this point, he nevertheless possessed the skills of a master. Three murals, in particular, caught her attention.

The first was a sensuous tableau that juxtaposed cruelty and languor. On the left, the artist depicted a pair of ancient Egyptians carrying off a dead slave, as another captive, presumably soon to die, writhed under the lash of an overseer. Behind, in a seemingly endless procession, loomed gigantic temple pillars recalling those at Karnak near Luxor in Egypt. Foregrounded on the right, reclining on a spacious couch in an ornate pavilion, a young noblewoman stretched luxuriantly. An exquisite bloom dangled from her right hand. Her arm extended over the cushions that supported her as she surveyed the scene. A scantily clad handmaid, her bare back to the viewer, wielded a fan. In front of the pair, crouched on the pavilion's carpet, was a leopard—an incidental touch of menace?

Amanda's second choice was a depiction of the ancient naval Battle of Salamis. Here, not far from Athens in 480 BC, the Greeks had scored what must have seemed to Persian King Xerxes a miraculous victory. How could their puny forces have defeated the greatest armada in the ancient world? Spaniards of the Armada would pose the same question in 1588, a little over two thousand years later. The Greeks, like the English, had done it through a combination of cunning and pure, dumb luck. Giovanni Genoa conveyed the chaos—and perhaps the exultation—of spears, shields, helmeted crests, and swords with a brio that left the viewer in awe. "Score one for western civilization," Amanda thought—otherwise the Iranian president might not need an interpreter on his visits from Tehran to the United Nations in New York.

And, finally, there was the series on ancient Rome. The artist had clearly favored this time period, with more scenes devoted to Roman subjects than to any other. Cannae was there, with the humiliating defeat of Rome by the would-be conquistadors, the Carthaginians, in 216 BC, when over seventy thousand men perished in less than six hours. Next was Julius Caesar, falling at the base of Pompey's statue in the Senate House on the Ides of March, with Shakespeare's "three and thirty wounds" all too visible. A depiction of the Jewish uprising in Israel highlighted the slaughter by the Roman army. Emperor Nero's persecution of the Christians, executed in thorn baskets and illuminated as human torches, displayed his horrific reprisal after the Great Fire of Rome in AD 64. Genoa had clearly read his Roman history in Tacitus. Even the sack of Rome four centuries later, when poetic justice reared its head, was painted in excruciating detail, with barbarians looting and burning the city as they exterminated its population.

One of the largest Roman murals struck Amanda as especially notable. Occupying a central position in the group, it seemed as if the artist had given it primacy. The mural depicted a scene in the Colosseum, Vespasian's amphitheater completed by his son, Titus, in AD 80. The proverbial venue for early persecution of the Christians, the Colosseum still figured on the top ten tourist sites in modern Rome—and, she reminded herself, it had given its name to Luc Renard's villa.

What distinguished this mural from many of the others, though, was the individualized presentation of one of the Christian captives. A semi-clad, red-haired woman, surrounded by snarling lions, stood stoically in the face of certain death. Others crawled around her in the dust of the arena. It was as if she were an island of peace in a stormy sea of suffering. Amanda briefly wondered if she could be so composed in such horrifying circumstances.

"So you think my rendering of the Colosseum is *giusto*, Signorina James?"

The white-jacketed artist was at her elbow, so abruptly as if to resemble an apparition. His bushy eyebrows seemed to bridge the space between them.

Amanda extended her hand. "It is an honor to meet you, Signor Genoa. What a magnificent occasion. A triumph for your talent. Your portrayal of the Colosseum is certainly...powerful."

The painter received her assessment with a courtly bow. "It is my signature mural."

"I could not help notice that it alone remains unnamed," she politely stated.

"Indeed, Mr. Renard has a couple of ideas in mind for this painting, but he remains undecided whether to title it after the scene or for its principal character."

"I see, so the woman martyr represents an actual historical figure?"

"Yes, but she was known by different names," Genoa added.

Then admiring his own handiwork and glancing up at Amanda, Giovanni quipped, "It must have been a great time to be alive—that is, if you were not the sacrifice! Grazie, signorina." His smile was quizzical as he deftly stepped around her and continued working the room.

Amanda's circuit of the great hall had now taken her almost 360 degrees. She was due on the balcony at seven forty-five for her second conversation with Luc Renard, and there was no way she could be late for her airport departure at eight fifteen. With such concerns, it did not even occur to her to wonder how Giovanni Genoa had known who she was.

Amanda threaded her way through an increasingly noisy crowd and reached the balcony at exactly seven forty-five. She looked around for Luc. Barely a minute later, she spied him exiting the library doors and walking directly toward her.

"I beg your pardon, Amanda. I was detained with the mayor. He wanted to renege on his earlier commitment to hire Giovanni for the Los Angeles City Hall renovation. I fear that angels are not Giovanni's specialty," Luc mused.

"Perhaps the mayor had his breath snatched away like so many others tonight," she offered. "Maybe he's afraid the conservative city council won't approve of Mr. Genoa's vivid images?"

Luc seemed to file the matter away for later, and he focused all his attention on Amanda. "I know you're on a tight schedule," he said. "Have you considered my proposal?"

"Yes, but I'm not sure about becoming a celebrity. It would be quite a step for me."

"You are the perfect host for this show. I guarantee you will have all the support you need. The Tokyo people are a media executive's dream team. Benedict, unlike you, was not the brightest bulb in the socket. However, they made him look and act like a movie star."

"Ah...when would they like to interview me?"

"Right away. We've got to be back in production within a week. In fact," he added, as he reached into an inside pocket of his jacket, "I have made arrangements for you to leave tonight. Please examine this envelope."

Opening the folder inside, Amanda saw it was a one-way ticket from LAX to Tokyo on Japan Airlines. First Class.

"I know you had planned to leave LAX for Italy," Luc continued. "But I need you to land in Tokyo. This flight departs LAX at ten thirty. You'll be met at Narita when you arrive and taken to the five-star Mandarin Hotel. Mr. Ito, our head producer, has been authorized to take you shopping at Mikimoto on the Ginza. There is a $25,000 gift certificate there in your name. Your belongings will be collected from your apartment and air-freighted overnight. When you get the job, we can explore more permanent living arrangements."

Amanda noticed he had said *when* and not *if.* She glanced at her watch. "Isn't this cutting it very close?"

Luc grinned broadly. "I've arranged late check-in at LAX. Meanwhile, one of my limousines will take you to the airport. I took the liberty of having your luggage transferred from your car to the limo. Your jeep will be stored here."

She extended her hand. "I still haven't made up my mind, Luc. But I accept your kind offer of a ride to the airport. I'll let you know what I decide."

"Very well." Luc clasped her hand in both of his. "I know you will make the right choice. Many of us are depending on you."

She could barely look away from his stare as the charming host backed away and disappeared into the crowd.

Ten minutes later, Amanda emerged onto the floodlit esplanade and peered into the driveway, looking for a Renard Enterprises limo with the golden crest *RE* on the doors. Then Rob appeared, sprinting out of the darkness.

"Your limo is just coming now, miss," the valet informed her. "I put your luggage on the backseat."

"Thanks, Rob." Amanda pressed a couple of bills into her young admirer's palm.

Opening her door, the limo driver politely introduced himself as Harris and informed Amanda that he was replacing Mr. Renard's usual chauffeur. As they passed through the gates of the estate and turned onto PCH headed south, Amanda asked if he would raise the tinted glass partition to seal off the passenger area for privacy. She might not have the time to change clothes at the business class lounge, she thought. She unzipped the Louis Vuitton, changed into a comfortable outfit for the flight, and extracted both her British Airways and Japan Airlines itineraries, as well as her passport, from the backpack.

Her mind was flooded with conflicting thoughts as she considered both options. How could she decide something this important so quickly? "Follow your heart," she remembered her mom repeating to her several times as a young girl.

Four miles down PCH, the intercom chimed softly.

"Miss James?"

"Yes, Harris?"

"Mr. Renard is on the phone. He would like to speak to you."

"Can you put the call on speakerphone back here?"

"Certainly, Miss James."

"Amanda?" Luc's normally resonant voice sounded a little strained, but it was crystal clear over the eight Blaupunkt speakers.

"Yes, Luc," she replied.

"Everything okay? Is Harris taking good care of you? He's new."

"Oh, yes. Excellent. And this limo is awesome."

"One of the latest models. State of the art. I had the Ferrari people deliver two of their stretched F1 360s last week. Anyway, I'm calling from the observation deck on the roof of Villa Colosseum. It was great meeting you, and I can't wait to see you in Japan next week. We'll have dinner together."

Silence on Amanda's end before she finally spoke.

"You're making this very difficult for me. The offer is so generous and tempting, but I'm afraid I just can't accept, Luc." She wondered if she would ever tell Johnny what she'd just passed up, as she softly bit her lower lip.

Silence, on both ends of the phone.

"Amanda," Luc finally murmured. "I don't think you realize what a big mistake you're about to make. It could be life altering. Please reconsider, I beg of you."

"Your confidence in me is extremely flattering. But for now, at least, I see myself in archaeology, not in TV. I don't know how to thank you, Luc. I'm sorry if this is a disappointment."

At that moment, the limo accelerated and then swerved abruptly. Amanda lost her balance and found herself pressed hard into the corner of the backseat against the side of the door.

The speakerphone went silent. "Harris?" Amanda screamed, hoping he could hear her through the smoked glass partition.

"Yes, Miss James?" as the partition lowered.

"What was *that*?"

"Oh, nothing much. Just a careless truck driver."

The partition rose again, giving Amanda her privacy back.

What Harris did not say was that, with pinpoint judgment, he had narrowly avoided a nasty collision with a Pacific Oil & Gas tanker. Just south of Malibu, the enormous vehicle had crossed the double yellow line and headed directly for the limo. Only Harris's counterintuitive push on the gas pedal and his sudden veer to the right had avoided what would surely have been a fatal crash.

The limo sped onward, so Amanda was not to see what happened next. Trapped by its vector and momentum, the tanker plunged over the seafront cliff, falling 150 feet to the beach and bursting into an enormous fireball that mushroomed over 500 feet into the air and was visible for miles.

The speakerphone came back on.

"Is everything all right, Amanda?" said Luc, who heard her yelling and then speaking more softly to Harris.

She could hear a tumult of shouts and screams in the background.

"Yes, Luc. But what's all that noise?"

"I think someone's holding an illegal fireworks party near Malibu pier, and my guests are admiring the show. I'm sorry about your decision. I truly am. Have a good flight. Good-bye, Amanda."

On the observation deck of Villa Colosseum, Luc Renard pocketed his Blackberry and surveyed the inky Pacific for several moments. Polberto politely ushered the muralist and the other distinguished guests off the deck and down to the main library to distract them from the burgeoning fireball in the distance. Retrieving his phone, Luc scrolled down through a list of numbers, selected one from Italy, and dialed.

"We have a problem," he said. "You need to be at Fiumicino Airport tonight. I'll call you in a couple of hours with the details."

CHAPTER 5

Italy

"**L**adies and gentlemen, we are beginning our initial descent to the Fiumicino Airport in Rome. Please check to see that your seat belts are securely fastened."

The British Airways flight attendant's crisp voice impinged on Amanda's drowsy reverie about Plato swatting a fly, and she awoke with a start. Dead tired when she boarded in LA last night, she had slept for most of the flight to London. During the stopover there, all the passengers were required to deplane so that the aircraft could be serviced. So she had occupied herself in the lounge at Heathrow with a *New York Times* crossword she brought with her and a sudoku puzzle she found in the *Daily Telegraph*. The Saturday crossword, always the most difficult, was no match for Amanda; she polished it off in twenty minutes.

During the layover, she had thought of calling Juan Carlos to tell him the flight was on schedule, until she realized that her first-generation iPhone wouldn't work in Europe. Never mind, she was sure he'd be on time at the airport in Rome.

Night had fallen before she reboarded the plane for the flight's second leg. She must have dropped off to sleep again.

During the final half hour before landing, she reviewed what little she knew so far. Juan Carlos had mentioned that the new site in Ercolano was near the Villa dei Papiri, the principal model for the Getty Villa in Malibu. Although the ancient structure remained unexcavated, enough was known about it to establish that this region, just outside the town walls, was the site for the seaside mansions of some of Herculaneum's wealthiest citizens in ancient times. Juan Carlos had also spoken of a bronze door with inscriptions in several languages, including Chinese. "Now that," Amanda thought, "is the real puzzle."

She knew that Herculaneum's ancient residents had possibly included Jews and Christians, so inscriptions in Hebrew and Aramaic, as well as Latin and Greek, would fit plausibly with the rest of the historical and archaeological record. But Chinese? How could that be explained?

Contact between Europe and China along the Silk Road had begun in the early third century BC, around the time of the first Chinese emperor. Could such ties have encompassed a small seaside town on the Bay of Naples? Depending on what the inscription said, the hypothesis would have to be entertained, at the very least.

Amanda absently doodled a few characters in Chinese on a paper napkin on her tray table. She had first learned the language when her family lived in Hong Kong in the early 1990s, a two-year stint for her father's job. Before the British handover to China in 1997, Pacific Oil & Gas had built a big refinery there, and Roger James was placed in charge. While she was at UCLA, Amanda had taken several Chinese language courses, hoping she might go on an excavation there one day.

As the aircraft continued its descent, Amanda glanced out the window. Lights along the Italian coast signaled that the landing in Rome was not far off. Her thoughts turned to Juan Carlos and their sixteen-month romance. How much, if at all, had he changed over the years since she'd last seen him? In college, he'd been passionate about everything, from soccer to motorcycles to his fervent religious faith. Certainly there was nothing in their conversation this morning to suggest he'd become any less intense. She wondered if he'd found a steady girlfriend.

After passport control and customs, Amanda stepped outside the baggage claim. There was no sign of Juan Carlos, probably because the plane had arrived twenty minutes early. And, Amanda recalled, traffic in Rome, even this late at night, was notorious. Inside the airport it was sticky, even with the air conditioning, and Amanda decided to step outside and stand near the taxi line, perhaps saving Juan Carlos the trouble of parking while she enjoyed some fresh air.

As she exited the glass doors, Amanda saw a tall, uniformed man at the curb. He was holding a large placard stenciled with her name, A. James. "Did Juan Carlos get held up and send a chauffeured car for me?" Amanda wondered. But surely he would have notified British Airways and had her paged soon after arrival. As she was wondering whether to approach the driver, she felt a tap on her shoulder and heard her name. Turning around, she was caught up in an embrace and, almost immediately, kissed European-style on both cheeks.

"Amanda!" Juan Carlos exclaimed. "You're really here! You look fantastic! I am so sorry, there was a bottleneck on the way, and I'm late. Scusi, per favore."

His curly black hair was much longer now, Amanda noticed, but his rugged features and dazzling smile had not changed.

"Juan Carlos, don't be silly! You're not late. The plane was early. It's wonderful to see you!"

"Let's get going right away," he said, scooping up her bag. "My car is about fifty meters down from here. I saw you as I pulled in, but the limos were lined up in front of me."

Amanda and Juan Carlos strode briskly down the pavement to a small but powerful-looking sports car, parked with its hazard lights blinking. She was so glad to see him that she didn't even mention the chauffeur with the placard. Probably just a coincidence, she told herself.

"Young lady," Juan Carlos said gallantly as he opened the passenger door. "Step into my *bambino*!"

"What a gorgeous shade of red!" Amanda gushed as she slipped into the seat. "I've never seen a convertible like this in America. What is it?"

"Not many of these make it to the States. It's a limited edition Alfa Romeo—the 8C Spider," he replied as he shut her door and stowed her bags in the compact trunk space. "Some of the roads we'll take down to Ercolano will show you what she can do."

Sliding behind the wheel, he smiled at his passenger. "Now, please keep your arms and legs inside the vehicle and fasten your seat belt!"

With a push of the start button and a tap on the gas pedal, the engine screamed like a horde of banshees, turning the heads of nearly everyone in the passenger loading area.

"Still a show-off, I see," she teased, playfully pretending to plug her ears. Juan Carlos merely shrugged and eased the Alfa away from the curb.

❧

It was after midnight. As they cruised through the suburbs of Rome, Juan Carlos filled Amanda in on the plan.

"It's about a two-and-a-half-hour drive. It's late and you must be tired. Otherwise, we could stop in Piazza Navona for a gelato and some people watching."

"Let's go direct, if you don't mind. We won't even get there until nearly three in the morning." Amanda recalled her twenty-hour day in California before departure.

"*De acuerdo.* We'll go straight to Silvio's place in Ercolano. Of course, he's invited you to stay with us there. Now tell me about your life in California. You know, being together again makes me realize how much I've missed you. It's amazing that the scavi have been responsible for this reunion. Are you still enjoying the Getty work?"

"Yes, I love the job. I can't say the same for my boss, but the work is great. And I feel the same way about our reunion, Johnny. You know, I'll always be grateful for your help when my dad died. You rescued me, but it took me quite a while to get my emotional footing. I've always felt guilty about the missed phone calls and closing myself off from you and the world. And then you left to join Real Madrid..."

There was a brief pause as Johnny wove through the traffic.

"Real Madrid was a good ride. I could never have afforded these wheels without my signing bonus. But I've decided my knee injury did me a favor. The team schedule is relentless. Don't get me wrong, being a celebrity is fantastic. I enjoyed those years, but I'm happy to be back in archaeology."

Amanda couldn't help but think of Luc Renard, and her own crack at celebrity. She decided not to bring it up, instead delving into what was really on her mind.

"Well, now that you're done with soccer, have you decided to settle down?"

"Oh, I'm still playing the field, at least a little bit. How about you?"

"My best friends are my papyri," she joked. "And Plato, of course."

They exchanged glances with a grin.

They were now on the *autostrada*. With no speed limit that any Italian driver took seriously, Juan Carlos opened up the throttle. Amanda sneaked a glance at the speedometer needle, which hovered at the 160-kilometers-per-hour mark. One hundred miles an hour—and other motorists were still passing them! Amanda allowed her mind to wander as Johnny inserted an Italian pop CD and drove into the night.

❧

It was nearing two a.m. when blinking caution lights alerted them to a motorway mishap. With a sigh, Juan Carlos braked steadily, and the Alfa soon slowed to a crawl. It looked as if the entire autostrada had been shut down in their southerly direction.

"Where are we?"

"Just north of Caserta," he replied. "It's not too far to Naples and Ercolano. But I think they've shut down the road. Maybe the rain caused a big accident earlier tonight." Multicar pileups were more than occasional on Italy's major roads.

True enough, all traffic was being diverted at the Caserta exit. Even at this late hour, the line of cars was considerable.

"We're probably being diverted to Nola. Then we can take another side road back to the A1 and continue on the direct route. Here, take a look."

Juan Carlos switched on the car's GPS. She saw that to get to the E841 to Nola, they would have to make a number of turns on local streets.

It was then that he noticed the headlights.

He murmured, "That's funny."

"What do you mean?"

"I know this area very well. To save time, I'm taking a shortcut to get to the main road. But every time I make a turn, this guy behind me does the same thing. I'm almost certain we're being followed."

"Maybe he knows the same shortcut?"

"Not likely. I think we may have the Camorra on our hands."

"The Camorra?"

"They're the mob, the Neapolitan *cosa nostra*," he said softly, not wanting to alarm her. "Lately there's been an outbreak of carjackings. They go for luxury sports vehicles like the 8C. There's an international market, all over Europe. It's often easier to carjack a vehicle with a high-tech alarm system than to steal it off the street. They tried it with this car once before, in fact."

Amanda felt rattled, despite his calm tone. "That's not very reassuring. What do we do if they catch us?"

"Don't worry, cara mia. This bambino can outrun anything."

Juan Carlos picked up speed, cornering expertly, until they gained a stretch of country road. They were nearing the E841, which the GPS showed as a divided highway. The occasional streetlights had given way to pitch blackness. The headlights in the rearview mirror grew steadily closer.

He shut off the CD player and gripped the steering wheel hard. "Hang on," he smiled.

The whine of the engine and the shriek of the sport coupe's powerful braking system ruled out further conversation. Amanda prayed they could make the E841, where more frequent traffic and the presence of toll plazas would make carjacking risky, if not impossible. Whoever was following them, she thought, must have a powerful vehicle to be able to keep up with the Alfa.

A mile short of the E841, they hit a straightaway, and Juan Carlos floored the accelerator, gaining distance from their apparent pursuers. Blurred fencing on each side of the road showed they were in farm country.

Suddenly, just beyond a shallow curve in the road, an apparition ambled into the Alfa's headlight beams. It was colored dirty white, with light gray shading toward a huge horned head. It stood on stumpy, sturdy legs that inched obliviously toward the broken white line in the center of the road. Whoever wanted to get past would have to veer either left or right.

Juan Carlos turned the wheel deftly and the Alfa raced past, seemingly grazing the bovine's tail.

"What in God's name was that?" shouted Amanda, gripping Juan Carlos's shoulder. They were still traveling almost one hundred miles per hour.

"Oh, that? That, cara mia, was a *Romagnola*, the Italian version of a Texas Longhorn steer. It must have gotten outside the fence somehow."

"Johnny," Amanda said urgently, looking back over her shoulder. "The headlights are gone."

And, indeed, the rearview mirror was dark. Juan Carlos grinned to mask his relief. "I guess the Camorra got served a fifteen-hundred-kilo steak dinner," he said wryly.

"That's terrible," said Amanda, thinking of the poor beast.

They resumed a reasonable speed. On the E841, once her adrenaline had done the same, Amanda questioned Juan Carlos.

"Shouldn't we report this to the authorities?"

"Normally I would. But if we go to the police tomorrow, you have no idea about how Italian bureaucracy would tie us up. They'd want endless forms and probably a personal appearance or two, maybe in Caserta or perhaps even in Naples. Your American nationality could add a complication, with the consulate becoming involved. It's one of the reasons why the Camorra has such a free hand. People simply don't want the hassle.

And the time that a report takes will mean that we won't be able to work on the scavi."

"Well, if you're sure we're doing the right thing..." Amanda's voice trailed off.

"Let's just think of it as an adventure. *Benvenuta in Italia*," he said, turning to her with a grin. "But let's not tell Silvio and Renata—we don't want to scare them. It'll be our secret." He reached over and placed his hand reassuringly on her thigh.

"Now I owe you for another rescue." She covered his hand with her own, giving it a squeeze. "I can't wait to get to work—let's see if we can arrive in Ercolano in one piece tonight!"

Juan Carlos switched the CD player back on and slotted in an old Luciano Pavarotti disc. They turned up the volume and sang "Torna a Sorrento" along with the great tenor as the Alfa hummed quietly toward the Bay of Naples.

CHAPTER 6

Ercolano, Italy

Amanda had hoped to get started in Ercolano as soon as possible. But when Juan Carlos knocked on her door midmorning that Saturday, she still felt exhausted. She had slept fitfully, her bizarre dreams punctuated by a herd of Romagnola crossing a pitch-dark road. Jet lag from the long airplane journey also didn't help. Still, Amanda roused herself and stumbled down to breakfast, lured by the smell of strong coffee and fresh rolls.

At breakfast, Silvio Sforza, Juan Carlos's grandfather, vetoed any suggestion they start the project that day. Amanda needed rest, he said. The exploration might prove to be physically arduous, depending on what lay behind the bronze doors. Deferring to his judgment, Amanda silently thanked him for the extra day of rest.

The Sforzas' hospitality made her feel genuinely at home. Silvio and his wife, Renata, owners of a large apartment in Naples, had rented a modest but comfortable house in Ercolano for the excavation season from early April to late October. Amanda was installed in a cozy room on the top floor, whose sparse furnishings suggested it had once been a nursery.

Although in their late sixties, both Silvio and Renata looked much younger. Silvio was of average height, portly and aristocratic, with aquiline features, a classic Roman nose, and thinning gray hair. Renata was almost as tall as Amanda, with wavy salt-and-pepper hair. They had reared six children, and their second daughter Diana, Juan Carlos's mother, lived in the Spanish Mediterranean city of Valencia, where Juan Carlos was born.

As Amanda cupped her hands around her second mug of coffee, Silvio suggested that Juan Carlos squire Amanda around on a private tour of the excavations.

"Since you were last here," Silvio began, "there have been a number of major finds. Some of them remain unpublished and have not yet been exhibited. Even with the resources shared with us by the Getty," and here he bowed graciously, "it is so hard for us to keep up with antiquities in Italy. We simply don't have the funds. And some of my colleagues are not as assiduous as they should be in making their discoveries public."

Amanda nodded sympathetically.

"If you can crack the code on those doors—and I am pretty sure it is a code—we have no idea what you'll find. But that is tomorrow's business. Today, Juan Carlos will do an excellent job of updating you on the local context. He's nearing the end of his second season with our excavation team."

"Why not get started after breakfast?" suggested Renata. "I'll have lunch ready at two o'clock. Then we'll all relax with a siesta."

She turned to Amanda.

"It still gets quite hot here in the afternoons."

"Sounds like an excellent plan," Amanda smiled to Juan Carlos.

"Then we are decided," concluded Silvio. "Amanda, I leave you in the capable hands of *il cocco della nonna*."

Amanda's puzzled expression evoked a literal translation from Silvio.

"It's—how should I say?—an expression that means something like 'the apple of the eye of the grandmother.'"

As they all laughed, Amanda thought she could detect a trace of a blush on her friend's cheeks.

They spent the next three hours weaving between ancient and modern, marveling yet again at the way present-day Ercolano lay on top of Roman

Herculaneum. Over three centuries, since the first traces of the ancient town were found in 1709, less than one half of it had been excavated. Scanty budgets, public opinion, and fiercely defended property rights made it doubtful that excavations would ever be complete, or even reach the level of neighboring Pompeii. Most of Herculaneum's important public buildings, such as the *palaestra*, or sports complex; the suburban baths; the *basilica*, or courthouse; and the theater remained either partially or totally buried.

"Don't think it doesn't have a lot to offer, though!" enthused Juan Carlos, listing for Amanda a litany of attractions: frescoes, mosaics, wall paintings, furniture, jewelry, everyday kitchen implements, and partially excavated buildings. The excavations at Herculaneum continued to offer a unique panorama of daily life as it was over nineteen hundred years ago.

They concluded their tour with an inspection of the new site. Just one hundred yards outside the ancient town walls lay the Villa dei Papiri, still mostly covered by sixty-five to eighty-five feet of volcanic matter. After a seven-minute walk to the north, Juan Carlos pointed to a deep declivity where excavations had been in progress for the last three seasons. Near the bottom of the rough-hewn stairs used by the excavators, the recent earthquake had split a huge wall with a narrow crack. This fissure was sixteen to eighteen inches wide and, he explained, extended several hundred feet into the slope. Juan Carlos mentioned that it was here that the robot with the fiber-optic cable had been inserted.

"Silvio will show you the pictures over lunch," he told her. "You will probably find them helpful. But he thinks they pose as many questions as they answer."

They arrived back at the house at one forty-five, when it was already ninety degrees in the shade. After a brief washup, they joined Silvio and Renata, who were busy making preparations in the small dining room.

Lunch was long and leisurely. Renata had prepared a delicious seafood stew as the main course. There were bowls of fresh vegetables and fruits and pine nuts, and flaky round loaves of bread. Glasses brimmed with Lacryma Christi, the local white wine.

Between courses, Silvio gave Amanda a brief tutorial on the photographs
the robot had taken. He explained that some distance inside the narrow crack,
the way was completely blocked by a set of tall double doors that looked as
if they were made of bronze. On each side of the doors were inscriptions. On
the right, these seemed entirely textual, while on the left there were a number of images.

What had been deciphered so far suggested that the right-hand door had
been inscribed with a group of quotations or proverbs. How these related to
the images on the left—if indeed there was a relationship—was difficult to
say. Many of the images were partial, and some of them were doubtless hidden by volcanic dust or other debris.

The robot, Silvio explained, was no longer operative. It had been disabled
by one of the earthquake's many aftershocks.

"What kind of code might the inscriptions contain?" Amanda wanted to know.

"My best guess," replied Silvio, "is that it constitutes a key for the doors.
We know that combination locks existed in Roman times."

"But could this one possibly still function after all these years?" she queried.

"A lock was found in the Kerameikos in Athens," he told her, "dating from the
Roman era there. It wasn't made of metal that can rust, but rather, it used a series
of finely polished stone cylinders. Remarkably, it worked perfectly. And look
here," he handed Amanda one of the photographs of the doors, pointing to a partially hidden row of symbols. "It's hard to be sure, but it looks to me as if at least
some of these symbols are three-dimensional, extending outward slightly from
the door's surface. I believe these doors may have the same type of mechanism."

"So, you're suggesting that the symbols can be pressed in some sequence
to open the doors?"

"Precisely. Let's hope you can determine the sequence."

The group gave over the late afternoon to a refreshing siesta. When they
reconvened for a cup of tea at six o'clock, Silvio suggested that they dine
that evening at a local trattoria. Renata, who had spent most of her day in the
kitchen, enthusiastically seconded this motion.

"Let's spend the time before dinner making a list of the equipment you will need, Amanda," said Juan Carlos. "Then we can send Carmelo to pick up the stuff at the excavation office." Carmelo was the trusted foreman of the digging team.

Later, over an aperitif and with the list completed, Silvio explained to Amanda that he had another, more selfish reason for postponing her mission until the following day.

"As you know, Amanda, Ercolano is a small town. Archaeology takes center stage here, and not only because of the tourist industry. The residents, quite naturally, are always on the watch for what the authorities are planning to do next. There is very little trust on their side. They worry about the town government condemning their homes and businesses for new excavations. Rumors fly. So I've done my best to keep this mission low-key.

"Frankly, we think we have some major finds in store. Nothing quite like this has come to light before, at least during my tenure. The biggest recent bombshell was in the eighties and nineties, when my predecessor Dr. Maggi uncovered all the lava-encased bodies in the marina boathouses. That generated a lot of publicity—not all of it good—so we want to keep a low profile until we know exactly what we're dealing with.

"I have planned for us to start early tomorrow morning. On a Sunday, there will be fewer people on the streets. The diggers have the day off. We'll have only Carmelo and a few expert excavators. We're nearing the end of the season, but there are still quite a few tourists. We'll do our best not to attract attention, okay?"

"Absolutely. I sympathize with your position," Amanda said.

The conversation turned to her work at the Getty. She filled Silvio in on the antikythera restoration, taking care not to share anything that would violate the Getty's confidentiality agreement with the Vatican. Silvio said he had a foggy recollection of the ancient computer, mentioning it had been decades since he last saw it. Amanda noted that Juan Carlos was following the discussion with keen interest. "I guess he has made a full conversion back to archaeology after all," she thought.

Dinner at Trattoria Viva lo Re was festive. A strolling accordion player took requests, and even Silvio, who had seemed to Amanda a trifle formal throughout the day, unwound, tapping his foot in time to the music. After the meal, Renata ordered a round of espressos, prompting Juan Carlos to reach into his jacket and extract his leather pocket case of Montecristo No. 2s. Silvio deftly employed his cigar cutter and accepted a light from Juan Carlos's S. T. Dupont lighter, the distinctive *ping* from its cap blending with the strains from the accordion. Juan Carlos proffered the case toward Amanda, who politely held up her hand.

"Thank you, Johnny, but not tonight. I'll tell you what—if I can decipher the language puzzle, I'll gladly indulge tomorrow with you, and we'll celebrate our success!"

At ten thirty p.m., early by Neapolitan standards, Renata suggested they call it a night. With a final ring of smoke punctuating his words, Silvio concurred, pointing out that they needed to make a six thirty a.m. start in order to beat the first church bell calling early worshippers.

To her great relief, Amanda slept soundly, even though before nodding off she had a few butterflies in her stomach about the mission—especially when Silvio had mentioned the aftershocks from last month's earthquake. But the challenge and potential reward were worth the risk. Yes, such an adventure had its dash of danger. But thousands of people—she thought of miners, firemen, skydivers, and spelunkers—operated under hazardous conditions. Besides, she smiled to herself as she drifted off to sleep, exploring this site was probably safer than big wave surfing.

CHAPTER 7

Near the Nuovi Scavi Ruins—Ercolano

Her wristwatch alarm awakened Amanda at five thirty a.m. She dressed in jeans, a blue and gold UCLA T-shirt, and a thin pullover. Half an hour later, she knocked on Juan Carlos's door, and the two of them went downstairs to the kitchen together. Renata had prepared a simple breakfast of rolls, fruit, and coffee. Silvio, freshly shaven and immaculate in a starched white long-sleeved shirt and khaki slacks, appeared a few minutes later. During breakfast, the group reviewed Amanda's chief objectives.

"If you get the doors open," Silvio said, "just make a quick survey of what lies behind. I know it will be tempting for you, as a professional, to begin a detailed inventory. But the season has only thirty days to run, till the end of October. We won't be able to fit a large project into the schedule. It will be much better if you can give us an overview, so that we can plan for next season—and try to raise funds for larger equipment to widen the crack if we need to."

Amanda nodded.

"How much time do you think she should spend in there, *nonno*?" Juan Carlos asked his grandfather.

"No more than three hours," Silvio replied. "If we can't get the door open by ten o'clock, we'll have to call it quits. There's too much chance of attracting attention. We also have to reckon with the danger of Amanda's inhaling poisonous gases. At the slightest hint on the gas meter, Amanda, you get out fast."

"Okay," she agreed. "Anyway, if I can't crack the code, at least I can brush away a lot of the debris and get better photographs than what we have now."

With breakfast finished, Silvio donned a light jacket, while Juan Carlos fetched the tote bag that Carmelo had delivered last night with Amanda's equipment: notepad, pens and markers, copies of the robot's digital pictures, headlamp attached to a wireless headset and microphone, digital camera for stills and video, miniature digital tape recorder, measuring tape, trowel, brush, a small pick, a gas emissions meter, a gas mask, a clinometer for measuring slopes, a prismatic compass, and an alidade for showing degrees of arc.

Renata met them at the front door. Kissing Amanda on both cheeks, she murmured, "*Buona fortuna*, Amanda. See you at lunch time."

"Arrivederci, Renata," Amanda replied.

The streets of Ercolano were deserted. A brisk fifteen-minute walk brought the archaeologists to the site, where Carmelo and three other team members were already waiting.

"*Buongiorno, amici*," Silvio saluted them. All the men shook hands formally. "*Cominciamo bene*" (let's begin).

They all descended the makeshift steps. Amanda transferred the contents of the tote bag to her backpack, and then attached the pack to a strong cord that she wound around her waist. Juan Carlos handed Amanda one last item: his fancy S. T. Dupont lighter.

"In case you need it. A good luck charm," he said, kissing her softly. "*Coraggio*, Amanda. You'll do just fine," he said. She looked at him with a smile. The concern in his eyes would be her best ally.

"Remember," warned Silvio. "Not more than three hours. Use the wireless headset to keep us informed, and try to be back here by ten at the latest."

She nodded, tapping her Timex.

Juan Carlos chimed in, "And then we can head to the eleven o'clock mass, just like old times!"

Amanda paused, then smiled. "All this working on a Sunday was making me wonder about you, Johnny. Just don't expect me to remember all those hymns!"

Facing the jagged crack, Amanda waved to the group with a thumbs-up sign, placed her backpack on the ground, squeezed through, and then dragged it after her.

She found herself in a long, narrow corridor. She paused, let her breathing settle, and began to step gingerly over small cracks. Switching the headlamp on, she oriented herself by comparing what she saw with some of the robot's digital pictures. About twenty meters ahead the corridor curved abruptly to the right.

Following the route and making the turn, she discovered the robot's remains. It had indeed been crippled, apparently by a chunk of debris dislodged by an aftershock. Examining the crumpled machinery now would be a waste of time, so Amanda continued onward.

Fortunately, the ground she needed to traverse within the crack was relatively level bedrock. She shuffled along, at one point turning sideways, removing her backpack, and exhaling completely to navigate through the tightest space. "This must be the spot where Johnny had to give up," she said to herself.

As she gradually ventured deeper into the crack, only the sound of her breathing punctuated the eerie stillness. About three minutes after negotiating the turn, her headlamp picked up a glimpse of the double doors. Then, after about ten more feet, the corridor widened enough to allow a full view of the ornate bronze portals. Impressive in both scale and design, they were approximately thirty feet tall and each about ten feet wide.

"Here's where I really go to work," Amanda thought. She extracted the brush from her backpack. After twenty minutes of careful cleanup, she stepped back from the doors to acquire an overview and ponder the possibilities of decipherment. She drew her notepad out of the backpack and began to compare the known with the unknown.

Two of the texts had already been transcribed by Silvio's team. The first, in Latin, was a traditional Jewish proverb: "The story is truer than the truth."

The second text, in Greek, was a quotation from the historian Plutarch: "Time is the wisest of counselors."

After brushing away the dust, Amanda counted a total of five inscriptions on the right-hand door, all within about a two-foot space just below eye level. She pored over the Aramaic expression, scribbling possibilities onto her pad until she arrived at a coherent translation: "Death may be the greatest of all human blessings." The source, if she was not mistaken, was the Greek philosopher Socrates.

That left the Chinese and the Hebrew. Moving a bit closer and studying the Chinese characters, Amanda read: "You shall eat dust all the days of your life."

"That's odd," she murmured. The words were those of God to Satan in the book of Genesis. They were part of the divine punishment on the serpent for the temptation that led to the original sin of Adam and Eve. What were they doing inscribed on an ancient door in Italy in *Chinese*?

She tackled the Hebrew text last. Reading from right to left were these words: "The truth uttered before its time is always dangerous." Amanda recognized the proverb as a saying attributed to the Confucian philosopher Mencius in the fourth century BC. Stranger and stranger. Here, in the final two texts, was almost a mirror image: a Hebrew scripture rendered in Chinese, and a Chinese saying written in Hebrew.

After recording the texts in her notes, she turned to the left-hand panel, where her cleanup had revealed multiple images. There were five rows, each with five pictograms. Silvio had been right about their formation. All the pictograms were in 3-D—slightly raised above the surface of the door.

It was a reasonable hypothesis that the five texts on the right were somehow related to the images on the left. After all, they were all inscribed on the same set of double doors, and the numbers were similar. If Silvio's guess was correct that the inscriptions figured in a pattern to release a combination lock, there had to be certain critical points of contact between the sayings and the pictograms.

Or between the *correct* pictograms, since there were five for every saying. As far as Amanda could see, each of the symbols suggested a certain idea or conceptual field. She ransacked her brain for what she had learned about symbolism, both in the ancient world and in more modern eras.

She knew that symbols could be generally divided into two broad categories. The first was universal and conventional, at least for a particular time period or culture. Symbols of this type included the rose for love, the dove for peace, and the flag for a nation state. The second type was more specialized and particular: for example, a tiger or a pirate for a local sports team.

Amanda decided she had to look for universal symbols. The proverbial texts were multicultural and multilingual, crossing boundaries of the ancient world. If there was a matchup, the symbols would also resonate across a broad spectrum.

She therefore ruled out any narrow interpretations, such as the well-known symbolism for the Christian apostles that matched each of the Twelve with a weapon that indicated his martyrdom. Thus, a knife was used for Bartholomew, who was flayed to death, and a saw for Simon, who was cut in two. Besides, she thought, none of the texts on the right-hand door was overtly Christian.

The first break occurred when her glance fastened on a symbol at the far right of the fourth row. It was a sword. Could the sword be matched with any of the quotations?

Amanda's eyes eagerly scanned the right-hand side once more. "Death may be the greatest of all human blessings" read the middle proverb. Socrates, she well knew, was put to death by his fellow Athenians in 399 BC by being forced to drink hemlock, and not by the sword. But the sword was the closest symbol for death among any of the images on the door.

"If this line of reasoning is valid," Amanda thought, "I could comb the visual symbols for persuasive correspondences with key words in the texts."

Bingo. The Chinese character for *truth*, on the left-hand door, offered an obvious match with the proverb from Mencius, rendered in Hebrew, on the right-hand side: "The truth uttered before its time is always dangerous."

Amanda glanced at her watch. It was eight fifteen and she had not reported back to the team. "I'm not going to tell them anything until I'm reasonably sure," she thought. And she continued to attack the puzzle.

There were many images to choose from. A balance scale, for example, suggesting fate in the Homeric epics and justice in more recent times. An apple and a sparrow, used in ancient Rome to suggest erotic love. "The challenge here on both sides of the door," Amanda thought, "is to winnow the irrelevant from the important."

"Time" and the hourglass made up her third match. That covered the Plutarch quotation. Likewise, "You shall eat dust..." from Genesis and the depiction of a serpent. Finally, the Jewish proverb about stories suggested to Amanda the depiction of a papyrus roll. As she knew better than almost anyone else, papyrus was the writing medium for ancient storytelling.

She stared at her notepad. She had translated all the proverbs. She had identified the symbols that credibly matched each one. Where to go now?

Amanda decided to experiment. The order of the quotations, from top to bottom, correlated with the following symbols: hourglass, sword, "truth" character, serpent, and papyrus scroll. She pressed each raised symbol in turn. Nothing happened.

She was momentarily stumped. "There must be a further layer in this puzzle," she mumbled.

Then she remembered—a combination lock. If the raised symbols were like numbers on a combination dial, they had to be depressed in a certain order to activate the lock's tumblers. And if each symbol correlated with a key word in each of the five texts, maybe the proper sequence depended on a combination of the key words.

"What combination would be appropriate?" Amanda asked herself. "With over three thousand possibilities, I could be here for a long time."

She thought through some simple approaches, such as alphabetic or chronological sequencing, but none seemed to match the sophistication of the overall puzzle. Then an idea occurred to her: a combination that produced yet another proverb, consistent with the overall meaning of the five maxims she had in hand.

Five words to play with, if her evaluations were correct: time, death, truth, dust, story.

It was now eight forty-five. She spoke into her voice-activated microphone and relayed a progress report.

"Silvio, can you hear me? I've made progress, but I need more time."

Silvio's warm voice came through clearly.

"Take your time, Amanda. We're here for you. Any sign of gas?"

In her linguistic zeal, she had forgotten all about the silent, invisible enemy. She hurriedly extracted the gas emissions meter from her pack and switched it on. The needle remained at zero.

"No, there's no indication on the meter and I feel fine. Just let me get through this last stage of the puzzle."

"*Brava*! Keep us current."

So now, how to fit the five words together into a statement that made sense? Thinking this language puzzle was created by a learned scholar thousands of years before, Amanda devised three criteria: the expression would have to be proverbial in nature; it would have to reflect on the relationship of time with human life and death; and it would have to stress the importance of storytelling and truth.

She stood before the doors calmly, as if they could telegraph the solution to her. Her mind was as receptive as she could manage.

Then it came to her.

"Neither *time* nor *death* can turn a *story*'s *truth* to *dust*."

Where had she heard such a saying? She couldn't think of the source. But it was compelling.

Taking a calming breath, she firmly pressed the symbols in sequence: hourglass, sword, papyrus roll, truth, and serpent. For a split second there was only silence.

Then she heard a click and a low rumble, and the massive doors parted in front of her.

Through her headset came Juan Carlos's concerned voice. "What was that noise, Amanda? Are you okay?"

"I'm great, Johnny! I got the doors to open, and I'm going inside."

"Fantastic," chimed in Silvio. "Please be careful in there."

Grabbing her backpack from the ground, Amanda stepped over a marble threshold into a cavernous chamber. She gasped at the scale as she shined her light around. The space was so large that her headlamp didn't allow her to discern its overall dimensions from where she stood inside the doorway. Pyroclastic flow from Vesuvius impeded the swing of the doors and also enveloped some of the contents; other furnishings, though, stood free and clear.

"That's odd," she thought. She knew that every other dwelling in Herculaneum had been totally enveloped by the eruption. How could only a small amount of volcanic flow have made it inside this structure?

She had only an hour before she was due to leave. She remembered Silvio's admonition about making an overall survey rather than a detailed inventory. She would have to hurry, now that she was inside.

She walked toward the middle of the space, which she could now make out as a circular room, yet she could not see the ceiling. As Amanda neared the center of the rotunda, she noticed what seemed to be a pair of human figures standing frozen in space and time. She decided to walk the perimeter of the chamber and return to the figures at the center as she was leaving.

There was a lot to see on her brief inspection. Silvio was not going to be disappointed. There were frescoes, marble statues, mosaics, maps, papyrus scrolls in metal tubes, and display cabinets with artifacts. The exhibits, like the inscriptions on the doors, seemed to cover huge arcs of history, from ancient Egypt and China to Greece and Rome. The Museo Archaeologico Nazionale will have to create a new wing, she thought, if they could raise the money.

But why had all these objects been assembled? Perhaps a wealthy citizen of ancient Herculaneum had conceived the idea of constructing his own private art gallery. But how could this patron of the arts have known such a diverse spectrum of cultures, even in the cosmopolitan early Roman Empire?

Amanda made another report to Silvio's team, although there was increasing static the deeper she ventured into the buried chamber.

"I'm inside the chamber, and it's magnificent! There are all kinds of spectacular artworks here. Like nothing we've seen in Herculaneum. I'm taking notes and pictures. There are what look to be two bodies standing upright covered in volcanic ash at the center of the room, next to a large telescope. My small headlamp is not bright enough to see the whole chamber. Will you guys just give me a bit more time? Say until ten thirty or eleven o'clock?"

Before Silvio answered, Amanda's next footstep fell on an unstable portion of the floor, and she heard the rumbling noise again. She was now about fifteen yards from the bronze doors. She swung herself around so that her headlamp could pick them up in the narrow beam. She saw the doors slowly folding closed. Her exit was cut off.

And so was her wireless connection.

Alarmed, Amanda looked down at the floor. She was standing on a section that wobbled slightly and was shaped like a fish. It must have acted like a pressure pad, triggering the doors' closure.

Panic was foreign to Amanda's nature. Ingenuity had gotten her inside, she figured, and it would get her out okay, too. Turning again to the center of the room, she saw a glimmer of reflection from her lamp, so she slowly approached the central pair of figures, coated in volcanic ash.

Standing in a shallow, recessed area of the marble floor, they looked as if they were locked in combat, with a well-muscled wrestler on the left grappling with a smaller, leaner adversary on the right. Had they been mock wrestling at the moment of the volcanic eruption and then caught, like flies in amber, for all time? Or was this serious combat?

As she examined the bodies, Amanda noticed a peculiar detail. The figure on the left had what looked like a rectangular pendant dangling from a thick silver chain around his neck. The smaller figure's left arm extended outward, with its fingers curled behind the object.

What was this strange pendant dangling from the neck of the more powerful-looking wrestler? Upon closer examination with her headlamp, it seemed to be some sort of small ceramic tile. With its colorful red and green markings, it looked rather like the mah-jongg game tiles she had seen in the Far East, only larger. For some strange reason, it was not covered by any of the volcanic flow. Knowing well, as a professional archaeologist, that she should be more circumspect, she still reached out and touched the tile.

Immediately, a painless jolt of energy shot up her arm. Amanda flinched and tried to let go of the tile, but her thumb and forefinger seemed glued to the object. She then became aware of the chamber slowly dissolving around her, replaced by the purple twilight of a clear evening sky. Now standing on a narrow trail, Amanda saw a gently rolling landscape with a dense forest in the distance. Looking up, she noted the Big Dipper in the heavens above. Where was she? What had happened to the chamber? Even the tile that she could not release moments ago had disappeared as well.

Amanda could now hear the footsteps of someone approaching from just over a gentle rise nearby. It sounded like he was running. She could actually hear his breathing! Wait—how did she know it was a man? Was she in danger? She tried to run and hide, but her legs would not move.

She looked down to see why her feet would not respond to her mind's command, but she couldn't see her own body! Instinctively, Amanda reached for her face, but her hands didn't respond either. Yet her physical senses of sight, smell, and hearing were heightened. It seemed she could even taste the aroma of pine needles swirling in the night winds. How was this possible? Almost imperceptibly, she could read the thoughts and emotions of the man as he approached her location. She sensed the fear in him. In fact, he was being driven wild by terror.

Moving with feral grace, the man sprinted at full speed toward her and right past her. No—right *through* her! He was completely oblivious to her presence. As he passed, Amanda's mind was dragged along silently in his wake, down the trail and toward the forest like a leaf down a fast flowing stream.

"Wake up, Amanda!" she yelled inwardly. She tried to bite her own tongue to jolt herself out of what she assumed must surely be a hallucination. But she had no teeth, no tongue, and no body.

Against her will, her thoughts became one with the runner's.

That was how her vision began…

CHAPTER 8

East of Eden

Escape.

He had to escape. To flee the terrifying scene. His parents had not taught him fear. Now he felt it full force. Panic gripped him hard, driving him farther and faster than ever before. Down the dirt path and toward the east. He had to reach the forest before dark. The trees would give him shelter. There were mountains to the north, he knew, and to the south lay the desert. He could not venture westward, for that was the direction of the fiery sword and the garden.

No, he must run east to the forest. He must lose himself.

Thorns riddled the man's sinewed body. With each stride, they corkscrewed deeper into his flesh. He would have to get them out, but there was no question of stopping now. The pain was wrenching, but not as ghastly as the image that scalded his mind. He would run until he reached the forest.

Here, in the open fields, he was too vulnerable. He feared the gasps of his breathing and the drumbeat of his heart could be heard for miles. The noise of his bare feet slapping the ground would advertise his whereabouts. He would be followed. He would be found.

The tree line was near. The man looked backward over his shoulder. No one was in pursuit. He was alone. Steadily, relentlessly, he ran.

Now he was in the forest. Mixed pine, cedar, and juniper. The tree trunks soared to a blackening sky. He ran through the forest, colliding with branches in the dark. There was, he knew, a pond on this side. He would reach the pond before he stopped running. Silently, he embraced the trees for their protection.

Once at the bank, he plunged half-naked into the water. Despite his exhaustion, he swam to the other side with a vigorous stroke. The cool water was cleansing, perhaps even healing, he thought. It would wash away the blood; it would loosen the grip of the thorns. The pond would gain him some time if they were after him. It would take them a while to pick up his trail again.

On the other side, he listened hard. All he heard was the sound of wind in the trees. Looking upward, he saw the stars. A full moon had risen and shone through the forest. At the water's edge, he leaned over to drink.

After the ripples calmed, he studied his moonlit reflection. Now in his late twenties, the man had dark brown hair. He was tall and physically fit. Years of farm work had broadened his chest and strengthened his shoulders. Dark stubble on his chin matched the hue of his brown eyes.

The urge to press on returned. Heading toward the moon, he began to run again. He had never explored the distant edge of the forest. He knew that the woods could not stretch on forever. But he had to try to reach the other side. There, perhaps, he would be safe from pursuit. There he might escape.

Two hours later, he could run no more. At the edge of a small clearing, he lay down exhausted, staring up at the sky. Thousands of stars returned his gaze. Silently, he cursed them. Their sharp rays, he thought, were a reproach.

The majority of the thorns had worked themselves loose during his swim. But some remained embedded in his flesh. "No matter," he thought. He was too tired to tend to his body. Before he could form another thought, darkness closed over him.

❦

On the restless border between sleeping and waking, the man heard a voice. Yet the doubt that he might not be alone failed to unnerve him. The voice seemed somehow disembodied.

"You are safe here, Cain."

How did this voice know his name? Did it know what he had done?

"I will protect you. No one will follow you. No one will harm you."
The voice spoke softly, reassuringly.

"Who are you?" the man asked faintly. "Are you a spirit?"

"I am the master of spirits," the voice replied.

"You know, then, of my crime?"

"Crime? He challenged you. The fault was your brother's."

"But why, then, am I punished?"

"He who cursed you has lied to you! Abel deserved his end."

"But God has made me a homeless wanderer, and cursed the ground so the work I love has been taken from me. I have lived my life in vain." Cain's voice grew bitter.

"Your life doesn't have to be that way, Cain. But do not expect forgiveness from him. He will never forgive you! You will only live in vain if you believe God. And then, in the afterlife, he will make you a slave. You will endure his torture for eternity."

"What do you want of me?"

"I will give you my protection. I will ensure your future. All I ask in return is your loyalty. Who else will shelter you?" The voice faded, as if the spirit was departing.

Cain fell silent. In his dream, he was looking again into the pool. He saw a face that was, and yet was not, his own. The water rippled slightly, the color of blood. Then, with a start, he awakened.

The sky was beginning to lighten. A brilliant morning star adorned the eastern horizon. Looking down at his hands, Cain saw with amazement that all the thorns embedded there had fallen out, and any puncture holes they had left behind were completely healed. The same miracle was true on his arms and chest. A gash on his right leg appeared to be much less pronounced than yesterday. Although his sleep had been disturbed by the conversation with the spirit, he felt vigorous and fresh.

And so, with pain and fatigue at bay, and at least to some extent the guilt as well, he rose to travel again. Stepping over a small pile of thorns next to his grassy bed, he walked rather than ran.

The spirit had said no one would follow him. Perhaps the spirit was right.

❧

Cain became a wanderer. He had never traveled far from his parents' settlement, but he learned to live off the land differently. Once a farmer, he now fashioned rough tools, including spears for hunting and fishing. He gathered nuts and whatever fruit he could find. He built temporary shelters but never stayed long in one place. He studied the animals' behavior, and learned from it. Life became almost normal again. He could, he felt, become accustomed to almost anything.

Even loneliness.

Periodically, the master of spirits visited Cain in his sleep. The spirit's voice was always reassuring, always consoling. The message was the same. Cain, the voice said, was a victim. He had been cursed by a tyrant, a being who created only to destroy. The master of spirits knew this tyrant well, he said. That knowledge had been the path to freedom for him. Cain, he suggested, was ready to follow this path as well.

Yet Cain was coming to identify freedom with self-reliance. Without parents, brother, or God, he depended now only on himself. His resources and survivor's instinct kept him alive. He needed no protectors. He feared no one and nothing. Gradually, a steely confidence grew inside him—a trust that would see him through anything.

So it was that Cain traveled, alone, for decades, growing ever more capable yet isolated. Until the day he found himself in a sunny valley, following the course of a stream that was rich with fish. That was when, at the confluence of the stream with a broad river, he heard something that lit a fire of longing inside him.

It was the sound of human voices.

Around the next bend, the rooftops of a great city hove into view. As he would soon learn, Cain had arrived in the land of Nod.

CHAPTER 9

The Land of Nod

Cain spent his first few months in the city at the house of a grain merchant named Omak. Since he had no money, he offered his services as a laborer, helping his host build a new storage barn. Thankfully, Omak didn't seem to care about his guest's past. Cain had no need to use the fable of kidnapping, slavery, and escape that he had concocted just in case. He saw no reason, however, not to use his real name.

Omak seemed to enjoy his new acquaintance's company. Perhaps he was lonely, Cain thought. The merchant had been married, but his spouse had died many years before. All the children, now grown up, lived on their own and seldom visited their father. Indeed, the social structure of Nod, for all its technological advancement, seemed to lack cohesion. People went where they liked and did as they pleased. There appeared to be no civil government of any sort.

One morning Omak suggested that they put the building work on hold and walk the city and its environs. Cain accepted eagerly. He had already seen and learned enough to know that he would make this city his home.

The two set out toward the great edifice at the city's center. On the way, Omak explained that the imposing structure had formerly served as a royal palace. Now, after the bloody revolution that had toppled the monarchy of Nod, the circular hall balanced on the flattened apex of the pyramid-shaped building functioned as a temple.

"What gods do the people worship here?" Cain inquired.

"No one really worships gods," Omak replied. "There are idols of gold and silver in the temple. But no one pays them much attention. People do anything that comes into their heads. The only god anyone takes seriously is Lorac."

"Lorac?"

"He rules the weather. Or so people think. And the weather makes the difference between good crops and bad."

When they reached the entrance, Omak encouraged Cain to climb the interior ramp that led to the temple. He himself would remain below, he said.

"I am afraid I am nowhere near as spry as you," Omak said. "I will wait for you here."

Curious to see what the idols looked like, Cain briskly ascended the ramp. At the top, he found himself in a ring-shaped corridor lined with gleaming statues. Some were clearly male or female; others seemed androgynous. The hall was protected from the elements by the translucent substance that Omak had referred to as "glass." The glass wall afforded spectacular views of the city in every direction.

Cain walked slowly around the hall twice—first to inspect the statues, and again facing outward, to appraise the city. What a vast place Nod was! He guessed that the population must be at least one hundred thousand—maybe closer to a quarter of a million. Beyond the city gates—he counted twenty-one—lay a broad expanse of grain and cotton fields on every side. Farther in the distance were vineyards and orchards. On the horizon to the north and south were snow-capped mountains.

Returning down the ramp, Cain realized he had many questions to ask of Omak. Were there other cities like Nod nearby? If so, did the inhabitants of Nod make war? How had they acquired the knowledge to quarry and build their massive, one-piece stone monuments? What inspired their stadiums? Now that the king was gone, who ruled the city? And what was this thing called a "calendar" that he had over-heard people talking about?

But he didn't want to seem too eager. Omak was a taciturn sort, seldom initiating conversations and usually replying to questions tersely. It would take Cain time to establish the contours of Nod, and to appraise the opportunities.

Meanwhile, if he really was to settle here, there was the issue of a mate. Omak raised the subject several months later.

"People here," he said one evening, "are live and let live. But if you really want to stay and be accepted, you will have to find a wife. You are of the age to marry. You will not grow younger."

Cain mulled this over for a moment. Then he replied, "And where would I find a wife, Omak?"

The older man grinned wryly. "Here in Nod, you may take any woman you like. No one will object. But I have a better plan. You will meet my old friend Tutok."

"Tutok? And who is he?"

"I have told you that no one really rules our land, now that the king is no more. But certain people have more influence than others. And the most influential of these is Tutok."

"Is he also a merchant?"

"Hardly. He is the head of a large clan. And very rich. Perhaps you could describe him as a priest."

"I thought no one here paid attention to the gods."

"You forget, young man, that I said there was an exception. Lorac, the weather god. Tutok speaks to Lorac. And that is why he is rich."

"What can he do to find me a wife?"

"You will see. It will not be a difficulty," replied Omak enigmatically.

And so Omak and Cain found themselves, several weeks later, within the palatial home of Tutok—as close to an authority figure as anyone in Nod. And it was soon clear why Omak had brought his young, handsome guest. Tutok had three daughters, each of marriageable age but still single.

Tutok, Cain thought, was very much Omak's opposite, and he wondered how the two had become friends. Whereas Omak was uncommunicative, even dour, Tutok was suave and voluble. He spoke to Cain about his priestly "duties." He recalled the lightning strike that he had survived when he was a child and how Lorac had saved him.

In response, Cain hinted that he, too, had an interest in speaking with spirits. Not with the master of spirits, Cain thought, but he kept that to himself.

The evening banquet was delightful. Entertainment was provided by Tutok's nephew, who told lighthearted stories accompanied by drummers and dancers. Platters heaped with delicious meats and fruits were presented by a cadre of handsome servants. As the banquet neared its end, Tutok's daughters sang for the guests. Cain thought that Ushar, the middle child, had an especially lovely voice.

"Why are these daughters still unmarried?" Cain asked as he and Omak retraced their way in the darkness back to Omak's house.

"This is Tutok's great sorrow," Omak answered. "I have told you before that people here are not religious. But they are superstitious. And envious. Tutok has enemies because of his wealth and reputation. He had no sons, but daughters instead. The soothsayers have foretold that these women will doom the men they marry. No young man in Nod will marry them."

"How absurd!" Cain blurted out. "Do people here really believe that nonsense?"

"Do not underestimate the average man's stupidity," muttered Omak. "The husbands of those girls would be heirs to a fortune."

❦

"Cain, do you sleep?" questioned the familiar voice.

In the mists of slumber, Cain replied, "Why do you come to me?"

"I come to you because I love and care for you," replied the master of spirits. *"It is I who protect you here in the land of Nod."*

"Really? It is Omak who shields me here. What are you in Nod?"

"If only you saw things as they truly are. Who is it that disposes Omak kindly toward you? Do you think he would shield you without my tending?"

"Leave me, spirit!"

"Yes, I will leave you now. But I cannot leave you to die. It is I who keep you alive. You will serve my purpose. Never doubt that you and my purpose are one."

❦

Four months later, Cain and Ushar were united in a marriage ceremony at Tutok's mansion. The prominence of the bride's father ensured a large attendance.

As Tutok's son-in-law, Cain found his reputation in Nod enhanced. He and Ushar moved into a pavilion attached to Tutok's mansion. Tutok let it be known that Cain assisted him in weekly vision quests with the god Lorac. Six months after the wedding, Ushar became pregnant. Tutok began to speak confidently of a grandson.

Cain had done nothing to deserve his reputation as a shaman, but he did nothing to disclaim it, either. Indeed, feeling as though he had escaped his fate as an outcast and a wanderer, he rather enjoyed his improbable status as a pillar of the establishment. Yet imaginary dialogues with the weather god hardly fulfilled his ambition. His marriage, he felt, was a beginning of a new life, but by no means a final destination.

So it was that he began, with Tutok's support, to accelerate Nod's economic vitality. The first venture was corn—a crop that had first been developed by a nearby city. Messengers had brought kernels, and the soil of Nod had received them hospitably. Cain had pointed out the plant's myriad uses, and Tutok enthusiastically assigned several thousand acres of his estates to the new enterprise. He even offered his son-in-law a large plot of land as a wedding present, but Cain politely demurred.

He could show others how to till the soil, he knew, but he would never be able to do it himself—not since the curse.

The second venture was banking. The inhabitants of Nod had long made loans in kind to their less fortunate fellows in the form of olives, dates, seeds, or animals. But now, upon Cain's urging, the more wealthy citizens added a premium. Usury in Nod was born, at first amounting to an annual rate of 10 percent, but swiftly climbing to 20 percent and higher.

The third venture was slavery. Nod did indeed have neighbors, and Cain was quick to see that the city's resources equipped it ideally to dominate the region. Slavery had existed in the city before, but not on the massive scale envisioned by Cain. All it took, he told his compatriots, was a little organization.

While these developments took shape, at home Ushar gave birth to a baby boy at the beginning of the harvest season. In an elaborate ceremony several weeks later, Cain named his son Enoch. He proudly held the boy up for the crowds to see.

"*You*, Enoch, are my harvest," he proclaimed.

CHAPTER 10

Ercolano: Present Day

As the bells from a nearby *campanile* pealed their summons to the faithful for Sunday mass, Juan Carlos and Silvio shouted Amanda's name down the crack in the wall through which she had entered. Only echoes came in reply.

"I heard the sound of the bronze doors closing," said the young Spaniard. "That's why we have no communication with her."

"What do you think we should do then, Grandson?"

Juan Carlos checked his watch. "We gave her three hours maximum. It's now nearly nine o'clock. I say we should call for a government search and rescue team. Maybe one of the rescuers will be small enough to fit in the crack and reach the door. Then they can use a blowtorch to open it. Otherwise, Amanda may run out of breathable oxygen."

"Let's not panic. If we are patient, she'll probably find her way out."

"But it'll take some time to get the team here," Juan Carlos objected. "By the time they go to work, she may be in deep trouble."

"No, no, don't worry," Silvio reassured him. "She's not going to run out of air. That chamber is vast. Besides, a rescue call will alert the media. You remember why we scheduled this project for a Sunday morning, so as not to attract attention."

"Yes, but now…" Juan Carlos pressed his case on the older man.

"And besides," Silvio broke in as he lowered his voice. "There is another concern. The entrance to the crack lies on a site we have full rights to excavate. But according to my calculations, the chamber lies underneath private property. Technically, we are trespassing."

Juan Carlos thought for a moment. Then he said, "Wait a minute! You said the chamber was vast. How do you know the dimensions?"

With a heavy sigh, Silvio drew a photograph from his jacket pocket. "I want to show you something. Let's take a walk so we can ensure we're in private."

With his arm around his grandson's shoulders, Silvio ambled casually down the pathway, which paralleled the rock wall through which Amanda had slipped several hours earlier. Then he showed Juan Carlos the picture.

"I found this fresco three years ago. But I never reported or published it. It came from a nearby dig, where possibly another villa lies buried by the ash of Vesuvius. Take a look."

Juan Carlos examined the colorful image. It was clearly in the style of Roman wall painting of the mid-first century AD. The artist had evidently employed a wide-angle perspective to portray an elderly looking man and a younger woman with long red hair, standing in front of an enormous set of bronze double doors. These portals, incised with inscriptions on the left and images on the right, appeared to be five or six times the height of the human figures. Looming above was a huge dome, and in the distance far beyond was the summit of Mount Vesuvius.

"This chamber is where Amanda is now," said Silvio. "I think it's a massive, ancient observatory. Read the inscription at the bottom of the picture."

Although his Latin was a trifle rusty, Juan Carlos quickly pieced the words together.

TULLIA MADE THIS.
TRUE FRIENDSHIP IS MORE PRECIOUS THAN
THE DIAMONDS IN A HEAVENLY VAULT.

"It looks like some sort of offering or tribute," Juan Carlos said. "You think this Tullia knew the couple shown in the fresco?"

"I am sure of it. The real question is, what did the artist mean by the reference to diamonds? If this structure really was an observatory, it's quite possible that the architect decorated the interior of the dome with scenes of the night sky, maybe using *real* diamonds for the stars and planets."

"But why didn't you tell Amanda and me what to expect in the chamber?"

The archaeologist shrugged his shoulders. "I didn't want to sound premature," was all he said. "But now matters are different. I learned late last week from a friend in the land office here that an international company is in the process of purchasing this site. They have also filed a mineral claim for anything found below ground. They are scheduled to take title tomorrow. Then they say they will turn around and donate it to the Getty Museum."

"So *that's* why you sent her in on a Sunday!" exploded Juan Carlos. "This is nothing more than a treasure hunt! You want the diamonds, if they are really there, and Amanda is your way of getting them. You don't give a damn about her safety!"

"Calm yourself!" Silvio rejoined. "Nothing could be further from the truth. Who knows if there are really any diamonds? Besides, I think you are allowing your feelings for Amanda to get in the way of clear thinking. She is obviously highly resourceful and should be perfectly fine. Nevertheless, Amanda's safety is paramount. If she's not out by noon, I'll do as you ask."

"Where is this fresco now?"

"Safe back at the Naples apartment. The only people to know of its existence are Renata and Carmelo. And now, you."

Juan Carlos stared at the ground with a perplexed frown etched on his face. He could not bring himself to look at his grandfather.

"Now let's get back to the site," Silvio said. "Carmelo and the other team members may think we're keeping something from them."

As they began to retrace their steps, there was a chime on his mobile phone.

CHAPTER 11

City of Enoch

With the passing years, the city grew more and more prosperous. When his grandson was on the verge of manhood, Tutok assembled the shadowy council of elders that made all the community's important decisions. Ill and frail, he formally designated Cain as his successor. A grateful council gave its assent and voted to change the name of the city. Henceforth, it would be known as Enoch.

Cain was thus confirmed as the founder of a dynasty. There was little doubt that Enoch would become the de facto ruler of the city after his father, and his descendants would inherit after him.

As Enoch's wealth expanded, so did its population. Cain estimated that, fifty years after his arrival there, the city was home to half a million people. Travelers flocked to Enoch from distant lands. Legends of instant riches held them in thrall. Enoch, it was said, was the land of heart's desire.

Wealth was not the only magnet, either. One could live life with no restraints imposed by legal or moral codes.

Through the generations that followed, Enoch experienced astonishing advances in technology and culture. Cain took full advantage of the city's expanding ranks of scholars and engineers, soaking up their knowledge and mastering its applications for the civilization he ruled.

And so Enoch embarked on an ambitious building program. Giant, water-powered mills rose up to grind grain, and numerous flood control projects greatly expanded the arable lands. Cain expanded the markets to facilitate trade and constructed stadiums and communal public baths of an unprecedented scale. He commissioned an observatory to study the heavens and refine the calendar, and he ordered a great library built so that knowledge could be stored and disseminated. Cain also enlarged Tutok's mansion to become a royal palace.

As a leader, Cain was careful to avoid nepotism, always seeking to allocate responsibilities by merit rather than family ties. Yet, some of Enoch's remarkable advances were ushered in by Cain's own descendants. Of these, perhaps the most significant was a son of the sixth generation who introduced metallurgy to the city. Cain was quick to exploit this development, building large foundries for the production of weapons, armor, and mining tools, thus cementing Enoch's economic and military dominance over a wide region.

Shortly after Tutok's death, Cain and Ushar had moved into the palace as his heirs. Enoch, their firstborn son, lived with them until he reached manhood and took a wife. Then Enoch and his family occupied the adjunct pavilion that had been the house of his parents. Ushar had five other children by Cain. He had even more progeny by his other wives, but he resided with Ushar because their union suited him.

Then came the time when Ushar passed childbearing age. Cain gave this little thought. His own vigor seemed undiminished. Many women offered themselves to him, if only to share in his aura of wealth and power.

From time to time, the voice in his night visions would demand his gratitude, but Cain ignored it.

Yet one night a different voice resounded in Cain's dreams. A voice he had not heard for many years, but one that he could never forget.

What have you done? Listen! Your brother's blood cries out to me from the ground! Now you are cursed and banished from the soil, which has swallowed your brother's blood. No longer will the ground yield good crops for you, no matter how hard you work! From now on, you will be a homeless wanderer on the earth. And I will give a sevenfold punishment to anyone who kills you. I will set a mark on you to protect you from those who would kill you.

A homeless wanderer? But he had foiled that curse, had he not? He lived in a mansion. He ruled a city wealthy beyond the people's wildest dreams. And what difference did it make if he could not farm the soil? Others farmed it for him. Furthermore, of what use was God's so-called mark of protection? Armies marched at his command, and slaves trembled at his word.

He prepared to return to sleep, yet a small corner of his razor-sharp mind was troubled by something unusual.

It was doubt.

❦

The next morning, as Cain ambled over to a fig tree in the courtyard to pick breakfast, Ushar stared at him, perplexed at her husband's youthful appearance. How could it be, she asked herself, that he did not seem to age? She knew of his other wives and children, and she had taught herself to accept his "wandering" from the marriage couch. But while Ushar, now entering her five hundredth year, was beginning to look old and gray, her husband appeared virtually the same as on the day of their wedding two centuries earlier. Had he some secret he was not sharing with her? Had Lorac, as so many others had speculated, really blessed Cain with knowledge of a fountain of youth? She pondered these questions, but said nothing, wishing to avoid the wrath of his temper.

For Cain, that day marked the beginning of a weeklong absence from the city. His project was a thorough inspection of the fortifications, as well as paying a visit to several remote outposts. Enoch had become a militaristic state, and its armed aggression against its neighbors required a constant state of readiness in case of counterattack.

Accompanied by his generals, Cain was eager to see personally the progress that had been made on the "reapers"—a system of large, scissor-like metal cutting arms that projected from the city's gates. These arms had been designed to form slashing machines that could destroy an enemy force that attempted to enter the city. During his inspection tour, Cain lodged with a series of powerful landowners, whose plantations surrounded the countryside outside the city.

On his third evening away, Cain was at the home of a clan leader who had also designed several of Enoch's new aqueducts, when an urgent message arrived. A young man whose facial resemblance to Omak was unmistakable was ushered into Cain's presence. Omak was long dead, but Cain had never forgotten how the older man had helped him. Now, here was Yorak, one of his grandsons, earnestly requesting that he be allowed to speak with Cain in private.

"Leave us," Cain said as he waved the servants and guards away.

"Sir," said Yorak in a low voice. "Omak held you in great respect. He commanded all of us to aid you. I hope you will not be angered at my warning."

"What is this warning?" Cain asked with a frown.

"Yesterday a new caravan arrived in Enoch. The travelers claimed they were traders from a settlement in the west. They said they had heard an ancient legend about a man named Cain, a man who had murdered his own brother."

Yorak's voice trailed off, and he shifted his feet nervously.

"Go on," said Cain firmly.

"The coincidence of the name seemed surprising. But there is something else. Some of these travelers were seen at the palace. The Lady Ushar was said to have given them an audience."

"To what purpose?"

"I cannot say, sir. Yet why would the lady speak to anyone bringing such a malicious charge?"

"Why, indeed," replied Cain in an undertone. "I thank you for this news, my friend. You must tell no one of our words together."

Yorak placed his right hand over his heart, bowed silently, and left the room.

Cain suddenly recalled the soothsayer's prophecy he had previously dismissed: "These women will doom the men they marry." Now he could take no chances. However incredible Ushar's betrayal might be, he thought with grim irony that Enoch's success, and his own, had probably played some part in it. But that couldn't be helped now. His return to the city would have to follow a different script from the one he had planned.

Two days later, Cain sat alone in his palace in Enoch. His trusted guards had arrested Ushar, rounded up the traders, and secured the residence. Cain could not bring himself to order Ushar's execution. She was the mother of his firstborn son. And she was Tutok's daughter. Besides, with no clear proof of treachery, the supreme punishment would have been impolitic. He therefore pronounced a sentence of exile for life. She could, he told her, make her bed with the traders she had befriended.

CHAPTER 12

City of Enoch

It had been a speedy victory. The forces of the land of Ergot had been no match for Cain's veteran troops, and Enoch had prevailed in a matter of weeks, rather than months. Ergot's defeat meant that Enoch would now control the largest and most productive silver mines in the region, as well as thousands of new slaves to work them.

Cain had launched this military venture shortly after a visit by Ergot's economic emissary, who had been sent to Enoch to propose, for the first time, an increase in the exchange price of silver. The visitor had explained to Cain's ministers how Enoch's accelerating consumption was creating production bottlenecks at the mines and requiring diversion of laborers from other sectors.

"How much do they want?" Cain asked Samek, Enoch's minister of trade, as they walked along a balcony overlooking the city.

"They are asking 15 percent, majesty. The good news is they indicate a willingness to fix these terms for ten years."

Cain knew as well as anyone that the proposed terms were reasonable enough, but the mere thought of adding to a neighbor's prosperity sparked a fit of jealousy. Yet, as he returned to his throne room, his face and voice betrayed nothing to Samek of the rage that welled up within him.

"Ask them to give us thirty days to think the matter through," he told the emissary.

Precisely one month later, Ergot received its answer, personally delivered through its gates by Cain and fifty thousand elite invaders.

❦

As the first citizen of Enoch, Cain now exercised unquestioned authority. Part shaman and part military leader, he had now ruled the city for centuries. For the most part, his contemporaries accepted and even lauded his seeming immortality as validating the efficacy of his communication with the spirit world. All of Enoch's original citizens were long dead, but Cain was able to convince the newer generations of his skill in communing with the weather spirit Lorac—a relationship that closely linked their fate to his "powers."

Thus, at the celebration of the victory over Ergot, he was accorded special honors. As Cain's war chariot drew to a halt, his fifth-generation descendant Lamech ceremoniously placed a crown of laurel on the commander's head and a solid gold chain with a medallion of lapis lazuli around his neck. Lamech's son Jubal, whose inventions included both the harp and the flute, led hundreds of musicians in a joyous serenade. A delegation of Enoch's wealthiest and most influential citizens then escorted Cain to his palace. During the parade, Cain reveled in his role as the ruler of the known world's most powerful kingdom. There was nothing more important in life than the love of wealth, power, and fame, he thought. Basking in Enoch's praise, he was the possessor of all three.

What made it even sweeter was that he'd done it all himself.

As the nobles prepared to depart, Cain asked one of them, a trader named Marek, to stay behind. Marek was a descendant of Omak, whose family had always enjoyed a special relationship with Cain. Trading was Marek's profession, but his most important duties, in fact, were to keep Cain informed about all that transpired in

Enoch. To this end, Marek administered a staff of several hundred trusted informants. The covert organization was tantamount to a secret police force.

When the two men were alone, Cain began as he always did.

"What news, my friend?" he asked.

"The city has been mostly quiet since you departed for Ergot," Marek replied. "But there were several instances of discontent concerning isolated food shortages from the recent weak harvests. Further, your kinsman Lamech has caused some disturbance. It seems he killed a man in a drunken brawl. Nothing remarkable there. But then he boasted publicly of the killing. He said that if any of the dead man's clan dared to attack him in revenge and killed him, that person would be punished, not seven times, but seventy-seven times."

"That was not wise of him, Marek," Cain noted impassively.

"No, sir, but the real concern is the tale Lamech has been spreading about the harvest failures. He asserts that your relationship with the spirit Lorac has been at the root of the problem. He suggests that you are using Lorac to augment your own vitality and youth at the expense of the city's prosperity. According to Lamech, you are draining Lorac of his power to produce ever greater harvests. While most people think that Lamech is simply arrogant, I must tell you that he is attracting a following with some of his generation."

Cain listened with seeming detachment, but inwardly he bristled at this budding challenge to his authority.

"Is there anything else to report?"

"Yes, sir. Four days ago, one of my lieutenants met with a traveler from the western region. This man, it seems, wanted to buy some building equipment. Saws, hammers, wood fasteners—that sort of thing. He had purchased such items in Enoch before, but his regular supplier became ill and the business was suspended. He was therefore inquiring who might give him the best terms."

"I assume we accommodated him in a profitable manner," Cain smiled.

"Of course, sir. But the next part of the report is mysterious," Marek continued. "My operative asked the traveler, whose name was Tarn, what the building material was being used for. Tarn told him a strange story about an old man named Noah. This man claims that a great flood is about to occur and that it will wipe out everything on Earth. To save himself and his family, Noah is building an enormous ship of advanced technology called an ark. The ship is supposedly finished, but Noah wished to procure a few more replacement parts. That's why Tarn was sent to Enoch."

Cain leaned forward with interest.

"Is this traveler still within our walls?" he asked.

"Yes, sir. Do you wish to see him?"

"I think it would be prudent. Have him brought here tonight so I can interview him personally. But do it in a way that does not attract attention, and be certain that Lamech learns nothing of this."

Nodding assent, Marek stood up and took his leave.

Cain considered these developments. Since the banishment of Ushar, his first wife, his longevity and vitality had simply been attributed to his relationship with Lorac. But now his youthful regeneration was surfacing again as a potential threat to his power. Periodically, Cain wondered if perhaps the mark that God had supposedly placed upon him could have extended his lifespan. The mark, he thought, might be symbolic rather than literal, since there were no unusual physical marks on his body.

If God was capable of such a thing, why would he have done it? So far, living several times longer than all other human beings had been a blessing, not a curse. Cain also remained skeptical of the master of spirits' claim of credit for his longevity. After all, he did none of this master's bidding, so why should that supposed master continue to aid

Cain? Along with this so-called curse of not aging, Cain had discovered that his body regenerated at a highly accelerated rate from abrasions, cuts, and even occasional broken bones. He seemed immune to infections, poisonous insects, and even snakebites. A by-product of his bodily regeneration was an enhanced memory that permanently recorded every day of his life in perfect detail.

Fortunately, being a powerful ruler meant that no man would dare try to kill him. Thus, he had rendered moot God's promise of sevenfold vengeance on would-be assailants. Also, the kingdom of Enoch itself was testimony to what he could accomplish on his own. Perhaps humans did not need any god or spirit to protect them or help them through life. Cain certainly didn't.

The ostensible threat from within his family, Cain thought, was not to his physical well-being, but to his authority. Until now, he had dismissed Lamech's occasional resentful outbursts as those of a spoiled, impatient heir. But Cain understood that believers in spirits could be as fickle as they imagined the spirits themselves to be. Could Lamech succeed in mounting a challenge to his rule? Cain knew that he could not control the weather, and the kingdom of Enoch for the most part had been blessed with an amazing run of favorable growing seasons. If a truly catastrophic series of harvests came about, Lamech might gain widespread support. He was popular with the younger generation, and silencing him would not be as easy as banishing a treacherous wife.

Perhaps an answer lay with this rumored ark. Could its technology afford access to the remote seas and thus provide the means for a monumental expansion of Enoch's military and economic might? Cain reasoned that the successful exploitation of distant lands would offer further insurance against the vagaries of local growing conditions. If Cain brought the secrets of the ark back to Enoch, his feat would quickly silence Lamech and any supporters he might gather one day. He determined to quietly investigate the ark on his own.

In his interview with the traveler, Cain learned much. Noah, Tarn said, was eloquent but eccentric. He insisted that there was only one God, and that this deity spoke directly to him. According to Noah, God had commanded him to build a giant ark. The ship would enable its occupants to survive the coming flood. No one in the western region took Noah seriously, but neither did they interfere with the old man's obsession. If he wanted to prophesy doomsday, so be it.

Cain thanked the traveler courteously and wished him a safe return to his land. In a separate interview, he ordered Marek's lieutenant to find out all he could from Tarn about the location of Noah's ark. The lieutenant was even to imply that successful negotiations for further supplies would be contingent on an accurate description of the ark's location.

Based on the report of Marek's lieutenant, Cain calculated it would take them ten days to reach Noah's building site. The patriarch lived near the ark, together with his wife, their three sons, and the sons' wives. It seemed as if Noah was at least several hundred years old and had been working on this advanced ark for nearly a century. Strange that the news of this ship had only now reached Cain's ear.

❧

A month later, under cover of night, Cain and a handpicked military battalion rode through the city's main gate. Marek had spread the story that the commander was traveling to Ergot to inspect the mines. In reality, their destination was the western region to find and seize the ark, if it truly existed.

On the day after they left Enoch, storm clouds enveloped the sky and it started to rain. This was odd for the season, Cain thought, but he was accustomed to traveling in any weather.

On the fifth day out, the rain had still not abated. The horses were becoming restive. The force had entered a mountainous region, and the soil there was less hard-packed than the mounts were used to. Their hooves were making deep depressions in the mud, and the pace of the expedition slowed considerably.

On the twelfth day, they entered a vast old-growth forest. It was here, according to Tarn's directions, that they would find Noah and his ark. Day by day, the rain had been growing harder, and visibility was poor. Still, from the forest craft he had accumulated over time, Cain was confident they would reach their destination.

Toward evening, the expedition was traveling westward along a high ridgeline. In the lead, Cain felt the ground shake and heard an ominous rumble from below. He peered down to his right. North of the ridge, and quite close across a small river, lay a huge ship. It was not a rumor anymore, Cain thought. It was true. He was determined to claim this ship for his own purposes.

They could see a procession of animals slowly making their way up a massive ramp door that led into the belly of the vessel. From this distance, Cain could make out only the larger animals. There were pairs of lions and a group of ibex, with their recurved, ridged horns. But there were many animals in the procession that he did not recognize.

The downpour increased. The men saw that the river separating them from the ark had begun to rise appreciably, even in the brief time they had been there. If they were to reach the ark, they had to act now. Before their departure, Cain had worked out a plan with his senior officers that provided for a small, elite band of soldiers to accompany him in situations such as this one. He signaled now that the designated troops should follow him.

Spurring their horses into a canter, the men descended from the ridge and forded the stream. Just as the horses found their footing on the opposite bank, a sudden surge of water cut off most of the party on the other side, making their crossing impossible. Several bolts of lightning and loud claps of thunder boomed across a darkening sky. With a shout and a crack of their whips, Cain and his five remaining companions called on their horses for renewed effort to exit the rapidly rising river and make haste to the nearby ark.

They were now within fifty meters of the massive vessel. At the top of the ramp just inside the doorway, Cain spotted a tall, white-bearded man with outspread arms, seemingly in greeting of the beasts as they entered inside. The procession was nearly at an end. After the last pair of animals stepped over the threshold, the huge doorway to the huge ship quickly closed as if on its own power. As they arrived at the ark, the men faced an enormous wall of wood, with no visible way to get aboard. Close behind them, the waters were rising fast.

"Get to the ship and look for a way in," Cain shouted. "It is our only hope to survive!"

Without warning, the river's rapid current overflowed its banks and gripped Cain, his men, and their horses. Their mounts screamed in fear. Horses and riders were borne by the current along the side of the ark, with Cain desperately scanning the expertly joined timbers for another doorway, a window, a trailing line of rope—anything that would afford him an entryway or even a toehold. His horse was now swimming with Cain on its back. If he could not cling to the ship somehow, he would be swept away by the current and drown.

In the twilight, he saw three of his men shed their swords and grab hold of a thick, dangling rope that had escaped his attention. Stout veterans of many wars, they started to pull themselves up toward the railing high overhead, kicking one another as they inched slowly upward. Once aboard, Cain was confident they would quickly gain control of the ark.

Cain was now almost parallel to the stern of the ship, where he spotted another rope dangling from the transom. Without warning, an enormous wave propelled him toward the ark, lifting his legs from the doomed horse and thrusting him toward a porthole in the boat's stern. He could see that the same wave stripped the trio of soldiers from their lifeline and propelled them screaming into the raging torrent below.

He had barely managed to grasp his rope when a broken tree branch whizzed by and tore a large gash in his shoulder. Ignoring the pain, Cain hauled himself up the line and crawled through the porthole, which seemed like the exit point of some wooden tunnel or chute. Heaving with painful breaths, blood streaming down his arm, he lay in the darkness as the great boat began to float on the rising waters.

CHAPTER 13

The Ark

"...on that day all the springs of the great deep burst forth, and the floodgates of the heavens were opened." (Genesis 7:11, NIV)

Crouching inside the dark tunnel, trying to collect himself, Cain was suddenly jolted by a violent motion. His stomach dropped as the ark surged upward at dizzying speed, and when the vessel abruptly slowed its ascent he was catapulted against the top of the tunnel. Steadying himself, he crawled to the transom and stared out at a terrifying scene.

Torrential rain fell from storm clouds. Blinding flashes were accompanied by earsplitting thunder, causing the ark to shudder from bow to stern. The powerful wind made the deluge seem almost horizontal. Cain noticed that the nearby hills from which they had descended to the ark were gone, buried beneath the torrent. The ark was already hundreds of feet higher, and the waters were still rising.

Where dry land was still visible, he could see giant, yawning cracks that spidered outward with horrifying speed, like canyons that had taken on preternatural life. Before his eyes, some of these chasms grew to a width of a mile or more. From inside the earth, huge jets of water spewed through the apertures, rising thousands of feet into the roiling sky. The springs from below and the rain from above seemed united with a single objective: the undoing of all creation.

As Cain gaped in astonishment, the stern of the ark began to rotate slowly. The variable gales seemed to have trapped the vessel in a spiraling orbit atop a maelstrom. However, before it had made a full revolution, the ark's motion diminished, and a break in the clouds revealed an amazing sight—his beloved city, Enoch!

Although he had traveled many miles from Enoch to the ark, the gap in the clouds seemed to magnify his view, and from the ark's loftier vantage point he was now offered a panorama of the city walls as well as the great pyramid at its center. At that moment the ark's motion ceased altogether, and Cain saw a gigantic crack in the earth racing toward the city, a crack that fragmented into a spidery web of fissures and surrounded Enoch.

What Cain saw next sickened him.

From beneath the city, an explosive water column of incredible power rocketed his pyramid-shaped palace thousands of feet into the air. Hundreds more clefts created a huge gulf many miles wide. As massive quantities of water spiraled inward, the entire city literally dissolved and crumbled into the belly of the earth.

Cain was now trembling. Where Enoch had stood, a huge whirlpool now spun. But, amazingly, the destruction was not yet complete. The tall, snow-capped mountains, once the perennial source of the city's water supply, began to topple from their foundations and avalanche into the vortex, burying the remains of Enoch under thousands of feet of rock. His great city of wealth and power and technology—the most glorious of all civilizations on Earth—had been annihilated in a matter of moments.

The ark now resumed a slow spin. Cain, exhausted and mortified, lay back with his eyes closed. He could not begin to comprehend his loss. The torrential rain turned even more violent, as if the entire atmosphere itself was liquefying. If he were outside, he probably could not even breathe, such was the force of this tempest. The noise of the downpour grew deafening, even through the thick, protective timbers of the ark. It was as if a million troops were marching on the vessel's roof. Any skepticism about Noah and his prophecy was erased by what Cain saw and heard—God most surely was destroying the world.

Overwhelmed by this catastrophic realization, he could barely drag himself through the tunnel to the inside of the ark. Collapsing behind a large support post, Cain hyperventilated for several moments before spinning into unconsciousness.

CHAPTER 14

En Route to Naples, Italy: Present Day

The long-range business jet had taken off from Van Nuys airfield near Los Angeles promptly at noon on Saturday. Luc Renard instructed the pilot to file a flight plan taking them directly to Naples, where a chartered helicopter would ferry him and his passengers to Ercolano. Since the Bombardier Global Express XRS had no need to refuel en route, Luc anticipated a midday arrival on Sunday. They would be in plenty of time for the transfer of the land title and Monday afternoon's dramatic press conference.

The fifty-foot-long flight cabin had been laid out for eight passengers, but even so it was only half full. At the front of the cabin reclined Giovanni Genoa, hitching a ride back to his native country and evidently fast asleep. In the row behind Genoa sat Luc Renard, idly flipping through a stack of his company's glossy magazine *Tattletale*. On the other side of the aisle, within hailing distance of Renard should he be needed, was Rudolph Schmidt, Esq., a powerful Beverly Hills attorney who had been brought along to assist with title transfer papers and other legal matters during the trip. Schmidt, a seasoned litigator and passionate jazz fan, was immersed in his iPod.

At the rear of the cabin was Dr. Archibald Walker of the Getty Villa. He had deliberately chosen his seat, both to flirt with the voluptuous flight attendant and to consume more than his fair share of the cocktails that she was winsomely dispensing.

"Another Bombay Sapphire and tonic, Dr. Walker?" the attendant inquired.

"Why not?" Walker asked with a rhetorical grin as he pressed the young woman's hand. "But mum's the word, my dear!" he cautioned. "What did you say your name was?"

"Sharon," she answered with a broad smile.

"Ah yes, as lovely as a rose of Sharon in high summer," Walker purred. Then he giggled at his own fatuous analogy as the attendant glided away to fetch his drink.

⚜

Two hours before the plane was due to land in Naples, Walker awoke from his boozy slumber. After tucking in to a scrumptious breakfast of crabmeat Benedict on croissants, he glanced at his watch. Then he used the XRS's sophisticated communications system to place a call to Silvio Sforza.

Walker dispensed with elaborate salutations. "Silvio? It's Archibald. I have a surprise for you. We're arriving a day early. Mr. Renard wishes to inspect the site this afternoon. I expect we'll be in Naples Airport by eleven o'clock."

Silvio cleared his throat as he walked alongside Juan Carlos. "Well, Archibald, that is a surprise. Ah, I look forward to seeing you, and meeting Mr. Renard. Is there anything you need?"

"Thank you, but Mr. Renard has us well taken care of. Is everything arranged for the press conference tomorrow afternoon?"

Silvio hesitated while he thought of Amanda, inside the chamber and possibly trapped.

"Yes. The podium and sound system will be set up this evening, and I've reconfirmed all the attendees from the media."

"Delightful! Of course, I'll want you on the podium with me in front of the television cameras when the donation to the Getty is announced." Walker made a mental note to have someone get him fresh hair gel for his appearance. "Now, the cameras will focus on me slipping into the crack just before I open the doors to the chamber, correct?"

Silvio shook his head. Archibald sure hadn't changed. "Absolutely. We'll have several handheld cameras in addition to the fixed locations near the podium."

"Perfect. Now, what about Amanda's progress in evaluating the doorway?"

With Walker's arrival imminent, Silvio had no option besides candor. "We're at the dig now. Amanda succeeded in breaking the door code much faster than we anticipated. She's actually inside the chamber as we speak… just to take a brief look around."

Walker irritably complained, "But we agreed that no one would…"

"I know, I know. But now we have a problem. She must have triggered some mechanism inadvertently, because the doors have closed again. She's been in the chamber for over two hours, and we can't get through to her wireless."

"*What*?" Walker forced down a spasm of acid reflux. "We specifically agreed that I would be the first person to enter the chamber, Silvio! How dare you let this happen! Amanda is a junior colleague. A *very* junior colleague, I may remind you!"

"I understand. But we had to get a head start, and the main thing is that she successfully solved the combination lock."

Walker sniffed. "I'm sure that, had I been there in person, I would have cracked the code as well. But listen to me. Renard has chartered a helicopter. We'll be at the site by noon, or a little afterward. You had better figure out how to extricate her from the chamber—or she can figure it out herself, if she's that clever. But she must be out by noon, and *no one* at the press conference needs to know she was in there first!"

"We'll do our best, Archibald. See you later today. Have a safe flight." Silvio ended the call before Walker could say anything else and turned to Juan Carlos.

"I need to make another quick call. Could you please go find Carmelo and tell him to come see me?"

As Juan Carlos departed, Silvio dialed a telephone number in Rome.

Aboard Renard's jet, Dr. Walker clicked off the connection and rose from his seat. He found Luc Renard deeply engrossed in his laptop. From all appearances, Giovanni Genoa, sprawled in the row ahead, was still fast asleep.

"Excuse me, Mr. Renard. I hate to interrupt you," said Walker, keeping his voice low so as not to wake the sleeping painter, "but I think there is something you should know."

Luc gazed up from his work and then motioned Walker into the adjacent seat.

"What do I need to know?"

Dr. Walker rubbed his hands nervously on the legs of his slacks. "I was just on the phone with Silvio Sforza. He's at the excavation site. Amanda James succeeded in cracking the language code on the door."

"That's great news! Good for her. It certainly simplifies our task."

"But there's one more thing. Amanda explicitly violated my understanding with Sforza. He allowed her to enter the chamber. Then the doors closed, for whatever reason. She's trapped inside."

Luc's eyes narrowed. "How long has she been in there?"

"More than two hours."

The icy stare that greeted Walker made him wish he'd brought a fresh cocktail along for this conversation.

"Dr. Walker," Luc intoned sternly. "We've known each other for, what, six or seven years?"

"I...uh, yes, I believe so."

"I would think by now you would have learned from me how to keep subordinates under control!"

Expecting no response, Luc looked at his watch and then waved Walker away.

"Well, don't be concerned, Doctor. We'll be arriving there shortly. Then we'll sort things out."

CHAPTER 15

The Ark

Cain awoke several hours later, greeted by waves of pain from the deep gash in his bleeding shoulder. As his consciousness returned, so did a torrent of the horrific images he had just witnessed. Attempting to suppress them, but with only limited success, he rose slowly to begin exploring what he now realized was his lifeboat.

Yet it was a boat full of danger as well. Noah and his sons were unknown quantities. They could be zealots, or even fanatics. Still in shock from what he had seen, Cain felt intensely vulnerable. He was now nothing more than a stowaway. He had no way of telling if the ark's makers were armed, or what action they might take if he were discovered. Cain had only his small knife to defend himself, as his larger weapons were torn off his body by the rogue wave that deposited him in the tunnel.

He had no idea how long he had been unconscious, but he noted that the deafening sound of the downpour outside had subsided, and the motion of the ark was more languid. He wasn't certain, but he guessed he was on the bottom deck of the ark. Peering around the support post, Cain stared down a long aisle of cages and stalls. At the end of this aisle, he saw a tall haystack and noted it as a promising hiding place. As he walked by, he gathered a handful of fresh straw and dressed his bloody shoulder as best he could. Gazing down the row of cages, he saw hundreds—no, thousands—of birds. In the dim light that filtered down the stairwells from the vessel's upper decks, they clucked, chirped, and twittered. Species after species stood in pairs, like the large animals he had seen on the ramp before the ark's door closed. Cain wondered if their annoying din would go on and on, but it soon trailed off. After a while, only an occasional screech could be heard.

Still apprehensive about being discovered, Cain inadvertently mumbled in a low voice that Noah's sons might "throw me overboard if they find me." With a start, he heard an echo: "Throw me overboard!" When he looked for the source of the echo, he spotted a large green bird with a red streak on its belly, perched on a wooden bar nearby. He was stunned to hear the bird repeat the phrase. A talking *bird*? Was this the master of spirits tormenting him, or God?

"Who are you?" demanded Cain, but the bird simply continued to scratch its molting plumage.

He was tempted to retreat back behind the post, lest the bird draw attention to his whereabouts. But with no sign of human activity, Cain pushed onward. Inside, the ark seemed far larger than outside. Walking down the aisle from the stern to the bow, Cain reckoned the length at many times the height of Enoch's inner wall. He realized that a ship on this scale was an exceptional feat of engineering and construction. He admired how the impossibly thick timbers were expertly milled and joined, forming a robust interior frame from bow to stern and side to side.

It seemed likely that the ark could accommodate tens of thousands of animals. But how would they be fed and watered? And what would be done with the tons of waste they would produce each day?

Cain carefully examined a stall holding sheep and goats. Water was dripping from a channel that ran up to the slatted ceiling and then, presumably, to a tank on the middle or upper deck. Feed had been placed in baskets around the stall. Like the ceiling, the floor of the stall was slatted and angled at a slight slope. Thus the animals' excrement would either be trampled into a pit below the cage or would roll into a gutter that ran outside the cages all the way from the bow to the stern. Investigating further, Cain realized he was wise to have extricated himself from the chute at the stern. For the tunnel that had afforded him entry to the ark was, in fact, one of the ship's main sewage outlets.

Amidship in the lower level of the ark, in a pool of bilge water, Cain saw what looked to be a large, vertical metal tube with several projecting bars. The dangling chains at the end of the spokes were fitted around the neck of several beasts walking in a circle to power the mechanism. The sound of water rushing through pipes at the top of the device gave away its use: a giant water pump. For even a ship as expertly crafted as the ark leaked water and needed to be pumped dry to stay afloat.

Glancing upward, Cain noticed several ramps and ladders leading to an upper level. He wanted to explore further, but he had no way of knowing the whereabouts of Noah and his family, nor what they might do if he were discovered. Might there be others on the ark like himself—stowaways who had sneaked aboard at the last minute? But back in Enoch, the traveler Tarn had said that no one in the region took Noah's flood prophecy seriously. Cain thought it likely that he was the only extra passenger.

As he stood indecisively by the ramp, Cain's mind buzzed with further questions. Even if he could stay hidden, how would he feed himself? Killing an animal was out of the question; the risk of detection was simply too great. A better choice would be to eat the animals' food. After all, with apparently ample provisions for thousands of beasts, one more stomach to feed would hardly deplete the supply.

Where were they headed, he wondered, and how long would the voyage last? Any flood that could destroy cities and mountains could take many months to subside—not that there was anything for Cain to go back to outside the ark. The world as he knew it was gone, and Cain understood that if and when the journey ended, he would be starting over.

The whole world would be starting over.

Shaking his head, Cain banished such thoughts. He would live as he always had, with survival as his chief goal. Within a single day, his fortunes had brought him from a position of royalty to that of a penniless stowaway. Yet he had not drowned but lived. His confidence rekindled, Cain gingerly mounted the ladder.

On the next level, Cain found a setup that very much resembled the arrangements on the bottom deck. Whereas birds, reptiles, and small mammals had predominated below, here there were larger creatures, including cattle, donkeys, pigs, monkeys, great apes, and many kinds of horses. To Cain's surprise, several species of the big cats, including lions and leopards, were lodged very close to the cattle, whom they eyed with interest.

Also on this level were several types of large mammals. Cain had heard his father's description of elephants, although he had never seen one himself. He stared in fascination at the huge beasts, lazily flapping their ears and exploring the feed baskets with their trunks. On the other side of the ark, he was equally intrigued by pairs of large, powerful looking beasts with thick skin, enormous snouts, and either one or two protruding horns. He did not have a name for them, but he knew he would not enjoy being the target of such an animal's charge. The elephants looked decidedly better tempered.

Just as on the bottom deck, ramps and ladders stretched upward from points about halfway down each of the main aisles. Standing at the foot of the starboard stairway, Cain hesitated to climb further, for he heard the sound of human voices. For the moment, at least, he could probably learn more by eavesdropping than by exploring.

Noah was evidently instructing his sons in their duties.

"Ham, Shem, and Japheth, my sons! We all must pitch in with
the food and water supplies. Remember to check every cage and stall
for signs of a sick animal. And keep in mind that this is a temporary
sojourn for these creatures. We will not have to give these beasts long-
term care, only an emergency rescue."

So Noah envisioned an end to their voyage sooner, rather than
later, thought Cain.

"As you know, my sons, many of these animals are free-ranging
by nature. Unaccustomed to confinement, they may grow nervous.
Do not become severe with them, my sons. Like you and me, they are
God's creatures."

The silence that ensued was Cain's cue for departure. Ham,
Shem, and Japheth might well be preparing to descend below decks.
Cain retreated down a level to the haystack.

❦

During the next few weeks, he fell into a hide-and-seek routine,
eluding Noah's sons on the bottom deck and venturing out only in
search of food. His shoulder wound had quickly healed and left no
trace of a scar. Cain had been careful not to leave drops of blood
creating a trail back to his hiding place in the haystack. To lessen the
chance of discovery, he jettisoned the bloodied straw dressings out
the back of the ark.

His best source of sustenance was the bird cages, where ample
quantities of seeds were provided. He also pilfered from the squirrels,
whose supply of nuts diminished rather more swiftly than expected,
thus puzzling the well-muscled but somewhat ingenuous sons of
Noah. From the monkeys, Cain procured roots and dried fruit.

One day, while hiding in the haystack, Cain overheard Japheth
and Shem talking. Like Ham, the third son, both of them were much

taller and more physically powerful than Cain. Brawny from the years of physical labor in building the ark, they could easily overpower him if he were discovered. Perhaps they would even throw him overboard.

"Throw me overboard!" came an echo. As Shem and Japheth stared at the green bird in disbelief, Cain could not suppress a grin. Was the bird a mind reader?

Periodically, great waves of noise washed over the ark. Provoked by some unaccountable trigger, and joining in chorus to outdo each other, the animals howled, brayed, roared, and trumpeted. After a brief pause, they took up the calls again: barking, squeaking, shrieking, bellowing, whinnying, bleating, grunting, and caterwauling. They neighed, hissed, and whined. When it happened at night, Cain was forced to stuff crushed hay into his ears.

It was another month before he thought it safe to venture upward to the top of the ark. Here Cain glimpsed another collection of smaller mammals, including rabbits, hares, mongooses, small wild cats, and jackals. Around the ark ran a semi-enclosed balcony, affording light and adequate ventilation to the whole vessel.

Cain gazed in amazement from the balcony. Rain was still falling. By now the height of the waters was staggering. There was not a single trace of dry land to be seen. Just small islands of tangled vegetation floating in the water. Logs, branches, and sticks mainly. But more disturbing were the bloated carcasses of cattle and other animals, along with what looked like human remains in those clusters. Cain grimaced at the occasional sight of large, saw-toothed fishes with gaping jaws frenetically feeding on the corpses. It was a ghastly image he hoped not to remember, but he knew his perfect memory would record its every detail for future nightmares, as it had for more than a millennium.

Angry at God's vengeance, Cain made his way back to the haystack, which was beginning to shrink as time wore on. Having just witnessed a fate far worse than drowning if he were discovered and thrown overboard, he dug even deeper into the remaining straw pile before falling asleep. Thankfully, none of his wives or mistresses had ever mentioned to him that he snored.

Several days later, after night had fallen, Cain ascended surreptitiously to the middle deck and crouched at his listening post to eavesdrop again. He overheard Noah delivering what sounded like a sermon to his sons.

"My sons, as you tend these animals, remain mindful of God's mercy and his care for us. Life after this great deluge will be hard. We will have to rebuild everything we had before the flood. We are still alive because God found us righteous in his sight. All the others succumbed to corruption and evil, and that is why they have perished."

"But Father," Shem asked, "why did God create all peoples only to destroy them?"

"The flood grieves God's heart," Noah replied. "He had no wish to destroy humanity. But human beings rejected God by their actions. Murder and lust, greed and theft, and betrayal and idolatry had no end. False idol worship especially angered the Lord."

"Why did God spare the animals, Father?" asked Japheth.

"Animals cannot commit idolatry, Japheth. They follow their instincts. Animals may slay each other, but we would never call their violence acts of murder. God has made them so that they live by the laws of nature. God had mercy on them, just as he pitied us. That is why he gathered them from all parts of the earth and brought them to the ark."

"And how long will the flood last?" Ham wanted to know.

"God has his own purposes, my son. We will know that the deluge is near its end when the waters from above and below recede. Then, after the ark comes to rest, we will send out winged messengers to explore the Earth."

Silence signaled that the conversation was over. Cain crept back to his hiding place and lay down to rest. Before he fell asleep, he could not help but reflect on the paradox Noah seemed to embody. Cain had never heard such confidence mingled with such dependence. Noah, too, believed in survival, but only at the will and pleasure of his God.

Cain had kept only rough track of his days on the ark, but he knew that months had elapsed since the ship's great doorway closed. The animals were becoming noisier and ever more restless. The thick odor of animal waste smothered the ark like a fetid blanket. In contrast to Noah's steely resolve, Cain was beginning to despair at, what for him, were the prisonlike conditions he had no choice but to endure.

❧

One evening at his listening post, Cain overheard Noah speaking to his sons about an "altar" and a "covenant." Cain shuddered at the remembrance of his own disfavored sacrifice and the curse it had brought upon him, but he had no idea what a covenant referred to.

"The rains have ceased!" Noah announced with joy. "A drying wind has been sent from God. The floodwaters will begin to recede. Within the next week or so, our ark will come to rest."

Noah proved correct. One week to the day after he had made his prediction, the ark lodged on a mountainside with a loud thud. But release for her passengers was not imminent. The waters would still have to retreat far enough to make disembarking—and spreading out afterward—practical and safe.

More than three months passed on the stationary vessel. For Cain, this was the most trying part of the whole ordeal. He was desperate to leave the ark. Indeed, he had devoted most of his time over the last several weeks to planning how he would explore the earth. On his mind as well was how he would escape from the ark unobserved. If Noah stood at the only doorway to bid the animals farewell, as he had stood there to greet them months ago, Cain could not avail himself of that exit. He would have to improvise, depending on circumstances. In any case, he thought with a grimace, he could use the chute leading through the transom if he had to, lowering himself by means of a rope to the ground.

During this time, Cain also pondered what Noah had revealed about God's purposes. It seemed clear that Enoch had been targeted for supreme punishment, and part of Cain seethed with resentment at the annihilation of his life's work. Had God willed Cain's destruction as well, and, if so, was it just a matter of time? Although he had been protected by the ark, was his destiny to be obliterated once he left the vessel? And how would this be consistent with the mark God had placed on him and with his apparent longevity—perhaps even immortality?

Finally, Noah declared that he had received God's command to leave the ark. As the patriarch, his family, and the animals began to disembark, Cain bided his time, and his patience was rewarded. Noah's first act on dry land was to build an altar of thanksgiving. He and his sons prepared a sacrifice. As the smoke from the altar rose to the heavens, a brilliant rainbow appeared in the sky. After months of clouds and rain, the colors shocked the senses with their intensity and beauty.

Noah and his family gazed up at the glorious phenomenon. Rapt, they failed to notice a man leading a pair of horses down a narrow path behind the ark. Strapped to the backs of the beasts were some caged chickens, several sacks of grain, a spear for fishing, and a bow and arrow.

As the rainbow burned in the sky, Cain set his face toward the horizon and walked without looking back.

CHAPTER 16

The Great Wandering

etermined to put as much distance between himself and the tribe of Noah as possible, Cain traveled as swiftly as he could. As the ark faded into the distance behind him, he turned and raised his fist in a final gesture of indignation. He had survived, but for what? Noah's God seemed to have blessed the ark builder and cursed the stowaway.

Cain navigated by the sun and the stars. The horses were fresh and eager for the journey, though they traveled through a world that was eerily silent, save for the occasional call or wing beat of a passing bird. He almost missed the cacophony of the ark. Its protection had been welcome. Now he was free to travel anywhere, yet with no fixed goal to give him purpose, nor human companionship to give him solace.

With game animals not yet available, he headed for open water, following the banks of the nearest large river toward the sea and watching for the flight of marine birds. Fish were his diet for some time. When he reached the nearest coastline, it proved hospitable. Gathering vegetation and the trunks of dead trees, Cain fashioned a rough-hewn camp. Clams and other crustaceans along the beach offered sustenance, and with practice he managed to spear a good number of fish in the shallows. In the first year, the horses foaled.

As an abundance of plant life returned to the world, Cain wondered if the great flood had wrought any change in his punishment. To probe the matter, he decided on a test. Although God had said the earth would never be fruitful for him, he tried planting the seeds he'd taken from the ark. But the effort was in vain. The result was a patch of ugly, stunted weeds with dark green leaves and blood-red veins.

Cain could not bear to look on what he had sown. Ripping the accursed plants out of the ground, he buried them in a shallow grave on the beach. The next morning, a violent itching burned his hands, kindling a fresh rage at his tormentor as he realized anew the gravity of his destiny—he could survive in this world, but only as a wanderer.

The eternal wanderer.

※

The master of spirits visited Cain as he slept.

"You are happy, Cain?"

"What have I to do with happiness, spirit? No, I am angry."

"As well you should be. What kind of god is this destroyer? He vaunts that he has created all, and then he annihilates all. How can such a god deserve our allegiance? He is malicious and malevolent."

"But I did not drown. The ark kept me safe."

"And to whom should you be grateful for this outcome, Cain? It is I, and I alone, who saved you. The huge wave, the dangling rope, the port-hole—I led you then. And I preserve you now."

"For what purpose, spirit?"

"I safeguard you against a natural death. God has punished all of humanity for your parents' ambitions. You can blame him for the sorry plight of mortals."

Death. Punishment. Blame. The words rose to a crescendo even as the voice of the master of spirits dimmed. Another voice replaced it, a voice from far in Cain's past.

Where is your brother? Where is Abel?

"I don't know. Am I my brother's keeper?"

From now on you will be a homeless wanderer on the earth.

"My punishment is too great for me to bear! You have banished me from the land and from your presence. Anyone who finds me will kill me!"

No, for I will give a sevenfold punishment to anyone who kills you.

Cain wrestled in his sleep. Whom did he believe? Whom *could* he believe?

❦

As the earth regenerated, animals spread once more across its face. Cain surmised that Noah's descendants were likely spreading as well, but where were they? Where was he?

Cain paced the world with restless steps, seeking something he could not quite name. Traveling the length and breadth of the postdiluvian landscape, he discovered marvel after marvel: a great inland sea that stretched beyond the reach of his eyes, yet came together at a narrow strait to empty into an even more vast body of water; mountains that seemed to reach past the clouds, some spewing fire and ash from their highest reaches; sections of beaches transformed into glass by the fearsome power of lightning; a mighty river that flowed through a desert and flooded the sand with life-giving water; beautiful crystals in a shallow cave that shone like stars in the morning sun.

And so the years became decades, and the decades flowed into centuries like rivers into the ocean. Cain stayed for a time in places— long enough to hunt, or fashion pottery, or sing melancholy songs by the shore of a lake, accompanied by an animal-skin drum or a hollow reed—but always a distant urge called him onward. In the great stretches of silence, when he could hear the desolate moan of wind on some towering desert spire, Cain understood what he was really listening for.

The sound of human voices.

The gulf between his past and present was anguishing. Having used people to further his own ends for untold generations, Cain now longed for the simple pleasure of human contact. Not to control, or command, but simply to converse. Yet all he heard was the sound of his loneliness.

Most terrible of all was the void of his future. Nature could sustain him indefinitely, Cain knew, but was a future without human fellowship one in which he wanted to live? Immortality, he understood for the first time, was a curse, not a blessing.

❦

Having wandered for eons, Cain sought rest. In the desert, south of the great inland sea and west of the great river, he found a giant depression in the earth. It contained a massive freshwater lake, perhaps two weeks' journey in circumference. Finding no source feeding the oasis, he figured these waters remained here from the flood. Cain lingered long at this spot, for the hunting was excellent. Migratory flocks of birds and land animals congregated here in huge numbers. He also decided that he would now simply wait here for people to find him.

Remaining at a fixed location for decades on end, Cain took advantage of the clear desert nights to track the movements of stars and planets. On windless days, he drew celestial maps in the sand. Many clusters of stars resembled animals, he thought, and he named the patterns for his own amusement: lion, bear, crab, scorpion. And then there were rare exceptions to the usual routine: full eclipses of the sun and moon, meteor showers, and—most spectacular of all—comets. Even these long-tailed wonders, though, seemed to obey laws and be subject to patterns. An especially bright comet that Cain observed recurred every seventy-five or seventy-six years. Eventually he stopped counting how many times he saw it grace the heavens.

What he did not lose count of, however, was the diminishing number of animals visiting his now significantly shrunken oasis. Reluctantly, he reached two conclusions: First, God was apparently compelling him to resume his wandering. Second, and more galling, Noah and his clan must have died off long ago.

He would never see another human being.

ஐ

One torrid morning, a few days after an unrelenting sandstorm had swept past, Cain climbed to a high point to scan the environs for a passing herd of beasts in search of water. Approaching the edge of a tall cliff, he noticed how mighty the lone cypress tree there had become. Long ago—or was it yesterday?—it had been a sapling. In his abject solitude, Cain had lost all sense of time.

So it was that he called out in daylight on the master of spirits. Cain decided he would assent to the spirit's claim that it was he who sustained life—and if that was true, Cain determined, he would tell the spirit he was ready for the afterlife.

"I am weary, spirit. I cannot face a life of wandering anymore."

"Yes, Cain, it is so. God has punished you unjustly."

"You have told me many times that I am not to blame for Abel's death."

"True, my friend. God's mistake of rejecting your fine offering caused Abel's death, not you."

"But now, I am ready to join my brother."

"And how will this come to pass?"

"Release me, spirit. You claim to be the cause for my survival. I no longer wish to live."

"Death may not be the end of God's punishment. It is possible that death may be only the beginning."

"I don't care about possibilities. My life now is barren torture. I can't go on."

"Then I will help you. But I will not cancel your restorative powers. Your life on earth will end only if you have the courage to take it yourself. That is your very greatest power, Cain."

"What would you have me do, spirit?"

"The means are at hand. A leap from this cliff is the act of only a second, but it is also an eternal act. It is fitting that your grave will be an oasis. Death will be the source of life. You will join me forever!"

The voice dissolved in air. As Cain stood near the edge of the cliff, he pondered what the master of spirits had called the act of "only a second."

Then the other voice, the voice from long ago, resounded in Cain's head.

I will give a sevenfold punishment to anyone who kills you.

He was trapped. Paralyzed. Would God's sevenfold punishment extend to him if he took his own life—and for eternity? Breaking down, he sank to his knees.

"I curse you, master of spirits!" Cain cried. Pounding the sand, he called on God himself to end his life, but the long-absent voice remained silent. He planted his face in the dust of the earth and wept bitter tears. Just as the grains of sand inexorably slipped through his clutched fingers, so too had all meaning been emptied from his life.

Looking again over the edge of the cliff, Cain was shocked nearly witless—not by what he saw, but by what he heard.

A thin, high-pitched voice. A *human* voice.

It echoed from a short distance away to his left. The language was foreign, but its tinge of fear was palpable. Was this a trick of the spirit to entice him over the cliff's edge?

Cain crawled on his hands and knees to the very edge of the overhang with its dizzying vista. Just below the drop-off, but not visible until now because of the angle, a small boy clung to a rocky outcropping. Far below, at the base of the cliff, an older boy stared upward, extending his arms in a pleading gesture.

The boys had evidently been separated. Playing near the edge of the cliff, the younger child had taken a misstep and then, by some stroke of good fortune, managed to grab hold of the outcropping to avert a fatal fall. Meanwhile, the older boy had caught sight of him from the floor of the oasis and was shouting advice or encouragement from below.

It was clear that the child was tiring fast and would soon be unable to sustain his hold. Just as the boy's arms buckled and his feet grated along the gravel, Cain stretched full-length at a downward angle and grabbed him by the wrist.

Cain and the boy locked eyes. This was the first human face into which he had looked since before being saved by the ark. In that split second—as the boy's thin frame dangled from the end of his rescuer's powerful arm—Cain decided that he would not end his own life.

He had snatched this boy back from the edge of death. But the boy had saved him as well. Hope welled inside him—he had found human civilization again. The earth was no longer his to roam alone.

He pulled the boy all the way to safety and stood up to brush the dirt from his chest and legs. As he did so, he looked over the edge of the cliff and saw a gathering crowd of people. From their pack animals, Cain understood that it was a trading caravan—and a caravan meant that there were once again cities.

The group clambered up the steep trail Cain had taken on the other side of the cliff, and they soon joined him, smiling and laughing, at the summit. One of the men, whom he took to be the child's father, lifted him gently out of Cain's arms and kissed the boy's cheeks repeatedly.

More and more people emerged, seemingly out of nowhere. Cain was soon surrounded by men, women, and children, all happily greeting him in an unintelligible tongue. Sign language eventually cleared up the mystery of their sudden appearance at this spot. Their caravan had become lost in the sandstorm, and they had ended up in the same oasis that he was calling home.

But to where had they been traveling when the storm disoriented them? The boy's father drew a picture in the soft sand. It showed a long river, crowned by a broad delta. It was, without much doubt, the great river Cain had surveyed so long ago to the east.

Elated to join these travelers, Cain made the man understand that he could serve as their guide. The caravan adopted him, though this time not as a stowaway. His rescue of the child meant that they would treat him as one of their own. The great wandering had reached its end.

On the way to the river, Cain happily learned a new language: Egyptian.

CHAPTER 17

Malibu, California: Two Days Ago

It was just after eight o'clock on Friday morning when Laura Mendez reached Amanda's apartment. Although not a morning person, she had set her alarm for an hour earlier than usual to keep her promise to feed Plato. As she rubbed the remaining sleep from her eyes in the slanting rays of California sunshine, Laura noticed the yellow Jeep Wrangler in its usual parking slot.

"Hmmm…she must have taken a cab to the airport last night," Laura murmured as she turned the key in the door.

"And left in a hurry," she added, noticing a heap of dirty clothes on the floor. Amanda's place was normally a bit untidy, save for her immaculately organized desk and bookshelf, but Laura had never seen this much disarray. After giving a few brief strokes to Plato, who was sprawled on the center of the desk, Laura scooped up her friend's laundry and went to the bathroom to toss it in the hamper. As she passed the bedroom, Laura noticed the unmade bed with Amanda's childhood teddy bear and her XBox game controller on it.

In the bathroom, a wetsuit hung in the shower next to Amanda's surfboard, which was emblazoned with a Marine Corps logo. "Roger James holding his daughter up on the waves," Laura thought with a pang, remembering the charismatic ex-Marine. The sentiment only magnified when she began making Amanda's bed, as a paperback her friend had been reading tumbled out of the covers to the floor and ejected its bookmark—the memorial card from Mr. James's funeral service.

On the card, beneath the decorated Marine's photograph, was the Bible verse: "What good is it for a man to gain the whole world, yet forfeit his soul?"

Laura reflected back to that sad day, recalling how her friend handled the sudden tragedy of her father's death. Amanda was so grief-stricken that, in planning the funeral, she had only this verse, her mother's favorite, to draw on.

She remembered Mr. James's funeral clearly, but even more so the aftermath. She recalled how the words of that Bible verse on the memorial card had triggered several anguished, late-night conversations between her and Amanda. The phrase troubled her friend deeply, who had confessed to Laura that her mom and dad were at odds over religion. He had always boycotted the Sunday services Amanda attended regularly with her devout mother until her death. Amanda had desperately wanted to know whether her dad was in heaven, but Laura didn't have much of an answer to comfort her with.

At least during those terrible days, Amanda had Juan Carlos.

A sudden clatter punctuated by a thud broke Laura's reverie, and she returned to the living area just in time to see Plato leaping from the desk and emitting a series of plaintive meows. He had dislodged several framed photographs, which now lay strewn on the floor. Fortunately, no glass was broken.

"Have patience, my little philosopher king," Laura reprimanded. As she opened the can of food for him, Plato rubbed rapturously against her leg.

After she fed him, Laura began replacing the photographs, trying to remember where they belonged on the desk. There was a picture of Amanda at the age of twelve with her parents at the Great Wall of China, just before her mom passed away. Next in chronological order, another photo showed a blue-gowned Amanda at high school graduation in Japan. "Braces still on," commented Laura as she shook her head affectionately. More recent snapshots included a group photo of the Kappa Kappa Gamma sorority girls at a beach volleyball game, and a picture of Amanda and Laura after they won their first nine-ball tournament.

"But what's this?" Laura asked out loud as she examined a picture she hadn't seen for years in the apartment. It was a shot she herself had taken of Amanda and Juan Carlos outside the Body Electric tattoo parlor on Melrose in Hollywood. It had evidently been taken out of hiding—and recently.

"So, J. C., you really have resurfaced?" Laura mused as her mind traveled back more than seven years…

❦

The beautiful evening in late May was supposed to have been a celebration. Both the lovebirds were ecstatic. That morning, Amanda learned she had been admitted to the prestigious work-study program at the Getty—which just happened to include a full-tuition scholarship for doctoral studies at UCLA. The award letter, signed by Dr. Archibald Walker, strongly implied that a full-time position on the Getty's staff would be hers upon the receipt of her PhD.

"Talk about a gold-plated graduation present!" Amanda high-fived Laura after she read the letter aloud to her for the second time.

"Have you told J. C. yet?" Laura asked.

"Are you kidding? I called him right after I left a message for my dad—with the time difference between here and Nigeria, I'll probably hear from Dad tomorrow. Johnny was thrilled, though. He said he also had some pretty good news, but wouldn't tell me until after today's exhibition game. Something about a Castilian superstition. Anyway, he should be here by five."

They were waiting at the Kappa house, where Juan Carlos had promised to pick them up when he got back from the game.

"You guys really want me to tag along to Body Electric? I feel like a third wheel."

"Laura—you're my best friend! Besides, how often do I do something like this?"

"I still can't believe you're actually getting a tattoo."

"Johnny has been asking me for a while. I guess I just needed a good excuse."

"Okay, I'll join you. I think I really *do* need to see this!"

At a quarter past six, Juan Carlos finally rumbled up to the house on his Harley. "Am I late?" he asked with a smile. Both Laura and Amanda pretended to scowl.

"I'll take my moped and follow you," Laura said as Amanda climbed on the Softail's rear seat, her arms wrapped around Juan Carlos's waist.

At the Body Electric, Amanda went first. Within half an hour, she emerged from the parlor into the waiting room, proudly displaying a small rendering of a papyrus scroll tattooed on her right ankle. After Laura and Juan Carlos had duly admired the artist's handiwork, Amanda gestured toward the inner sanctum.

"Your turn, Johnny!"

"Mine will definitely take longer," Juan Carlos told them. "Rather than just sit in the waiting room, why don't you two go for a coffee across the street?"

"But I want to watch," Amanda protested.

"Sorry, chica mia. It's part of the surprise."

An hour later, Juan Carlos strolled into the Starbucks, rolled up the sleeve of his T-shirt, and peeled back a bandage on his shoulder.

Amanda stared quizzically at the image.

"What is it?"

But Laura instantly recognized the distinctive red, blue, and gold crest she'd seen countless times in her native, soccer-crazed Guadalajara.

"Real Madrid!" she exclaimed. "So that's the big news?"

Juan Carlos beamed. "I guess they found themselves desperate for attacking midfielders this year."

Amanda jumped up and hugged him tightly. "That's wonderful, Johnny! When did you find out?"

"They e-mailed me the contract offer yesterday. I'm sorry to have kept it from you, but I wanted this moment to have some magic."

As she watched them embrace, Laura's euphoria began to fade. She didn't want to prick the balloon, but she realized the implications: there was no Real Madrid in Los Angeles, and no Getty Museum in the Spanish capital.

"Well, we'd better capture this magic moment," Laura said, trying to recover her mood. "Hey, how about that biker bar next door? That would make a pretty cool backdrop for a photo of you two."

Juan Carlos scooped Amanda up into his arms and struck a pose in front of the bar. Laura snapped a few closeups and wide shots and then declared, "I've got to get going, guys. Sorry, but that accounting exam tomorrow is supposed to be a bear. Have a great time this evening. You deserve it!"

∽∘✦∘∼

Early the next morning, Laura knocked on Amanda's door at the Kappa house. The two girls always exchanged a hug before either one took an exam. To Laura's surprise, there was no answer. Opening the door a crack, she could see that Amanda's bed was empty.

"Oh, my! Well, I guess they really *did* go celebrate!" she smiled.

Laura then joined half a dozen other Kappas at the breakfast table. Needless to say, speculation about their missing sorority sister was rife.

Ten minutes later, Amanda sheepishly opened the front door and tried to head for the stairs.

"Not so fast!" exclaimed Patsy Marshall, the sorority's social chair, in a playful tone. But when Amanda turned her head to face her sisters, a collective gasp ensued. Amanda had a fat lip and several livid bruises on the left side of her face.

"Ouch! What happened?" asked Laura as Amanda sat down wearily at the table.

"It was so stupid. We decided to go into the biker bar to shoot some pool. We thought we'd blend right in with our new tattoos. Bad idea. Around eleven o'clock some guys there started in on us. You know, the names, the rude remarks. Then this one ape grabbed me and that's when Johnny went ballistic."

"The biker gave you the fat lip?" asked Patsy.

"No, that was a gift from his ultrarefined, drunk girlfriend. While Juan Carlos was dealing with the jerk, she sucker punched me and knocked me down to the floor. I must have bruised my ribs when I hit the edge of a table during the fall."

"What happened then?" asked Laura.

"The manager called the cops and the bouncers broke up the fight. Johnny got off with some bloody knuckles, but he messed the biker up worse. Then, we had the privilege of spending our night at the police station. I finally convinced the cops that we were the victims, and they let Juan Carlos go. But it took hours. I'm soooo sleepy," Amanda winced as she stifled a yawn. Her ribs hurt so badly she could not take a deep breath.

"Come on, let's go clean you up. Then I'll get you to the health center for some pain meds." Laura put a gentle hand on Amanda's shoulder and led her up the stairs.

Amanda was able to sleep, but only until later that afternoon.

That's when she finally heard from Nigeria.

☙❧

Laura could simply not believe all that her friend had gone through in less than twenty-four hours. Just then, Amanda's desk clock chimed.

"Yikes! It's already eight thirty. I've got to get moving."

Giving Plato one last backrub, she wistfully headed out the door and on with her day.

CHAPTER 18

Egypt, circa 3100 BC

As was his custom, Cain rose before dawn. Here in the city of Memphis, not far south of the Nile delta, he liked to watch the sunrise over the great river. At the advent of each new day, he enjoyed seeing the town surge into life as the sun began to grace the streets and markets.

As always, the river remained the center of human activity. Beginning just before dawn, a steady stream of people of all ages flocked to the Nile—some to bathe, some to fish, and some with their donkeys and oxen, brought along to work the irrigation canals that watered the wheat and barley fields surrounding the city.

Ever since he had traveled to Memphis with the caravan, Cain had been overjoyed to be reunited with people. The length of the journey afforded him the opportunity to learn the essentials of the Egyptian language. Now, a settled existence in Memphis was a source of great satisfaction and relief to him.

Dressed in his best linen garments, Cain left his house soon after daybreak to visit Snefru, the father of the lad he had rescued on the cliff face six months before. When they reached Memphis, the grateful Snefru had facilitated Cain's assimilation into Egyptian life, much as Omak had done in Enoch long before. Snefru offered him a substantial plot of land to farm, but Cain politely declined, informing his new patron that he had engineering experience and inquiring if there was a construction project of some sort he could join.

That morning, addressing Cain by his adopted Egyptian name, the tall, slender Snefru greeted him warmly.

"Good day, Kha 'ten! I have some excellent news to share with you."

Cain returned his smile. "What news could possibly match the beauty of this morning, Snefru?"

"Well, my friend, I have been giving considerable thought to your aspirations, and I have arranged for a meeting this afternoon between you and my cousin, Menes."

Cain knew from their earlier conversations that the nobleman Menes was one of the town's most prominent citizens. And Snefru had also commented on Menes's own ambitions. He wanted to make Memphis the capital of all Egypt and unify its many tribes and cities into one great empire. Menes had the kind of visionary, charismatic dynamism that Cain—were he given to self-flattery—might have recalled he had embodied in Enoch.

Menes was not a native of Memphis, but rather had origins upriver in the vast district far to the south, universally referred to as Upper Egypt. Shipbuilding had made him wealthy. Many of the traders who plied the great river used his vessels. First made of papyrus reed mats and caulked with pitch, trading ships were now constructed, due to Menes's entrepreneurial drive, from massive cedar logs imported from Byblos in the Levant, nearly four hundred miles northeast of Memphis. Reputedly, Menes's knowledge of the river's geography was encyclopedic.

Cain replied, "Why, it will be a great honor to meet your esteemed cousin. What will be the subject of our discussions?"

"My cousin and I were dining last evening, and I was privileged to learn a great deal more about his designs to power our city to preeminence. Menes envisions an immense earthen dike on the Nile to protect a large part of Memphis from the river's annual flooding. This would give the city scope to expand our population and acquire

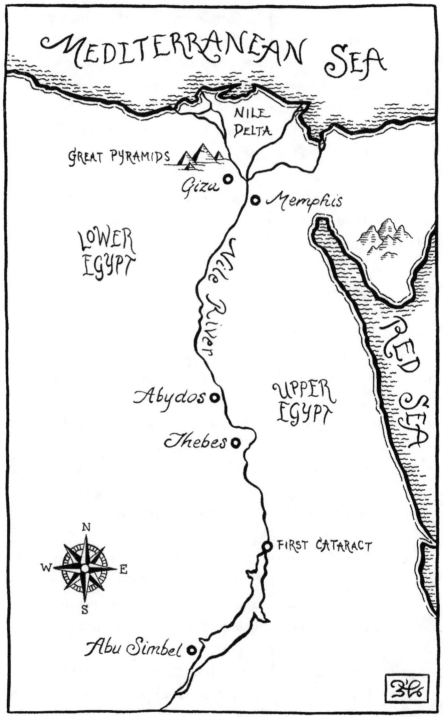

additional economic clout. The fertile lands surrounding the city are capable, in his view, of producing crops with far greater efficiency."

"From what I have seen during my stay here so far, I would say that makes a great deal of sense," replied Cain.

"That is precisely why you two should meet. My cousin is a gifted administrator and a successful merchant, but he is no engineer. When I mentioned your background to him, his interest was roused."

"As is mine," Cain replied.

☙◦❧

Menes's compound was expansive. The sprawling main house was constructed of bricks made from Nile mud and strengthened with straw and pebbles. The exterior walls were plastered with limestone, and inside the residence a series of nature paintings decorated the principal rooms.

In front of the main house was a spacious garden centered around a pool containing lotus plants and several ornamental species of fish. It was here that they found their host. Menes was just finishing dictation of a message to a Nubian king. He rose and, as was the custom, bowed to his guests, who saluted him with their hands over their hearts. Dismissing the scribe, Menes waved them to finely carved, ornamental chairs flanking the pool.

"Welcome, Snefru," the short, thickset Menes beamed in greeting. Cain made him to be about thirty years old. "And you must be Kha 'ten. I am so pleased to finally meet the man whose heroic exploits my cousin speaks of endlessly!"

"Snefru is prone to exaggeration, noble sir," Cain responded.

"Please, call me Menes. Snefru already considers you a kinsman. And you may trust that the gratitude for your selfless act extends throughout our family."

"Thank you, Menes." Cain began to relax a bit.

"I am fascinated to know how your path crossed that of my cousin's in the middle of the desert," Menes inquired.

Cain recounted what now had become the standard fabrication of his prior history.

"As your cousin has probably told you, I hail from Syria. You have heard of the civil war that broke out there two years ago? The conflict forced me and my entire clan into exile. We were unaccustomed to such harsh conditions, so exposure and famine took a brutal toll. Eventually we were separated and had to fend for ourselves. In reality, it was I who was fortunate to have encountered Snefru and his caravan at the oasis, for I believe I would soon have perished." Cain lowered his watery eyes as if in remembrance of his deceased clansmen.

A look of concern crossed Menes's face as he replied, "The desert is harsh and unforgiving. I myself never venture any distance from the river. And actually, I had feared the worst when Snefru's caravan was so long in returning. But perhaps we can regain our festive mood this afternoon. Will you both join me in a beer? Just *listening* to your saga has made me thirsty."

Without waiting for a response, Menes's hands issued two sharp claps, and momentarily a servant girl appeared with a tray holding three mugs of murky, amber liquid. Cain learned of the Egyptians' fondness for this unique beverage promptly upon his arrival in the new land, although he had yet to sample any that he found agreeable. Perhaps in the house of a nobleman he would encounter a more delectable brew.

"Ahhh," exhaled Snefru and Menes, almost in unison after each taking healthy gulps. Cain politely echoed their sighs following his more modest sip, while masking his true reaction to the bitter, chalky taste.

Menes leaned toward Cain after a second swig. "My cousin informed me last evening that the skills you employed in Syria rival your bravery and compassion. I understand you were an engineer?"

"Yes, that is so. I have some familiarity with ship design, though of a different sort than your merchant vessels. Mainly, I was involved in a variety of construction projects there, from fortified walls to bridges and water control."

"Indeed, Kha 'ten, may I explore with you some ideas I have in regards to the latter pursuit?"

Cain listened intently as Menes described his vision for the dike project. As he concluded the outline of the basic concept, his voice stiffened.

"Some of my advisors contend that these plans cannot be accomplished. Others have endorsed their feasibility but question whether the investment of money and labor is wise. May I have your opinion?"

"Well, Menes, in Syria nothing of this scale was ever required, much less attempted. But if a river as vast as the Nile can be harnessed, how could the benefits for Memphis not be equally impressive? This is as noble an undertaking as I have ever encountered."

Seeing Menes's face brighten, Cain paused for a brief sip of beer before adding, "May I suggest that there is another possibility beyond the irrigation and flood control potential of the project?"

In the midst of another quaff from his mug, Menes arched his eyebrow as he gestured for Cain to continue.

"In my homeland we had begun to experiment with additional ways to channel the water, not just to the arable lands, but also to the city center for domestic and commercial uses. To my mind, you could exploit the power of the great river to provide civic enhancements that would propel the economics of your project well beyond levels your advisors have considered."

Snefru cast an encouraging glance toward Cain while his cousin leaned back in his chair and pondered the newcomer's words for a few moments. When it came, Menes's rejoinder was framed with a winsome smile as he raised his mug in a toast.

"Syria's loss is Egypt's great fortune. Kha 'ten, may you long remain our guest here in Memphis!"

CHAPTER 19

Egypt, circa 3100 BC

Cain's new vocation suited him perfectly.

Initially, Menes arranged for him to collaborate with his chief engineers to assist in refining the design of the earthen dike. After about two months of work, the team settled on the main parameters, and Menes approved a project that would be two miles in length, with a thickness of two hundred feet and a height of fifty feet.

However, a debate continued to rage between the advisors about the proper composition and layering of materials. When Cain proposed a solution that all agreed was both structurally and economically sound, Menes became convinced that the newcomer's abilities would help to make his vision a reality, and so he appointed Cain the overseer for the entire project. The post assured Cain of a handsome wage, payable in grain, and secured for him a healthy social status in Memphis as well.

Eight months later, Cain and Snefru were again invited to Menes's compound. Cain assumed that his employer would want a thorough report on the progress of the dike. But when he raised the subject, Menes merely asked Cain to provide a time frame for the dike's completion so that he could consult with the priests about an auspicious date for the dedication ceremony. Other than that, he showed little interest in the details.

"I know you will master the challenges, Kha 'ten. What I wish now to discuss, my friends, is an even more ambitious goal."

"Just tell us, cousin, and we shall be at your side in full support," Snefru declared.

"You have heard, I assume, that Nubian forces have lately threatened the independence—the very livelihood, even—of dozens of communities in Upper Egypt. I have weekly reports from my contacts in the region. The towns to the south are being pressed hard."

Snefru and Cain listened attentively.

"Now is the time," said Menes, "for all Egyptians to stand united. We are people with a common culture: the same gods, the same customs, the same writing system, and basically the same economy. I believe, with all my heart and mind, that the moment is right for an alliance between Lower Egypt and Upper Egypt. Perhaps even for a union of the two."

Menes held his right hand aloft, extended with the index finger pointing upward, as if he were addressing a wider audience. Snefru and Cain maintained a respectful silence.

With a meaningful glance at Cain, Menes pronounced, "And, when our dike project is completed, Memphis will be ideally situated to be the capital of this alliance—and the crown of all Egypt!"

The rest of their meeting was devoted to a more personal matter. Menes informed them of the sudden, grave illness of his younger sister, Cena. Her doctors suspected she had contracted some type of malady from the river. Both Cain and Snefru expressed their concerns, although Cain remained politely quiet as Menes and Snefru then offered up prayers to various healing gods.

After two hours or so, Snefru and Cain took their leave, returning to their respective houses by the river. "So Menes has dynastic aspirations after all," thought Cain, as he strolled beside the other man. In this visionary's mind, the city's glory was harnessed to his own ambitions for power. Cain had seen such aspirations in Enoch. Indeed, he had lived them. But Memphis was tiny compared to

Enoch, and now it was another leader's turn. Cain had tasted all he
wanted of political power.

On entering his house, Cain reflected on the dour news concerning Cena. Despite his best efforts to remain upbeat and encouraging
in front of Menes, he'd learned that death was an ever present fact
of life in this new land. Cain calculated that perhaps a third of the
children here died in infancy. The great majority of adults did not
live past thirty-five. A people who lived by the river also died by the
river—not only from waterborne diseases, but also from the jaws of
hippos and crocodiles. What a contrast to the long-lived generations
Cain had known before the flood!

Cain pondered the deeper reasons, if any, for this contraction of
the human life span. Was God, offended by the rampant paganism
and idolatry of Egypt, once again showing his displeasure with mortal
beings? Was another flood, perhaps, on the way? What had happened
to the pious preaching of Noah and his warnings on the subject of
false gods?

Again, Cain confronted the recurring dilemma of his own longevity.
Here in Egypt his immunity to the ravages of time would become
obvious much faster, and would likely cause suspicion, envy, or hostil-
ity. For some time now, he had debated the issue within himself. On
the one hand, he had no wish to leave the safety of Egypt. Although
very different from Enoch, Egypt had achieved an enviable level of
prosperity and culture. Cain could see that there were vast opportunities here. Thanks to the Nile, agriculture was thriving and transportation was relatively easy. Shipbuilding and weaponry had reached
the point where it was indeed possible to imagine Menes succeeding
in making Egypt the preeminent power in its region. It was surely
tempting to abide near his new patron.

On the other hand, if Cain remained in one community for
even a relatively short time—say a decade or two—suspicion would

inevitably grow about him. After all, he appeared to be in his late twenties—senior citizenship for an Egyptian. He had never forgotten his first wife's treachery in Enoch, and he had no wish to suffer a repetition.

He walked outside and stared at the late evening colors dancing on the Nile. He was intimately acquainted from his wandering with the river's vast extent: four hundred miles and more from his house at Memphis, upriver to the Nubian region, and then many hundreds of miles again, ever southward, thrusting up to the ultimate source in a mountain lake deep in Africa.

Then it occurred to him. As with so many things in Egypt, the great river offered an answer. After fulfilling his obligations to Menes, he would become a nomadic trader, with the Nile as his lifeline.

CHAPTER 20

Egypt, circa 3100 BC

After three and a half years of steady labor by four thousand slaves and hundreds of citizen supervisors, Cain was in a position to promise Menes that the dike would be completed before the next flood season, and he was as good as his word. All of Memphis and many of its neighbors crowded to attend the dedication ceremony, which was conducted by dozens of priests in splendid regalia. Special reverence was accorded to the god Ptah, who was worshipped in Memphis as the patron of craftsmen, particularly of those who worked in stone. A giant image of the deity was unveiled, revealing him with his trio of sacred symbols: the *ankh* representing life, the *was* representing power, and the *djed*, standing for stability.

In the interim since the past fall, Menes had steadily promoted the union of Upper and Lower Egypt. Everyone in Memphis knew that, were this alliance to come to fruition, Menes himself would emerge as the new nation's leader. So Cain was not surprised when, at the dedication of the new dike, he glimpsed Menes wearing headgear that blended symbols associated with the two regions. Although Menes did not call himself pharaoh, he had become king in everything but name.

The mutual benefits of the friendship between the two men grew steadily. Just as Cain had proved a helpful resource for Menes, the new ruler offered useful counsel to his deputy. Unlike most citizens

of Memphis, Menes had traveled widely. In this, of course, he unwittingly resembled Cain. The two men found common ground in their
knowledge of, and appreciation for, distant regions. Menes had begun
to encourage Cain to consider his next endeavor following the dike's
completion. Although he was somewhat surprised that Cain seemed
interested in trading as opposed to further engineering pursuits,
Menes was nonetheless happy to provide Cain with extensive insights
into the commerce of the day. Menes possessed an intimate knowledge
of the great river, and he described its various bends and currents with
a facility that even Cain, with his flawless memory, had to admire.

☙❧

During the summer flood season, Cain personally inspected the
new dike several times each day. The thousands of slaves had done a
commendable job of layering several types of alluvial sand, clay, and
loose gravel on the structure, finally positioning large rocks on the
dam's face to prevent erosion.

But ceaseless work had eventually become tedious for Cain. For
companionship, he took a young wife, the niece of Snefru, whose first
husband had been killed in a skirmish with the Nubians to the south.
Her name was Layla. When she shyly inquired about his earlier life,
he told her the same narrative he had used with Snefru and Menes.
He regretted lying to her, but what choice did he have?

Cain was surprised by the necessity to sign a marriage contract. In
contrast to Enoch, where women had few rights, in Egyptian society
women were virtually equal to men under the law. They could own
and sell property, receive inheritances, divorce, and appear in court to
pursue legal disputes. The marriage contract protected Layla by estab-
lishing Cain's financial obligations to her and to their offspring, if any,
should the marriage end in divorce. Thinking it unlikely that he would

remain in Memphis for long, and knowing that Snefru would provide amply for her in any case, Cain gladly signed.

A month or so after their wedding, Cain discovered that Layla was a most unlikely mentor. He had long known that both women and men in Egypt made liberal use of cosmetics. But he never suspected that his new wife, at the tender age of eighteen, was a fountain of lore on the subject. When she suggested that the crow's feet developing at Snefru's eyelids could be more effectively concealed with a new variety of kohl, Cain listened intently. After Snefru had permitted Layla to make a preliminary application, Cain took her aside and quizzed her extensively on the sources, composition, availability, and effects of Egyptian makeup preparations.

Cosmetics were a way of life for all Egyptians—even the dead had to be mindful of how they would look at the last judgment. The Egyptian penchant for good hygiene complemented the widespread interest in products such as kohl, which was both decorative and practical. In the glare of the desert sun, cosmetics helped soften the fierce light, and also helped to repel flies, the source of much disease. It was no wonder, thought Cain, that magical powers were often attributed to cosmetics.

While most Egyptians used makeup to appear younger, however, Cain wondered if cosmetics could help produce the opposite effect. If he could make himself appear older, Cain reasoned, it might help him prolong his stays.

❧

After the annual flood of the Nile came the planting season—and Cain's dike held. A jubilant Menes asked Cain to supervise one more project: the construction of the largest river barge ever built in Memphis, a vessel measuring 250 feet from stem to stern. The barge would have three masts outfitted with lateen sails, equipped to take advantage of the prevailing northerly breezes in wintertime in order to make good progress upriver with cargoes of grain for Upper Egypt. Cedar logs imported from the Levant would be used for construction.

Cain agreed to the undertaking, thinking that at the very least he would profit from on-the-job experience. He could use the nautical construction techniques he had seen on the ark to build the greatest riverboat ever to grace the Nile. When Menes asked him in November when he thought the barge would be ready, Cain promised it for the beginning of April.

Once again, Cain did not fail his patron. By March, the beginning of the harvesting season, the vessel was nearing completion. One evening Cain traveled through the city to Menes's residence, which now resembled a palace, to present a report.

"My architect!" exclaimed the ruler of Memphis and, though it was not often publicly declared yet, of all Egypt.

"At your service, Pharaoh." Cain used the new term of respect, which meant literally "great house."

"Snefru tells me you will soon be a new father?"

"Yes, indeed," Cain replied. "The baby should be born in less than a month. Layla and I are overjoyed."

In reality, however, he was conflicted. With people's much shorter lifespans evident since the flood, Cain knew he would be facing much sooner the pain of abandoning or burying each of his offspring.

"That is wonderful news," said Menes. "May all your children bring you great joy. Now, please tell me about the progress with the ship."

"It will be finished by the very next new moon."

Menes rubbed his hands. "Excellent, Kha 'ten. You have never failed me. The dike holds. Memphis grows rapidly. Our people prosper. Now I wish to announce news to you."

Cain's brow furrowed. What had Menes held back from him?

"When the ship is finished, load her with emmer wheat and barley. Then, with the crew I shall provide, set sail for Upper Egypt before the flood. I will give you a list of ports. Trade well, great architect. You are a river merchant now. She is yours!"

It took Cain a few moments to fathom the man's lavish generosity. Menes was giving him the ship!

"We Egyptians believe that loyalty is a virtue given by the gods. You have been faithful to me and to Memphis, your adopted city, Kha 'ten. How can I not repay you? Your contributions to Memphis are plain for all to see. Now it is high time for you to build your own personal achievements, for yourself and your family. I have no doubt that those accomplishments will be profound."

Cain was at a loss for words. Placing his hand over his heart, he bowed deeply. Menes approached him and placed both hands on his shoulders.

"May the great river keep you in her care!"

CHAPTER 21

Rome, Near the Vatican: Present Day

Cardinal Alessandro Ravatti, president of the Vatican's Pontifical Commission for Sacred Archaeology, was seated comfortably at his desk in the cavernous office on Via Napoleone III when the call from Silvio came in.

"Yes, Notombo connect me right away," Ravatti directed.

"Stand by, *Eminenza*," replied the cardinal's assistant, a young monsignor from the Congo.

"What a pleasant surprise, Silvio!" Ravatti greeted his caller warmly. "I'm glad you got through on a Sunday. Notombo and I are catching up on an endless backlog. What are you up to these days? Still in Naples, I trust?"

The two men were old friends. For over thirty years, they had excavated catacombs and other ancient sites around Rome. Although not technically an archaeologist, the cardinal possessed an encyclopedic knowledge of church history and was shrewd in the ways of Vatican bureaucracy.

"Actually, Sandro, I'm in Ercolano this morning. At the new site we began to investigate after the earthquake a month ago. You remember, I told you about the pictures our robot took of those large bronze doors."

"Yes, I remember very well. But I also recall you were going to send them to me for analysis. It seems I never received your e-mail."

Silvio paused briefly. "Oh, goodness, my memory is not what it once was. If you'll stand by, I'll send them right now." He walked over to his laptop and e-mailed the photos to Ravatti.

"Okay, Sandro, they are on their way to you. Now, let me explain the purpose of my call. This morning we sent in a young archaeologist,

Dr. Amanda James, to evaluate the inscriptions on the doors. She's on loan to us from the Getty in California. We've partnered with them many times before, as you know."

"Yes, they are very capable people. Was Dr. James able to shed any light on the inscriptions?"

"Indeed she did, Sandro. In fact, she deciphered the complex code for a combination lock much faster than any one of us could have expected."

"So she succeeded in opening the doors?"

"Yes. She is making a preliminary survey of the chamber at this very moment. But I have lost contact with her."

"She is trapped inside?"

"I'm afraid so, but we are working on that problem. In the meantime, before her wireless went dead, she said something about the chamber's possibly being a catacomb. I thought you should know."

Cardinal Ravatti's ears pricked up. Anything related to crypts, catacombs, or sacred cemeteries fell squarely under his commission's jurisdiction.

"Did Dr. James mention any evidence for this inference?" he asked.

"She didn't have time to go into detail. Before she went in, I emphasized that she should restrict her mission to a very brief survey," Silvio said. "But now, Sandro, we may have another problem."

"And what is that, my friend?"

"Because of my work, I am on very good terms with the land office here in Ercolano. At the end of last week, one of my best contacts there informed me that an offer to purchase the property next to the excavation site is on the verge of closing. The doors and the chamber lie beneath this adjacent tract. And the corporation that tendered this offer has also filed a *mineral* claim."

"How interesting," Ravatti murmured. "And did your informant disclose the name of the purchasers?"

"It's a large corporation named Renard Enterprises. They are based in the United States but do business around the world. The CEO is a man named Luc Renard."

Cardinal Ravatti switched on his computer. "That name seems familiar. I'm going to put you on the speakerphone for a moment, Silvio," he said. "But I'll turn down the volume so we can talk in private. Just bear with me while I check something."

From his desktop menu, Ravatti selected an icon that linked him to the databases maintained by the Vatican Museums. After typing in several passwords, he clicked on another icon labeled Acquisitions and Deaccessions. After a brief search, he found what he wanted.

Scanning the screen rapidly, the cardinal said into the phone, "I've found it, Silvio. I'll turn the speakerphone off now. You know, of course, that the Vatican Museums maintain files on every acquisition and deaccession they've made over the past five hundred years."

"Yes, but that information is very closely held, is it not?" Silvio asked him.

"Normally, yes. But let's just say that I, too, have contacts, my friend. Now, as to Luc Renard and his company. Five years ago, the museums decided to deaccession a half dozen ceramic madonnas by Andrea della Robbia, dating from the fifteenth century. Renard Enterprises put in a bid. Normally, the Vatican requires that purchasers sign an indemnity pledging to respect the known facts about an object's origin if they choose to resell the item or donate it to another collection. Otherwise, irresponsible art dealers can compromise our museum's integrity."

"Perfectly understandable, Sandro. But what happened with the della Robbias?" Silvio asked.

"That's the trouble. Within a year, Renard Enterprises proceeded to offer them for sale at large auction houses, along with utterly fictitious descriptions of their pedigree. They realized a huge profit. Vatican advocates have filed a claim. In fact, my database includes a recent note about the company's efforts to gain control of the adjacent site in Ercolano."

"And so what do you conclude?"

"I smell a problem brewing. Let me check my calendar and see when I can get to Ercolano. We should probably deal with this side by side."

"Can you ensure that the site will be preserved, Sandro?" Silvio asked urgently.

"If the site turns out to be a catacomb, you need not worry, my friend. Arrivederci."

Clicking off the connection, Cardinal Ravatti turned back to his screen, which had just beeped to alert him to the arrival of Silvio's transmission. He noted there were five pictures attached to the e-mail. Opening the first, which appeared to be a wide-angle shot of the doors, he could barely make out any detail. The next photo was a closeup of the upper left quadrant, where some of the inscriptions Silvio had referred to came into clearer view. Skipping back and forth between the left side and the right side photos, he began to marvel at the ingenuity of Dr. James in deciphering the complex puzzle.

Then, he opened the fourth picture, which revealed the lower right quadrant. He saw little of significance until his eye fell on some impressions near the bottom. Ravatti's pulse quickened as he zoomed in on the markings. Instead of viewing the final attachment, he reached over to the side of his desk and pressed the intercom button.

"Monsignor Notombo! Call the airport and ask them to clear a helicopter for us immediately!"

CHAPTER 22

The Nile River, circa 2630 BC

"One more game, sir?"

"Are you sure you wish to risk another defeat, Captain Nakht?" Cain chuckled, as he rolled the knucklebone dice and then placed his marker firmly on the board's opening square. The two men were passing time as the massive barge and its hundreds of crew members floated slowly down the Nile. They had picked up their precious cargo weeks ago, a single four-sided piece of stone weighing more than a large herd of cattle. The obelisk was hewed from the rock quarry in Aswan and loaded by over a thousand men using rollers and levers. Cain was hired to deliver the pillar of red granite to one of the pharaoh's temples downriver.

Cain and his young captain were engrossed in yet another game of senet, perhaps the most popular diversion in all of Egypt. From the pharaoh to the peasantry, senet was a universal distraction. Like almost everything in Egypt, the board game was bound up with religion, holding the status of a ritual for at least some players. Successful senet fanciers like Cain were widely thought to enjoy the protection of the gods. With its grid-like panels of thirty squares, arranged in three rows of ten, the senet board and its ornate playing tiles were talismanic objects, often placed in graves so that the deceased could indulge during the afterlife.

As Captain Nakht contemplated his own opening move, Cain's thoughts drifted. The brilliant rays of a late afternoon sun sparkled on the Nile, where a northerly breeze helped to moderate the heat. He had now traversed the river more than a thousand times. His original investment, supplied by Menes's stake, had multiplied handsomely. He was currently the owner of a dozen barges for the transportation of heavy stones. These were much in demand for building pyramids, the latest fashion in funerary monuments. The vessels also had the capacity to handle the much larger stones from which obelisks were crafted to adorn the pharaoh's temples.

In addition to his trading successes, Cain felt pleased that his strategy to avoid detection of his longevity was working. His routine seldom varied. He would choose a commercially promising river port as his base, remaining there for five years or so—just enough time to familiarize himself with the community and to garner profitable trading contacts. Much of this time would be spent in river transit, however.

Cosmetics proved an indispensable tool in maintaining the charade, and Cain often blessed the name of Layla, now long dead. Another ruse he occasionally employed was the impersonation of his own sons after prolonged absence from a port. If he felt that discovery of his secret was likely, he would simply move to another base on the river, taking care not to return to any community where people might be still alive to recognize him. Before each relocation, he would arrange for a trusted servant to implement a long-term trust agreement for the maintenance of family members and for the administration of his business interests.

For Cain, family relationships presented some of the most troubling aspects of his curse, much as he anticipated when Layla first became pregnant. Although his kinships in Egypt afforded a welcome contrast to the abject loneliness of the desert oasis, his ability to bond with wives and children suffered in numerous ways. His length of years brought the inevitable grief of the deaths of generation after generation of loved ones, and he felt himself becoming increasingly callous over the centuries. Moreover, there could be no real intimacy with relatives whom he was presently misleading and ultimately abandoning.

Cain found that his life had hollowed into something like a game of senet, where successfully maneuvering within its required elements of strategy, deceit, and blind luck brought him at least some satisfaction. At the same time, however, if his life was like a game it could never quite be normal—and he wondered at what point would he finally lose.

After besting Nakht, Cain looked up and saw they were nearing their destination. He stood up and motioned for the captain to follow. They walked the length of the barge to ensure the preparations for arrival were complete. Reaching the base of the obelisk at the far end of the vessel, they noticed a young crewman staring at a narrow, horizontal rectangle Cain had chiseled into the base of the stone several days earlier.

"Have you never seen a shipper's mark before, my friend?" Cain asked.

"Oh, yes sir," answered the startled sailor. "But I cannot make out the inscription on this one. It doesn't look like any hieroglyph I know. May I ask its meaning?"

Cain paused for a moment, noticing that other nearby ears had pricked up, awaiting his response.

"In my travels far and wide, I have encountered many languages and writing systems," he replied cryptically. "But this is no time for a translation lesson. Look, we are nearing port. Now, all of you, prepare to unload our cargo!"

Weeks after delivering the obelisk, Cain stopped in at Abydos on the way back to his base in Thebes. Menes had been born here, and fittingly enough, it was in Abydos that he was buried. Although Cain did not adhere to Egyptian religious beliefs, he made a tomb offering for his patron out of respect, in accordance with standard practice.

But his visit had a more commercial purpose as well. Ever since uprooting from Memphis, he had pondered the entrepreneurial potential of beer manufacturing. Like senet, beer was a universal feature of Egyptian life. It was the beverage of choice for nobles and farmers alike. To Cain, however, beer brewing in Egypt seemed curiously backward and cumbersome. For one thing, it was regarded as women's work, confined to individual households. Closely linked to the baking of bread, the brewing of beer was a domestic task which, given the ubiquity of the beverage, cried out for economies of scale. In addition, never forgetting the bitter brew he'd managed to choke down during his first interview with Menes, Cain thought the product itself could be considerably more refined.

So his time in Abydos was largely devoted to locating a suitable site for the beer factory he was contemplating. Rather than acquiring land in the town, he decided early on that he should build the brewery by the riverside, taking advantage of abundant water and easy transport facilities. After all, this would be a factory not just for Abydos and its environs, but for distributing beer to all of Egypt.

After several weeks, he found an ideal site for the factory and its requisite grain storage and docking facilities. Negotiations with the landowner bore fruit, and Cain signed a contract to purchase a two-hundred-acre riverfront tract. From local fishermen he obtained detailed descriptions of the river's levels and currents in that locale. Much work lay ahead, but the foundations for his new enterprise had been laid.

It was now the beginning of the planting season, and Cain intended to depart from Abydos for his home in Thebes. He missed being with his local wife and his three young sons after several months of absence, and he longed for some relaxation from river plying and constant business activities.

Yet he lingered in Abydos long enough to witness the municipal festival in honor of the god Osiris. This deity, whose cult was starting to gather momentum throughout Egypt, was widely worshipped as the lord of the dead. He was also the god who, according to local legend, had taught the Egyptians how to make beer.

Osiris was the subject of a detailed mythology, at the center of which was the tale of his murder by his jealous brother Set, the god of evil. Coveting Orisis's throne, Set had killed his sibling and carved his body into many pieces, scattering the gory fragments all over Egypt. Osiris's grieving sister and consort, Isis, searched for the body and reassembled its parts, whereupon Osiris was miraculously resurrected. Because the heart of Osiris was believed to have been deposited in Abydos, the city developed a special veneration for the deity. And every year, the theatrical performances presented at the festival dramatized the life-death-rebirth cycle of the myth.

From the back row, Cain watched the dramas in the town's open-air theater with a mixture of fascination and mounting anxiety. The memories reawakened by this primordial story tempted him to abandon the spectacle, yet he couldn't tear himself away. The notion that here in Egypt, of all places, fratricide was intimately bound up with the human condition struck a dissonant chord in Cain. Several thousand spectators cheered and applauded at the end of each play, but Cain felt racked by anguish and alienation.

Back aboard his vessel, long after midnight, Cain fell into a deep and dreamless sleep. But toward dawn, some intuition woke him with a start. Had the anchor chain given way? No, the barge was sound. A last-quarter moon glimmered on the Nile, whose waters were calm.

A familiar voice materialized out of the shadows.

"You still think of your brother, Cain?" asked the master of spirits.

Cain was silent for some time. He decided to parry one question with another.

"Where is Abel, spirit? Is he like Osiris, in the afterlife?"

"Abel sleeps well. You will find him again when you finally have the courage to end your own life."

He was angered by the spirit's reference to his fateful invitation at the cliffside oasis.

"You saw what happened. I saved a life, rather than taking one."

"And you expected some kind of reward, but instead received only more of the same curse. Restless wandering up and down the river without end. You merely exchanged the lonely sands for even lonelier waters. I am the only reason you live well in Egypt, enjoying great wealth, but without power's hazards and its obligations."

"You do not know the memories that gnash at me, spirit. I bid you depart!"

"Yes, Cain, the memories. I will leave you now. But the memories— they are yours forever."

A predawn mist drifted over the river. Cain had sat bolt upright during the conversation, but now he sagged backward, exhausted.

He feared the memories would always torture him.

CHAPTER 23

The Nile River, circa 1400 BC

The years wheeled around for Cain, mounting into decades and generations. His trading as a river merchant flourished, ably aided by successive ship captains. He acquired lands under many different aliases in every district of Egypt. Though a stranger to the courts of power, his many names were known by the pharaohs of every dynasty. His pathway to material success in his adopted country met no obstruction. Cain was, if anything, an advertisement for the beneficent prosperity of pharaonic rule and the dominance of Egypt in the known world.

The brewery eventually became a triumphant success. After centuries of trial and error, Cain perfected a two-part process that produced a more refined beverage than Egypt had ever consumed before. Instead of lightly baked bread as the main ingredient, Cain used bread made from emmer wheat and slightly flavored with coriander, dates, and figs. This base, in turn, was combined with barley and yeast, and the medley was then fermented. The beer that resulted was golden-hued and slightly cloudy, but filtering and straining rendered it almost translucent. Egyptians, headed by the royal family, loved the new taste, and grain payments flowed ever more generously into Cain's silos up and down the river.

Yet, no amount of wealth seemed to satiate Cain, so he immersed himself in plans for the brewery's expansion. Calling in his supervisors, he reviewed a set of drawings that would enable the plant to triple production within a year. The market seemed inexhaustible. Cain hoped to ship his product overseas as well, perhaps to ports as distant as the island of Crete.

The construction of new warehouses, silos, copper fermentation tanks, and lifting cranes proceeded apace. Then, one evening just before sunset, Cain found himself on the loading dock, discussing personnel issues with his foreman, Sapra. While he was away on one of his many trips, some of his laborers had recently defected to take work with a rival grain merchant named Horus. This man, now nearing sixty and notorious for nursing long-standing grudges, regarded Cain as an upstart. Although these defections involved only a small minority of the employees, Cain inquired if Sapra had been able to determine the causes.

"Horus is fiercely envious of your success, sir," replied the foreman. "He spreads ugly rumors that you are not even an Egyptian. His resentment has rubbed off on some of the workers, I'm afraid."

As Cain paused to absorb this news, a strange sight presented itself. A medium-sized barge was swiftly approaching from upriver, seemingly laced with tongues of fire. At first he thought it was some kind of optical illusion, or a reflection of the flame-like rays of the setting sun. Yet as the vessel drew steadily closer, both men could see she was loaded with an immense mound of burning refuse, fanned even more briskly now by an early evening breeze on the river.

"A fire ship!" shouted Sapra. "Quickly, sir, we must summon the entire staff to help! If she hits the dock, the brewery will burn!"

But it was too late. Cain and Sapra jumped clear in time, but the rogue barge, as if guided by a diabolical hand, crashed into the loading dock, soon triggering a deafening explosion in the nearest grain silo. As workers ran in all directions, Cain and Sapra were knocked backward to the ground by the force of the blast. Both were burned on their face, arms, and chest. Cain helped his superintendent off the

flaming pier and was forced to watch his cherished investment consumed in the inferno. It had all happened so quickly that Cain struggled to comprehend the malice that had reduced most of his brewery
to a charred ruin. This enterprise was his most thorough attempt
yet to work around God's curse of the ground. It seemed his maker
would grant him no such reprieve.

By dint of some heroic firefighting, Cain, Sapra, and the rest
saved about a quarter of the brewery. The consensus was that the
sabotage was the work of Horus. But nothing could be proved. The
fire ship, itself destroyed, was of untraceable origin.

Meanwhile, Cain grimly accounted for the casualties. Several
dozen of his workers, trapped inside exploding silos, had been killed,
and compensation would have to be paid to their families. Cain himself, as well as Sapra, had suffered additional severe burns as they
fought the flames, and many staffers were similarly injured. Luckily,
the salves and herbs available in Abydos sufficed to alleviate the pain.

But in the midst of such travails, he overlooked the risk that now,
willy-nilly, he was running. After Cain's burns healed within a week,
the regeneration of his skin was impossible to conceal, even with cosmetics and bandages. Sapra and the others bristled; perhaps Horus
had been right about Cain after all. What had been a series of mur-
murs against Cain became a chorus of angry shouts.

Reluctantly, he left Abydos behind.

CHAPTER 24

Abu Simbel, Egypt, circa 1255 BC

Cain thought that he had never seen a more splendid procession in all his centuries in Egypt. It was the first day of the *heb-sed* festival of Ramesses II, the public celebration of the pharaoh's continuing vitality after thirty years of rule. While Cain had attended many such festivals before, for most Egyptians the *sed* jubilee was a once-in-a-lifetime event. Thousands of cheering spectators packed the riverside esplanade in Thebes, where the principal rituals of the festival would unfold.

The sed festival had ancient origins, he recalled. Pharaoh Djoser, for whom the Step Pyramid was completed in 2611 BC, celebrated such a jubilee, as did most of his longer reigning successors. But the first sed of Ramesses II outdid all its precursors in lavish pomp and splendor. The traditional religious rituals and narratives had been firmly reestablished. The priesthood of Amun-Re again had deep roots among the nation's elite. Now more than ever, the pharaoh embodied the secular dominion of the state with the majesty of a god on earth.

As the priestly procession made its way around the perimeter of the esplanade, Cain noted with satisfaction that his friend Khaimudi had been promoted to the ranks of the high priesthood. The special insignia on his robe, as well as his presence in the front ranks of the procession, testified to Khaimudi's new eminence. He had met the priest shortly after reinstalling himself in Thebes three years prior. Several days before the festival, Cain, who now called himself Senejer, received a message from his friend urging him to attend the opening ceremonies so that Khaimudi could present him with a special request. He wondered what his priestly friend had in mind. The two met that evening near the Red Chapel.

"Why did you not inform me of your promotion?" Cain asked.

His friend shrugged. "I am a religious man, not a merchant. Boasting is frowned upon."

Cain chuckled. "I think we have more in common than you realize, O holy one," he teased. "But, that aside, what is this request that brings us together this evening?"

Khaimudi placed his hands on Cain's shoulders, his features bearing an uncharacteristically earnest expression.

"First I must have your vow of silence. No one outside the highest ranks at court knows what I am about to disclose to you."

"You have my word."

Khaimudi glanced over his shoulder to ensure they were alone. "Well, then, are you acquainted with the site of Abu Simbel? It lies on the western shore of the Nile in Nubia, some 175 miles southwest of Aswan."

Cain nodded.

"Ramesses wishes to build a colossal temple there. Two temples, actually. One shrine will celebrate his mightiness, and the second will glorify his beloved wife Nefertari. The temples will be literally carved out of the mountainside. Preliminary estimates call for a construction period of twenty years. Who knows if he will live that long, the sed notwithstanding. But that is not my chief concern at the moment."

"Then what worries you?"

"The Mighty One has charged the high priesthood with the task of devising an unprecedented plan for the main temple. Of course, the construction serves the ends of propaganda, both religious and national. We want the Nubians to know that it is fruitless for them to challenge Egypt's power. But Ramesses has another motive as well. He wishes this temple to surpass all others ever built in Egypt. It must not only be distinctive—it must be unique."

"And how will you make it thus?"

"I have racked my brains. At the most senior level, the priests have combed records reaching back in time for more than fifty generations to the earliest dynasties. We have not found an answer. Everything that *can* be done *has* been done, it seems."

Cain murmured with the trace of a smile, "If you can't solve this puzzle, why turn to me?"

"You have seen more of Egypt than any man I know," Khaimudi declared emphatically. "It is said that you are more than just a river trader—you are a builder and a scientist as well. I need your advice, Senejer. If anyone can develop a master plan for this temple, it is you."

Cain glanced across the river to the west bank. Here was the Valley of the Kings, where Egypt's pharaohs had been interred in rock tombs for several hundred years. The sun, dying in the west, fitfully glinted on the river's rippling current.

"Why not consider the sun?" Cain said to his friend.

☙❦☙

Three months later, Cain found himself drawing sketches on a sand dune perched atop the proposed building site at Abu Simbel. His plan was as simple as it was ingenious.

Two dates in the calendar were more significant to Ramesses, and to the public support of his kingly authority, than any others in the year: his birthday and his coronation day. These sacred days occurred in late October and late February, respectively. The four-month interval between them, Cain calculated, possessed an alluring symmetry.

The pharaoh had been born almost exactly one month after the autumnal equinox. And he had been crowned one month before the vernal equinox. The angled rays of sunrise on these two dates, therefore, would be parallel. Cain's idea was to orient the axis of the large temple so that the sun would brilliantly illuminate the inner sanctum, or holy of holies, on these two days alone. Not only would colossal statues and laudatory engravings celebrate Ramesses as Egypt's eternal ruler, but the celestial firmament would do likewise. The symbolism was unmistakable: Egypt's perennial vitality was linked to the sun's regenerative powers on the earth. Heaven itself approved of Ramesses.

Khaimudi's gratitude was boundless. Cain had encouraged him to present the plan to the priesthood as his own, which the priest agreed to do, provided that Cain promised never to disclose the plan's true source. The pharaoh's commendation was swiftly forthcoming. When the chief priest succumbed to a lung infection several months later, Khaimudi assumed his place—despite the fact that he lacked the customary seniority for such an elevation. Cain was gratified that he now had a close contact at the very highest level of the court. Who knew when such a connection might come in handy?

As construction on the new temples at Abu Simbel proceeded, Cain continued to enjoy his life in Thebes. Consistent with the usual pattern, he had taken a local wife who bore him a son, Jacuna. For Cain, this boy was special. From the time Jacuna was a small child, father and son enjoyed an easy camaraderie, free of the stifling formality that so often straitened the relationships of parents and children in Egypt. Jacuna possessed a healthy mischievousness, but also, as he grew older, a keen entrepreneurial insight.

Proud of his boy, Cain eventually accorded Jacuna the ultimate tribute: he treated him as an equal partner in the trading business. Cain felt confident that, with Jacuna's help, the family business could outstrip all its competitors in Egypt—perhaps even in the eastern Mediterranean region. As for Jacuna's mother, Cain had little familiar feeling. Her limited world of experience held no mystery for him, and thus she secured no special place in his heart.

Cain's pleasure in Jacuna's companionship, however, caused him to remain in Thebes much longer than normal. Over the generations, he had become increasingly adept at concealing his longevity. New cosmetics had become available, and he experimented with them deftly. As Jacuna drew near to marriageable age, Cain eagerly anticipated the arrival of a grandchild. He was not disappointed. Nine months after the wedding, Jacuna's bride gave birth to a son. They named him Hati.

With Jacuna now approaching twenty, Cain decided his son had sufficient maturity to superintend the business interests in Thebes. He therefore reverted to his usual pattern, informing his family that he had decided to go on an extended business trip. Once again, his destination was Memphis, where he would be far downriver. Bidding Jacuna an especially affectionate farewell, he imparted final instructions and assured his son he would remain in touch by letter. Well aware of how people tended to die young in Egypt, he knew he might never see Jacuna again, and as Cain left his family compound he choked back tears.

❧

While he was based in Memphis, four hundred miles north of Thebes, Cain wrote regularly to Jacuna, checking on Hati's well-being and monitoring the family's commercial interests. Fortunately, Jacuna never traveled to Memphis, since he was focusing his time on contracts and deals with Nubia to the south. Cain reported that he had fathered another son by a young Memphite woman, a child named Seti, who was thus Jacuna's half brother. In almost every letter, he promised to visit Thebes soon, but somehow business commitments always intervened.

Late in Ramesses's reign, Cain did, in fact, return to Thebes, but not as Senejer. As he had done so often before, he impersonated his own son. "Seti" reported that their father had died in a sudden Mediterranean storm while on a trading mission. A grief-stricken Jacuna was comforted by his "half brother," who bore a distinct resemblance to their common "parent."

Cain settled into life in Thebes once again, partnering with Jacuna as a merchant. Now grown to adolescence, Hati also aspired to carry on the family business. Seeking companionship, Cain took another young wife, who bore him a son, Nefran.

Their trading enterprise grew to such prominence within Egypt's economy that Cain was afforded a private audience with Ramesses, at which he presented Nefran as his firstborn to receive the pharaoh's royal blessing.

Little did Cain know how fateful the eventual consequences of that encounter would be.

CHAPTER 25

Thebes, circa 1230 BC

I t was while he was living in Thebes as Seti that Cain first heard of Moses.

Khaimudi, still in office as Ramesses's high priest after twenty-five years, was in close contact with Jacuna, whose business interests often coincided with those of the pharaoh. When Cain, as Seti, first arrived in Thebes, Jacuna promptly arranged a visit to the royal palace to make a proper introduction of his half brother.

"Welcome, Jacuna," the chief priest smiled warmly. Cain thought that his friend, though obviously advanced in age, carried the dignity of his office well. "Ah, and what a pleasure at last to meet Senejer's long absent son! My, Seti, I must say that you are the very image of your father." Khaimudi then caught himself and continued, more solemnly, "The entire court of Pharaoh mourns with you. Your father served Egypt selflessly."

"Thank you, your holiness. My father spoke of you often. And, of course, the great marvels you conceived at Abu Simbel. The sudden circumstances that took him did not permit my father a dying wish, but may I be so bold as to express one for him?"

"I would honor the noble Senejer in any manner you suggest," the high priest replied earnestly.

"It would bless me, as well as my father's memory, if the revered architect of the temple would himself accompany me on my first visit there."

"It would be my great privilege to do so," Khaimudi answered. "I regret, however, that arrangements may be difficult in the near term. Pharaoh has restricted many of us from travel while we address an unusual issue."

Jacuna inquired, "Is there any way we may be of service?"

Khaimudi politely declined the offer, but went on to explain that a leader who called himself "prophet" had begun pressing the pharaoh to liberate the Hebrew slaves. This was a ludicrous demand, of course. But anxiety still swirled in the halls of power. Any slave rebellion would have to be ruthlessly suppressed, declared Khaimudi. Yet how to do so without compromising the slaves' work?

Furthermore, the high priest stressed, Moses posed a threat to the heart of Egyptian culture: the nation's religious beliefs. The Hebrew leader championed monotheism. And not only did Moses worship just one God, but it was said he actually *spoke* with him as well. Such a claim directly challenged the pharaoh's sacred authority.

It was said that the prophet bore the name Moses because he had been raised as a royal prince. He was drawn as a baby from the waters of the Nile in a reed basket by the pharaoh's daughter and adopted by the royal family. But as his birth mother had raised him in his early years, he considered himself a Hebrew. As a young man, Moses had frequently taken issue with the captivity of the slaves, and he notoriously killed an Egyptian overlord and then fled to Midian, where he dwelled in the safe company of his Hebrew brethren.

Cain puzzled why God would even speak to a murderer, much less appoint him as a prophet or a leader of the Hebrew people. God certainly no longer spoke to Cain, and he was no more guilty of taking another man's life than Moses.

❧

Months later Moses issued an ultimatum. Either Pharaoh would let the Hebrew people go, or Yahweh, their God, would punish all Egypt with a series of grave afflictions. As an especially potent first sign, declared Moses, Yahweh would turn the river Nile, Egypt's nurturing, beneficent tide, into blood.

Just before the flood season, Cain, Jacuna, Hati, and young Nefran had set out from Thebes on an upriver expedition. The party pursued a leisurely course past Aswan all the way to Abu Simbel, for Cain wanted to revisit the scene of his labors for the pharaoh some decades before—though of course as Seti he had to pretend that he was viewing the spectacular monuments for the first time.

At Abu Simbel, benefiting from introductions furnished by Khaimudi, the party lodged comfortably with the main temple's senior priesthood. Cain was pleased to see that the colossal statues of Ramesses had weathered well. While the toddler Nefran was cared for and coddled by the head priest's wife and daughters, Jacuna and Hati admired the great relief depicting Ramesses's victory over the Hittites at the Battle of Kadesh on the Orontes River in Syria.

So near to such a powerful example of Egypt's dynastic power, Cain could scarcely imagine anything threatening the empire, and certainly not the strange delusions of an upstart murderer.

৩৩৩

By August, the Nile was in full flood. Cain and his party had decided to spend the next few months upriver, until the receding waters would make the journey back to Thebes less turbulent.

And then, as Cain strolled with Jacuna by the banks of the Nile early one morning, the two were greeted by a strange sight: the silvery blue ribbon was tinged distinctly scarlet. Jacuna breathlessly recalled Khaimudi's account of Moses's grim warnings. Cain listened carefully to his son, but remained privately unconvinced. From the centuries he had spent wandering, he knew that the Blue Nile, rising in the Ethiopian highlands, might be the source of powdery, carmine-colored soil, flushed downriver by unusually heavy rains. This effluent, or perhaps red algae, might afford a natural explanation of the phenomenon that seemed to exhibit an uncanny match with Moses's "first plague."

Cain's certainty began to erode. That year would be long remembered in Egypt. In close succession, trial followed trial and curse followed curse. Fish died, frogs overran the land, and dust turned into noisome clouds of gnats and lice. Domestic animals ran amok as wild and then dropped dead in piles, the victims of plague. People and animals alike suffered from incurable boils. But Cain's, of course, were healed immediately, so he covered himself in long robes during those few weeks.

The plagues grew ever more fearsome. Fiery hailstorms burned houses and set dry fields ablaze. Swarms of locusts, billions of them, consumed all the remaining crops in Egypt. And finally, sepulchral darkness engulfed the land for three days.

Throughout these trials Pharaoh refused to release the Hebrews. In his skepticism, Cain had attributed each successive plague to natural causes, but now even he grew intrigued. He wanted to meet this Moses, to see where the source of his power really lay. The darkness was as difficult to explain as Noah's great flood.

Whatever the powers of Moses, or of Yahweh, to disrupt Egyptian life, Cain was, as always, on the watch for economic opportunity. The natural disasters that plagued the land for over half a year meant that Ramesses in his old age had to confront an economic and social crisis. Drought and famine had been known before in Egypt's long history. But now, after the devastation of farmland and livestock on an unprecedented scale, there was a real uncertainty about whether Ramesses could feed his people. If he could not, he would face civil unrest far worse than the mere disaffection of Hebrew slaves. Already tens of thousands of Egyptians were moving toward the capital, demanding that the Pharaoh provide food and put an end to the plagues.

Calculating that Ramesses would be amenable to any solution, even at an exorbitant cost in gold, Cain sent a message upriver, where most of his largest barges were moored. In March, he ordered the vessels loaded with grain and livestock he had secured long ago in Nubia. Located outside the borders of Egypt to the south, these grana-ries and stockyards were not only exempt from the usual tribute that Egyptian producers were accustomed to paying the pharaoh, but they had escaped the plagues as well. Ramesses could not object to paying for food he did not possess in his own right, Cain thought. In fact, he expected that Ramesses would accede to virtually any price. There was scant hope of any other food source. Cain's hopes remained high that he would strike one of the most lucrative bargains of his long career and place the pharaoh in his debt.

One day, on the return journey downriver to Thebes, Cain awoke before sunrise. Just as he was finishing his breakfast of bread and dried dates, the eerie stillness shrouding the vessel was suddenly interrupted.

"Come quickly, sir!" the captain's mate exhorted.

"What is it, Menotep?"

"I cannot awaken them, sir. Your brother, Jacuna, and his son. They do not move."

Alarmed, Cain jumped up from the table. "And Nefran?"

"He is awake, sir. The stewards are bathing him now."

Cain trembled as he rushed below decks to Jacuna's cabin. His son's deathly pallor was unmistakable, yet Cain rustled the cold body repeatedly, in vain hope. After an identical episode at Hati's bedside, he collapsed in tears. Then, from cabins elsewhere on the barge, shrieks and wails merged with Cain's cries into a dreadful chorus, as other crewmen discovered their loss.

Cain staggered back up to the ship's deck and found little Nefran. Staring listlessly at the waning stars above, Cain struggled to understand how the firstborn sons of many crewmen on his barge had died at the same time. Heartbroken, he ordered a halt to the journey so he and his stricken crew could bury their dead near the banks of the Nile.

⦿⧫⦿

Upon arriving at the Egyptian capital, Cain's fleet of barges was met at the docks by smaller pilot boats. Nearby, hundreds of the pharaoh's soldiers were busy holding back a huge crowd of people thronging the wharf area. Everyone along the river could see Cain's barges laden with sacks of grain and fat farm animals. In a time of famine, the Egyptian capital was in a state of panic. He knew he had to strike a deal quickly to prevent his barges from being looted. Cain had already drafted a contract for the official signature of the pharaoh's scribes, stating prices four times higher than normal.

Fortunately, moments after the mooring lines were secured, the elderly priest Khaimudi appeared out of the crowd. Walking down the gangplank, Cain held Nefran in his arms to keep the small boy from getting trampled by the unruly mob.

"Welcome, Seti. You have arrived just in time. Pharaoh is awaiting you at the palace." Pausing for a moment while he eyed little Nefran, Khaimudi motioned to his female servants.

"They will attend to Nefran as they did back at Abu Simbel," Khaimudi promised. Cain nodded in gratitude. One of the servants lifted the boy from his arms, and the two men walked to the palace.

Cain stood in the audience hall while Khaimudi proceeded into Pharaoh's chamber to present the contract. At length, Ramesses and

Khaimudi entered the hall, as usual to a flourish of trumpets. Cain was always surprised by the pharaoh's short stature. By now, his flaming red hair had grizzled into grayish-white. The monarch's arthritic knees and ankles caused him to limp noticeably. Nevertheless, a powerful aura emanated from the man.

Ramesses began the discussion abruptly.

"You have come to help Egypt, Seti?"

"My duty is to the nation, Mighty One, and you are its embodiment."

"We are told your glorious fleet of barges is docked at our piers, freighted with grain and livestock."

Cain bowed low in assent.

"But now, there is one matter that takes precedence."

Unsure whether to question the pharaoh, Cain remained silent.

"You are aware of the latest outrage that the traitor Moses has devised for Egypt. He and his God are murderers, Seti. And their victims are strewn across our land. I have lost my own firstborn son, and his firstborn male descendants with him." At this, the ruler's voice cracked slightly.

"All of Egypt grieves with you," Cain responded hesitantly, surprised to learn of Moses's connection to the slaughter.

"Why, then, have you cast your lot with Moses and his tribe of Hebrews?" Ramesses demanded sharply. His upraised right arm seemed to claw at the air, a tic that Cain had noticed long years before.

Caught off guard, Cain stared at the ruler blankly. With a snap of his fingers, the pharaoh commanded the palace guards to fling open one of the chamber's side doors. To his amazement, Cain saw the attendants of Khaimudi lead in a dazed-looking little boy. It was Nefran, his young son.

"This is your son, your firstborn?" Ramesses's reedy voice quivered between a question and a statement.

"He is mine, Pharaoh."

"And he did not die. Death passed him over. You have sold your-self to Moses and his God. How else to explain the curious survival of your son?" Pharaoh then held up Cain's contract and glared at him. "And in Egypt's darkest hour, you would come to my court as a profi-teer? You are a traitor, Seti!"

Cain was silent. How could he refute this accusation? Would the story of the deaths of Jacuna and Hati avail him? His own ingenuity had become the jaws of a hideous trap. By passing off Nefran as his firstborn in front of the Pharaoh, Cain had sealed his own doom.

"I could order your execution," said Ramesses, painfully pulling himself up erect on the throne. "But your father Senejer served me well. And you bear the name of my own father. I will therefore exhibit more mercy than the Hebrew God. Seize him, guards!"

Cain was instantly surrounded. At his side, Khaimudi stepped away, smiling. Cain knew at once that his old friend had betrayed him, doubtless to curry Pharaoh's favor and to seal an even more prestigious promotion.

"Your fate will be exile. Just as the Hebrew slaves will trudge through the sands and thornbushes of the wilderness, you will be bound and set adrift on a raft beyond the delta in the open sea. Thus will Egypt rid itself of traitors."

Cain's thoughts flashed back to the ark.

"Your stores of grain and plantations throughout Egypt shall be seized as the property of the state and distributed to the people. Now, guards, take the boy Nefran! Whatever your destiny, he shall not sur-vive you, Seti. You, too, must bear the pain of losing a son."

Cain's tortured scream rang across the throne room as he and Nefran were led in bonds from the chamber, each in a different direction.

CHAPTER 26

The Nile Delta, circa 1230 BC

Their faces grimly determined, the pharaoh's guards strapped Cain securely to the raft. Made of stout Phoenician cedar, it measured twelve by eight feet. With the raft in tow, the guard ship, rowed by a crew of thirty marines, made its way out into the lagoon toward the open sea. On one of the islets they passed, he could see three enormous Nile crocodiles sunning themselves in the sweltering heat.

Cain knew they were in the East Delta of the Nile, somewhere near the town of Bubastis. But all his questions of the guards had been met with a stony silence. When he had pronounced the punishment of exile, Ramesses had spoken of being set adrift on the open sea. The sentence was now being carried out. Only time would tell just where the crew would jettison the raft. Naked, Cain flinched as the brackish water stung the wounds on his back and legs where the guards had repeatedly flogged him.

The Nile was now in full flood. Cain knew that the strong river current might carry the raft twenty or even thirty miles out from shore. His chances of rescue would diminish with each mile, since seafarers of the day preferred to hug the shore for safety. Meanwhile, he had to contend with numerous, more immediate dangers, such as storms, hunger, thirst, sunstroke—and crocodiles.

"I should have seen it coming," Cain thought with acid hindsight. What was more predictable than for Khaimudi to fortify his own position by denouncing Cain as a collaborator with the Hebrews? The charge of treason also allowed Ramesses to claim a treasure trove of supplies at no cost to the state. Both the king and the priest emerged as winners. Cain ruefully reflected that his taste for the halls of power, as well as his greed, had cost him dearly once again.

Not to mention little Nefran. He thought bitterly of how God had taken his beloved Jacuna's life, and that of Hati, only to "spare" Nefran for what would probably turn out to be a far more ugly fate. How could God justify such deaths, but punish Cain with endless wandering? Or was there a higher purpose to God's actions in Egypt? Moses, after all, had not been punished for his act of killing.

At least not yet.

They were now at the seaward margin of the lagoon. Cain could see large clusters of whiskered terns, shovelers, and cormorants combing the coastal sands. After loosening the towrope and casting off the raft, the guards murmured a few prayers with their arms stretched out to sea. Cain knew that they were beseeching the gods not to hold them accountable for his death.

Propelled by the Nile's current, the guard ship made steady progress in the open water, where a freshening offshore breeze capped the waves with crests of white. As the raft bobbed in the sea, Cain could see that land was rapidly receding. At the crest of the next wave, he saw the guard ship in the midst of its turn back toward the coast. As the ship streamed past him, the oarsmen sat stone-faced at their benches, and the pharaoh's guards pointedly turned their backs to him. It was as if he no longer existed.

It was now midafternoon. With no way to control the raft's speed or direction, Cain reckoned that his only chance of survival was rescue by a merchant ship. Lying flat on his stomach was a crippling disadvantage, however. A ship might pass very near by the raft, but it was entirely possible in this turbid water that the crew would fail to spot him. Even if he were plucked out of the water, who was to say that such a rescue would be benign? Pirates, Cain well knew, were as common as merchants in these waters.

The powerful river current pushed the raft onward. As land became steadily more distant, Cain saw fewer and fewer birds overhead or in the water. At least the crocodiles had also been left behind, he thought. Still, there were other dangerous sea creatures that might be on the prowl. Cain knew that the Mediterranean was home to several dozen species of shark, some of them measuring over ten feet in length. It would be child's play for such a predator to heave his raft into the air. He fervently wished that his recuperative physical powers would operate with greater than usual speed to heal the wounds on his back and legs and stanch the flow of blood.

Night descended quickly. At the dark of the moon, the blackness was absolute, and Cain's only companion was the wind, which blew ever harder. A rare summer storm was brewing. He would have to discipline himself to hold his breath at the trough of each wave in order to avoid swallowing too much seawater. Only at the crests could he breathe freely. It became a monotonous, repeated alternation: trough and crest, trough and crest.

And there was no end in sight.

As the eastern horizon began to lighten, Cain was surprised by two things. The first was that he was still alive; the second was that he could move more freely. Countless soakings of warm seawater had loosened the bonds that lashed him to the raft. Perhaps that was one mistake the guards had made, he thought. This time of the year, the sea was usually placid. His captors had probably anticipated that the prisoner, held immobile in place, would die of hunger, thirst, or exposure before the ropes would begin to disintegrate.

Wriggling free of the restraining bonds, Cain experienced fresh optimism. But his hopes were short-lived. No sunrise adorned the eastern sky. Instead, the dreary firmament glimmered fitfully in gray walls of water stretching to every horizon. The wind, if anything, grew heavier, and it started to rain.

His bonds had been a blessing in the rough sea, Cain now realized—at least they had ensured that a giant wave could not sweep him off the raft.

Just as that realization dawned on him, an oversize swell crested and crashed down on the tiny vessel. With a slamming thud that propelled him into a grotesquely elegant trajectory, he found himself lifted into midair and then plunging toward a yawning trough. When he had shaken the seawater from his eyes, mouth, and nostrils, the raft was nowhere to be seen. He began to tread water, but the struggle against the towering waves and gale force winds quickly wore him down. His head bobbed lower and lower as he swallowed more seawater.

"Oh God," he cried inside. "Oh God, is death by drowning what you have saved me for all this time?"

Utterly exhausted, Cain's head slipped beneath the surface as he lost consciousness.

___

CHAPTER 27

New Hampshire, Sixteen Years Ago

Amanda scanned the storm-tossed waves from a great height, searching in vain for any sign of Cain. Was this the end of her vision? Would she continue to soar upward until she left the world of Cain entirely? Instead, she suddenly seemed to rush toward the water, and even as she plummeted, the tumultuous waves morphed into a glassy smooth surface. She was no longer looking at the sea, but rather at a lake surrounded by the glorious ambers, reds, and greens of early autumn. With only sparse wisps of cirrus clouds high overhead, Amanda could feel the sun's warm rays penetrating the cool air.

A dock came into view, and as she traced it toward the shore, she recognized the log cabin home of her grandparents on Lake Winnipesaukee in eastern New Hampshire. Familiar voices began to reach her ears, and then she was inside the cabin, watching a young girl tap gently but insistently on the blue jeans of Roger James.

"Dad, can I go down to the dock?" begged the pigtailed preteen.

"Uh…sure, but be back in fifteen minutes. Grandma is setting the table in the front yard for a picnic lunch," her dad said. Inching a bit farther under the sink to position his pipe wrench on the leaky drain, Roger smiled to himself. Amanda had been virtually glued to him during the past week since the funeral services down the street. He felt relieved that his grief-stricken daughter was finally willing to venture out on her own. And on a small island, she could not get lost.

"Take Ruby along with you, sweetie. She needs to get out of the house," he added, referring to the Irish setter who lounged at his feet, chewing on an old tennis ball.

"Thanks, Dad." Amanda grabbed the ball and opened the screen door. "Come on, girl, let's go!" Ruby sprang to her feet, eyes fixed on the yellow object as her tail lashed back and forth in eager anticipation. Amanda hurled the ball down the pebbly trail leading to the shoreline, and Ruby shot out of the cabin in pursuit of her bouncing prey. The spring-loaded door slammed behind her as she gave chase.

Amanda and Ruby soon arrived at the low-slung dock that jutted about fifty feet onto the lake. Located on Bear Island, the second largest of the hundreds of cays that dot New Hampshire's most scenic lake, this quaint property had been in the family for generations. Amanda came here with her parents every summer and occasionally in winter for as long as she could remember. Except for this trip, the memories were very fond.

Crossing the lake to the island had always been fun. Depending on the season, Bear Island was either a short ride in a small motorboat or a breathtaking dash by snowmobile across the thick ice. However, this visit required a ferry large enough for the many relatives who accompanied Amanda, her father, and Jennifer James's casket on the short, somber voyage.

The chapel and graveyard on the island were both tiny, yet the service was packed with dozens of distant relatives, people Amanda either barely remembered or did not know at all. They kept telling her how sorry they were for her. It seemed everybody was sorry.

She recalled the moment after the guests exited the chapel and the family was invited for the final viewing. Through tears, her father gazed at his beloved Jennifer one last time, but Amanda looked away. She simply could not tolerate that ghastly image of her mom as her final memory.

That was a week ago, and all the strangers and relatives had left a few days later, giving Amanda, her dad, and her grandparents some time alone. On the night after the funeral, her father called her out to the cabin's front porch and gave her a surprise gift, handing her a light blue box. She opened it to find a heart-shaped gold locket containing a tiny black-and-white picture of her mom. Her father wanted her to have it, and Amanda obliged him, but she carried it around in her pocket. Somehow it didn't feel right looped around her neck, at least not yet.

Torn by these remembrances, Amanda distracted herself by throwing the ball toward the end of the dock and seeing if the fleet-footed setter could retrieve it before it dropped into the water. Three straight successes, but then Ruby froze halfway up the dock on the fourth attempt, wheeling around into a pointing stance and growling in the direction of the woods. As the tennis ball splashed over the distant edge, Ruby raced past Amanda and disappeared into the trees.

Figuring a squirrel had gotten the better part of the dog's attention, Amanda walked to the end of the dock and sat down. She dangled her feet over the side, her tennis shoes just barely above the surface of the water. A couple of months earlier, the rusty swim ladder to her left would have beckoned, but the water temperature was now too cold for a comfortable swim.

With barely a breath of wind near the tree-sheltered shoreline, the lake surface directly in front of her looked like a polished mirror. In the distance, Amanda could see the breeze drawing tiny cat paws across the water, yet they seemed to fade before they reached the dock.

The old icehouse on the distant shore brought a thin, brief smile to her face as she recalled her grandpa's oft-repeated story of the historic landmark, one of many such structures ringing New England's lakes and ponds. In the late 1800s, ice blocks could be sold in the summer for a small fortune in New York and Boston. Today, this relic across the lake still stood as a tourist attraction to support the locals.

Amanda shifted position and flopped over onto her belly to watch the tadpoles jetting around just below the surface. She squirmed and reached into her pocket and removed the locket. She flicked it open and shut repeatedly, testing the grip of the tiny clasp. She tried to imagine her mom being there with her. She stared at the picture, wondering what her mom was doing and where she was when the photo was taken. Trying to recall the sound of her voice, Amanda drew a blank. How could the memories of her mother be fading already?

A distant staccato series of barks from Ruby startled Amanda, and she fumbled the locket. She watched in horror as it bounced onto the dock and disappeared through the crack between the weathered planks.

"No!" she cried. Instinctively, she tried to snatch it back in time, but the faint splash sent a chill down her spine. Squinting through the small gap, she watched helplessly as the locket offered only a tiny last glimmer before she lost track of it.

In a panicked reaction, she rose and leaped feet first into the chilly water. She could not disappoint her dad by losing her priceless gift. Her jeans and sneakers felt heavy, but she was trying to get her mom back—and she wouldn't fail. She inverted her body and kicked downward toward the bottom, fortunately only six or seven feet below. Opening her eyes, she couldn't see the locket amidst the underwater forest of weeds, but she guessed it must have dropped straight down through the calm water.

Her searching fingertips produced clouds of silt that completely obscured her view. After what seemed like a full minute of frenzied clawing through the mud and weeds, Amanda was becoming desperate for air when her left hand felt the contours of the locket. Success! She clutched her prize, planted her feet on the bottom, and thrust upward with all her might.

That was the last thing she remembered from that day until she regained consciousness on the shore. But now the older Amanda watched from above as her younger self broke the surface of the lake, her head impacting with a dull thud on one of the dock's low-lying crossbeams. Moments passed as she floated facedown, completely motionless.

Then came another bark from Ruby, who was chasing after a man sprinting out of the woods toward the end of the dock. He reached down and secured the twelve-year-old beneath both her shoulders and effortlessly lifted her out of the water. Swiftly, he carried her back up the dock and laid her on her stomach in the tall grass at the shore. Turning her face to one side, he touched the spot where she'd hit her head and then began pushing gently on her back. Lake water gushed from the unconscious girl's mouth.

The man then looked up and smiled in the direction of the older Amanda, who immediately recognized his face. It was Harris—the limo driver who had brought her from Villa Colosseum to LAX three nights earlier! What was he doing in New Hampshire sixteen years ago?

Harris stood up, petted Ruby, and then ambled up the bank and disappeared into the woods. Ruby began licking Amanda's face, urging her back to consciousness.

A minute or so later, Amanda sat up. Soaked and starting to shiver, she did not remember swimming to shore, but she must have. She opened her hand. There was the locket and gold chain! Out at end of the dock, her dad was pacing back and forth, scanning the lake and calling out her name with concern. Wiping the wet hair away from her face, Amanda prepared to answer him.

Before doing so, she opened the clasp on the delicate chain and secured the locket around her neck. Amanda thought for a moment. No, she couldn't possibly inform him of the mishap with the gift he'd given her. Nor could she explain to herself, much less to him, her memory lapse between finding the locket and ending up on land. She decided to tell him that she'd accidentally slipped off the dock and swam ashore.

"Daddy! I'm over here!"

CHAPTER 28

The Mediterranean Sea, circa 1230 BC

Cain felt a vague sensation of being pulled by the hair. Some time later, he heard a woman's voice and felt strong hands compressing his chest firmly under his ribs. Someone was trying to coax him back into consciousness.

"I think we have revived him, Father," said the voice.

Cain opened his eyes. He lay on the deck of a boat, with a robe decently covering his nakedness. Over him bent a young woman with long brown tresses. Her gold necklace, intricately studded with semi-precious stones of carnelian and jasper, instantly revealed to Cain that she was a Phoenician. At his gaze, her full, round lips spread open in a dazzling smile.

"My name is Tanith," announced his rescuer. "Our lookout saw you struggling in the storm just before we almost ran you over. Luckily, I was able to drag you to safety. What were you doing alone in the middle of the sea?"

Cain grimaced but found himself unable to speak as a coughing spasm took hold.

"No matter," said Tanith. "You are safe now. My father, Ahiram, is the captain of this vessel. We are Phoenicians, from Tyre. We will care for you. Can you understand me?"

Gratefully, Cain signaled comprehension, closed his eyes, and let himself drift to sleep.

☙❦☙

The Phoenicians, Cain found, were as good as their word. By the time
they reached their homeport of Tyre, he had fully recovered from his
ordeal at sea. Naturally, Captain Ahiram and Tanith had inquired
about his past in Egypt. Cain summarized his experiences, saying
that he had led a successful career as a merchant before becoming
unwittingly caught up in a plot against the pharaoh. Judged guilty
of treason, his life had been spared because of his previous services
to the monarch. As a reduced punishment, he was flogged and then
consigned to the sea.

As he recounted this narrative several days after his rescue, Cain
could see that Tanith hung on his every word. If she had a husband,
he thought, she would surely be living in Tyre, and probably supervising the household and raising their children. So it was very likely
that she was still unmarried. But why, with her gazelle-like grace and
voluptuous figure, would she still be unattached?

Learning that Cain had some experience in seafaring and in
trade, Captain Ahiram gladly showed the castaway around the ship. A
round boat merchant vessel, she was about eighty feet in length and
powered by a single bank of oars and a small sail. Her professional
crew numbered twenty: fourteen oarsmen, a cook, and five marines.
Tanith was attended by a single maidservant. At the stern were two
oars that served as a rudder. Attached to the stem post at the prow was
a large clay container called an amphora, which held an ample supply of drinking water. Most of the deck space was occupied by similar
ceramic containers, held in place by sturdy railings. Inside these vessels was the ship's reason for being: the trade goods that had made
Phoenicia one of the wealthiest civilizations in the entire region.

Ahiram explained that they were returning from the western edge of the Nile delta, when they rescued Cain. It had been a

MEDITERR

SPAIN

Rome
Herculaneum
MT. VESUVIUS

Carthage

Leptis Magna

N
W E
S

prosperous journey. Outbound from Tyre on the eastern edge of the Mediterranean, they had been laden with cedarwood, embroideries, fine linen, wine, salt, dried fish, and glazed pottery. Now the cargo containers held papyrus, ivory, spices, and incense—all of which could be sold in Tyre for a handsome profit. Despite his recent debacle with the pharaoh, trading was in Cain's blood, and he listened eagerly to Ahiram's recital.

It took them ten days to cover the route to Tyre. Although they hugged the shoreline for the journey's later stages, Ahiram was not at all reluctant to shave off the distance by plotting a more direct course on the open sea and by traveling at night. He explained to Cain that the Phoenicians had steadily improved their navigation techniques, using a detailed knowledge of the night sky at various seasons of the year. Listening politely, Cain recalled the years of his great wandering during which he had learned to navigate by similar means.

As Cain spent more time with his rescuer, he discovered that he had a great deal in common with the beautiful young woman from Tyre. Like Cain, Tanith had traveled far and possessed an innate curiosity about other cultures and customs. She entertained him with amusing stories about the ports she had visited, and he regaled her with some tales of his own about life on the Nile. The economics of trade were second nature to Tanith, and Cain quickly recognized a merchant mentality akin to his own.

While Ahiram was communicative, even chatty, on the subjects of seafaring and trade, he remained somewhat aloof when it came to Cain and Tanith's growing attachment. They seemed to be in constant company during the day and, Ahiram suspected, for much of the night. Ahiram was too much of a realist to believe that he could rein in his daughter. Even as a child, she had displayed a forceful, independent spirit. But Ahiram was also privately skeptical of Cain's account of events in Egypt. Why had Ramesses spared his life? Plots against the pharaoh, in Ahiram's experience, were always punished with death. Ahiram suspected there was another dimension to Cain's past. Perhaps he had even been a Hebrew slave. After all, when his crew pulled him from the water his body clearly bore the marks of a severe flogging. Who was this mysterious man for whom his fearless daughter had dove into the sea?

No such misgivings troubled Tanith, though. Both she and Cain sensed that their shipboard romance was ripening into deep attachment. Yet their intimacy was not unfettered. Cain did not confide the secrets of his past, and neither did Tanith speak of the ill-fated, arranged marriage that had been dissolved in Tyre seven years before when it was discovered she was barren. A wife who could not produce an heir was unacceptable in Phoenician culture, and Ahiram was forced to bear the shame of taking his daughter back to live under his roof. The short-lived marriage was one reason why father and daughter spent as little time as possible in Tyre. They preferred a seafaring life, where wagging tongues could cause them less pain.

Besides their conversations about enchanting ports of call and the economics of trade, Cain and Tanith also delved into several lengthy discussions of the new Phoenician alphabet. It had been many decades since Cain had been in contact with Phoenicians, although of course he had visited their city-states on some of his Mediterranean excursions as a trader. Now he learned, to his amazement, that they had invented a writing system vastly superior to Egyptian hieroglyphs.

"Aleph, beth, gimel, daleth, he," Tanith drilled him.

Cain promptly repeated the names of the first five Phoenician letters, and then used a makeshift stylus to inscribe the symbols on a papyrus sheet.

"You have an excellent memory!" Tanith complimented him.

"You are an inspiring teacher," he diplomatically replied.

"All right, my handsome pupil. Write me the symbols for the next five, and say the letters aloud."

Cain pronounced the letters as he wrote them: *waw, zayin, heth, teth, yodh.*

"Who invented this marvel?"

"If it was a single individual, he or she is not known," Tanith replied. "But for my part, I think it was a woman."

"How so?" Cain asked with a hint of teasing.

"Because women are more economical than men. Look at how much papyrus our alphabet saves!" she glowed.

Once they put in to the island of Tyre, Ahiram courteously invited Cain to stay with the family for the week's layover. The city's twin harbors, one on the island's north side and the other to the south, had made it one of the great trading centers of the Mediterranean. Contact with Egypt had commenced soon after Tyre's foundation, some fifteen hundred years before. Perhaps its best-known product was Tyrian purple dye, derived from the shell of a native sea snail. Outlandishly expensive and produced only in Tyre, the dye had become the exclusive emblem of royalty and nobility, for only the extremely wealthy could afford it. The purple powder had even given the Phoenicians their name, courtesy of trade with Greece, where the word *phoinike* meant "the land of the purple."

Cain and Tanith spent the days exploring the city and its environs, while Ahiram attended to commercial transactions, winding up affairs from the previous voyage and preparing for the next one. The city had grown considerably since Cain's last visit. In the bazaar, for example, there were now literally hundreds of food stalls. Grilled fish with garlic, large tureens of steaming lentil soup, and baskets heaped with freshly baked bread emitted mouthwatering aromas. The busy hum of a thousand conversations was punctuated by the shrill cries of vendors hawking their wares. Stately men, attired in their belted,

pleated skirts with multicolored, embroidered borders, strolled among
the stalls. Even in the warm sunshine, they wore their cone-shaped
hats. Women wore long tunics tied at the waist with tasseled belts.
Like Tanith, they braided their hair down the back with two shorter
braids on each side. But Cain saw no woman who could compare to
Tanith in his eyes.

Cargo for the new venture began to accumulate in short order, as
Ahiram's crew loaded grain, Phoenician glass, and gaudily embroidered textiles onto his ship. Cain helped with the purchasing, and
his negotiating ability was welcome to the captain, allaying his appre-
hensions somewhat about the new addition to his team. This would
be the longest expedition the captain had ever undertaken. In addition to Cyprus, Lycia on the southern coast of Asia Minor, the island
of Crete, and the Greek mainland near Athens, Ahiram had set his
sights on the western Mediterranean, where the prize commodity
was silver from Spain. After that, if all went well, he would venture
outside the inland sea, all the way northward to Britain, in quest
of tin. This metal, smelted with copper from Cyprus, had already
yielded bronze for the Phoenicians, another mainstay in their pros-
pering economy.

The night before departure, Cain improvised an Egyptian senet
board from a piece of wood in Ahiram's workshop and taught Tanith
how to play over goblets of sweet white wine. To his astonishment,
she beat him on the very first try.

"Beginner's luck," he murmured with a slight smile.

"Nonsense, my sweet," she countered, but her liquid brown eyes
softened the retort. "You too are an inspiring teacher, that's all."

After a few more games, they strode to the large stone terrace of
Ahiram's estate, which enjoyed a panoramic view of the water separating the island city from the mainland. Large flowerpots contained
a profusion of lilies, poppies, camelias, and roses, affording the

terrace a riot of color in the daytime and a gentle mosaic of scents by night. A gigantic full moon, just gliding from copper into gold, hung in the eastern sky. Cain drew Tanith close.

"Where are we headed together?" he asked her.

"I do not know our destination," she whispered as his arms encircled her. "It is the journey that matters."

CHAPTER 29

The Voyage from Tyre to Cyprus, circa 1230 BC

Favored by a steady southeast wind, they made the 125-mile journey from Tyre to the large island of Cyprus in only three days. Ahiram's oarsmen were grateful for the respite, although the captain, ever mindful of discipline, ensured that they were kept occupied with shipboard maintenance tasks.

On the second day out, the first mate was supervising a small detachment of marines on a cargo inspection. Discovering a faulty seal on one of the grain containers, he opened the amphora only to confront the beady eyes of a pair of rats, who scurried across the deck in search of a new hiding place. Cain, looking on, made a mental note to suggest that Ahiram acquire a cat or two in Cyprus. As he well knew, the Egyptians had used these animals for centuries to protect their grain from rodents. In fact, cats were so prized in Egypt that they were mummified, buried lovingly with their owners, and sometimes even worshipped.

Cain thought it strange, but in all his travels as a seafaring trader he had never visited Cyprus. After he admitted this to Tanith, who had been to the island often with her father, she assumed with alacrity the role of storyteller and guide.

"Cyprus is very ancient," she told him the next day as they sat under an awning at the stern of the ship. "It is said that the island had water wells seven thousand years ago, when villages first sprang up. The Greeks have been colonizing there for several centuries now.

We Phoenicians share stories with them about our greatest goddess, Astarte. The Greeks call her Aphrodite. Like the Greeks, we believe that she was born on Cyprus."

Cain smiled. From their exploration of Tyre, he knew that Tanith was a fervent devotee of Astarte, the Phoenician goddess of love, fertility, and war. When his companion shyly lowered her eyes, Cain decided it would be diplomatic to change the subject.

"What were you sketching so busily this morning?" he inquired. One of Tanith's many accomplishments was her talent as an illustrator. Since she favored marine subjects, she had plenty of inspiration on her voyages. Opening a protective metal tube that lay beside her on deck, she showed Cain a sketch of a smiling bottlenose dolphin. The likeness was uncanny. The unfinished shape was so vibrant that it looked as if it might leap from the papyrus roll onto the deck.

"But we haven't seen any of these so far on the voyage, have we?"

"No, but all my past sightings of them are engraved on my memory since they are so graceful."

Cain stretched out lazily on the deck in the warm sunshine.

"Tell me a story," he murmured.

"There is a famous tale about dolphins told by the Greeks. It's about a poet and musician named Arion. I wonder if you have ever heard it?"

"No, please go on."

"Well, Arion, who lived once upon a time in Corinth in Greece, decided he would enter a poetry competition in Sicily. So he traveled westward and, lo and behold, won the contest. The Sicilians awarded him rich prizes, and these were loaded onto the ship that would bring him back to Greece. But fate had other plans."

She was a natural storyteller, Cain thought. A woman like Tanith should have the chance to beguile her children with bedtime tales and lullabies.

"And then what happened?" he urged.

"You know yourself that life at sea can hold many surprises. The greedy sailors plotted to kill Arion and steal his new riches. They gave the musician a choice: either kill himself with his own dagger and be buried on land at their next port of call, or throw himself into the water, where he would surely perish. You know that the Greeks have a horror of remaining unburied."

Cain thought fleetingly of Pharaoh, reflecting dryly that the monarch had neglected to accord him any choices—not even unpalatable ones.

"And then," Tanith continued, "how do you think Arion answered them?" Cain furrowed his brow in curiosity and gestured for her to tell him more.

"Even under such pressure, he remained calm. All Arion requested was permission to sing one final song. He took up his lyre in praise of Apollo, the god whom the Greeks revere as the patron of poetry and music. The song was so beautiful that a school of dolphins collected around the ship. I can picture them, Cain. Did you know that dolphins sometimes kiss each other on the beak?"

Cain shook his head in disbelief.

"Well, they do. They love both music and humans, which perhaps amounts to the same thing. If Arion saw such a kiss, maybe the sight made him leap into the water. Because, according to the story, that's exactly what he did after the song's final notes."

"So he drowned among the dolphins?" Cain asked.

"Not at all, my dearest. One of the dolphins offered its back to Arion and saved him. His rescuer took him to the southern tip of the Peloponnesus. And then, through the blessings of Apollo, the dolphin was transformed into a constellation. On clear nights, you can see her in the sky."

"Before the dolphin set him on her back, did she drag him by the hair, by any chance? And by the way, how do you know that the dolphin was a she?" smiled Cain.

Tanith shrugged her shoulders casually, just as the lighthouse on the coast of Cyprus hove into view. "How do you know she wasn't?"

⚮

They stayed in Cyprus four days. Cain and Tanith spent time sightseeing, while Ahiram supervised cargo off-loading and purchased a consignment of copper ore, for which Cyprus was famous. Copper, the principal element for the durable alloy bronze, was highly prized for weapons manufacture in Asia Minor and on Crete, the next two stops on the ship's itinerary. In his negotiations, Ahiram also ensured that the suppliers would provide him with an even larger quantity of ore on the return voyage, for delivery back in Tyre.

By now it was past midsummer. There was no time to waste, since the sailing season in the Mediterranean would end in early October. Ahiram planned to spend the winter months in Greece with his ship in dry dock, then set out the following spring for the westward excursion to Spain and then past Gibraltar into the open ocean, northward to Britain. With luck and hard work, he could figure on making the return journey to homeport in Tyre by the end of the following season. It was an ambitious itinerary, but Phoenician mariners lived ambition as an article of their faith. After all, Phoenicians had circumnavigated Africa before Ahiram was born.

Their next port was Patara in Lycia, located near the mouth of the yellow-hued Xanthus river on the southwest coast of Asia Minor. The water owed its peculiar color to the golden tint of the alluvial soil. Here Ahiram moored his cargo ship in the harbor, transferring the goods for trade to a barge for delivery upriver in the town of Xanthus. During the transfer, Cain admired the speedy, well-coordinated teams of dockworkers as they passed the amphoras from hand to hand to the tune of sea shanties sung in chorus.

It was in Lycia that the travelers first heard of a lengthy war unfolding hundreds of miles to the northwest. The Greeks, it was said, had united under the leadership of a Mycenaean king, Agamemnon, to lay siege to the wealthy city of Troy on the coast of the Aegean Sea. Two Lycian chieftains named Glaucus and Sarpedon had allied their troops with the Trojans. Cain and Tanith speculated on the outcome of the struggle. They suspected they would hear far more about the conflict after they arrived in Greece.

"What is said to have been the cause of this war?" Ahiram wanted to know one evening, as they sat together enjoying some of the local wine.

"Some are blaming it on the abduction of a Greek queen by a Trojan prince," Tanith replied. "The queen, named Helen, was the wife of Agamemnon's brother. Prince Paris was the son of Priam, the Trojan king."

"You don't really believe that story, do you?" Cain asked teasingly.

"Why not? Are women not worth fighting for?" Tanith answered with a smile.

"Some are, and some are not." Cain answered with measured deliberation, as if he were methodically assessing the issue. "But from what they are saying about the gold and horses of Troy, I am willing to bet this war is being waged for wealth, and not for a woman."

"Nevertheless," Tanith rejoined, "you have to admit that the Greek version makes for a good story."

❧

They covered the two hundred nautical miles to Crete in a single week, coasting the large island of Rhodes en route, as well as the smaller islands of the Dodecanese. After mooring the ship at a stone quay in the harbor of Heraklion, Ahiram and Cain once again directed the off-loading of trade goods for the marketplace. After three days, their business was concluded. With large amphorae of Cretan wine placed on deck for delivery in Athens, the crew prepared to set sail. This time, however, the winds were less favorable. The oarsmen would have to pitch in for much of the voyage if the ship were to reach Athens by the autumnal equinox.

The first part of their route lay across the open water of the Sea of Crete. Then they would be able to island-hop in the Cyclades, with Santorini, Sikinos, Sifnos, and Serifos in sight for much of the time. The final stretch would take them west of Kithnos and Kea, thence to Cape Sounion, the tip of the Greek mainland. From there it would be an easy stage to Piraeus, the port of Athens.

Late one afternoon, they were halfway to Santorini when Baltsar, one of the oarsmen, slumped forward at his bench. Cain hastened to his side, thinking that perhaps the man had succumbed to a hangover from the sailors' revelry in port. When he questioned Baltsar, however, he discovered that the man had barely been ashore at Heraklion, preferring to remain shipboard.

"Do you feel any unusual aches or pains?" Cain asked.

"Yes, some painful swelling that I've never felt before," Baltsar replied.

"Where is the swelling, man?"

When Baltsar raised his bare arms aloft, Cain felt a wave of dread. The swollen lymph glands in the armpits were a sure sign: the plague. He remembered the rats in the grain amphora shortly after they had set sail from Tyre. They had acquired cats in Cyprus, but the felines had obviously not been able to control the situation. Now the rodents were apparently spreading the disease.

Baltsar pointed also to his neck, where the swellings were painfully apparent. Knowing that there was only a slim chance that the oarsman would recover, Cain patted his shoulder and ordered him to his bunk for a night's rest. One of the other marines would take his place.

Before the evening meal, Cain sought out Ahiram and confided his suspicions. The captain accepted the news with stoic calm. When Cain pointed out that many more crewmen might already have been infected, Ahiram quietly reassured him. They could stop at any number of the islands, he said, if they needed to replenish the crew. Cain decided not to touch on the possibility that the plague, no respecter of rank, might not limit itself to the crew. Instead, he objected that acquiring fresh recruits would be difficult if word got out that the Phoenicians were piloting a "plague ship."

Captain Ahiram put his foot down. "We have made a large investment in this voyage," he said sharply. "We must stick to our schedule. If there are problems with the crew, my young friend, I will handle them."

Seeing that Ahiram would tolerate no dissent, Cain backed down.

Overnight, two more oarsmen became ill. One could not stop vomiting blood, while the other had developed a rash of lurid red spots on his skin. As rumors circulated among the men, the afflicted crew members were ostracized by their fellows. Cain spoke urgently to Tanith.

"There is no cure," he said. "We will have to find a way to isolate these men."

"How is that possible on a ship this size, Cain?"

"We could leave them ashore at Santorini. Ahiram has the resources to pay for their care on the island, or for their burial there."

Tanith shook her head. "These men have families. We cannot abandon them on a foreign shore."

"You have to remember the risks of contagion. The plague is the master traveler of trade routes. Within a week, most of the crew could become infected. Who knows if you and I are immune? And your father..."

Tanith broke in. "Panic is a more dangerous enemy than any plague. Let us keep our heads. When we land at Santorini, we will see how things stand."

❦

At Santorini the situation became even more urgent. Now six crewmen lay ill, and Melita, the faithful maidservant who had tended Tanith since childhood, had died. Baltsar's illness had progressed to the point where his skin was actually decomposing, causing excruciating pain. Ahiram faced a cruel dilemma. On Cain's advice, he discreetly inquired if the afflicted men could be cared for on the island. But he needed replacement oarsmen. How was he to hire them if the plight of the "plague ship" became public knowledge? Somehow, aided by Cain and Tanith's persuasive powers and a full purse, the necessary brokering was accomplished. The Phoenicians, now reinforced by half a dozen Greek mariners, weighed anchor a few hours after their arrival.

The following days, Cain thought afterward, were like a descent into an abyss. In fact, he fully expected a night vision from the master of spirits, but there was an even more ominous silence instead. As the vessel called at island after island, usually at night, clandestine replacements renewed the crew. By the time they reached the island of Serifos, seventy-five miles from Athens, only two of the original Phoenician oarsmen were left.

And then, the unthinkable, which had festered unspoken in the minds of both Cain and Tanith. Ahiram, whose health had always been robust, fell prey to violent bouts of coughing. Cain was virtually certain that the captain had at last contracted the plague.

As the ship got underway at sunrise from Serifos, the last stop before the Greek mainland, Cain and Ahiram sat together under the awning at the stern. Though seriously ill, Ahiram had lost none of his composure. He gazed at Cain directly with penetrating gray eyes.

"Please take care of her when I'm gone."

"You can't be serious, Ahiram. You're not going anywhere."

"Well, I don't think I'm going to Athens, at any rate," the older man replied, with the trace of a smile.

"I want to tell you something," Ahiram continued. "You and Tanith have grown close over these few months. I know she loves you, Cain. You have treated her with the respect I always hoped for my daughter. But in our home city, back in Tyre, she never received that honor."

"How not? She has beauty, wit, intelligence... Any man in his senses would prize her for his wife, Ahiram."

"Until such a man discovered her curse."

Ahiram's failing eyes missed Cain's startled reaction. "Curse?" he asked in as calm a tone as he could manage.

"She prays to Astarte, our great goddess. But Astarte did not grant that my daughter would ever be a mother. She is barren."

Cain looked down as an unaccustomed empathy touched his heart.

"That was the end of her marriage as a young woman. Such news spreads quickly in a city like Tyre. More rapidly than the plague, perhaps."

"I love her for herself, Ahiram. Not for children from our loins. And remember, she saved my life."

The older man smiled wanly. "I've never asked too much from you. But now I ask you for my beloved daughter's sake. Keep faith with her."

Cain bowed his head and pressed the sick man's hand as another fit of coughing shook Ahiram's body.

◦◦◦◦

Three days later, they buried him at sea. When Cain had assured Tanith that he could maintain the morale of the remaining oarsmen until they reached land for a proper burial, she merely answered,

"He is a Phoenician. Let the sea be his in death, as it was in life." As tears welled in her eyes, Cain placed his arm around her shoulders in silent comfort.

With Ahiram gone, Cain became the de facto captain of the vessel. It was up to him and Tanith to plan the final act of the voyage that had begun so auspiciously and then turned into a nightmare. Cain understood what was needed.

"We need to scuttle the ship at least a mile offshore," he told Tanith. "Everything that can spread the plague has to go down in the sea."

"And the sailors?" she asked, wide-eyed.

"If they are already infected, they will probably not survive. But the grain and the rodents—they must all be cast off."

"How will we make land?"

"We will swim for it, my dolphin. You saved me once. Now we will save each other."

Privately, he was amazed that Tanith, unlike her father and the crewmen, had not so much as a trace of a symptom. From eons of experience, he well knew his own immunity and powers of recuperation. But Tanith, who had ministered to dozens of ill sailors, also seemed immune.

The couple decided to be candid with the remaining crew members, telling them of the necessity to sink the ship and warning them of the dangers of any alternative course. The crew understood the severity of the situation, accepting the news with grim resignation.

At the first sight of Cape Sounion, four of the oarsmen would abandon their benches and venture below decks. There they would hack out gashes in the hull, and seawater pouring into the ship would sink the vessel within minutes. The entire crew would abandon ship. Improvised rafts would help the refugees gain the beach, or so Cain hoped.

Soon the plan went into effect. The prow began to tilt upward at a bizarre angle. As he and Tanith jumped from the deck, Cain thought of the story she had told him about Mot and Yamm, the Phoenician gods of the sea and of death, respectively. The two were brothers, and Cain hoped that they were on cordial terms that morning.

CHAPTER 30

Greece, circa 1230 BC

The hour-long swim to shore proved easier than Cain had imagined. Strong, rhythmic swells helped propel them landward, and their only real challenge was avoiding the flotsam and jetsam from the scuttled ship. He and Tanith could hear breakers booming on the rocky coast near the headland of Sounion, but to the left they could see a broad, sandy beach where the water was calmer.

Gaining the beach, the castaways encountered some local fishermen, who informed them that a small village was close by. After a ten-minute walk along a dusty track, the travelers were greeted by a grizzled local elder who emerged out of nowhere only seconds after they arrived. Wearing a wide-brimmed, blue woolen hat to protect himself from the hot sun, the old man welcomed them courteously, identified himself as Nikandros, and led them to a small farmhouse. Inside the stone wall that circled the property, goats browsed and hens cackled, busily running about. A slight breeze rustled the gleaming, silver-gray leaves of four sturdy olive trees. The man introduced his wife, Adonia, to the visitors, and she warmly embraced Tanith. Cain knew from his journeys that travelers, strangers, and guests were sacred in Greek eyes. The Greek gods, led by Zeus their king, firmly upheld the age-old tradition of hospitality. Nikandros and Adonia, he thought, were certainly good examples of the custom of the country.

Tanith and Cain, who both spoke Greek, were easily able to make themselves understood to their hosts. They explained that, en route from Phoenicia, their cargo ship had foundered on rocks close to the coast. They had been forced to swim for it as their boat sank. Nikandros, a farmer by trade but well acquainted with the local fishermen, accepted their explanation, commenting only that the travelers were lucky to have escaped the perils of the sea.

Before they scuttled the ship, Tanith had told Cain that her father had rented a small house in Piraeus, the port of Athens, for many years. There was basic furniture there for Ahiram's layovers in Greece, as well as a small stash of coins. Cain agreed they would go there as soon as possible. Athens was only forty-five miles from Sounion, and they could make the journey, even on foot, in two days. But they would need fresh clothes before they started. Cain decided to broach the subject with their host.

"Nikandros," he said, gesturing to the short tunics that he and Tanith were wearing, "we lost all our possessions in the shipwreck. Is it possible for us to purchase fresh clothing in this village? Or in a nearby town?"

"It is not only possible, but necessary! And I will help you. You need to see Philemon, the traveling peddler of this region. As a matter of fact, he should be visiting our village this very day. I will introduce you. But first, you must enjoy our local wine."

After sampling what Cain had to admit was a delicious vintage, mixed with water as was the custom, the men passed the time with a long walk through the vineyards and orchards surrounding the village. Cain could see that farming was far different here than it was in Egypt. The soil was rocky, and most fields were situated in hilly terrain. The principal crops were barley, olives, and grapes. Now, in late September, it was grape-picking season. Later in the fall and over the winter, olives would be harvested. When Nikandros remarked on a vexing manpower shortage in the village, Cain gladly brokered an arrangement whereby the six Phoenician crewmen would find a temporary home there as farm laborers.

As they returned to the village, they could see that a small crowd of people had collected outside Nikandros's dwelling. The reason was soon apparent. At the center of attention was a bulging, battered oxcart so heavily loaded that one or two more items on either side might have toppled it. The peddler Philemon had arrived.

Amidst the cooking utensils, children's toys, looms, wine strainers, brooches, helmets, and robes, Cain and Tanith found what they sought: a long, maroon-colored chiton, or dress, for Tanith, and a cream-colored woolen tunic, together with a cloak, for Cain. But then came the issue of payment.

Declaring that he and Tanith were headed for Piraeus, Cain inquired when Philemon would next visit Athens, hoping that the peddler would agree to sell them the clothes on credit. Philemon replied that he planned to set off for Athens the very next morning, and he invited the couple to travel with him. Far from being a burden, Philemon said, their company would serve as extra insurance against brigands along the way. As for credit, he readily agreed to Cain's request.

The next morning, after availing themselves of Nikandros's hospitality for the night, Cain and Tanith set out with the peddler for Athens. At Philemon's invitation, Tanith scrambled to the apex of the pile of goods on the oxcart and perched there precariously. Cain barely concealed his laughter as he saw her being jostled from side to side, somehow keeping her balance, but just barely.

"Let's hope that the travelers we meet don't draw the conclusion that you too are for sale!" he jested, giving Philemon a playful slap on the back.

She only glowered at them in reply.

෨෨

Candles flickered and guttered as Cain opened the front door of a typical Athenian house. As he stepped inside from the courtyard, a chilly November wind preceded him. But the gust could not compete with the cozy, mouthwatering aroma of the barley bread Tanith was baking at their improvised oven.

"It's almost ready," Cain told her.

Outside on the grill, a merry fire was slowly burnishing a roast leg of goat. Their meals were seldom elaborate, but this evening they had two reasons to celebrate. It was Tanith's thirtieth birthday, and that very morning Cain had landed employment at the fishing docks, thanks to one of Ahiram's contacts in Piraeus.

Cain settled himself in their small dining room. As he watched Tanith, almost in silhouette, go about her practiced movements before the oven, he reflected on life's paradoxes. They had been in Piraeus almost two months now. Ahiram's rented house, though comfortable, was very small—especially for a man like Cain who had lived in his own palace, but also for Tanith, accustomed from childhood to the spacious seaside villa in Tyre. Now they lived in a confined, distinctly dark, three-room cottage made from mud-brick and nestled on a busy and noisy working-class lane. Yet Cain was happier than ever, and Tanith seemed to share his exhilaration in the joint reinvention of their prior selves. Above all, Cain thought, life's challenges demanded resourcefulness. Better than anyone, he knew the imperative to survive. He was glad that Tanith knew it, too.

Yet there were two faint misgivings in his mind. Like a high, wispy cloud tainting the purity of bright sunshine, the fact that he had not been entirely candid intermittently bothered Cain. Why, he wondered, could he not bring himself to tell her about his past, giving her a full account of all he had been—and of all he wanted the two of them to be? Reluctantly, he was forced to confront the link between this reservation and his other worry: that one day, he would lose the woman to whom he had given his heart. Yet the inescapable destiny of his solitary immortality could not deter him from savoring his present happiness.

"What shall we do after our meal?" he asked her as he sliced the meat and she placed the rolls of bread in a large basket on the table.

Tanith's eyes glowed as she ran her fingers through his locks, "Drink wine, my love! Later, what do you think of strolling down to the harbor? I learned today that some war veterans are expected to return. If the ship arrives on time, they will certainly be at the taverna tonight."

"These veterans are from Troy?" Cain asked.

"Yes, they served under Menestheus, the commander of the fifty ships from Athens. They are the first to be furloughed home to Greece. We shall hear some interesting stories, at the very least."

"Good idea," he nodded eagerly. "But before we go, I have a better idea. Let's warm our bed and enjoy our cup of wine."

The taverna was crowded, as usual. The sounds from panpipes, drums, and lyres could barely be heard over the hubbub of voices. Sunburned fishermen and sailors rubbed elbows with merchants from the town and farmers from the outlying countryside. Among the patrons were a fair number of women—whose presence would have been frowned on, or outright forbidden, in the more straitlaced setting of Athens. Cain and Tanith greeted several of her father's friends, accepted their condolences, and then seated themselves at a small table.

After an hour or so, a loud cheer rippled through the crowd, and a group of tall, lightly armed warriors entered the taverna. The men wore body armor but no helmets. Cain thought that, for troops who had been fighting in a siege abroad for ten long years, they looked to be in remarkably good condition. He wondered absently how long it would take the Athenians to find recruits that would be sent to Troy in their place.

Alexiou, the thick-bearded taverna owner, let out a shrill whistle for silence, and the noisy hum of the patrons subsided.

"You all know Sostratos," he declared, gesturing to a soldier in his midthirties who was clearly the leader of the group. "As a boy he was the finest athlete in Piraeus. Menestheus chose him personally to lead our detachment at Troy. Now he has returned in glory! Hear his news!"

Sostratos, who was obviously not accustomed to speaking in public, was edged forcefully by Alexiou to the center of the crowd, which eagerly pressed forward to hear his tidings. Scanning the rows of faces, he hesitantly raised his goblet of wine. Taking a sip to fortify himself, he announced some shocking news:

"Friends of Athens and of Greece, you are the first to know...Troy has fallen! We return home not on furlough but as victors! Troy is ours. The long war is over!"

As Sostratos thrust his cup aloft, it was knocked from his hands by the embrace of delirious onlookers, whose deafening cheers might have been heard in Athens, some six miles away.

Cain and Tanith remained late at the tavern until the full story could be pieced together. Sostratos and his troops recounted the master stratagem of the Trojan horse, the inspired ruse devised by Odysseus, king of the western island of Ithaca. Under the guise of a sacrificial offering to the gods, the wooden horse had concealed in its belly an elite corps of Greek troops. The Trojans, tricked into believing that the Greeks had abandoned the siege, had dragged the monstrous equine image inside the city's gates, thus permitting the Greek saboteurs to exit by night and open the city gates to their comrades' invading force. The vengeful Greek assailants burned the wealthiest city in Asia Minor to the ground, butchering its king and queen along with many of the inhabitants and enslaving thousands of others. Troy was no more.

On the way home through dark lanes, Tanith asked Cain what he thought of the news.

"It is an almost unbelievable story," he replied. "And yet, for that very reason, it will probably be told for decades to come. We can both tell it, my love. You are a far more compelling storyteller than that fellow Sostratos."

"As are you, my handsome pupil. Perhaps we have found a new calling together!" She wove her arm around his waist and brought him close as they strolled slowly through the night.

CHAPTER 31

Athens, circa 1225 BC

n the years that followed, Cain continued to work at the fishing docks, and Tanith was hired by a local merchant to help keep his accounts. Their income was nominal, but it was enough to support their modest lifestyle. They supplemented their wages with Cain's occasional appearances as a bard. His new vocation as a singer of epic tales gave him great satisfaction.

After that first evening in the taverna when he had heard the narrative of Sostratos, Cain added more stories to his repertoire about the Trojan War and the return journeys of the Greek heroes. In this venture, Tanith was a partner behind the scenes. In endless rehearsals, she critiqued Cain's arrangement of the tales and his presentation. He sang the stories in prose, interspersing the narrative with dialogue and using a lyre for musical accompaniment. His audiences were small—seldom over a hundred listeners at any one performance. But they were enthusiastic, and like the patrons of musicians of every time and place, they gladly rewarded a pleasing singer with coins.

With their income on a solid footing, Cain designed a meager savings plan, which he hoped would suffice to buy their rented house from the owner one day. There had been no wedding ceremony, since neither of them had relatives in Greece, but all the townspeople of Piraeus accepted Cain and Tanith as man and wife by common law.

One fresh spring morning five years after the first veterans' return to Greece, the couple found themselves on horseback headed

for Athens. Lilies and iris dotted the roadside, a gentle breeze
caressed the trees, and a brilliant blue sky heralded the return of the
sailing season. Tanith was bent on shopping for a new table for their
dining room, while Cain sought a new seven-stringed lyre, as his old
instrument had become almost impossible to tune.

They broke the six-mile journey almost exactly halfway at a small,
roadside shrine to the goddess Aphrodite. During their years in
Greece, Tanith had retained her devotion to this deity, whose mythology and rituals so closely resembled those of her native Phoenician
goddess Astarte.

As they approached the shrine, Tanith turned to Cain.

"Let us stop here for a prayer," she said. "Will you come inside
with me?"

Cain smiled but shook his head. "You know how I feel about the
Greek gods, my dearest. The Egyptian ones, as well. An unbeliever
like me will contaminate your prayers. You go inside, and I will tend
the horses. When she sees you, Aphrodite will smile. If she sees me,
she will frown."

Tanith dismounted and disappeared inside the small temple,
while Cain led the horses to the shade of a tall olive tree. He knew
the goal of her prayer. Ever since their arrival in Greece, Tanith had
often broached her desire to bear Cain a child—hints that Cain, well
knowing from Ahiram about her barrenness, had gently deflected. But
Tanith seemed determined. She really believed, Cain thought, that
supernatural intervention from Aphrodite could remedy her condition.

"But why not pray for such a thing?" Cain asked himself. While
he was no believer in Aphrodite, he was forced to admit from experience that, for the real God, nothing should be impossible. And so,
sitting under the tree with the horses quietly quenching their thirst
from a small stream, he closed his eyes and muttered a prayer to the
God whom he had seldom addressed over all the centuries.

"May she achieve her wish, Almighty One. May my beloved conceive and bear our child."

As he said these words, Tanith, with her devotions concluded earlier than he expected, was at his side.

"You, too, were praying after all?" she asked softly.

Cain felt embarrassed but was bound to respond.

"Yes, my beloved," he admitted. "But my prayers were to a different God. A deity more powerful than Aphrodite. I asked that your wish would come true."

Tanith smiled with pleasure at the thought that her "unbelieving" husband had offered a prayer. The two mounted their horses and set out again for Athens.

Several months later, in high summer, Tanith complained of feeling nauseous. Initially, both she and Cain were hopeful that their prayers had been answered. However, her condition soon worsened. Tanith began to show an intense aversion to bright light, and when her symptoms grew to include headache and drowsiness, Cain's anxiety increased and he called a healer. The diagnosis was ominous.

"I am not completely certain," said the doctor, a tall, soft-spoken man with salt-and-pepper hair and a hooked nose. "But what exposure has she had to plants and animals recently? Does she spend any time at all outdoors?"

Although she knew that Greek women were seldom to be seen outside the house, Tanith replied candidly in her own behalf. "Yes, I love growing plants in our courtyard. You have seen my flowers. Are they not beautiful?"

The healer nodded his head gravely. "They are worthy of Pan and all his companions of the forest," he said. "But unfortunately, illness sometimes lurks beneath beauty. I fear your flowering plants may have betrayed you, lady."

As Tanith covered her face with her hands, Cain led the healer into the courtyard. Locking eyes with him, Cain demanded, "What betrayal do you mean?"

"She has all the symptoms of brain fever," he replied. "It is triggered by the bite of a tiny insect. Once the tick bearing the infection has passed it to a human being, very little can be done. Just try to keep her as comfortable as you can," he said, putting his hand on Cain's shoulder briefly before walking slowly toward the courtyard gate.

Cain was left alone in the courtyard, and it seemed that the bright flowers surrounding him had lost all their color.

⚬⚬⚬

When he reflected later on his loss, Cain decided that Tanith knew her fate that very afternoon. Despite his pretexts about a minor infection that would heal with time, he realized that it was futile to try to beguile the woman he loved so passionately.

Yet the two of them passed the final weeks of Tanith's life in a strange aura of make-believe. Since to say otherwise would cause them to break down in despair, they both assured each other that she would recover. Cain thought of the prayers, both hers and his, at the shrine of Aphrodite. He remembered with tears the deaths of his family in Egypt. Once again, the ways and purposes of God were a bitter mystery to him.

Tanith's death was quiet. Just before dawn she exhaled her last breath. Leaning down to kiss her lips, Cain raised her hand and placed it on his breast. "I shall never forget you, my darling," he murmured, as hot tears scalded his cheeks.

Funeral rites were prompt. After taking Tanith's body to be cremated in Piraeus, Cain bore the ashes out beyond the entrance to the harbor, accompanied by a flotilla carrying not only his fellow fisher-men but also many of his loyal audience members. Cain scattered Tanith's remains into the sapphire of the Saronic Gulf, while his fellow mourners adorned the waters with thousands of white flower petals. It was fitting, Cain thought, that Tanith would rejoin Ahiram in this way. The sea had been home to both father and daughter, and now it would be just a bit deeper with his tears.

———

CHAPTER 32

Greece, circa 750 BC

"Time heals all wounds."

Cain had heard the Greek proverb numerous times, but it was centuries after Tanith's death until he could bring himself to acknowledge its truth. To assuage his grief, he immersed himself ever more deeply in other times and places. Now oral history and the entertainment of a live audience became his main interest, eclipsing his work at the fishing docks and leading to a string of ever more gratifying successes. Because so many of his listeners in the port of Athens were transients from other parts of the Greek world, word of his artistry spread. Invitations began to stream in for Cain to travel abroad, and he became widely known as the "Athenian bard."

During the period after Tanith's death, all of Greece experienced a significant cultural decline due to the ravages of the plague. Population diminished, trade contracted, and the art of writing was lost. But the people's appetite for entertainment never waned, possibly because storytelling was a welcome distraction from the harsher realities of life. Cain—and his storytelling—were at the center of this desire.

Athens eventually began to grow again, from a small settlement into a vibrant metropolis. As Cain moved around the Mediterranean to conceal his secret, he saw fresh evidence of an upswing in Greek society and culture. Most notably, cities in Greece were founding colonies abroad, especially to the west in Sicily and southern Italy, but

also on the western coast of Asia Minor. The region of Magna Grae-
cia, "Great Greece," was being born.

It was in the context of this burgeoning empire that Cain became
increasingly aware that his longevity, while presenting personal challenges, provided a singular benefit to the wider human world.

He was keeping history alive.

☙❧

In the mid-seventh century BC, Cain journeyed to the island of Chios
at the request of the local inhabitants. By now, his stories of the
Trojan War had become so widely acclaimed that his performance
fees sufficed to sustain him. A stone's throw from the Anatolian
coast of Asia Minor, Chios was close to the ancient site of Troy, and
the island's inhabitants had always maintained a lively interest in the
storied conflict that unfolded four centuries before.

As he often did, Cain performed his tales in a taverna during
the early evening, and then continued, depending on the particular narration, later into the night. The performances in Chios, as
he later recalled, were especially notable in one respect. Each time
Cain began his tales, he was met by the piercing stare of a twelve-
year-old boy, seated in the front row of the audience. Children were
not a rarity at such performances, since fathers often brought
their sons along to enjoy the tales of bygone times. But there was
something exceptional about the intense concentration displayed
by this youngster.

After the conclusion of his fourth and final performance, Cain
strode over to the sandy-haired boy, who was escorted by a tutor, and
asked his name.

"I am called Homer," said the boy.

"You are from this island?" inquired Cain.

"Yes, I am from Chios, but I would see other shores if the gods grant me the chance."

Cain ruffled the boy's long, curly hair. "May your wish be granted," he said gently. "And may you, too, become a singer of tales!"

❧

With the ever-increasing popularity of the Trojan War stories, Cain's travel schedule expanded. It seemed as if the public's appetite for the glory days of Greece and the age of heroes was insatiable.

Some years after the visit to Chios, he was invited to perform in the new Greek settlements in southern Italy and on the island of Sicily. There, he especially enjoyed Croton, a new city on the Italian peninsula already renowned for its excellent physicians, and also Syracuse, a Corinthian colony in southeastern Sicily that boasted a spectacular site and a superb harbor. After three months of strenuous travel and oral performance, he returned to the house in the port of Athens.

Despite his fatigue from the long sea journey, Cain was loath to decline an invitation from Leandros, the owner of a new taverna, who was intensely eager to attract an enthusiastic clientele. Therefore, two nights after his return, Cain arrived at Taverna Yassou with his lyre, assuming that the crowd inside would be eagerly anticipating his appearance.

But the spotlight that evening shone elsewhere. Leandros had hedged his bets.

"Oh, he's just a warm-up act for you!" the pudgy innkeeper squeezed Cain's shoulder in reassurance.

"Who's your other storyteller, then?" Cain asked.

"A man from Chios. His name is Homer. A fresh talent, but he's captured the Aegean. I was lucky to get him here. But, of course, you are the king of storytelling in Athens. Not to worry, my friend!"

However, listening to Homer's presentation, Cain did worry.

The young boy Cain first met thirty years earlier had developed into a charismatic bard. His resonant voice was spellbinding, the music from his instrument hypnotic. And, most remarkable of all, Homer was telling the story entirely in poetry—verse with a six-beat line that conveyed the emotions of the characters and events far more suggestively and vividly than prose narrative could ever hope to achieve. Transported back to the island of Chios in his mind, Cain now visualized himself sitting in the front row with an unwavering gaze, the same way the boy had done in childhood.

After an interval, Cain rendered his own performance. He was gratified to see Homer sitting in the front row. They were competitors, to be sure, but also colleagues, at least in Cain's mind. Yet he worried that Homer would think it strange that he showed no signs of aging. Perhaps, after this long interval, the rival singer's memories would be somewhat blurred. Nevertheless, Cain took the precaution of wearing a cloak and a broad-brimmed hat, ostensibly for warmth on this cool evening. At the conclusion of Cain's performance, Homer waved the Athenian bard to his table.

"A splendid performance!" Homer exclaimed. As Cain acknowledged the accolade in a muted tone, he noticed that Homer's clouded eyes were staring a bit off to the left. It was only then that he realized that the visiting bard, whose beard was streaked with traces of gray, had become blind.

"So, you *have* become a singer of tales! I well remember the curly-headed boy on Chios." Cain now relaxed as they sat down together.

"You were an inspiration to me then," Homer responded. "I still remember your recital with gratitude. But I knew that something else was missing. I wanted the verse and the meter, as well as the words and the music, to be part of the story, part of the performance. Other epic singers came to Chios. They had the six-beat line, and I became their apprentice."

"Where did that verse line come from?" asked Cain.

"No one knows for sure, but many of the singers I met said they thought it had come down from the time of the war itself."

"How are you able to sing the same song in exactly the same way at each performance?" asked Cain.

"I can't claim that every performance is identical to every other. But the verse line helps me to fix my thoughts in place. There are certain rhythmical groups of words that recur time and again. Once I know their positions in the line, I am able to handle the components of each verse more easily. I am able to tell the events of each story episode in the proper order. Every performance is one part memory, one part improvisation."

It had never occurred to Cain, given his own powers of recollection, that poetry could aid in the process of memorization. His affinity for Homer grew.

"But what if you could make your best performances permanent? What if you could set them down for future generations?"

Homer shrugged sadly. "The Mycenaeans of whom we sing possessed writing," he said. "We have lost the art."

"No, my friend. The art is there to be reinvented. Let me show you. Come outside to the courtyard."

Away from the crowd, Cain scratched Phoenician letters in the clay soil of the taverna's courtyard. Then he took Homer's hand and lightly rubbed his fingers over the indentations.

"It would not take much to adapt these Phoenician letters to Greek," Cain told him. "The most important changes you would need are new symbols for vowel sounds." He sketched two examples, *epsilon* for short *e* and *iota* for *i*. "If your songs are recorded for posterity this way, Homer, they will be nothing short of immortal."

The singer of tales replied slowly, quizzically.

"But then, if audiences can read these tales, performance will languish and die, will it not? Bards like us will not be necessary."

Cain sighed. "Even with progress," he said, "there is always a price to pay."

☙❦❧

During Homer's three-month visit to Athens, the two men talked every day, sometimes for hours. Homer's approach to the epic story of Troy fascinated Cain.

"I did not set out to recount the whole war," Homer explained. "How could a singer include everything that happened in ten years' time? And I am not a cheerleader for the Greeks. The backbone of my *Iliad* is the quarrel between two leaders with different values."

"And that's why you started out with the verses about the 'wrath of Achilles'?" Cain asked. They had spent much of their time together refining the new alphabetic system of writing. Now, absentmindedly, Cain traced the alphabetic letters for the first line of Homer's epic poem in the sand.

> Menin aeide thea Peleiadeo Achilleos
> Sing, Muse, of the wrath of Achilles, son of Peleus...

"Exactly. I also wanted to use the war as a backdrop for what every man, Greek or Trojan, must come to terms with—his own mortality."

Cain betrayed no emotion, although inwardly he registered the irony of his own position. "Your poem is not really a history, then, but something else?" he hazarded.

"Yes, my friend. But I would not know precisely what to call it. I don't think the word has yet been invented." Somehow his statement conveyed modesty, not arrogance.

"What about the homeward journeys of the Greek heroes after the fall of Troy? Have you sung tales about those voyages?" Cain inquired.

"I once heard a story about the wanderings of Odysseus, but it was so full of gaps I could not piece it together. It would not make a song in my mind."

"I also have heard of Odysseus's journeys," replied Cain. "And I too have been a wanderer. Let us compare what we know."

Cain called for a flagon of wine and two cups. And so it was that, on a sunny afternoon by the sea, Homer's *Odyssey* was born.

CHAPTER 33

Rome, Near the Vatican: Present Day

"Yes, Notombo?" Cardinal Ravatti responded to the blinking intercom light on his desk. Late on a Sunday morning, the office of the Vatican's Pontifical Commission for Sacred Archaeology was as hushed as the catacombs that lay within its jurisdiction.

"I've just spoken to the airport, Eminenza," his assistant reported. "There's a backlog on helicopter flights departing from Fiumicino, but I have secured the necessary approvals to depart instead from the Vatican heliport. We can leave in half an hour."

"This monsignor will go places," thought Ravatti, as a chopper with the yellow-and-white papal insignia hovered appealingly in his mind's eye. But all he said was, "Good work, Monsignor. Let's pass the time with a cappuccino in my office. I have already called the kitchen."

"Thank you. I'll be in as soon as I finalize our clearance into Ercolano. Apparently there has been some activity from Vesuvius that is disrupting the local airspace."

Before Notombo's arrival, Ravatti withdrew several photographs from the top drawer of his ornate sixteenth-century marble desk. Spreading the pictures out on the gleaming surface, he placed beside them a color printout of the image e-mailed from Silvio Sforza a few minutes beforehand.

"*Ebbene, se non è vero, è certamente ben trovato*," Ravatti murmured to himself. "So, even if it's not true, it surely hangs together."

When Notombo entered, followed by a white-jacketed waiter with a tray bearing the coffees and assorted biscotti, Ravatti motioned the monsignor to one of the chairs on the other side of the desk. As he waited for the servant to withdraw, he savored the rich aroma of the frothy beverages.

After the door clicked shut, the cardinal leaned forward and spoke with the affection of an uncle. "Gabriel, before we fly to Ercolano I want to share some background. One day, you may well be sitting in this chair, my friend. But for now, this is strictly confidential, you understand?"

Notombo, taken aback, sat up very straight. Ravatti had addressed him by his first name. He had also speculated favorably on his future. It was rare in the notoriously secretive Vatican for a cardinal to be so willing to share a confidence.

"*Assolutamente*, Eminenza," he reassured his mentor.

Ravatti pointed to the first photograph on the desk. "Do you know what this is?"

The monsignor looked at the picture momentarily, his eyes widening.

"I gather they did not cover this when you were at Harvard. It is an anti-kythera mechanism, Gabriel. I hasten to add that, aside from its name, no one knows its purpose, including me. But I have a special connection with this intriguing gadget. Over forty years ago, when I was fresh out of seminary, my superiors sent me to a dig in Libya for further on-site training. It was there that I first met Silvio Sforza. We were fledgling archaeologists, flush with all the enthusiasm we needed to conquer the world."

"Were you digging at Leptis Magna?" inquired Notombo. The site, eighty miles east of the modern-day Libyan capital at Tripoli, was one of the most renowned in the ancient Roman world.

"Correct, my friend. Silvio and I discovered the device almost completely intact. It lay in the hold of a buried ship in an ancient dry dock, a few hundred meters inland from the Mediterranean. Possibly a powerful desert sandstorm covered it so that it was lost to time."

"How old is the device?"

"Coins found in the wreck indicated a date of about 250 BC. There is only one other surviving antikythera mechanism, discovered more than a century ago by sponge divers near the island of Antikythera. It is now in the National Archaeological Museum in Athens."

"It looks remarkably intricate," observed Notombo, as he peered at the dozens of miniaturized interlocking gears.

"It has been described as the world's first mechanical computer. But despite the minute lettering in Greek and Phoenician, which may be some sort of instruction manual, nobody really knows what it was used for. It could have been a navigation device, or possibly a calendar. It might have been an instrument for astronomical observations."

Extracting a powerful magnifying glass from his desk, Ravatti handed it to Notombo. "Now, look carefully at the narrow rectangle in the lower right-hand corner. What do you see?"

"It looks to be some sort of mark. It's quite different from the alphabetic lettering elsewhere."

"Correct again. When Silvio and I found the device, we noticed the difference immediately. We speculated that the mark was some sort of signature—perhaps a personal symbol used by the maker. Similar, possibly, to the individualized crests you find today on signet rings or coats of arms. As you know, signing artifacts of many kinds was a common practice in the ancient world."

"What happened to the device? Where is it now, Eminenza?"

Ravatti sighed. "Before Silvio and I could study it further, our superiors ordered it boxed up and sent to Rome. Here, too, it was lost to time for many years, due to a cataloging error in the Vatican Museums."

"A cataloging error?" Notombo raised an eyebrow.

"Well, that is the *official* explanation. In any case, it only surfaced less than a year ago. Of course, I contacted Silvio immediately. He suggested that we send it to the Getty Museum in California for further analysis, since they are experts in such matters and possess all the latest technology."

"Isn't it a bit unusual for the Vatican to deploy outside assistance in a matter such as this?" Notombo asked.

"Typically, yes. But because I head the Pontifical Commission, a loan to the Getty was not difficult to arrange. They are studying the piece now," Ravatti told him. "But that's not the end of the story."

They sipped their cappuccinos appreciatively. Then the cardinal resumed.

"For many years, I had only my memory of the artist's mark to rely on. We had no digital cameras in those days. But the mark, if that's what it was, had made a very powerful impression. So you can imagine my amazement when I saw this."

Ravatti gestured to the second photograph, which Notombo dutifully inspected.

"More than twenty years after I worked at Leptis Magna, this stunning map came into the Vatican collections. The material is exquisite: silk paper. The chart is of ancient Xi'an, the capital of the First Emperor of China. From what we can tell, it is astonishingly accurate. From the silk paper and the inks, it is estimated that the map was fashioned just a few decades before the birth of Christ."

"Where did it come to light?" Notombo asked eagerly.

"You'd never guess. It was found in the late 1980s, slightly singed, inside a metal tube recovered from the basement of a first-century AD estate right here on the Palatine Hill. The cellar was apparently situated above the entrance to a catacomb. That's how our Pontifical Commission got involved. From a stone with the name carved on it, archaeologists have established that the place belonged to a nobleman named Marcus Flavius Pictor."

Notombo's expression betrayed his astonishment.

"Yes, I know. It does seem supremely unlikely to encounter such a possession in Rome," the cardinal told him. "Yet we are certain there were trade contacts between ancient Rome and China, even in those days. Now, please use the magnifying glass to examine the lower right-hand corner of the picture."

"The identical artist's mark!" exclaimed the monsignor.

"When I first saw it, I was confounded. So baffled, in fact, that I confided in a senior colleague, Cardinal Luigi Bertoli. You wouldn't remember him. He died in 1990. He was archpriest of Santa Maria Maggiore, the basilica right around the corner from here. I was not yet a cardinal, and he was one of my kindest mentors. After I summarized the story and showed him some photographs, he invited me to lunch. We went to a small trattoria in the Piazza del Popolo.

"'I have something to show you, Sandro, before we sit down,' Luigi told me.

"We strolled from the restaurant across to the center of the piazza. When we were in the shadow of the obelisk, he pointed to its northern face.

"'Now, look very carefully at the lower right corner. Describe to me what you see there.'

"I could not believe my eyes." Ravatti slid the third photograph, a telephoto snapshot of the base of the obelisk's northern face, over toward Notombo, who scrutinized it carefully.

Notombo let out a low whistle. "You have ruled out a *graffito*, Eminenza?"

"According to the Egyptology experts, the mark probably predates the original inscriptions. They believe it was chiseled right after the stone was quarried. You know the history of the obelisk, of course? It was originally erected by Ramesses II around 1200 BC. Then it was brought to Rome by Augustus in 10 BC and was placed in the Circus Maximus. It's been in Piazza del Popolo since 1589."

Notombo considered for a few moments before commenting, "With the tremendous disparities in time and place among these artifacts, I can understand your astonishment over this mark."

"Indeed, my friend. This mystery that began over four decades ago, and still remains to be solved, has become a personal quest for me. The artifacts all bear the same mark, yet they cannot possibly be the work of a single artist. My working hypothesis is that they are the products of a society of skilled artisans and engineers, a secret guild that is still unbeknownst to modern archaeology and that must have endured for centuries."

"I know of no historical precedent for such a group, Eminenza."

"Nor do I. Certainly not in the particular time period in question. For lack of a better name, I have dubbed this artisan 'society' the Incogniti. It's scarcely an original name," Ravatti chuckled. "There was a group of intellectuals called *Accademia degli Incogniti*, the Academy of the Unknowns, in Venice in the mid-1600s. But if my Incogniti are shown to be historical, the discovery will be a major revelation. Think of multiple incarnations of Leonardo da Vinci, extending over more than a millennium!"

"And what is the relevance of this last item?" asked Notombo, as he picked up the color photograph from Silvio Sforza's e-mail.

"This digital photograph came in this morning from Silvio," clarified Ravatti. "It is a picture of the large bronze doors leading to the central chamber at the new dig in Ercolano. I think you know where to look, Gabriel."

There, in the lower right-hand corner of the photograph, Notombo recognized the same artist's mark. Even though he had expected its presence, it still caused him to shiver slightly.

"What Silvio has discovered could hold the key to the entire mystery. I surmise that behind these doors may lurk many more artifacts of the Incogniti. And that, my friend, is why we are flying this morning to Ercolano," declared the cardinal as he rose and looked at his watch.

"Let's get underway. It's only a fifteen-minute drive to the Vatican on a Sunday. Come, we'll stop on the way at the Piazza del Popolo so you can see the mark on the obelisk for yourself!"

CHAPTER 34

Greece, 520 BC

"You are aware, sir, that the games started with a single footrace?" the man walking alongside Cain asked him. While strolling through the sanctuary of Zeus on his way to the opening ceremonies of the Olympic Games, Cain chatted idly with a spectator.

"You don't say!" Cain affected astonishment. Of course he knew about the footrace.

"Hard to believe, isn't it?" the man rattled on. "A footrace of two hundred yards. Exactly two centuries ago. Hercules won that race. He was accustomed to victory. Then he ordered that games be held every four years. No one dared to disobey him."

"I expect not," Cain replied. "But I thought there was a different story about how the games began. Something about Zeus and his father Cronus wrestling for control of the world?"

"You can believe that one if you want to, sir," the man sniffed haughtily. "The story about Hercules is historical *fact*."

Cain chuckled to himself at the man's comment. For many centuries he had felt a satisfying sense of purpose in recording and sharing human history and tales from the past. In addition, the blurring of mythology with reality so common to the era had earned him a comfortable living. Yet, soon after collaborating with the master poet Homer, he began to experience a decline in his passion for, and eventually outright boredom with, the vocation he and Tanith had jointly discovered.

With the onward march of technology and the development of city-states, life as a wandering bard had now become obsolete, he thought. Largely due to Cain, the Homeric epics had been committed to writing. Although most Greeks still regarded Homer as their encyclopedia, new forms of literary expression were emerging. These ranged from lyric poetry to philosophy and natural history.

Simply put, there were so many entertainment options on the menu that few people ordered what Cain was serving any more. Yet, even as the literary scene exploded in Greece, interest in athletics had never been stronger. Greeks could now travel to sporting events of the finest quality every summer. There was a vigorous energy in all this, and Cain realized that the adulation of a stadium crowd of thousands was of a higher order of magnitude than late-night listeners' praise of a storyteller in a small taverna. And so he had committed himself to finding a new vocation, a search that had brought him to Olympia.

His first efforts to qualify for the games had begun six years ago. He focused on the footraces, especially the two-*stade* race wherein competitors ran the double length of the stadium, approximately four hundred meters. After a grueling eighteen months in solo training, he had succeeded in qualifying for the Olympics of 524 BC as a representative of Athens. But he underestimated the competition and lost to a competitor from Croton, a colony the Greeks had established recently in southern Italy. The evening of his loss, his mind circled back to a footrace improvised long ago.

"Anyone can run a single length of the field, Abel. You need a bigger challenge. Try racing for two lengths, then three. Let's start today. I know you can do it. I'll be your trainer."

"Would you teach me racing, Cain?" Abel asked. "You are so swift-footed... I don't know if I could ever compete with you."

"You can if you have the desire, brother. We will turn your superior strength and size to your advantage. You will make me proud."

This second return to Olympia for the games of 520 BC marked a turning point in Cain's aspirations. Although he narrowly won his event this time, his victory was overshadowed by the exploits of a man whose name was now on everyone's lips: Milo of Croton. At the age of eighteen, long before Cain's first Olympic competition, this youth had emerged as the victor in the boys' wrestling. Most seasoned spectators agreed that he had not only won, but also displayed the confidence and technique of a prodigy. Milo, it was said, would mature into the greatest wrestler in Olympic history.

This prediction had turned out to be accurate. Over the next twenty years in the men's wrestling, Milo triumphed five times. Tracking his career, Cain had to admit that he had fallen into the category of a fan as Milo captured larger-than-life celebrity status.

And so, at these Olympics of 520, when Milo was in his late thirties, a fascinated Cain finally sought out the legend. For a sports celebrity, he found the great champion to be surprisingly accessible. The two men chatted at the final champions' banquet, with Milo cheerfully volunteering news from Croton and Cain countering with the talk of Athens, where citizens were experimenting with a novel form of government called democracy.

"So when will you visit Croton?" the wrestler asked Cain. "It would be a pleasure to have you stay with me and my family. You have heard of Pythagoras?"

"The man from Samos, the founder of the *mathematikoi*?" Cain asked. After his self-imposed exile from his native island, word of the storied philosopher's secret society in southern Italy had spread throughout the Mediterranean world.

"Indeed," Milo replied. "I am married to his daughter Myia. A strange alliance, is it not? A wrestler and a mathematician. Yet in a curious way we do the same thing. The opponents with whom

GRE

Croton

IONIAN
SEA

N
W   E
S

ECE

GREECE

AEGEAN SEA

Olympia

Salamis

Athens

Cape
Sounion

Pythagoras struggles are formidable, but since they are numbers, they are also invisible."

Cain was mildly intrigued, but the chance to meet yet another luminary was hardly his motivation for accepting Milo's invitation.

"I will come to Croton soon. You have my word."

CHAPTER 35

South Italy and Greece, 520–516 BC

hortly into his stay with Milo, Cain decided to make Croton his home. The colony was burgeoning, and the Mediterranean climate, long favored by Cain, was even better on the Gulf of Taranto than it was in Greece. Milo was as good as his word, welcoming his Athenian guest, introducing him to friends and family, and eventually locating a small homestead near the harbor where Cain could live.

"I know my wrestling days are numbered," Milo confided to Cain one day. "This body is reluctant to yield up its secrets, but wrestling remains a young man's game."

"You will always be the ultimate champion," Cain replied, sensing the opportunity he had hoped for. "But if you can no longer compete, why not become a trainer? Who has more valuable insights and skills than you? It would be a way to remain involved in the sport that you love more than anything in the world."

The taller man looked distantly above Cain's head. "And whom would I teach? I can scarcely imagine anyone worthy."

"You are looking at your first pupil," Cain replied with a smile.

Milo looked at Cain incredulously. "Oh, is that so? Take off your cloak so that I may see if you are a fit enough young Athenian to serve under my tutelage."

Cain untied the knot under his chin and threw his tunic to the ground, revealing a perfectly proportioned body sculpted of solid muscle. His torso and back resembled chiseled stone, and his sectioned abdomen quivered with every breath he took while awaiting Milo's verdict.

"I have tried to keep myself in shape over the years," quipped Cain.

Milo's eyebrows arched upward in complete surprise as he appraised the physique of his younger apprentice.

"In the name of Zeus! For a runner, you have more brawn than any Spartan soldier I have ever seen! You indeed have the physical frame of a potential champion. Now we will see if you also have the heart to compete."

So the two of them embarked on a brutal regimen. Day after day, week after week, they haunted the palaestra in Croton. Anointing their bodies with oil and then sprinkling them with dust, they began each day with stretches, weight lifting, and rope climbing before progressing to an exhausting roster of wrestling moves that persisted well into each evening. Milo was a stern taskmaster, but Cain was more than up to the challenge.

☙❦❧

After Cain performed outstandingly at a tryout in Delphi at the Pythian Games of 518 BC, Milo pronounced him ready for training at the Olympic level. The two redoubled their efforts, right up to the day before the Olympic Games of 516 BC. Even for Cain, the pace was grueling.

Milo was especially aggressive in their last practice match before the games began. Catching Cain by surprise, Milo lifted his young apprentice over his head and brutally slammed him to the ground, landing on top of him. The sound of ribs snapping was unmistakable. Cain could hardly breathe, the pain was so intense. He waved off Milo's hand, outstretched to pull him to his feet.

"What was *that*?" Cain snapped. "You could have killed me with that illegal throw." He tried to speak softly to mitigate the sharp stabs racking his wounded torso.

"Sorry. I don't know what came over me," his trainer replied, but in a tone Cain did not like.

And then Milo dropped a bombshell. "And by the way, I will be competing one last time tomorrow—a farewell appearance for my legions of fans!"

"What? Are you sure? Perhaps it's time to get out while you're still undefeated," Cain sputtered, now realizing the depths of his master's competitive nature.

"Nonsense!" Milo thundered. "You are wise to be afraid of me, student. Just so you know, I had made up my mind to retire, but Croton won't hear of it. They are so used to boasting of champions that I would feel like a traitor if I refused. Why, even King Darius of Persia has sent a message urging me to compete. When the greatest king in the world bids you perform an action, it's dangerous to deny him."

Cain sat stunned. Milo was indeed a calculating man, and not just at mathematics.

Milo added, "I have wrestled with far worse injuries. Now we shall truly see if you have the makings of a champion, or are simply a goat."

Callously walking away from his breathless student, Milo glanced back. "In case you do wrestle tomorrow, don't think for a minute I've taught you everything I know. No master wants to be bested by a *former* pupil."

Recognizing psychological warfare when he heard it, Cain remained silent and sat stone-faced. Thoughts of revenge swirled in his mind.

That evening, his dreams brought a disturbing vision from a time long past.

❦

"Come with me to the wheat field, my brother. I have something to show you."

They walked slowly to the field, then entered a row of wheat together, until they reached a large, circular clearing of crushed stalks.

"How could you bring yourself to add insult to injury?" Cain demanded angrily of Abel. "You saw God reject my gift at the sacrifice, but he accepted yours. You showed me up at the altar, and now you've trampled my crops to spite me!"

"You charge me wrongly, brother," Abel replied with quiet urgency. "I haven't even been here. I'm a shepherd. You are the cultivator of the ground."

"Liar! Who else would have dared?"

"I do not lie to you," insisted Abel as he turned aside to leave. But his brother blocked his path. The younger, stronger man grasped Cain's shoulder to push him out of the way. All of a sudden, their arms were locked around each other. Stumbling over a rock in the wheat field, Abel fell to the ground with Cain on top of him. Wrestling in angry earnest, the two men rolled on thorns that neither one of them had seen underneath the stalks. Both men screamed in pain. Abel rolled on top and pinned his brother's shoulders to the ground.

"Let me up," yelled Cain. But Abel's wrenching hold tightened. Maddened by the accusation leveled so unjustly by the brother he had always looked up to, and enraged by the agonizing sting of the thorns, Abel pressed even harder. Cain felt a blinding wave of pain from the thorns beneath him, digging into his flesh. He tried to reach the rock a few feet away. Perhaps he could use it to free himself. But it lay just beyond his grasp.

Sensing he had gotten the better of his brother, Abel finally relented and brought himself to his feet. "Now get up!" he said breathlessly. "This has gone too far." Abel turned away and began to leave the field. "Let us forget the wheat..."

Grabbing the rock, Cain rose up and slew his brother Abel.

CHAPTER 36

Greece, 516 BC

With a bandage wrapped around his chest, Cain approached his match with Milo using a simple tactic. The Greeks called it *akrocheirismos*, or "high-handed" wrestling. Keeping Milo at arm's length was the way to defeat him, Cain realized. He would gradually wear the more experienced champion down, taking care to elude his bone-crushing embrace. Milo was six inches taller than Cain and outweighed him by thirty pounds. But Cain had superior reflexes and greater reserves of stamina.

In the ring, Milo laughed at his wounded opponent, who circled about him to avoid his lethal bear hug. He would need just one mistake from his former student and the sixth and final laurel wreath of his career would be secured.

The bout went on for the better part of an hour, with deafening roars from the crowd whenever each wrestler took a fall. Cain's incessant circling gradually began to frustrate Milo and forced him to spend his energy lunging, with Cain merely darting away at the last second.

"Afraid to come too close, are you?" Milo taunted, sweat pouring off his back in the sweltering Mediterranean heat.

"Don't waste your breath, graybeard!" Cain shot back. "You're going to need it!"

Milo had made it a point to jab repeatedly at Cain's ribs, and each time he connected, Cain reinforced his opponent's confidence with a suitable grunt and an agonized grimace. Gradually, the crowd's sympathies began to shift to the underdog, and a rising chorus of boos swelled each time Milo made contact.

With his opponent virtually gasping from the protracted exertion, Cain finally saw his opportunity. Cain's hand shot out for his opponent's leg behind the kneecap. Astonished, his face contorted, Milo was slammed to the ground. Cain pounced on top of him and rammed his knee into Milo's groin. Quickly applying a crushing chokehold to the agonized champion's throat, Cain now had only to wait for the inevitable. Summoning what little strength remained, Milo bucked and thrashed for almost two minutes before reaching the edge of consciousness. Finally, with a slap of his palm on the sand, he signaled his surrender.

Cain jumped to his feet. The obviously stunned referee first hesitated, then grabbed the victor's hand and raised it high for all the crowd to see.

"Take this back with you to Croton while I wear the crown of a champion!" snarled Cain, tearing off his fake bandage and dropping it on Milo's face.

The dethroned Olympic champion lay writhing in the sand as the crowd went crazy with adoration for its new hero. For over an hour, they applauded the impressive skill and craft that had defeated a living legend. Cain was jubilant. Nothing quite like this had ever happened to him.

It was as though all of Olympia thronged the victor as they paraded him around the gymnasium-palaestra complex on their shoulders. From his higher vantage point, Cain smiled as he watched a defeated Milo limp off into the night, never to see him again. He then turned his attention to enjoying the love of all Greece.

The adulation was exactly what he had been seeking—and it had been worth every effort.

❧

Late that night, after the celebratory banquet, Cain settled into bed. He had given no more thought to the vision from the past that had so troubled his sleep the night before. As with all ghastly memories, he would have to balance it against more soothing distractions, both present and future. Instead, he lay awake, savoring in his mind the scenes from his incredible victory. A column of moonlight angled through the window, bathing his bed in a comforting, soft glow.

Almost imperceptibly, Cain's focus drifted from the images in the gymnasium to the surroundings of his small quarters. His finely tuned senses detected an unseen presence in the room, and the hair on his forearms stiffened. He bolted upright.

"Show yourself!" demanded Cain, while squinting to see who was lurking in the shadows beyond the foot of his bed. Was this some crazed fan stalking him in the night?

"I see you have taken up a most popular sport, Cain. Your wrestling days are not over after all!" scoffed the master of spirits.

"Why do you taunt me, spirit?" Cain sighed heavily as he slumped back against his pillow.

Ignoring his question, the master of spirits continued. *"And I see that, long ago, you prayed to God for a child. But he did not give you a child, did he? Instead, he took Tanith away from you. What kind of God is that, Cain? Can you not see how he hates you? Can you not acknowledge that his dearest wish is for you to suffer in solitude?"*

"Leave me spirit, or I will..."

"Wrestle me? That would be foolish. I am more resourceful than your former trainer." The spirit chuckled. *"But after your transitory taste of victory today, you will do well to consider: if you would like to see dear Tanith again, recognize your God for who he truly is, your sworn enemy. And do not remain so aloof with me."*

As the voice faded, Cain tried to drift off into sleep. But he remained wakeful, tortured by the spirit's taunts and by pangs of grief for his beloved Tanith.

CHAPTER 37

Greece, 483—480 BC

A haggard Cain returned to Athens some thirty-three years later, having spent the intervening decades wandering the remote Greek Isles in misery and anonymity. His wrestling career had ended almost as soon as it began, for each time he pinned an opponent he guaranteed himself a night of torturous memories of Abel.

Unable to stand the slow pace of life any longer, Cain was now returning to an urban environment, despite a new danger—he had learned that Athens and Sparta were the only cities left to defy the Great King of Persia, Xerxes, who seemed determined to conquer all of Greece in his expanding empire, now the largest on Earth.

Upon arriving at the docks, Cain immediately sought employment in the local shipyard, a job considered vital to the security of Athens, to protect himself from being drafted into either the army or the navy. He had no desire to be at the front line of any brewing battle and put his immortality to that sort of test.

A few months passed. While waiting for a sudden winter rainstorm to abate before completing a boat's keel, Cain tinkered on one of his inventions at his workbench in the back of the shipyard.

"You there, what is that strange device you hold in your hands?"

Surprised he had not heard the richly dressed, middle-aged man sneak up on him, Cain turned around and thus met Themistocles, Athens's leading politician, for the first time.

Neither man knew how much he would come to depend on the other.

"Sir, it's a finely geared timing device. I have been working on it with local metalsmiths. My hope is one day it may help ships navigate across the open sea," he offered.

"Hmm. Interesting how a simple shipwright spends his lunch hour. What is your name, sailor?"

"Agathon," replied Cain.

"Walk with me while I evaluate this yard's capability to produce warships. So far all I see are lazy Greeks content to build small fishing boats while Greece is slowly surrounded by our enemies. At least someone is thinking of ways to improve the military strength of Athens," he said in an exasperated tone.

❧

Over the course of the next few months, Cain discovered that Themistocles was unlike any politician he had ever known. He lived in a large, renovated house in the poorest section of town. He never forgot anyone's name. But underneath that guise, Cain learned, was a cunning general highly skilled in the ways of war from his younger days in the army.

One evening, to his surprise, Cain received an invitation from Themistocles to eat supper at his house with his family. Cain thought this was odd, as they had known each other only a short time and had talked only briefly. But unbeknownst to Cain, Themistocles recognized a bright and talented man when he saw one, regardless of his station in life.

"Every man, woman, and child in Greece will be put to the sword if these barbarians have their way. It will be a holocaust!" sputtered Themistocles. "It has now been a full seven years since the Battle of Marathon, and most Athenians have become far too complacent. They're not expecting another invasion." The politician's tone about his fellow citizens was acerbic.

The two men were sitting in the spacious dining room of Themistocles's house in Athens. As was the custom, Themistocles's wife had retired after dinner to the family's private quarters.

"You really think the Persians will organize another attack?"

"I have not the slightest doubt of it. Ever since he succeeded his father Darius on the throne three years ago, King Xerxes has considered punishment of the Greeks as his sacred duty. He gloats on our slaughter, Agathon. It is only a matter of time. My spies in Babylon tell me the Persians intend once more to bridge the narrow straits of the Hellespont and invade Greece."

"That will not be an easy task," said Cain.

"No, indeed," chuckled Themistocles dryly. "Their first attempt was washed out in a storm. Furious at nature's disobedience, Xerxes had the waters of the strait flogged. Can you imagine? The man is mad—but he is very dangerous."

Cain tried to imagine the scene as Themistocles continued, "It is not only time that runs short; it is money as well. You remember that I was one of the ten Athenian generals at Marathon? With all due respect to the courage and sacrifice of our troops, I will tell you, in confidence, that our victory there was an almost incredible stroke of luck. It will be very difficult, perhaps impossible, to beat the Persians on land a second time. They outnumber us several times over. We need warships, hundreds of them. Our best chance to repel another invasion is on the sea, before their overwhelming forces ever reach our shores."

"But how will you pay for such a fleet?" Cain asked.

"Exactly. And even if we had the money, I am not sure I could sway the legislative assembly to use it on building a fleet of huge warships.

My political rivals, especially Aristides, would vote to give the people handouts before they would spend any extra money on the navy."

"Well, your first step is to lay your hands on the funds," Cain pointed out. "Then you can deal with Aristides. Have you thoroughly explored the silver deposits at Laurium?"

Themistocles leaned forward. "You mean the mines near Cape Sounion?" he asked. "My own family has estates there."

Cain nodded, with a haunting recollection of his swim to shore with Tanith. He also remembered, from the time he wandered the earth, seeing chunks of high-grade silver ore washed into a canyon from an unexplored river valley. "In my travels years ago, I recall noticing that the production of silver there was rather lean. My advice is that you send a team of miners and engineers to look for fresh new veins of silver in the next valley to the south. You may find yourself with the money you need in a matter of months."

Themistocles, well known in Athens for his mercurial temperament, growled angrily. "What idiots we have in this city! No one has thought to explore Laurium further—including me! Such are the wages of complacency, and I am as guilty as the next man." He slapped his forehead in frustration.

Then Athens's foremost politician brightened, clapping Cain on the shoulder.

"If your prophecy comes true, my friend, Greece shall finally have its freedom from foreign domination!"

Cain smiled and bid his host good night.

⊙≈⊙

"I have an idea, Cleon," said Cain to the dapper young entrepreneur who employed him at the shipyard near Cain's old haunts in the harbor of Athens.

"You're good for one every day," Cleon complimented him. "But not all of them are necessarily practical, Agathon. Spell it out for me."

Their voices were nearly drowned by the grating handsaws that sliced through lengths of pine all over the yard, scattering clouds of sawdust that fluttered in the mild, harborside breeze. Nine months after Cain had alerted Themistocles to the potential of Laurium, revenues from silver were pouring into naval construction. Themistocles, ever persuasive, had used Athens's ongoing conflict with her nearby rival, the city-state of Aegina, as a pretext to sway the assembly. He had said nothing about the Persian threat, on the assumption that local rivalries would galvanize his compatriots far more than remote threats from abroad.

"I want us to build a special flagship for the fleet," Cain urged his boss. "I am sure we can get Themistocles to fund it."

"And how will this warship be different?"

"For one thing, it will have a crew of two hundred ten—seventy rowers on each deck—meaning an increase of forty oarsmen. So it will be slightly larger than the standard warship, without compromising speed or maneuverability. It will also have a triple rudder. There will still be a single pilot, but he will control three steering devices, rather than two, for more precise course changes that can be executed more quickly."

Cleon cleared his throat speculatively and stroked his beard.

"But the ship's most important innovation will be its weaponry," Cain continued. "It will have far more than the usual bronze-coated ramming spike at the bow. I have developed some new designs."

He held out several scrolls for Cleon's inspection. The shipbuilder was well acquainted with Cain's inventive streak. For some months now, he had briefed Cleon on his innovative designs for weapons that could be fitted to large ships.

"What's this?" Cleon pointed to the first drawing.

"A catapult to launch flaming balls of tar," Cain replied. "But now look at this," he gestured to a second, far more elaborate sketch.

"It looks like a threshing machine," said Cleon.

"That is not far from the truth," Cain smiled. "I call it a war reaper. Attached to a ship, it can be operated by soldiers on deck to repel enemy troops trying to board, or to reach beyond an enemy ship's rail in order to attack all the oarsmen on the middle and upper decks."

Cleon stared at the drawing, a design for death if he ever saw one. "And what name would you suggest for this vessel?"

Cain hesitated. "I haven't given that much thought. But how about *Phobos*?"

"Every warship in the fleet bears a feminine name. You know that, Agathon. *Phobos*, the word for 'fear,' is masculine."

Cain shrugged. "But this ship *will* be feared."

Cleon paused and considered the potential selling price of such an awesome battleship. "You find the money, and we'll build her!"

☙❦❧

By the late summer of 480 BC, the shipyards of Athens had turned out a hundred new warships, enlarging the total Greek fleet to nearly four hundred. Crews from Athens alone totaling more than seventeen thousand men had been assembled, ranging in a broad spectrum from aristocratic landowners to middle-class artisans to poor peasants. The Athenians' ardent belief in democratic government was mirrored in the diversity of their naval recruits.

At the very end of summer, in mid-September, Themistocles and Cain dined again. By now, they conferred with each other almost as equals.

"It is Salamis," Themistocles declared confidently. "The narrow straits between the island and the mainland must be the venue of battle. Our more maneuverable warships will have a critical advantage there. If we lure the whole Persian fleet into combat in that confined space, our ships will outmaneuver them decisively. Our smaller numbers will actually benefit us!"

Once he made up his mind, there was no arguing with Themistocles. Cain could see the logic of the Athenian leader's rationale. Themistocles had pondered naval strategy day and night for years now.

"But first we must lure Xerxes's fleet into the straits?" Cain asked.

"Correct. If we can achieve that, I know in my bones that victory will be ours."

"I have a suggestion, then. You remember the story of the Trojan Horse?"

"Of course, who doesn't know it?" Themistocles waved his hand impatiently.

"But listen, my friend. Odysseus won success at Troy long ago by planting a false rumor that the Greek forces were abandoning the siege. You and I know the story very well, but does Xerxes? Why not try a similar ruse?"

"And what do you have in mind?" Having funded the budget for the fleet's new flagship and marveled at the vessel's offensive capabilities, Themistocles knew Cain too well to doubt his friend's resourcefulness.

"I will pose as one of your trusted slaves and go to Xerxes under protection of being your private messenger with a story that sounds credible: that disputes have fractured the Greek resistance and that you, Admiral Themistocles, are sympathetic to the Persian cause. This should lead Xerxes to believe that if he enters the straits of Salamis now, before the other Greeks retreat, a victory that will annihilate the bulk of their forces will be his. But if he waits, that opportunity will slip away. I can hint that the Athenians, urged on by you, will defect to the Persian side."

Themistocles sat silent for a full minute. Then he leveled the piercing gaze of his gray eyes on Cain.

"It is a brilliant plan, wrought with treachery and betrayal. If you succeed in this mission, I will be in your debt when I am acclaimed as the man who saved Greece. You may expect my gratitude. But I warn you, Agathon. If you betray the city of Athena to the barbarians, I will hunt you down, torture you, and slay you myself."

Cain was, for once, at a loss for words.

❧

On the morning of September 24, an earthquake struck in the vicinity of the island of Salamis. The night before, Cain had rowed a small boat across from Salamis to Phaleron, the harbor near Athens where over a thousand Persian ships were arrayed. He told Xerxes exactly what the Great King wanted to hear. After hearing Cain's report that Xerxes had taken the bait, Themistocles, superstitious like most Greeks, interpreted the earthquake as a favorable omen.

Soon after midnight on September 25, by the light of a moon waning to last quarter, the Persian vessels silently rowed westward from Phaleron. Miles of them stretched in ghostly formation. Rounding the curved headlands near Athens, the fleet passed the small island of Psyttaleia and prepared to enter the Salamis channel, barely a mile wide at its narrowest point.

Toward dawn, Xerxes summoned his chariot and rode to a golden viewing throne, which the Persians had set up on the slopes of Mount Aegaleos on the mainland. He would observe the battle from there, just as a spectator seated high up in an outdoor theater on a hillside might view a play. The king's presence on the hillside was well advertised. It would motivate maximum performance from his troops, who knew well that any slacking might imperil their heads. Confident of an overwhelming victory, Xerxes had ordered that not one Greek sailor or marine be spared. He prepared to rejoice at the dismemberment of Greece.

Themistocles had publicly invited Cain to accompany him on the new flagship *Phobos*, from which the admiral would command the Athenian contingent of 180 vessels on the left wing of the line. Although he was reluctant to place himself in harm's way, Cain could find no plausible excuse for refusing. After all, he had designed the flagship himself. And besides, every escape route from Greece had been sealed by the forces of the invading Persian Empire.

It was fight or die.

"When will you give the order to launch?" he asked Themistocles as they stood near the ship's mast in the predawn darkness.

"Not until an hour after sunrise. The Persian vessels are still arriving," Themistocles gestured toward the opposite mainland shore. "The fishermen on Salamis have told me that a sea breeze from the south, an *aura*, can be expected in early to midmorning. The wind will favor us. It will make the water choppy—better for our maneuverable ships and worse for their taller, top-heavy vessels."

"You have thought of everything," Cain complimented him.

"Not quite, Agathon," Themistocles replied grimly. "There is no escape plan if we lose."

CHAPTER 38

The Straits of Salamis, 480 BC

The battle lasted all day long. Nearly a quarter of a million men and twelve hundred ships clashed at Salamis. For the Greeks, the stakes were nothing less than the survival of freedom, of language, of a culture: of an entire way of life.

After the first assault, Cain watched in silence as Themistocles dealt with a rapid-fire series of messages and orders. While their oars swept the water, the rowers of every Greek warship raucously chanted a song of praise to Apollo, mingling their prayers with cheers and fiercely stoking their courage against the foe. The rowing master and the bow officer yelled orders to keep the oarsmen stroking in unison, while a piper marked time by playing rhythmically. Striking a ship and disabling or sinking her was the prize in such a battle, and the thud of bronze rams and the splintering of wooden hulls split the air. As the men warmed to their work, the mild breeze could not diffuse the stench of their sweat.

High on his throne of royal state, Xerxes of Persia, the king of kings, surveyed the scene in the straits. The course of battle was not what he had expected. Far from deserting the narrow channel, the Greek fleet glided with sleek determination in an unbroken line, and here and there they succeeded in breaking the front row of opposing Persian vessels and fouling these as the leading ships retreated clumsily through the second and third rows.

"Are there messages from the Athenians, Mardonius?" Xerxes

queried his top general and senior advisor. "Have they proposed terms of alliance?"

"No, sire," replied the seasoned warrior. "It appears as if that talkative slave Themistocles sent has misled us."

"*Misled* us, you fool? He has *tricked* us! Artemisia was right. She begged me not to do battle in the straits. Now see where your stubbornness has led us!" The monarch looked darkly at Mardonius, who lowered his eyes in submission.

"Now, then!" Xerxes rose and pointed downward into the distance. "Isn't that her ship? Do you recognize the insignia?"

Mardonius looked out through the smoke of the battle in time to see what they thought was a Greek vessel being rammed, certainly a rare occurrence that day. The attacking ship was commanded by Artemisia, the queen of the Carian city of Halicarnassus in southwest Asia Minor. A Persian ally, she was the only woman commander at Salamis.

"She's done it!" shouted Xerxes. "Brave queen! Oh, gods, my men have turned into women, and my women into men!"

A scribe standing beside the throne dutifully recorded the Great King's words, along with a memorandum of honorary tribute to Artemisia.

❧

It was now midafternoon. The battle still favored the Greeks, but their Persian opponents had not yet shown any signs of retreat. Suddenly, the flagship's pilot shouted, "Two vessels in pursuit, sir!"

"Full speed!" ordered Themistocles. Because of the flagship's larger crew and greater speed, outpacing the Persian pursuers would not be difficult. But the Persians had caught Themistocles in a pincer movement, forcing him to draw closer to one of the largest clusters of enemy vessels.

"Launch the catapults, and activate the reaper!" Themistocles shouted, and the order was passed from stern to bow. "Now we'll clip the tails of these dogs!" the commander cried.

As the flagship plunged forward, six marines churned a gear-studded apparatus and the gigantic metal arms of the war reaper extended from the vessel's starboard side.

"Will you risk a ramming from them?" Cain shouted to his commander.

"They'll never get the chance!" Themistocles rejoined gleefully. "*They* would be running the fatal risk."

At that very moment, the flagship sideswiped a Persian ship in a daring maneuver. With grinding efficiency, the reaper shredded the port side of the enemy ship. Cain could see scores of mangled bodies—young Persian oarsmen literally torn to pieces by the lethal weapon he himself had engineered. The sight of their body parts—severed arms, legs, and heads—revolted him. Blood spattered the Greek oarsmen. Cain felt a painful twinge of guilt. Designing this carnage machine was not at all the same thing as seeing its murderous capabilities in action.

But the Athenian flagship was still not in the clear. During the time consumed for the reaper to accomplish its gory work, a Persian warship had approached from the port side. Themistocles's pilot took evasive action, but too late to prevent two zealous Persian marines from swinging down a rope from their vessel over the rail of the flagship.

Cain, whose attention was riveted on the reaper's operation to starboard, was oblivious of the Persian threat. One of the attackers launched a spear at his back, but it was somehow deflected in mid-flight. Simultaneously, Themistocles shouted a warning. The string of his bow twanged, skewering one of the Persian assailants with an arrow in the chest.

The other marine leaped at Cain from behind, and both men crashed to the deck with a thud. Momentarily stunned, Cain quickly gained the advantage, rolling on top of the now helmetless Persian while raising his knife. The eyes of a boy in his late teens darted up at Cain, who hesitated. But his young adversary felt no such compunction, freeing his own knife hand and stabbing Cain in the thigh, then reversing positions to prepare a mortal strike.

Instead, the attacker's blade dropped feebly to the deck as Themistocles's sword found its mark in the youth's back.

❧

By sunset, it was clear that Themistocles had calculated the Greek chances correctly. Crushingly outnumbered, the Greeks had managed to disable or sink nearly three hundred Persian ships while sustaining only moderate losses themselves. As the blood-red rays of the dying sun tinted the waters of the strait, the Persian vessels limped eastward, rounded the promontory at Piraeus, and regained the refuge of Phaleron harbor, where land troops would shelter them.

Meanwhile, in the narrow straits of Salamis, thousands of Persians were desperately swimming for shore after their ships had been sunk and their own fleet had abandoned them. Greek archers mercilessly hewed them down.

Xerxes had indeed presided over a huge massacre—but not the one he had ordered.

❧

On the shore of Salamis that night, Themistocles and Cain witnessed a sacrifice of thanksgiving to the gods and then reviewed the day's events before a roaring bonfire surrounded by hundreds of cheering soldiers. Though Cain shared their joy of victory, he suppressed his anxiety at the sight of their "sacred" offering of Persian soldiers being roasted alive in the blaze. He felt as if the eyes of his young assailant were still staring out at him from the flames.

"You have more reason than most to give thanks!" Themistocles exclaimed to his friend. "I cannot explain why the Persian's spear didn't find its mark. The gods must keep you under their protection!"

His friend's jubilant words triggered a remembrance of God's pronouncement to him thousands of years before:

I will give a sevenfold punishment to anyone who kills you. I will set a mark on you to protect you from those who would kill you.

Cain was amazed. It occurred to him that today, for the first time ever, an assailant had made a direct attempt on his life—yet God had not forgotten his promise! Instead, it seemed his comrade Themistocles had become the human face of his mark of protection. His gaze remained fixed on the blaze in the distance. Was God now exacting, through Greek hands, his manifold, fiery vengeance on Cain's behalf? He shuddered at the thought.

But could Cain "give thanks" for all of this? He was not exactly caught up in gratitude. Yes, his life had been saved, but for what? Thousands of years of wandering, deception, loneliness, and sadness had now culminated in his signature accomplishment of the day, the slaughter of young warriors made possible by his latest innovation. No, thanksgiving was far from his mind. Nevertheless, he felt duty-bound to acknowledge his debt to the man who had slain his attackers.

"I would not bet on the god who challenged you in archery!" he managed to quip.

Just then, a messenger arrived on the run. Recovering his breath, he whispered into the commander's ear. When the emissary had departed, Themistocles breathed a long sigh.

"Your masterpiece has burned beyond salvage, Agathon. *Phobos* is no more."

"How did this happen?" Cain asked him.

Themistocles shrugged his shoulders. "Persian saboteurs may have infiltrated the docks. The firing of our flagship might have been a last-ditch attempt to intimidate us. Or perhaps it was the work of Greek turncoats."

"But you can surely build another if you need to. Are the plans on file with the naval registry?"

"No, I never filed those plans. I wanted to make sure that the Persians, if they were victorious, would not have access to our military secrets."

Or perhaps, thought Cain, you paid some Greek lackeys to carry out this act of arson for the same reason. Themistocles was indubitably mercurial, but he was also the most cunning politician Cain could remember.

"No matter," Cain said smoothly. "We can reconstruct the plans if necessary." But he felt a quiver of uncertainty as he voiced this reassurance, now pondering whether the demise of the flagship was also the will of God.

"Yes, my friend. But let us hope we have seen the last of the Persians." As the fire danced before their eyes in the night, Themistocles urged, "Come now, let us join our compatriots in their song to Victory, our goddess *Nike!*"

Cain joined the revelry around the roaring bonfire with his body, but his mind soared out over the wine-dark sea where the remains of ships and bodies still floated.

CHAPTER 39

Chicago: Twenty-Eight Years Ago

A s the bonfire on the shore of Salamis faded from sight, another fire by night took center stage in Amanda's vision.

She first saw the blaze from high above. But her perspective quickly zoomed in so that she could distinguish a burning four-story building, set on the corner of two densely developed city streets. Except for the crackling flames, however, the setting had nothing in common with ancient Greece. This was a modern American metropolis, and crews of firefighters were battling a five-alarm blaze.

From her vantage point, Amanda noted the block lettering of the Chicago Fire Department on a nearby hook and ladder truck. Seeing the puffs of frost emitted by the firefighters as they shouted orders and directions to each other, she could tell it was very cold.

Now she found herself inside a smoky stairwell. A firefighter with his oxygen mask tilted back on his head was arguing forcefully with a woman dressed in pajamas holding a wet cloth to her face. On her blouse was pinned a small silver cross.

"Sister, you can't go back up," the man said sternly, as he put his arm out to block the nun's way. "I won't allow it."

"Listen to me," she replied in a voice tinged with authority. A petite woman in her midfifties, she drew herself up to her full height. "I am Sister Kathleen O'Donnell, the director of this orphanage. I don't just work here—I'm responsible for all the children in our care!"

"But all of the boys are safe, Sister Kathleen. I already brought them out. Now please go back down to the front lawn and attend to the girls!"

"Are you *sure* they are all out? These children, especially the youngest ones, like to hide when they get scared. Let me go with you to find them."

"Out of the question, Sister. You have no oxygen mask. Look, I already told you they are fine. I led them out myself. I'll go back up and double-check any hiding places, but you must get out of the building now!"

Sister Kathleen bowed her head in assent. The fireman was right. The smoke and flames were spreading so rapidly that an escape might soon be impossible. Hurrying down the stairs to the ground floor, she strode through a long hallway and out the front entrance of Mercy Orphanage. As she descended a short flight of brick steps to the lawn, she was further unnerved by the blinding lights and blaring horns of a fleet of fire trucks, ambulances, and police vehicles.

Turning to look at the building behind her, she saw intense flames behind the windows of the third story, the floor where the boys slept. "Thank God the fireman got them out in time," she thought.

But when her eyes scoured the front lawn, not a boy was to be seen.

Another firefighter ran up to her. "Come this way, Sister," he ordered brusquely. Sister Kathleen acquiesced when he put a brawny arm around her shoulders and steered her rapidly toward one of the command vehicles. As they made their way to the street, she could see a group of several dozen girls being tended to by paramedics. She recognized several of the children whom she herself had led to safety fifteen minutes earlier when she woke up to the first whiffs of smoke.

Inside the mobile command and communications vehicle, she was greeted by the officer in charge. Captain Molloy was surrounded by a rescue unit, all dressed in heavy coats and equipped with oxygen masks, pike poles, axes, and halligan bars.

Without bothering to exchange introductions, she burst out, "Where are my boys, Captain?"

"What floor are they on, Sister?"

"They were on the third floor," she replied, gesturing toward the billowing flames.

With a puzzled look on his face, Captain Molloy reached for his radio. "Anyone in the building?" he demanded. Silence. Switching to another channel, he questioned the leader of the squad stationed at the back of the building.

"Dempsey, were any boys led out of the building on your side?"

"Negative, Captain. We're just going in now."

"But I don't understand," implored Sister Kathleen. "One of your men assured me that they had been escorted out of the building. Where are they now? I don't see them here." Fear now streaked her tone. "Please, God, let them be safe!"

Captain Molloy quizzed the nun. "Do you remember the fireman's name?"

Sister Kathleen shook her head.

"Can you describe him?"

"He was tall, but the light in the stairwell was dim and the air was becoming quite smoky. I didn't really get a good look"

A shadow crossed Molloy's face. He changed the radio channel once more. "Dispatch, it's Molloy. Make it a point to get an incident history from every fireman. Have the reports on my desk in the morning. Mercy Orphanage, West 103rd Street. Over and out."

Leaning over toward the nun, he said, "We'll see if we can get in there, Sister. We'll do everything in our power to—"

Just then, a loud explosion blew out half a dozen third-floor windows. On the edge of panic, Sister Kathleen leaped from the command vehicle and raced toward the circle of girls. All in their night dress, they ranged from four to fourteen years old. Swarming around the nun, they bombarded her with questions.

"Girls, please! Have you seen any of the boys outside the building?"

Rosa, one of the older children, silently pointed to a figure in the center of the lawn. Lying on a stretcher, a boy of about twelve was being treated by the paramedics. Even from a distance, the nun could see that the child was badly burned. His face was turned away, and a burly EMT partially blocked the view, so she did not know who it was. An IV tube was stuck into his arm.

"Do any of you know how he got here?" Sister Kathleen questioned.

"We'd been out here for about ten minutes," Rosa replied, shivering. "I saw a fireman carry him out and lay him on the ground. He was shouting for the paramedics to come over. Then he went back into the burning building."

Sister Kathleen left the girls and ran toward the boy, but the paramedics lifted the stretcher into an ambulance parked at the far edge of the lawn.

"Wait!" she shouted to no avail as the stretcher glided into position and the rear doors slammed shut. With its sirens revving up, the ambulance roared off in the direction of Cook County Hospital.

❦

Under his oxygen mask, the boy slowly came to. The young paramedic leaning toward him held his hand firmly.

"Don't worry, you're going to make it, buddy. The hospital has the best burn unit in the city. Tell me something, though. Do you know how the fire started?"

The paramedic lifted the mask so the boy could talk, but he merely closed his eyes and remained silent.

"Well, son, good thing you made it out of the building in time. You've got third-degree burns on your back and stomach."

The boy winced in pain as the man continued, "You know, in my rush to get you to the ambulance, I forgot to get the name of the firefighter who carried you out. You'll want to send him a nice note when you're able. Did you see his name badge?"

The boy muttered meekly, "I, uh…I can't remember."

His eyes closed once more, and he drifted out of consciousness.

❦

As the ambulance swung into the emergency entrance, the vehicle was met by a team of nurses and a doctor. Meanwhile, on the hospital lobby television, a live interview with Sister Kathleen O'Donnell back at the orphanage was being broadcast.

"But who told you that they were safe, Sister?" The reporter thrust her microphone close to the nun's mouth, twisted with grief.

"A firefighter in the stairwell. I don't know who he was." Sister Kathleen's voice trembled.

The reporter pivoted away from the nun and looked directly into the camera. "Fire department officials now confirm that all the boys are deceased except for one survivor, who has been rushed to Cook County Hospital. His name is being withheld because he is a juvenile. Officials have no comment on Sister Kathleen O'Donnell's claim that a firefighter represented the situation falsely to her. All we know now is that a fireman may have been responsible for the deaths of twenty-two male orphans. Victoria Thompson, reporting live from Mercy Orphanage."

CHAPTER 40

Athens, 465 BC

The letter arrived in Athens well after midnight. Cain had stumbled home from a taverna after drinking Greek spirits all night. Whereas Greece enjoyed its new peace, the ramification for Cain was unemployment, as the ship factory had been closed. Reluctantly, Cain had become a gambler to afford the rent on his small flat near the harbor. Lately, he found himself on a losing streak and had exhausted his savings. Receiving the small scroll from the waiting messenger's hands, Cain held up his oil lamp and squinted through tired eyes.

> *My dear Agathon, your presence is urgently requested! Take passage on the first ship at your disposal for Ephesus. I enclose a small sum for your travel expenses. I will have you met and conveyed via the Royal Road to Babylon. Here in Persia there are exciting opportunities, and an even more exciting future may be envisioned. Do not fail me!*
>
> *Faithfully, as ever,*
> *Your friend,*
> *Themistocles*

Cain was not entirely surprised. Themistocles was, if anything, resourceful. Seven years earlier, in 472 BC, he had been ostracized by the Athenian assembly, largely due to his abrasive arrogance in boasting that he was the "savior of Greece" at Salamis. The vote meant that Themistocles would have to leave the city for a minimum of ten years, with a penalty of death if he returned beforehand.

After this blow, the politician's troubles multiplied. An envious political party at Sparta had accused Themistocles of treason and had collaborated with his enemies in Athens. As a result, he no longer found it safe to remain within Greece, let alone in his native city. At first he withdrew to the northwestern kingdom of Molossia, then to Macedon, then to Asia Minor, and finally to Persia.

All this time, Cain had kept in contact with his old friend by letter. This in itself was extremely risky, since the Athenians had officially condemned the architect of their victory at Salamis as a traitor. But Themistocles, who still had numerous admirers in Athens, used trusted couriers for the correspondence.

Cain weighed his options. It was ironic in the extreme that Themistocles was apparently now consorting with his erstwhile mortal enemies, the Persians. Yet, years earlier, Cain had seriously considered the possibility that Themistocles, in the event of an impending Persian victory, might have been willing to do a deal with the Great King. If there were two qualities that marked his friend's mind and emotions, they were *cunning* and *ambition*.

What, Cain wondered, were these "opportunities" of which Themistocles wrote?

⁌⌇⌐

Two months later found the friends reunited on the shores of the Euphrates River in the city of Babylon. Cain had seen nothing as grand as the Persian capital since his days in Egypt. On each side of the Euphrates, arrow-straight paved streets led down to the river, flanked by ziggurat towers, ornamental columns, and magnificent four-story mansions. An enormous astronomical observatory bore witness to Babylonian expertise in celestial matters. Magnificent brickwork attested to this people's mastery of engineering and architecture.

"The perimeter of Babylon is said to be fifty-six miles," Themistocles declared as he and Cain strolled on an elevated promenade on the river's left bank. "Can you imagine? That is more than double the distance between Athens and Marathon!"

Cain recalled how Themistocles, one of the generals at the famous battle of Marathon a quarter century before, had always possessed a knack for folding into any conversation a flattering reference to his own exploits.

"In your letter you mentioned opportunities. What exactly did you mean?"

"My contacts in the royal court inform me unanimously that King Artaxerxes, the son of our old adversary, will look with favor on Greeks who support the Persian Empire. Not just any Greeks, mind you. *Distinguished* Greeks. Achievers."

"You certainly qualify for that title. But how would I be involved?" Cain asked.

"You are involved as my associate. Tomorrow I will be officially accepting the reward the king has offered for my defection. I am sure His Majesty will be happy to make your acquaintance at our audience with him."

"Our *audience* with him? You didn't tell me anything about a meeting with Artaxerxes!" Cain exclaimed.

"Life would be boring without surprises, Agathon. Come, let's head for the bazaar to get you some proper clothes. I notice, by the way, you are as trim as ever. You seem to possess the secret of per-petual youth!"

☙❧

The very next day, a phalanx of armed guards parted to admit the two Greek visitors, who passed through an enormous gate in the hundred-foot-high wall surrounding the royal palace. Inside, Artaxerxes sat on a golden throne, directly opposite a gigantic statue of the god Bel seated on an elaborately ornamented platform. The symbolism was unmistakable—the deity had chosen the monarch to aid and protect Babylon.

Themistocles had briefed Cain beforehand on the customary etiquette, and both men knelt before the monarch. As Artaxerxes extended his hands in greeting and motioned for the visitors to rise, Cain noticed that the emperor's right hand was slightly longer than his left. Of medium height, he had a closely cropped beard and heavy, jowly features. The only imperial-looking trait about him was the long plane of his nose.

"Welcome, Themistocles!" exclaimed the emperor. "The year we granted you to study our language and customs is nearly over. We trust you have spent this time profitably?"

"I have, Great King," replied Themistocles in Persian. "I am now ready to serve you."

Artaxerxes, wrongly assuming that Cain knew no Persian, now switched to fluent Greek. "And your colleague today, he is the one you told us of, the designer of the armored flagship that my father once mentioned?"

"He is, my lord. As I have informed you, Agathon's expertise in nautical engineering and metallurgy is unrivaled. With his help, it will be possible to outfit Persia with an invincible fleet of warships.

You will be able to carry out the conquest of which your father dreamed. All Greece will pay you tribute."

Artaxerxes smiled broadly, as if the taste of victory were already his.

"Themistocles," he said, "for your alliance with us we are pleased to grant you a reward. The bounty I had placed on your life will now be yours—the sum of two hundred talents. And we appoint you as our governor of the province of Magnesia. Three cities will pay you revenues: one for bread, one for meat, and one for wine."

"I humbly accept this appointment, my lord," replied Themistocles, striking his breast in submission.

"And now," said the emperor, turning to Cain, "we would gladly hear more of your armored warship. How is it constructed, exactly?"

Cain made a split-second decision. Having played such an important role in preserving Greek history through time, he would not participate in bringing it to a close.

"Your Excellency, I cannot help you build such weapons for the purpose of annihilating an entire culture. True, I designed a flagship for the Greeks, but that is when they faced invaders who threatened to enslave them."

Themistocles's jaw dropped in astonishment.

Indeed, life would be boring without surprises, Cain thought as he saw the look on his friend's face.

"Themistocles," said the emperor, "we wish to converse with Agathon in private. Let our ministers accompany you to the hall of maps, where they will brief you on the imperial administration in Magnesia."

Bowing deeply, Themistocles backed toward the doors of the throne room and made his exit.

Artaxerxes and Cain faced each other. "You have spoken of an invasion," said the emperor. "Who knows but that Persia herself may face an invasion from Greece one day?"

"I hardly think that likely, Your Excellency," answered Cain. "It was only with great difficulty that Themistocles was able to hold the Greeks together at Salamis." It occurred to Cain that Themistocles might have promised to deliver him as part of the defection deal.

"But our informants have told us of the new Athenian empire. Some of the Greeks, at any rate, do not lack ambitions for conquest. Athens now receives enormous tribute from many city-states. She uses the Persian threat as a pretext."

"All the same," responded Cain, "I refuse to escalate the chances of war. I have lived with these Greeks for seven hundred years. I would never betray them."

The emperor's puzzled expression made Cain realize his verbal blunder. Fortunately, Artaxerxes merely sighed. "I have dealt with patriotic men before, but never one with your strange sense of humor, Agathon. If you really were as clever as your reputation, you would follow your friend's lead and join the Persian side. I should have you tortured and executed for your insolence, but instead, I will give you time to think about the matter. Perhaps a year in solitary confinement will help you to change your mind. If you agree to share the flagship's designs with us and pledge your allegiance to Persia, your reward will be two hundred talents, the very same as the sum granted to Themistocles."

At a signal from the emperor, guards surrounded Cain and led him swiftly from the throne room.

CHAPTER 41

Babylon, 465–323 BC

To his surprise, Cain's jail cell was so spacious as to be almost comfortable. Located at the top of one of the hundreds of towers in Babylon, the cell enjoyed a splendid view of the city. Through a large barred window, Cain could clearly see the Hanging Gardens, the lush and legendary wonder of the world built by King Nebuchadnezzar over two hundred years before.

The emperor had given strict orders, which were inscribed on a bronze plaque placed on the wall outside the cell door. The prisoner was to be left alone inside the cell. Twice a day, he would be given food and water, passed through a small opening in the one-foot-thick, metal-reinforced wooden door. The cell would be opened only on the express order of the emperor, who personally retained possession of the key.

Cain reflected on his predicament. True, Artaxerxes had deprived him of his liberty. But the emperor's arrangements also meant that Cain had little to worry about. His food and shelter were provided for, and imprisonment ensured that Cain would not have to participate again in military conflicts such as the Battle at Salamis. Dryly, he reflected that, in contrast to Artaxerxes, time was on his side. He could break the routine of solitary confinement by reliving his memories of more pleasant episodes in his life, such as his beer venture in Egypt and his idyll with Tanith. And the cell was flooded with air and light, with spacious limestone walls perfect for etching or drawing designs.

Thus, when a messenger from Artaxerxes arrived exactly one year later to ask Cain if he had changed his mind, the prisoner said no. And Cain's answer remained the same the next year and the year after that.

☙❧

One year, the messengers stopped coming.

That was not the end of his human contact, however. Although he could not see their faces, Cain had befriended many of the young day jailers who guarded the cells in the tower. They informed him that the cell he occupied was intended for enemy generals—leaders whom the emperor regarded as precious commodities and potential allies. This gave Cain a certain status in the jailers' eyes. They told him of military conquests and foreign developments—in particular of a great war in Greece that pitted the Spartans against the Athenians. They also told him that the reason no messenger had come from court was that the king had died.

This news caused Cain to wonder what fate might await him at the hands of Artaxerxes's successor. But there was no change in the prison arrangements. According to the day jailers, the new king, who took the name Darius II, was intensely focused on the Peloponnesian War in Greece, following a policy first of aiding the Athenians and then the Spartans. For more than a century now, Cain thought, the mightiest empire on earth has been obsessed with a small collection of independent city-states.

"The war has spread to Sicily," a jailer told the prisoner one day.

"It goes well for the Athenians?" Cain inquired.

"Oh, no, Agathon, the Athenians have suffered a stinging defeat in the harbor at Syracuse. Hundreds of their ships are lost. The effects on Athens will be devastating."

Cain thought wistfully of another time, of another Athens. Accustomed to being free to participate in the course of human events, his only freedom now lay in his mind.

❧

A night jailer who called himself Cyrus had shown a particular interest in befriending Cain. The jailer had, in fact, offered to furnish the prisoner with writing tools, carving supplies, and candles. The offer raised Cain's suspicions, since passing anything except food and water through the slender opening in the door would most likely be frowned on by the authorities. But Cain was brimming with ideas for new designs. In particular, he wanted to explore developing a mechanical reaper to improve agricultural output, a peacetime counterpart to the horrendous war machine he had created for Themistocles before Salamis.

All the night jailer asked for in return for his good offices was information about what Cain was writing on papyrus and drawing on the walls of his cell.

"You are said to be a masterful designer," came the disembodied voice from beyond the door one night.

"And who compliments me thus?" Cain inquired.

"I have many contacts at court, Agathon. They tell me you are a wizard at war machines. What specific offensive weapons have you invented?"

The man was a bit too curious for a run-of-the-mill jailer on the night shift, and how could a mere jailer boast of contacts at court? Cain was on his guard. Perhaps this was a spy sent by the emperor.

"I don't know what you mean, Cyrus," he replied disingenuously. "But with the benefit of your supplies, I may be able to develop something promising."

"By all means, you may count on me. But be sure you describe for me the drawings you create on the walls. I am most interested in your plans." As Cain stood up from the small opening through which they were conversing, another possibility crossed his mind.

Was Cyrus the master of spirits?

Although he couldn't answer the question definitively, Cain's suspicions grew as the years passed. He used the supplies conveyed to him by the night jailer for purely beneficial projects—the mechanical reaper, for example, as well as refining the design for his geared navigational timing device. But the night jailer seemed interested only in weaponry.

It was also odd that, as the decades passed and night jailers came and went, one of the guards claimed that he was the son of a former night jailer who had died. Although Cain had to admit that the voices of "father" and "son" were somewhat different, he was unconvinced. He had, as he well remembered, employed the same ruse to disguise his true identity in Egypt.

As he weighed the motivations of those who guarded him by night, Cain decided on a test.

"I have devised a formula for creating an explosive powder made of natural minerals. The ingredients won't be easy to find, and they must be combined in proper proportions," Cain whispered through the two-way portal.

"And what will you use the powder for?" came the reply.

"I am working on my designs for an arrow launcher," Cain improvised. "I want to enhance the propulsive power. I'll need saltpeter crystals distilled from bat guano, and sulfur. Also some charcoal. But the sulfur needs to be freshly extracted from the mines in Sicily. The best quality."

"Splendid, prisoner. And what will we call our new mixture?"

"I've been more focused on the formula itself than the name. For now, I suppose the label 'black powder' would be apt," Cain replied.

When all the materials were passed through the small opening a mere two nights later, Cain concluded that he was indeed dealing with the master of spirits. He resolved to become more circumspect in his conversations from now on.

❧

His day jailers kept him informed about events in the wider world. The rosters of these guards rotated frequently, as jail duty was limited to one year, after which the young conscripts were sent off to battle. But none of them seemed curious about the longevity of their prisoner. As far as they were concerned, they were being paid to slide sustenance through a small opening, share some innocuous conversation, and little else.

One day an especially loquacious young guard told of a new threat to the empire.

"They say that King Philip of Macedon is planning an invasion of Persia," he informed Cain.

"What chance of success could such an invader possibly have?" asked the prisoner.

"No chance at all, in my opinion. The emperor will defeat him soundly."

The guard refrained from further comment on the matter, but Cain knew from other jailers that Persia's current monarch, Artaxerxes III, had come to the throne after plotting the assassination of eight of his half brothers.

"Agathon, did you know that my commander cannot find any records relating to your imprisonment here?"

"That's strange. Has there been some confusion?"

"Our detachment has been assigned to this tower only recently, and the commander was looking for verification of each inmate's original date of incarceration. But it seems that all your records have disappeared. We have no idea how this could have happened. But the emperor has not reversed the orders on the plaque outside your cell. So at least you know that you won't be moving soon!"

Unseen inside his cell, Cain smiled at the young man's naïveté.

That evening, shortly after sunset, the master of spirits appeared. He assumed an amorphous, dark shape in the corner of Cain's cell.

"*You are so comfortable, Cain? The Persians do not possess unlimited patience, my friend. Sooner or later they will force you to reveal your secrets, if only so that they can defeat Philip of Macedon. And consider this also. For the moment, I have concealed your prison records. But if the Persians should find and examine them, they may discover the secret of your longevity.*"

The prisoner ignored the veiled threat. "Where do you come from, spirit?"

"*Oh, I am never far from you. I go to and fro on the earth, and walk up and down.*"

Cain was repelled by the nonchalant, almost jaunty tone.

"And you are happy, spirit, in your quest to wreak woe upon human beings?"

"*You misinterpret me entirely. My own happiness is immaterial. I only seek to spread pleasure and share benefit. Right here and now, I offer you relief—an escape from this prison before the Persians can injure you further. You know what they are capable of, I presume?*"

Cain remained silent.

The master of spirits continued. "*As self-professed lovers of the truth, their treatment of liars is most unpleasant, Cain. One Persian soldier was recently accused of slandering the emperor. His punishment was to be stretched out between two troughs, one below his body and one above, and force-fed with delicacies and milk mixed with honey. Only his head and his feet remained visible. Unable to move, he was attacked by flies that*"

swarmed over his face. Inside the troughs, his excrement began to attract
worms and maggots. After seventeen days of exquisite suffering, he died.
When the top covering was lifted, the onlookers could see that his flesh had
been eaten away."

Even though he knew this was blackmail, Cain felt himself growing numb.

"They could easily inflict the same torture on you, Cain. Except you
wouldn't die, would you?" said the master of spirits.

"What would you have me do, spirit?" Cain burst out angrily.

"Swear allegiance to me, not to the Persians. I will arrange for your release."

"Depart from me, evil one. You will never have my allegiance!"

The dark shape in the corner vanished. What remained after the spirit's departure was an unnerving tableau acted out repeatedly in Cain's mind, dominated by the wrenching spectacle of the Persian soldier, his vitals destroyed by his truth-loving compatriots.

꒰ঌ⋆ᰔ

"He has brought peace to the world!" a day jailer reported.

Cain's ears perked up.

"Alexander is a great ruler, Agathon!" the young guard gushed. "Although he threatens my country, some of us wonder if he would not be a better king for us. Alexander has already vanquished the cities of Susa and Persepolis."

Cain was astonished. The cities he had named were, besides Babylon, the most important metropolitan centers in the Persian Empire.

"What else has this leader Alexander accomplished, other than conquest in battle?"

"It is said that he has great plans for a worldwide capital in Egypt. The city will be known as Alexandria. Two of its monuments will be wonders of the world, as surely as our Hanging Gardens here in

Babylon. In the harbor, there will be a lighthouse that soars higher than any other on the inland sea. And in the city itself, there will be a great library, a glorious temple of knowledge gathered by all humanity and a center for scholars from every corner of the world."

"How can this commander hope to construct such magnificent public works?" Cain asked with keen interest.

"For Alexander, such a goal will not be difficult. His wealth is boundless. He is on the brink of becoming master of the known world!"

From that day on, Cain's attitude toward his imprisonment changed. Originally stoic and passive, with ambition drained by a sense of detachment and relief, he was now consumed by a new passion for release. By day and by night, dreams of Alexandria fired his brain. The tempo of his wall designs quickened, as he sketched mathematical formulas and the blueprint of a great telescope to study the constellations. He envisioned learned colloquies with the scholars who congregated from every part of the world at Alexandria. He wanted—no, he *needed*—to be a participant in this remarkable new turn in the trajectory of human civilization.

Accordingly, he began a series of blatant appeals to his guards, using a range of blandishments. To one of the day jailers, he alluded casually to the location of buried treasure in Egypt. Cain had miscalculated. The young man reacted with shock and then threatened reprisal. To another, he hinted of diamonds and other precious gems as big as a man's fist. To no avail. And to the captain of the day contingent, Cain spoke casually of the silver deposits he had identified in Greece. Not interested. Reluctantly, Cain had to admit that these Persian jailers cherished duty and integrity. The one thing he would not do, however, was to mortgage his liberty to the master of spirits.

The jailers' integrity, however, soon became a moot point. Babylon fell to Alexander the Great in 331 BC. Eight years later, in mid-June of 323 BC, the conqueror succumbed to fever there at the age of thirty-two, breathing his last in the great palace of Nebuchadnezzar. Bells rang and shrieks of wailing echoed throughout the city. While Alexander's generals converged to divide the spoils, all of Babylon's nonviolent prisoners were ordered to be released, Cain among them. Abandoning the as yet unsuccessful black powder project, he dumped the ingredients down the cell's refuse chute so they would not be found. Two Greek soldiers unlocked the cell, using a key brittle with the rust of time.

Exiting the prison tower, Cain strolled toward the Euphrates River and breathed, for the first time in nearly a century and a half, the fresh air of freedom.

CHAPTER 42

Alexandria, Egypt, 285–250 BC

Soon after the turn of the third century BC, Cain received news that the Royal Library at Alexandria was nearing completion. A showcase for the city, the library enjoyed the direct patronage of King Ptolemy I, who had adopted the popular name *Soter*, Greek for "savior." As one of Alexander's three most senior surviving generals, Ptolemy possessed by far the most lucrative portion of the empire. The fertile lands and ample tax revenues of Egypt boosted Alexandria to worldwide prominence at an explosive rate.

Cain had secured full-time employment at the Royal Observatory of Babylon, but he was only marking time until the Great Library beckoned. At last, the moment was ripe for his return to Egypt. He booked passage on a caravan on the Royal Road through Asia Minor to Ephesus. From there it would be a leisurely voyage on the Mediterranean to Alexandria. He had no idea what sights would greet him, but his thirst for a journey of the mind was as strong as ever.

He arrived at Alexandria in the spring of 285 BC. What he saw astounded him. Since his last visit long ago, when Alexandria was an obscure fishing village, both harbor and city had undergone massive improvements. As he rode on horseback around the city, he admired the majestic civic buildings. Huge *stoas*, or colonnaded covered walkways, surrounded a vast marketplace on all sides. The city wall divided the residential areas from Lake Mareotis and the canal that stretched to the Nile. Alexandria boasted no fewer than six gymnasia, each with its attached palaestra, or wrestling practice ground. Cain marveled at the degree to which Greek architecture had become rooted on Egyptian soil.

The jewel in the city's crown was the library, its prominence signaled by its location adjacent to Ptolemy's royal palace. The library was an adjunct to the *Mouseion*, the think tank that Ptoelmy had established for scholars from all over the world. This institute for advanced study had attracted experts in every field, ranging from literary and textual criticism to geography, history, anatomy, geometry, and physics. The convergence of these savants in Alexandria had vaulted the city into the top tier of learning and made it the new Athens.

From Zenodotus, the head librarian, Cain learned that the library's first major project was to establish definitive, standard texts of Homer's *Iliad* and *Odyssey*. Identifying himself as Callias, an elderly scholar, Cain had used his credentials from the observatory in Babylon as an entrée, and Zenodotus had welcomed him courteously. As the two men strolled down a spacious, colonnaded stoa, lined with marble statues of Greek gods and punctuated by smaller rooms leading off to one side, Cain asked about the library's acquisitions policy.

"As you have seen," said Zenodotus, "more and more people are traveling here, some to settle permanently. We encourage book donations. Sometimes, these are not entirely voluntary."

Raising his eyebrows, Cain asked for clarification. Gesturing toward a narrower stoa that stretched down toward the harbor, Zenodotus explained, "That is the acquisitions wing. Every ship that docks here is inspected by His Majesty's harbor police. The books that are found aboard are brought here for copying." He lowered his voice and added, conspiratorially, "Of course, sometimes it is the copies that are returned, not the originals."

Cain smiled. "It is the King's goal, then, to amass a universal collection?"

"Exactly. We have everything in our collections from medical texts to accounts of ancient foreign wars to the works of Plato and Aristotle," the head librarian said proudly.

Zenodotus invited his visitor to examine some of the library's holdings, and they made a detour from the main stoa into one of the smaller rooms. There, on shelves that lined the chamber from floor to ceiling, were hundreds of papyrus rolls, neatly stacked in compartments. At the end of each roll facing outward was an identifying tab.

"This is, in fact, part of the Homeric collection," said Zenodotus. "These ancient scrolls have come to us from all over the world, from Sicily to Asia Minor. Because we have collected so many copies of the *Iliad* and *Odyssey*, we have tagged them alphabetically according to their place of origin."

Cain asked permission to open one of the scrolls, which contained a thousand lines or so of Homer's *Odyssey*. Running his eye over the text, he pointed to a line in a speech by the hero Odysseus to the divine sea nymph Calypso.

"Surely this can't be right, Zenodotus. This line violates several of Homer's metrical rules of poetic verse."

Skeptical, the librarian peered at the text. As he read the line to himself, comprehension dawned on his face. "You are absolutely correct, Callias! Why haven't we noticed this before? Any copyist who could make an error such as this has probably included dozens of other botches."

At the chief librarian's invitation, Cain made many repeat visits. He collaborated steadily with Zenodotus on Homeric questions—never revealing, of course, that he had firsthand knowledge of the epic bard's performance techniques. Within three months, Zenodotus had become so impressed by Cain's abilities that he offered him a part-time fellowship at the Mouseion. Cain's privileges would include a meal allowance and a small annual salary. Most important of all, he would enjoy unrestricted access to the library.

"I think I can persuade King Ptolemy's council to upgrade this appointment within six months," Zenodotus told him. "I would very much like you to become a full fellow. That would mean life tenure."

Cain gratefully accepted the probationary appointment. It was the fulfillment of a dream that had begun in his tower cell in Babylon.

By the following year, it was clear that King Ptolemy, now in his early eighties, had not long to live. Before his death, however, he presided over a council meeting at which Cain was promoted to a full fellowship at the Mouseion. The king, who had personally sponsored such brilliant scholars as Euclid, sent his latest superstar, "Callias," a special message of commendation along with an ornate signet ring. He now had tenure for life.

☙❧

Over the next ten years, Cain grew steadily happier in his life of scholarship. The library was virtually his residence. Every morning, as he ambled across the huge quadrangle in the palace quarter, passing green hedges and spectacular gardens of imported trees and fragrant flowers, he glanced upward at the library's front entrance. There, he glimpsed an inscription in Greek letters:

THE PLACE OF THE CURE OF THE SOUL

These were the very words he himself had used at the grand opening of Pharaoh Ramesses II's much smaller library in Memphis nearly one thousand years before. An attentive scribe must have been taking notes, Cain thought. But he felt no irritation at the lack of attribution for his quote. On the contrary, the notion that it would be reechoed after a millennium filled him with gratifying serenity. Some of the things he had done, Cain reflected, were becoming matters of record.

Together with dozens of other learned, multilingual scholars, he translated books from foreign languages into Greek. He became the envy of his peers for his ability to translate from virtually any tongue. He also worked on his own engineering designs, producing a prototype of the mechanical grain reaper that he had planned while in prison in Babylon.

At the intersection of Europe, Africa, and Asia, as well as at the junction of numerous overland trade routes, Alexandria was a bustling, cosmopolitan metropolis, both by day and by night. Needing little sleep, Cain would often work late into the night at the library by the light of oil lamps. To relax, he would stroll toward the harbor, where brightly lit shops, taverns, and businesses all hummed with activity long past sunset. The port of Alexandria was so busy that dockworkers often labored in double shifts loading and off-loading the cargo vessels anchored in the harbor. There were no limits, it seemed, to Alexandria's global reach and capacity for growth.

With the passage of the years, however, some of Cain's old anxieties resurfaced. How much longer could he avail himself of his disguise as a grandfather? Even with the increased longevity that recent advances at Alexandria's medical school had afforded, there were limits to his persona's credibility. Besides, the stirrings of envy at his achievements made his colleagues increasingly uneasy with him.

So in 250 BC, the "elderly" Cain petitioned the Royal Council to grant him a sabbatical. He had no intention of leaving Alexandria permanently, but he pleaded the need for an intermission in his scholarly activities. The council readily gave its assent, and Cain prepared to depart from the city. His destination was a new power on the horizon to the west: Rome.

CHAPTER 43

Ercolano: Present Day

"Buona fortuna!" Silvio called out to Carmelo as he watched the foreman depart. Resuming his walk back to the site, Silvio saw Juan Carlos rushing toward him.

"Silvio, I think I've got most of it!" Juan Carlos told his grandfather excitedly. "I've been reviewing the digital recording of Amanda's voice as she was assessing the doors. It's a good thing she usually talks out loud to herself when she's wrapped up in a puzzle!"

"Excellent—what have you come up with?" Silvio wanted to know. It was now ten forty-five a.m.

"Well, I worked backward from the proverb she ended up with: 'Neither *time* nor *death* can turn a *story*'s *truth* to *dust*.' This proverb cracked the code. But the five key words in the proverb also had to line up with the correct pictograms on the left-hand side of the doorway."

Juan Carlos took out a small notebook and drew a diagram for Silvio.

"Here are the four pictograms I heard her comment about on the recording." He drew an hourglass, a sword, a Chinese truth character, and a serpent. "And if we correlate these images with the key words, we get this chart." Juan Carlos laid out two columns to show the equivalents of words and images.

"What about the word *story*?"

"That's exactly it. I went back over the recording twice. I couldn't hear everything Amanda said because of occasional static. She must have identified the proper pictogram for *story*, but I can't recover what she found."

"But still, you've made lots of progress. I'm proud of you," Silvio complimented him.

"Well, Amanda deserves the compliment, not me. Can't we get someone through the crack now?" he pleaded. "Maybe there'll be an obvious solution on the doors."

Thinking about his earlier phone conversation with Walker, and then checking his watch, Silvio replied, "Just give Amanda a little more time in the chamber. After all, she has a gas meter."

"But, nonno, every moment is precious! I don't understand the justification for any delay!" Juan Carlos exclaimed.

"How about this, *nipote*? Dr. Walker from the Getty will be here within the hour. He's wiry enough to fit through the crack in an instant. And he's thoroughly experienced in matching up texts with images. He's perfect for the job."

"Let's hope you're right," said Juan Carlos a bit reluctantly. "I pray Amanda will be safe until Walker gets here."

"She'll be okay, I am sure of it."

CHAPTER 44

Rome, 250–238 BC

Cain leaned over the rail of the transport ship as it readied to depart the port of Ostia and sail up the Tiber River to Rome. At the time of his arrival, Rome was halfway through its first overseas war with Carthage, a Phoenician colony founded five hundred years beforehand that had burgeoned into the most important naval power in the Mediterranean. The bone of contention between the cities was Sicily, on which Rome had recently set its sights. The island lay squarely between the two contenders, and whoever controlled it would be preeminent in the region.

With no literary or visual arts to speak of, Rome was a cultural backwater, barely half the size of Alexandria. Yet there was no denying the Romans' military flair and their engineering resourcefulness. To do battle with Carthage, Rome had, within a few short years, raised a fleet of over three hundred warships. Many of these were outfitted with grapnets—swinging cranes equipped with spikes, so that the Romans could board enemy vessels and turn naval combats into land battles. When three-fourths of this fleet was lost in a storm off Sicily's southern coast in the year 255 BC, Rome, seemingly unfazed, had raised in short order a brand-new navy of two hundred vessels. "Themistocles, you would have been proud," muttered Cain.

His most immediate aim was to interest the Romans in his mechanical grain reaper, which would greatly improve their agricultural production. After making a few inquiries, he discovered that the aediles were the proper government officials to approach. Midlevel magistrates, the aediles were annually elected to supervise markets, temples, religious celebrations, gladiatorial games, the upkeep of the city, and the grain supply. Thus, on a crisp autumn morning, Cain found himself in conversation with Marcus Terentius Varro. They sat in Varro's austere office just inside the main entrance to the Roman Forum.

He introduced himself as Philo of Alexandria. After Cain had shown Varro the design for the reaper and explained how it could be used, Varro leaned forward. "By how much do you estimate annual grain production may increase, all other things being equal?" Varro asked.

"By a minimum factor of tenfold," Cain replied. "A trial period with a prototype has been underway in Egypt for three years. The harvests have been incredible. With my invention, keeping your citizens well-fed will not require the grain resources of your neighbors." Cain noted that this last remark seemed to fall on deaf ears.

"Egyptian soil is known to be the most fertile in the world," Varro remarked. "Still, that output, if verifiable, is most appealing." Cain could see the wheels spinning inside Varro's head. If the reaper arrived on his watch, Varro would surely be elected to the higher steps on the political ladder in the Roman Republic: the praetorship and then the ultimate prize, the consulship.

"And how much do you want for these plans, Philo?"

Cain began the negotiations with the astronomical figure of one hundred million sesterces.

Varro drew himself up and glared darkly at his visitor.

"You know that we are a city at war, my friend. For fourteen years now, our treasury has been severely strained to bear the costs of our navy. Even now, the expense of a siege in western Sicily is costing us dearly."

Yes, thought Cain, but there would be much less of a burden if Rome would rein in her imperialist ambitions.

"Of course," he told Varro, "but imagine what the reaper will do for your tax base and the morale of your citizens. We can talk about the numbers, but let us first consider an additional idea."

Preparing to reel in Varro, Cain extracted some new drawings from the metal tube he carried. Spreading them out on Varro's worktable, he addressed the aedile pointedly.

"You are, I believe, in charge of all public buildings here?"

"That is correct."

"We have talked about grain, the people's food. But what about fresh water, which is just as essential? Here in the city, I see very few public fountains or baths."

Varro glanced downward. "That is because our tunneled construction methods have severe but inevitable limitations," he lapsed into bureaucratic euphemism.

"But what if you could use *this* method?" Cain gestured to the graceful storied bridges of his aqueduct design. "Wouldn't you manage to convey a higher volume of water faster and at less cost? Several hundred million gallons a day, I should say. Think of the advantages for public hygiene, at the very least."

Varro stared at the drawings before him. Cain saw the official's eyes widen slightly, and he knew then the deal was only a matter of price. Now the aedile called in his colleagues, and they bent over the worktable. Cain knew that any agreement would have to be endorsed by the other aediles as well, since all of Rome's magistracies operated on a principle of collegiality, by which one official of the same rank could veto his counterparts. At length, Varro looked up and delivered his verdict.

"Philo, this scheme of yours looks workable. But the initial outlay will be huge. Now that my colleagues have arrived, kindly state your terms."

"For the reaper and the aqueduct designs, I ask a payment of fifty million sesterces. That is far less than they are worth, gentlemen. So I also ask you to supplement the payment with some tracts of land."

Relieved that the price was feasible, Varro settled back in his chair and asked for specifics.

"You don't mean land here in crowded Rome, do you?" the aedile inquired.

"Not at all. I mean in Spain and North Africa. You Romans are active in both regions, and I am confident you will soon take control there." Concise flattery was worth any amount of reasoned argument.

Varro called for maps and the group carefully examined the areas Cain designated. Their potential, for both silver mining and glassmaking, was familiar to him from his wandering so long ago. The aediles, however, thinking that this gifted but eccentric inventor was requesting ownership of a wasteland, barely suppressed their laughter.

"I see no reason to object to the inventor's request," Varro assured his colleagues smoothly. "We will accede to your terms, Philo. We will convey a prospective deed to the registration office, and you may then complete the filing procedure there."

With the negotiations complete, the men parted. The cash payment would be forthcoming the very next day. Both sides were convinced they had scored a coup.

※

With a portion of the money from his bargain with the Romans, Cain made two key investments. Satisfied that its design was perfected, he hired the finest craftsmen to help him construct a working version of his finely geared navigational device. After years of testing from a fixed location, and finding its mapping of celestial movements to be accurate, he was anxious to deploy the device for its ultimate purpose.

Then, when the Carthaginian conflict ended in 241 BC, Cain financed the construction of a small, two-masted exploration vessel. He discarded his disguise as an old man and hired a new crew. The

ship's completion coincided with the advent of the sailing season
three years later. Christening her *Pegasus*, he raised anchor at Ostia,
Rome's busy port, for the return to Alexandria.

Far from pursuing a direct route, however, he decided to begin
his journey by heading westward. Aided by the navigational device
and the ship's shallow draft, which was ideal for coastal navigation,
he intended to conduct a thorough survey of the Mediterranean's
western regions, which were much more poorly charted than the
ports and harbors to the east. For some time, Cain had been troubled
by the mediocre quality—and even the flat-out inaccuracy—of the
charts and maps he had discovered, not only in Rome, but also in
Alexandria, where scholarship was prized.

Cartography was his new passion. With the results of the western
survey, he hoped to raise the Royal Alexandrian Library's map collection, as well as his own, to a new level.

CHAPTER 45

Alexandria, 238–214 BC

"Watch for the light," Cain shouted up to his lookout as the ship neared Alexandria. "Inform me the minute you see it!"

They had been at sea for eighteen months. At every port of call—from Saguntum in Spain to the Pillars of Hercules at Gibraltar and Carthage in North Africa— the recently completed lighthouse in Alexandria was the topic of the day. Sailors, merchants, and travelers alike asserted that it had to be seen to be believed.

"There it is, sir!" cried the lookout.

An extraordinary sight greeted Cain. Soaring high above the small island of Pharos, just off the coast, was a building whose apex rivaled that of the Great Pyramid at Giza. From his conversations, Cain had heard that the brilliant shafts of light emanating from the structure's zenith were magnified by a system of reflecting mirrors. The fuel for maintaining the fire, he learned, was animal dung. Whereas only small quantities of wood were readily available in Alexandria, dung was plentiful and cheap. The dream of the first Ptolemy had been achieved at last. The lighthouse, Cain thought, was not simply a marker for sailors. It was a magnet, a beacon to attract the citizens of the world.

"Home at last!" he exclaimed to his Roman-born crew. "Now you men will get to see a *really* big city."

As the crew finished off-loading the *Pegasus*, Cain gave final instructions to his captain.

"After your week of shore leave, take her to the port of Leptis Magna. I trust their shipwrights more than the people here. She'll probably need to be placed in dry dock to fix the leaks in the hull. There are plenty of coins in the treasury for the repairs and provisioning of the crew while you're there."

"Yes, sir. I will see to it," replied the captain dutifully.

"I trust you'll be able to use the new navigational device without my assistance?"

"Of course, sir. I had a bit of trouble with it when we started the voyage, but I've figured out the instruction manual now."

A thought occurred to Cain. Since he planned to remain in Alexandria for the foreseeable future, what did he need the Pegasus for, anyway? Inspired by the actions of his erstwhile Egyptian mentor, he said to his trusted captain, "One last thing. When the repairs are finished, the *Pegasus* is yours."

The astonished captain was completely at a loss for words, so Cain continued, "All I ask in exchange is that, on your return visits to Alexandria, you provide me with copies of any new charts you make."

"Sir," the captain beamed. "I promise you a treasure of knowledge of the coasts and seas!"

Unbeknownst to Cain, he would never see the captain nor the *Pegasus* again.

❧

Alexandria was a new city to Cain. The population had passed the quarter-million mark and was growing exponentially. The Royal Library had expanded so that it now occupied seven wings rather than two on the palace grounds. An offshoot collection of the library was housed in the city's newest and most magnificent temple, the Serapeum, dedicated to a combined Greek-Egyptian god named Serapis. A composite of Zeus, king of the gods in Greek religion, and Osiris, the renowned savior and divine conqueror of death in Egypt, Serapis functioned for the ruling Ptolemy dynasty as a cultural unifier. Cain admired the splendor of the temple but was privately bemused by the invention of yet another false god by humankind.

Fortunately, though, there was still a lot more to do in Alexandria than pray. At the first opportunity, Cain approached Eratosthenes, recently appointed by Ptolemy III as the chief librarian. Before their initial meeting, Cain had discreetly inquired into his background. By all accounts, Eratosthenes was a polymath: poet, mathematician, athlete, astronomer, and geographer. He had calculated the circumference of the earth. He had created a detailed map of the Nile. The people Cain talked to wondered what the man *hadn't* accomplished.

"Please show me your charts, Philo," Eratosthenes said when the two men convened in the new map room of the library. Cain had introduced himself as Philo, the great-nephew of Callias, whose sabbatical, he regretfully reported, had ended in Rome after a long terminal illness.

"These are extraordinary!" the erudite librarian exclaimed. Eratosthenes invited Cain to meet with his slightly older colleague Archimedes. Over a lavish meal in the communal dining room of the Mouseion, the three men discoursed on a wide range of topics: physics, astronomy, engineering, and the scientific method. At a neighboring table, a collection of scholars were engaged in animated discussion. Cain recognized the language as Hebrew. While it was not at all unusual to hear foreign tongues and accents in Alexandria, he wondered about the presence of such a large delegation in the Mouseion.

"Are these distinguished visitors?" he asked Eratosthenes, gesturing discreetly in the group's direction.

"Yes, Philo, they are. They are engaged in a remarkable project that enjoys His Majesty's patronage. About seventy in number, these scholars aim to expand the audience for the Hebrew Scripture by translating it into Greek. It is a book about their God, and the creation of the world. It is also, I am given to understand, a manual of conduct."

Having just seen the Serapeum temple, which also enjoyed the patronage of His Majesty, Cain was bewildered.

"King Ptolemy, then, remains open to many different faith traditions?" he inquired.

"Oh, indeed, yes! Our city cannot hope to be a beacon for the world if we close ourselves off. I am convinced that these scholars will make a mark. There is already a nickname for the text they are preparing. Since there are about seventy of them, their book will probably be known as the Septuagint."

Cain's ready appreciation of the Greco-Roman pun on the word for "seventy" was not lost on Eratosthenes. More importantly, his cartographic abilities signaled that he would be a valuable addition to the ranks at the Mouseion. Just as Zenodotus, years earlier, had offered Cain a fellowship there, Eratosthenes eventually broached the subject of institutional affiliation.

"I can promise you, Philo, that King Ptolemy Euergetes lives up to his name," the librarian told him several months later. "He is a philanthropist who creates good works. I have recommended to his council that you be appointed a fellow of the Mouseion. That is, if you are willing."

With an amused sense of déjà vu, Cain declared himself ready to accept the appointment.

❧

The years passed happily for Cain. Cartography was his primary interest, but the efforts of the Hebrew translators also intrigued him.

The group worked slowly but methodically. For their initial effort, translation into Greek of the Pentateuch, the five books of Moses, they had budgeted twenty-five years. Although some of the scholars could be abrasive, haggling over petty religious sticking points, they eventually settled their differences.

The linguistic proficiency of "Philo" attracted the attention of the translators, and they regularly invited him to attend their seminars. They were working backward within the Pentateuch, starting from the time of the first entry by the Hebrews into the promised land of Canaan. Reflecting on his painful departure from Egypt, Cain was intrigued to learn of the exploits of the refugee slaves during their own exodus. As he encountered the Hebrews' endless complaints during their desert wandering of a mere forty years, he felt a certain sense of pride in his own resiliency during his own time of wandering.

Cain couldn't help but wonder at the richness of the historical detail that Moses, the putative author of these books, had retained. How could these accounts have accurately survived for over one thousand years? He knew well from his career as a bard how easily facts became blurred as oral tradition attempted to hand them down. Yet the book contained a description of the plagues of Egypt that matched his experience exactly.

However, as the scholars neared the end of their journey and began to work on the book they called Genesis, his fascination was inexorably replaced by mounting discomfort. Encountering the story of Joseph in the last portion of Genesis, Cain was reminded how his own greed during the time of the plagues had backfired on him before Pharaoh—in sharp contrast to Joseph's altruistic leadership during an earlier famine in Egypt. The accounts of Noah and his descendants after the great flood induced a tide of depression in Cain. How could God have showered these people with blessings and divine promises after their many misdeeds, and yet cursed him with such extremes of loneliness and isolation? And the lurid description of the flood itself only heightened his somber memories.

Cain needed an escape from these bitter recollections. He decided to avoid the Hebrews' sessions and busy himself in his maps. Gradually, his good humor returned.

☙

Several months later, as he was strolling in the halls of the library, Cain encountered a young Hebrew scribe.

"Philo! We have missed you. Where have you been all this time?"

"I apologize for my absence. I am afraid Eratosthenes has been a bit of a slave driver with me lately," Cain fibbed.

"Well, you must be with us at tomorrow's celebration. Our work is complete! Your many contributions should be honored alongside all those of our group."

Cain could not bring himself to decline the invitation, so the next afternoon he gingerly entered the room where the scholars were holding their festivities. Accepting a goblet of wine from the young scribe who had greeted him the day before, Cain strolled the perimeter of the room as the boisterous group exchanged congratulations. Just then, Mordechai, the leader of the translators, noticed his presence. Encircling Cain's shoulders with his right arm, he brought him into the midst of their gathering.

"To our esteemed colleague, Philo!" he toasted. "Who else has enriched our efforts with such skill and nuance?"

Cain smiled and accepted the accolade as the gathered scholars raised their goblets in appreciation. Perhaps he would be able to relax and enjoy himself at the party. But his feelings quickly changed when he overheard a dialogue between two of the scholars a few paces away.

"My view, as you know Ezra, is that the murderer was treated too leniently. We have chronicled far more severe consequences for lighter offenses than Cain's evil deed."

"Yes, Shimon, but you must admit that Yahweh did us a great favor by ridding our forefathers of the bastard's presence. It would have ruined their own agriculture to spill his accursed blood along-side Abel's."

"Fair enough. *But Cain's death goes unrecorded!*" Shimon growled with a raised fist. "I still would find it a comfort to know he was not blessed with the long lives of Adam, Noah, and Methuselah."

The room swirled as the sound of his name reached Cain's ears for the first time in a millenium. These men all knew of his crime! His deeds were recorded in the Hebrew Scripture and were being spread throughout the world. But they had no idea of the irony of their remarks, nor the true scope of his punishment.

"Philo, where are you going? Are you ill?" Mordechai called, but Cain was already fleeing the room.

❧❦❧

Cain secluded himself completely over the next several weeks until the Hebrews had departed Alexandria. But tortured night after night by tormented dreams about his past, he sorely lamented his return to the library and yearned for new horizons.

One morning, fate provided the answer. As he was strolling across the quadrangle outside the main library, he was intercepted by a delegation of half a dozen foreign visitors from the East.

The group's leader, attired in stylish and colorful silk clothes, bowed low. A tall, thin man about fifty years old, he spoke fluent Greek and Egyptian. Cain instantly recollected that he had encountered this man before—at a dinner party hosted by Eratosthenes two years ago, but they had only exchanged pleasantries. From his garb and demeanor, this foreigner was certainly a person of some consequence.

"Esteemed sir," said the leader. "I am sincerely hoping that this detainment is not awkward for you. We should have dispatched advance notice. I am Kwok-se."

Cain bowed in reciprocation. "Of course. I remember well our prior meeting, Kwok-se. May I know the purpose of your return to Alexandria?" he inquired.

"We are on a trade mission, honored sir. But my patron has asked me to seek you out. I have written to him about your unexcelled abilities in map and chart making, and he now earnestly desires your presence."

"And who is your patron, if I may ask?"

Kwok-se's poise faltered, shocked as he was by the ignorance of this westerner, but he quickly recovered himself.

"He is the First Emperor of China, honored sir. He is known in many courts and many cities. His name is Qin Shihuangdi, may that name be forever praised!"

Like Kwok-se, the others in the delegation smiled and placed their hands over their hearts.

"Your *emperor* desires my presence, you say?" inquired Cain, with more than a trace of curiosity. "How could I be of service to him?"

"If I may call you Philo, sir, I should inform you that His Imperial Highness wishes to construct accurate maps of all the world. In particular, his will is that a giant map of the western world be hung in the royal throne room so that he may study it at any time. He also has plans to commission a huge globe made of precious gems and gold to be placed in the royal burial chamber."

"He is anticipating death soon?" Cain asked.

"Oh, no! His Imperial Highness is building a kingdom that will last ten thousand years. Whatever this kingdom's extent in time, he has found a potion of immortality that will allow him to rule eternally! There is no doubt about this fact."

Cain's curiosity was piqued. Never, even among the ancient pharaohs, had he heard about another man so convinced of his own immortality.

"And suppose I should agree," he hazarded. "How would we travel to meet with your patron?"

Kwok-se waved his hand, in courteous dismissal of such naïveté. "On the Silk Road, of course!" he exclaimed.

Two weeks later, Cain submitted his resignation from the faculty of the Alexandrian Mouseion.

The East beckoned.

CHAPTER 46

Naples, Italy: Present Day

"This is Captain Scirocco from the flight deck," said the voice over the Global Express's public address system. "We have begun our initial descent into Naples. The tower has informed me that we are the last flight that will be permitted to land this morning, due to a mild eruption of gas and ash from Mount Vesuvius. The weather in Naples is sunny, with a temperature of seventy-five degrees. We should be on the ground in thirty minutes."

Having slept comfortably through the flight, Giovanni Genoa accepted a glass of 1996 Barolo from Sharon. Spotting her from the rear of the cabin, Archibald Walker rattled the ice in his crystal tumbler, his now familiar signal for Sharon to mix him a fresh gin and tonic. As Rudolph Schmidt was making his way back to his seat from the restroom at the rear of the cabin, Walker hailed the attorney genially.

"Will you join me in one for the road?" Walker asked. "After all, the sun is nearly over the yardarm!"

Schmidt paused and then, ordering a Perrier and lime, sat down in the seat adjacent to Walker.

"Smooth flight. Very comfortable. And these jets are so quiet," he observed.

"Yes, they're the top of the line, I'm told," agreed Walker. "Now tell me, Mr. Schmidt, what is the outlook for title transfer of the archaeological site from Renard Enterprises to the Getty? We at the museum are eager to get started."

"Unfortunately, Dr. Walker, the Italian land transfer laws are extremely complex. You might even call them Byzantine. Surveys, indemnities, non-objection certificates, transfer taxes, national heritage depositions—that sort of thing. We might find this taking sixty to ninety days, or even longer."

For the second time that morning, chagrin overwhelmed Walker. He had been caught off guard when Silvio disclosed on the phone that Amanda had entered the chamber. Now, nervously fingering his purple signet ring, he wondered if Luc Renard was also intending to undercut him. "Mr. Renard led me to believe that everything could be wrapped up by tomorrow. We have already scheduled the press conference," he reminded Schmidt.

"Yes, I know, I know," the lawyer replied smoothly. "But you can't expect Mr. Renard to be bothered with the legal niceties. There will be no harm, at any rate, in announcing the company's *intention* to donate the site to the Getty."

"Well, I would very much hope so," said Walker in a sulky tone. "Otherwise, I might just as well have spent the weekend in the Polo Lounge at the Beverly Hills Hotel."

Just then, Luc Renard strolled down the aisle, smiling expansively. "Ready for the big moment, Dr. Walker?"

"It will certainly be an historic occasion for the Getty, Mr. Renard," Walker answered. "Only Mr. Schmidt here informs me that the transfer—"

Renard broke in, shooting Schimdt a glance. "There, there, dear Doctor. You know from experience that things proceed at their own pace in Italy. After all, it was only under Mussolini that the trains ran on time. Rest assured, we'll get it done as soon as we can, and you will have top billing for the new discovery. You certainly deserve it." Walker smiled in acknowledgment as Luc continued down the aisle and Schmidt returned to his seat. Fastening his seat belt, the Getty's man of the hour finished his cocktail and willed a measure of confidence to return.

                       ာ◌ာ

At the airport, Giovanni Genoa wished the other travelers good-bye, and the painter climbed into a limousine for his ride home to Rome.

Meanwhile, an Italian customs agent on the tarmac accorded the visitors VIP treatment, and the formalities took less than five minutes. Then Luc shepherded Schmidt and Walker to a waiting helicopter for the brief flight to Ercolano. It was eleven forty-five a.m.

Just before takeoff, two Italian bodyguards wearing earpieces slid into the chopper and seated themselves directly behind the pilot.

"Why all the security?" Walker asked Renard over the mounting roar of the rotors, noticing the telltale bulge of shoulder holsters beneath the bodyguards' jackets.

"Routine procedure, Doctor," replied Luc reassuringly as he patted Walker's shoulder. "I always take them with me when I travel abroad."

Walker glanced across at Luc, but his eyes were unreadable behind his mirrored glasses. The helicopter rose into the air and headed out over the sparkling bay, southeast for Ercolano.

CHAPTER 47

The Silk Road and China, 214–213 BC

"I s there any sort of market there?" Cain asked as they were approaching Kashgar, the halfway point to the City of Xi'an on the Silk Road.

"In Kashgar?" Kwok-se replied incredulously. "Surely you jest, my friend! It is one of the finest markets in the world. Simply extraordinary what you can find there."

"Excellent! I am eager to try out my Chinese."

"Your Chinese, both spoken and written, is almost as good as mine, Philo. I cannot believe you have mastered my own language in a matter of months."

"You are a patient teacher, Kwok-se." Cain knew his own facility for languages, but a fluent command of more than six thousand Chinese characters had been a daunting goal, even for him. He had spent many late nights on the way to Xi'an huddled in a tent with a candle and a roll of parchment.

The sand-blown faces of the camel drivers brightened as the travelers' caravan approached Kashgar. An oasis city poised between the rugged mountains of the Tian Shan range and one of the most arid deserts in the world, the town would be their home for the next fifteen days, as they paused their journey to enjoy the festive celebrations of the New Year.

As they rode into town, Kwok-se recounted to his companion the legendary origins of the New Year's festival.

"Many of our New Year's customs are rooted in the story of Nian, a cruel and ferocious monster. The reason we paste red paper signs on doorways, for example, is to keep Nian away on New Year's Eve. We light torches and make loud noises for the same purpose."

"And why is Nian so much to be feared?" Cain wanted to know.

"Very simple," Kwok-se laughed. "He eats people!"

They stayed at an inn operated by an old friend of Kwok-se. After all the camels were unpacked and the horses stabled, the two men set out to visit the marketplace. Cain soon realized that his friend had not exaggerated. Kashgar was a bustling mercantile crossroads of the Silk Road, the five-thousand-mile artery that linked eastern China with the West. The faces and headgear of the merchants and shoppers told of their origins in India, Persia, Egypt, and Arabia as well as China. Cain even thought he could recognize a Roman or two. In the dusty alleyways, seemingly everything was available: sandalwood, lacquer, porcelain, woolen carpets, aloes, frankincense, and silk brocade. Donkey carts jostled for space with horses and herds of sheep, their drivers shouting commands and warnings in a babel of tongues.

While Kwok-se examined a jeweler's topaz collection with a view toward securing a gift for his daughter in Xi'an, Cain amused himself by bargaining with a Chinese trader for a small sandal-wood image of the Buddha. In addition to serving as a fulcrum for worldly goods, Kashgar was a Buddhist refuge, with dozens of monasteries dotted around the town. Bantering in Chinese, Cain offered to barter with the man, producing one of the small pocket compasses he had brought along for the journey. The trader had never seen such a device before and stared in amazement. After Cain briefly explained the uses of the magnetic pointer, the Chinese merchant readily agreed to the deal. "Kung-hsi Fa-ts'ai!" he exclaimed. "Happy New Year!"

During their layover in Kashgar, they spent many hours discussing the ways in which Emperor Qin Shihuangdi had forged a unified China. The emperor's father had reigned over the Qin state for only three years, with his son inheriting the succession at the tender age of thirteen. By the time he was twenty-five, the new ruler had foiled several coups and assassination attempts. He then subjugated seven warring states, achieving by the age of forty an accomplishment that few had thought possible. Now he was engaged in building a great wall to secure his northern frontier against invading nomads.

"Where does the labor come from for such a formidable undertaking?" Cain asked.

Kwok-se stared at Cain incredulously. "Surely you jest, Philo. He *is* the emperor!"

Inferring that the manpower was supplied by peasants, slaves, or conquered enemies, Cain changed the subject.

"Tell me more about the elixir of immortality. How has the emperor discovered such a wonder drug?"

Kwok-se's face was impassive. "When the time is right, you will be able to pose that question to His Majesty yourself," he replied.

"And what have been the results of unification?"

On this topic, Kwok-se was more forthcoming. "Unification of the states has been an epochal achievement. Weights, measures, and coinage have been standardized, permitting vast new commercial growth. Law and administration are applied uniformly and consistently. Most important of all, everyone now speaks the same language, by order of the emperor."

"The emperor's writ certainly runs wide."

"He has surely been sent to us from heaven," Kwok-se remarked gravely.

"When do you think we will arrive in Xi'an?"

"That is in the hands of fate. But we must be in the capital before next winter sets in. I have a wedding to attend."

"Who is getting married?" inquired Cain.

"You will see, my friend! Your honored self is on the invitation list."

☙❧

The travelers departed from Kashgar at the close of the New Year celebrations. They still had twenty-five hundred miles to go to Xi'an, the Emperor's capital, and it was bitterly cold in the desert. Slowly, however, spring crept across the face of China. When they arrived in Dunhuang, where the northern arm of the Silk Road rejoined the southern route, temperatures were positively balmy. Here they glimpsed the stone and earth fortifications of the emperor's great wall, as well as the delicate, colorful murals in the local Buddhist grottoes.

"Buddhism seems extremely widespread in your land, Kwok-se," ventured Cain. "I have heard tell, however, that the most influential social and ethical philosophy in China is the legacy of the teacher Confucius."

In a rare display of impatience, Kwok-se abruptly shook his head. "No, Philo, Confucius is not to the emperor's liking. Or I should say, he is not to the emperor's prime minister's liking. Li Si cannot tolerate Confucius. In fact, he has persuaded the emperor to outlaw Confucian books and scholarship. Whole libraries have been burned... and worse."

Recalling Alexandria a bit wistfully now, Cain decided not to inquire what "worse" might refer to.

They were halfway between Dunhuang and Lanzhou when bandits accosted them. "Don't worry," Kwok-se smilingly reassured his fellow traveler as their caravan was rapidly surrounded by several hundred horsemen. "I have something to show them."

SILK

Rome

Mediterranean Sea

BLACK SEA

CASPIAN SEA

Antioch

PER

Alexandria

EGYPT

Nile River

ARABIA

ARABIAN

N
W E
S

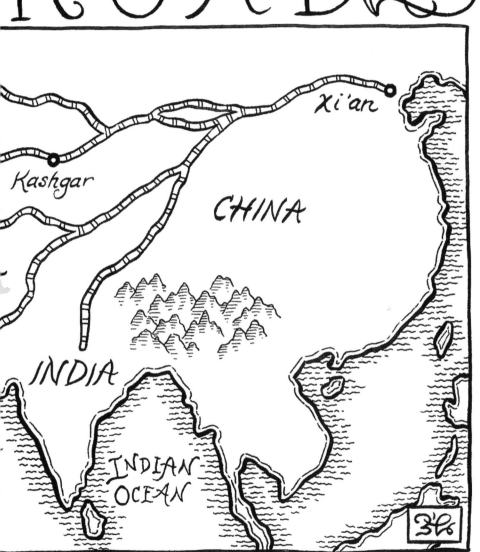

Cain watched closely as his friend, mounted on his favorite black Arabian stallion, calmly approached the bandit chieftain. Kwok-se withdrew several articles from his saddlebag, and within minutes the chieftain lowered his head in submission, murmuring a few words. With a jaunty salute to the chieftain's followers, Kwok-se rejoined Cain.

"What did you show him?"

"Oh, I simply displayed to him my golden passports from His Sovereign Majesty. Remember, I am a diplomat by profession," Kwok-se replied nonchalantly. "We shouldn't have any trouble from here on. In fact, they have offered to escort us the rest of the way to the capital. Since that is nearly eight hundred miles, the bandits are making a meaningful gesture." Kwok-se threw Cain a wink. "I told their chief I would be sure to inform His Majesty."

And so the caravan gradually neared Xi'an, the capital city of the First Sovereign Emperor, traveling on a system of excellent roads and canals that His Majesty had caused to be built. About fifty miles from their destination, a strange sight puzzled Cain. The broad highway was partitioned into three compartments, with walls constructed to seal off a center lane.

"What is the reason for the walls along this highway?" he inquired.

"Ever since an assassination attempt several years ago," Kwok-se replied, "the emperor has devised unusual safety precautions on his travels. He has ordered a network of walled roads for the imperial outings he undertakes from time to time. He also uses a suite of identical carriages."

A visionary, Cain thought. But also a man who was both hated and feared.

❦

The following morning, Cain and Kwok-se enjoyed breakfast on the veranda of Kwok-se's picturesque estate on the banks of the River Wei in Xi'an. Cain wondered how a midlevel diplomat could afford such palatial surroundings of this magnitude. But then he recalled that Kwok-se and the ruler had grown up together as children—a fact that his friend had revealed during a late-night drinking session on the Silk Road.

After their meal, they were escorted to the imperial palace by a detachment of ramrod-straight bodyguards, clad in sleek body armor and black pheasant-tailed caps. The emperor's palace, located in the northwest quadrant of the city with splendid river views and lavish gardens festooned in riotous colors, was built on an astonishing scale. Above the dozen wings of the principal structure, a kaleidoscopic series of pagodas formed a veritable skyline. It dwarfed anything Cain had ever seen, including his palace in Enoch.

The great bronze doors were adorned with pale green porcelain and lavender jade inlays depicting dragons, foo dogs, and demons in combat. As they slowly swung open, the imperial master of ceremonies bowed low to the visitors. "Please take your seats in the throne room, gentlemen," he intoned.

"Remember the motto," murmured Kwok-se. Cain had it on the tip of his tongue.

He estimated the throne room was two hundred yards by one hundred and fifty. On such a scale, thousands of people could be accommodated at imperial audiences. This morning, however, it appeared that the enormous hall had been reserved especially for them, with but one exception.

Li Si, the Emperor's prime minister, entered grandly dressed in flowing robes of gold-embroidered black silk. He bowed ceremoniously.

"Kwok-se, dear to His Majesty's heart, how happy is your return from foreign lands! The Emperor rejoices in your safe arrival here in Xi'an."

Something in the prime minister's manner signaled to Cain that the words were not entirely sincere.

Responding with exaggerated courtesy of his own, Kwok-se replied jovially, "Surely you jest! Of course we are safe! The imperial bandits accompanied us here all the way from Lanzhou."

Li Si raised an eyebrow. "Bandits, you say? I know of no such bandits in our precincts. In China, the rule of law is as universal as it is absolute."

At that very moment, with the reverberation of an enormous gong, the First Emperor entered the hall, surrounded by groups of scribes, guards, and ministers of state. All three men bowed low as His August Majesty, Qin Shihuangdi, ascended his throne of emerald, jade, and gold.

Cain studied the ruler's features. About forty-five, he had the body of a warrior, as well as a few facial scars, evidencing past combat. His head was surmounted by a tightly twisted topknot. He sported a double-edged Jian sword in a black brocade belt wrapped around his tunic. The "gentleman of weapons," as the Chinese saying went, the sword looked as if the blade had been carved from a single piece of jade. Altogether a commanding presence.

Cain had not anticipated the voice, however. In a booming, resonant bass, the emperor began the audience by addressing his scribes.

"Let the reports on the revenues from each commandery be in my hands no later than tomorrow evening," he ordered, referring to the administrative districts into which all China was now divided. "You are now dismissed, my scribes, so that you will not fail to fulfill my orders."

Turning to his prime minister, the emperor inquired if there were any matters deserving of the ruler's attention. Li Si, gesturing to Kwok-se and Cain, addressed the ruler in a fawning tone.

"The travelers from abroad attend on you, sire," he said, somewhat superfluously.

As if on cue, Kwok-se and Cain promptly straightened from their bows. The emperor cast a bemused gaze on both his visitors. He motioned to Kwok-se to address him.

"The bright virtue of the August Emperor aligns and orders the whole universe," the emperor's old friend recited.

"You are safely returned, Kwok-se! The sight of you gladdens my heart!" His affection for his schoolmate was obvious.

"Majesty, I have brought from the Far West some gifts for your inspection." Palace guards, who had transported a selection of the treasures from Alexandria, promptly laid them out directly in front of the throne. An appreciative smile brightened the emperor's face, although Cain thought it was peculiar that no papyrus scrolls were included in the collection of gifts.

After a few minutes, during which the emperor inspected the gifts, Kwok-se continued, "But the most valuable treasure I have secured in Egypt stands beside me in your presence, Majesty. I have the distinct privilege to introduce you to Philo of Alexandria, the most eminent cartographer of his, or any, age."

An even broader smile radiated from the emperor's face.

"A cartographer? How delightful! Is the foreigner perchance conversant with our language?" Qin Shihuangdi seemed afflicted with some sort of nervous tic, causing him to blink his left eye irregularly, but it did not detract from the man's imposing dynamism.

Cain again bowed low and then recited, "The bright virtue of the August Emperor aligns and orders the whole universe." His accentual, rhythmic tones were perfect. The emperor had not expected a visitor gifted with such fluency.

"You speak our language magnificently, Philo of Alexandria. I am delighted! May I see a sample of your cartographic work?"

Having been primed by Kwok-se, Cain withdrew from a satchel a papyrus roll on which he had created a beautifully detailed map of the Mediterranean coastline, ranging westward from ancient Phoenicia in the Levant to the Pillars of Hercules at Gibraltar. He spread the scroll out at the foot of the throne. The emperor signaled a servant to bring the map to him so that he could examine it more closely.

"This is extraordinary! Maps are my passion. Will you be able to accept a commission for some new projects?"

"I would be honored, Majesty," replied Cain, knowing that to refuse would be ungracious, at the very least. "What do you wish?"

"Here in the palace in Xi'an," the Emperor gestured around with a lordly sweep of his left arm, "we harbor large dreams. I have a dining room that accommodates six thousand guests for state dinners. On one wall of this room, I desire a map of the entire western world. Can you fulfill my desire?"

"I have traveled far and wide, Majesty. I will attempt to do your bidding."

"Excellent!" declared the Emperor. "Now, my ministers, you may depart." Bowing in salutation, all the attendees at the audience, including Li Si, processed from the room.

When they were gone, the Emperor rose and descended the steps from the throne. Throwing his arms around Kwok-se, he embraced him warmly.

"How I have missed you these five long years! You must never leave me again. And we have the wedding plans to discuss, Kwok-se. Winter is not far off."

To Cain's astonishment, the wedding Kwok-se had returned to Xi'an to attend, and to which Cain was invited, would unite Kwok-se's own daughter with the emperor's second son, Hu Hai, in marriage.

The emperor changed the subject abruptly and addressed Cain.

"The dimensions of the palace dining room will be conveyed to you by my secretaries. I hope you will be able to start on the map immediately. It will be an important addition. But for now, my wish is for you both to accompany me on a royal outing."

Gazing at Kwok-se meaningfully, the ruler imparted, "In your absence, I have accelerated a prized new project, old friend! There has been nothing like it ever before. Nothing!"

The emperor's left eye blinked rapidly, while Kwok-se and Cain bowed in assent. Placing his arms around the shoulders of his guests, Emperor Qin Shihuangdi swept them out of the throne room.

CHAPTER 48

China, 213–212 BC

They rode in rumbling, elaborately decorated imperial carriages down the highway's walled center lane to a destination nearly twenty miles east of Xi'an, just beyond Huaqing Hot Springs. The First Emperor was clearly relishing the suspense he had created in his guests.

"Have you any idea where we are headed?" he asked Kwok-se, poking him jovially on the arm.

"How could I, Majesty? It is you who have graciously planned today's itinerary."

They alighted in front of an enormous earthen mound. There were no buildings visible as far as the eye could see.

Kwok-se ventured a question to his old friend. "Have you brought us here, then, to appreciate this beautiful countryside?"

The emperor guffawed. "Surely you jest! You see, do I not remember your mercurial manner of speaking, old friend? Come, follow me."

Attended by the palace escort, they circled on foot to the back side of the towering mound. To the guests' amazement, the earth lay open, with tens of thousands of laborers working in a deep, subterranean pit in utter silence. As with everything undertaken by the First Emperor, the scale of the excavation was mind-boggling.

"What figures are those men fashioning?" asked Kwok-se as he pointed to an array of life-size statues.

"They are creating my army, my friend. Out of terra-cotta, but the warriors' swords and the other weapons are real." The emperor turned to inspect the clay army before continuing. "And so will be the soldiers, once the heavens endow them with the breath of life."

"But surely, Majesty, do you not already have a full roster of living and breathing troops?"

"Of course, of course," replied the emperor with an impatient wave of the hand and some more rapid eye blinks. "But *these* troops are special. Unlike my run-of-the-mill conscripts, or even my heroic veteran officers, *these* will live forever." He drew rapid breaths for emphasis.

Cain recalled Kwok-se's previous remarks on the subject of the emperor's obsession with immortality. He stared at the serried ranks of terra-cotta soldiers, each of them life-size and impeccably attired in studded plate armor. The workers were evidently using an assembly-line technique to create the torsos, with individual heads and limbs subsequently added to fashion an immense gallery of lifelike, realistically differentiated individuals. At least two thousand troops had been completed, with ample space in this pit for thousands more. Their robes, in brilliant vermilion and green, imbued them with an extraordinary vitality. Such a force could certainly withstand any hostile charge in the spirit world.

They continued on. Beyond a nearby hillside were factory buildings housing workshops for bronze chariots, terra-cotta horses, and the manufacture of clay acrobats and musicians. Exquisite bronze waterfowl accompanied the instrumentalists, a graceful embellishment for their never-to-be-heard melodies. Yet another factory was devoted solely to stone armor and helmets.

Cain, emboldened by the emperor's magnanimous mood and apparently close friendship with Kwok-se, sensed it might be the appropriate time to probe the ruler's interest in a life without end. Still, he took care to phrase his question tactfully.

"When we first met in Alexandria, Majesty, Kwok-se informed me that you had discovered a potion or elixir that confers immortality. Is it not so?"

The emperor turned to him and lowered his voice. "I was *hoping* to discover it," he confided. "I even made two visits to Zhifu Island—you must know it, yes?—and dispatched hundreds of inhabitants there to search Penglai Mountain on that quest. They never returned." He paused and chuckled. "But then, to return without the elixir would have required them to demonstrate their *own* mortality, wouldn't it?"

There was an awkward pause in the conversation. Then the emperor continued, "But we have not finished, gentlemen. Come this way!" He held his hand aloft, as if he were signaling a sizable group of visitors to follow him.

As they strolled briskly westward, the emperor explained that the entire burial complex occupied an area of approximately twenty-five square miles. Cain cast his mind back to the Egyptians. In comparison with the Valley of the Kings opposite Luxor, in whose graves many pharaohs had been interred, the emperor's complex was enormous. The First Emperor's necropolis dwarfed even the Great Pyramids.

Behind a strongly fortified wall in the distance there loomed an even more gigantic, mound-like structure. "Now *that* is the reason for all this. You see how well it is positioned. The slopes of Mt. Li guard it to the south, and the River Wei lies on the northern side. To the west, the Qinling Mountains protect it. And my terra-cotta army guards the eastern side."

The men entered a gate on the northern side of the outer wall. Then, after they passed through an entrance in the inner wall, the enormous mound lay directly in front of them. Roughly square-shaped, it covered over a million square feet and soared nearly three hundred feet into the air.

"If my life-mandate should ever expire, I shall be comfortable here, and well protected," declared the emperor with satisfaction. It soon became clear that the project was nothing less than the construction of an underground palace that would be impregnable, not only to enemies from the spirit world but to time itself.

In that special way, China's First Emperor would indeed be immortal.

With His Majesty leading the way, they descended more than two hundred feet into a vast subterranean chamber. By the light of seal-fat lamps, thousands of workers were busily carving a giant stone map of China on the floor. Teams of skilled craftsmen embedded pearls and other precious stones on the ceiling to create a gleaming heavenly vault.

Here, beneath the emperor's tumulus, earth and sky conjoined in an entire cosmos to form a facsimile of the living world. On the huge map, mountains of beaten copper had been placed, and clusters of precious stones marked the location of cities. Around the map's edges and traversing the interior ran silvery rivers and streams of mercury. As Cain and Kwok-se gazed in awe, they could hear the whirring noise of concealed machines, making the liquid flow.

Since the dawn of humanity, Cain had never seen such an elaborate building project—or a leader with such a grand view of himself.

◑◈◐

Not about to disappoint his new patron, Cain threw himself wholeheartedly into the map project for the state dining room in the palace. The emperor gave him carte blanche to hire skilled artisans, and Cain promptly interviewed and coordinated a team of two hundred craftsmen. He even enlisted the managers of a silk factory in order to explore new materials for the map. Tough yet elegant in appearance, the surface that he devised and called silk paper would appeal to the ruler, he thought, as much for its novelty as for its aesthetic qualities. In accordance with the dimensions relayed by palace officials, Cain designed the map to be seventy-five feet tall and three hundred feet long—large enough for the state dining room wall, but still puny in size when compared to the stone map of China on the royal mausoleum floor.

Every day he worked well into the night, not only on the map project but also on another commission the emperor had assigned him. This was the construction of a large, decorative globe, which the emperor intended for his tomb. There it would have a symbolic function, just like the great stone map of China, the starry heavens, and the rivers of mercury—believed by many astrologers and physicians of the day to be the base of all metals and a powerful element in prolonging life and health.

From a group of Chinese astronomers known to Kwok-se, Cain procured a stony meteorite that had fallen from the heavens many centuries before. From the perspective of both space and time, he considered it a perfect core for his globe of the world. Once again, the emperor would appreciate the novelty of the artifact. After his workmen had shaped and polished the meteorite into a perfect sphere, he had it coated in gold and then planned inlays of colorful minerals and precious gems for the outline of the world's known continents. The North and South Poles were shown as circles in white. Cain had not personally seen the poles, but he borrowed the idea from a conversation he once held with astronomers in Alexandria. He did, however, pay a visit to eastern China to verify the accuracy of charts showing the Yellow Sea coastline.

Cain's goal was to complete both the map and the globe before the royal wedding. Thus, cartography in two and three dimensions would constitute a special salute to the emperor for this joyous occasion. As the marriage day approached, he exhorted his artisan teams to work ever harder.

Cain was not the only person in Xi'an working overtime. For his tomb complex, the Emperor had conscripted over 700,000 laborers, ordering more than 120,000 families to relocate to the capital from other parts of China. Now, to cope with the wedding preparations, tens of thousands more workers streamed into the city. Facilities were strained, but the laborers were sorely needed, since it was anticipated that one million people would attend the ceremonies. The wedding festivities would stretch over a two-week period—by far the most spectacular celebration China had ever witnessed.

The fortune-telling masters had set the royal marriage day for two weeks after the lunar New Year, toward the end of February. Further, it was determined that the marriage would be celebrated in winter and also that all wedding gifts would be in monetary amounts divisible by six, the emperor's sacred number. These factors would ensure a happy and long-lasting union.

At the moment of the most important ceremony, the young couple would face north, the cardinal direction associated with the power of water, the emperor's element. Although Qin Shihuangdi mandated the use of black, his signature color, for flags, pennants, and garments at state occasions, he permitted the traditional use of red at weddings, since red was the color of happiness. Therefore the principal participants—the bridal couple and their parents and close relatives—would dress in red, which was also the color of many of the wedding decorations.

One month before the wedding, the map and globe were ready. To Cain's relief, the emperor's admiration was rapturous.

"I have seldom seen him so overjoyed," said Kwok-se to Cain after the formal presentation at the palace. The two were seated on the main veranda of Kwok-se's estate overlooking the river. "You may bask in your triumph," he continued. "You surely deserve it, Philo. The cartography on both artifacts is superb!"

Cain smiled at his friend's compliment. Kwok-se was certainly practiced in the art of diplomacy.

"Did you see Li Si's face when the attendants unveiled the map?" he asked Kwok-se.

"I did not miss his look of envy. Be cautious with him. That man is a schemer. His strict legal system has produced conformity at the expense of innovation in this country. And I suspect," said Kwok-se, lowering his voice and glancing around the veranda to ensure they were alone, "that he is ruining the emperor's health."

Cain thought these comments cryptic, but after working so intensively, he looked forward to enjoying himself at the upcoming marriage ceremonies. So he changed the subject, asking Kwok-se to describe some of the traditional wedding customs in China.

"My daughter Changying, who will be married precisely one month from today, was actually betrothed to Hu Hai before either of them was born."

Cain was amazed. "Isn't that somewhat unusual?" he asked.

"Oh, no, it happens often in wealthy families. Two wives pregnant at the same time will make an agreement. If the children are both boys or both girls, they will grow up as brothers or sisters. But if they turn out to be of the opposite sex, they will marry. The idea is to strengthen family alliances and finances. And, of course, the families want to ensure a succession with the birth of sons. My wife was pregnant with Changying at the same time as the emperor's most favored wife, and they were good friends."

"What do the actual wedding rituals include?"

"Well, one of my favorites is the hair combing," his friend replied. "The night before the wedding day, both bridegroom and bride instruct specially chosen attendants to comb their hair four times. Each combing has a symbolic meaning. The first stands for beginning to end, the second symbolizes harmony from now until old age, the third is for many sons and grandsons, and the fourth is for wealth and a long-lasting marriage."

"Yet it seems common in China for men to take concubines," Cain injected. "How is that consistent with a long-lasting marriage, Kwok-se?"

The diplomat smiled at Cain's naïveté. "Surely you jest, my friend! Many women increase a man's chance of an heir. Look at it this way," he said, gesturing to the lavishly lacquered tea table. "One teapot is usually placed with four cups around it. Have you ever seen one cup with four teapots?"

CHAPTER 49

China, 212 BC

O n the wedding day, Cain awoke to a deafening din of gongs and drums. The music signaled the approach of Hu Hai's procession from the palace to Kwok-se's estate. In keeping with tradition, Changying, wearing a red silk veil, was transported in a specially curtained sedan chair to the palace, where the formal marriage ceremony would take place. She was shielded by a crimson parasol, whose ritual opening signified her future conception of many progeny. At the rear of the sedan chair, a sieve was suspended to strain away evil, and a mirror would reflect sunlight. A young boy accompanied the procession—another harbinger of the bride's future sons.

On the bride's journey, no effort was spared to ward off evil spirits or inauspicious sights such as a widow, a well, or even a cat. Preceding the sedan chair, hundreds of attendants scattered grain, beans, and rice, symbolic of fertility. Care was taken that the bride's feet did not touch the bare earth at any point during the journey.

Kwok-se and Cain rode to the palace in a ceremonial carriage furnished by the emperor. The formal ceremony took place in the throne room and was surprisingly brief. In front of their beaming parents, Hu Hai and Changying approached the royal family altar and paid homage to the deities of heaven and earth, as well as the family ancestors. A profound bow to each other completed the wedding of bride and groom.

❦

That evening, under red-and-black striped tents on the palace grounds, the emperor hosted a sumptuous feast for twenty thousand of the most distinguished guests. Men and women were seated separately, according to custom. Musicians played, acrobats and jugglers performed, and jesters and storytellers entertained the company. Archery contests were held by the light of flaming torches mounted on poles. Kwok-se dragged Cain away an hour before sunrise. It was time for the bride's father to make his own preparations for the reciprocal banquet, scheduled for the following evening, to be held at Kwok-se's estate.

Although it was less elaborate, Cain found Kwok-se's feast more enjoyable. Several thousand guests streamed into the estate, but the crowds were not as overwhelming as they had been at the palace. Circulating among the guests, Cain felt like a celebrity. After all, few Chinese had ever encountered a westerner, let alone one fluent in their own language.

The emperor bestowed special favor on Kwok-se by attending the banquet personally. Late that evening, after the bridal couple had retired, Qin Shihuangdi invited Cain to return to the palace with him for more drinks and discussion.

"Let us travel on horseback," he declared. "We don't need the official carriages. We can take the black Arabian stallions that Kwok-se presented as part of Changying's dowry."

His slurred speech and erratic, lurching movements suggested that the emperor had been drinking a great deal at the party, but Cain knew him to be an excellent horseman.

"I am honored, Majesty. I will ask Kwok-se to order the grooms to prepare the horses immediately."

Qin Shihuangdi and Cain bade their host good night and cantered out side by side from the estate to the palace road, preceded and followed by military escorts. Halfway to their destination, as they rode through a stretch of highway overshadowed by a grove of plum trees, a careless soldier in the row ahead allowed an overhanging branch to snap back, cutting Cain's left cheek. Outraged, the emperor dug in his spurs and, with a single stroke of his Jian sword, sliced the man dead. He then returned, voicing concern for the inch-long gash his guest had sustained.

Shaken by the ruler's violent explosion, Cain reassured him, "It is only a scratch, Majesty."

❦

"Kwok-se is a dear friend, Philo, but the rice wine he served at the banquet was revolting."

They were standing in front of the great map in the state dining room. "Here, try this grape wine from the imperial cellar. A far superior vintage, I am sure you will agree."

With his own hand, the First Emperor decanted the ruby-red liquid from a bronze storage vessel into large porcelain goblets.

"To immortality!" the Emperor toasted. Cain, betraying none of the irony he felt, raised his goblet in salute to his host.

"Come now, tell me tales of the West," the Emperor exhorted. "Your map will inspire us as we walk up and down."

They talked long past midnight. Qin Shihuangdi's curiosity seemed insatiable. He was well informed about contemporary developments, even mentioning Rome's devastating setbacks in her Second Punic War against Carthage. He seemed especially interested in the military prowess of other states, along with their development of new technologies. Cain wondered if His August Majesty were not contemplating further additions to his empire.

After liberal quantities of Chinese spirits had topped the grape wine, the Emperor abruptly summoned one of his physicians. Lanky and balding, with a wispy beard and a crooked spine, the man bowed his head respectfully and then placed a vial in the royal hands. After the doctor silently withdrew from the room, Qin Shihuangdi confided in Cain, "He was recommended by Li Si. They feed me medications, you know. The preparations taste terrible, but they are sure to prolong my life!"

His voice was animated but strikingly uneven as he emptied the bottle's contents into a goblet of liquor. "To immortality!" he repeated.

"If I may ask, Majesty, what does the vial contain?"

"Why, mercury, of course!" replied the Emperor with a sly grin and sporadic eye blinks. "Do you not know that quicksilver is the sustainer of all life?"

☙❧

Qin Shihuangdi retired two hours before sunrise. After the emperor had staggered from the room, supported by a pair of burly guards, a group of uniformed attendants led Cain to his quarters, where servants had placed an array of fruits and accompaniments. Also waiting for him was a guest the emperor had not mentioned. She was endowed with sleek, raven tresses and a regal stature that reminded him of one of the emperor's bronze waterfowl in the mausoleum.

"I am Lijuan, honorable sir. I am here to see that your every comfort is provided," she murmured softly while bowing low. Cain thought the name was familiar. After a moment, he recalled that Kwok-se had mentioned this young woman, whose name meant "beautiful and graceful," as one of the Emperor's favorite concubines.

As she prepared the bed, Lijuan told Cain, "How unusual that you know Chinese! Where did you learn our language so fluently?"

Cain could only respond that Kwok-se had taken pains to teach him during their journey from the West to Xi'an on the Silk Road.

"And what was your profession in the West?"

"I was a cartographer and an engineer."

"An engineer! Such an inspiring profession. You must have been the builder of many great inventions."

"Sunrise is at hand," he pointed out, a bit superfluously. Gesturing to the bed, he added, "Let us enjoy it."

Lijuan smiled alluringly. "But before we retire, sir, allow me to treat your wound."

Removing the bandage from Cain's cheek, she smeared honey on the gash to prevent infection. Cain placed his finger on the honey, and then offered it to Lijuan's lips to taste. Drawing her close, he folded her into the soft pillows.

CHAPTER 50

China, 212–210 BC

The gilt-tinged rays of sunrise slanting through the bamboo slats failed to awaken Cain. But Lijuan, always a light sleeper, lifted her head from the satin-encased pillows and glided across the polished, inlaid floor. Donning a gorgeous peach-colored robe of silk brocade, she returned to the bedside and gazed at Cain's sleeping visage.

To her surprise, the wound on his left cheek was completely healed.

Slipping noiselessly from the bedchamber, Lijuan headed directly for the emperor's quarters, where the guards admitted her straightaway.

Two hours later, a peremptory knock on the bedchamber door forced its way into Cain's consciousness. A loud, officious-sounding voice informed him that his presence at the royal breakfast table was required, so he hastened to do the host's bidding. Before unlocking the bedchamber door, however, he took the precaution of examining his left cheek in the mirror. As he expected, the sunrise reliably heralded his complete recuperation from such minor wounds. Without the means at hand to re-cut himself, he promptly applied a new bandage to the area where the gash had been. Idly wondering about Lijuan's whereabouts, he opened the door and was promptly escorted by the emperor's attendants through the palace hallways.

"Have some kumquats!" the emperor invited in a hearty, welcoming tone as Cain arrived at breakfast. "Delicious, hardy fruit, and so good for the digestion. I consume great quantities of them each morning."

Flanked by Lijuan, who smiled sweetly, the Emperor presided at the head of a jet-black lacquered table in the sunny breakfast room. This part of the palace resembled a conservatory, for it was crowded with aromatic, brightly flowering plants. As Cain seated himself opposite the sovereign, an attendant immediately poured him a cup of steaming, fragrant tea and offered a glazed bowl of the pale, golden fruit. Something in the Emperor's gaze told him that His Majesty had more than dietary considerations on his mind this morning.

"So now, Philo, what of your cheek wound? I notice you have applied a fresh bandage. May I see more closely? I should have ordered my doctor to examine you last evening. You have served me so admirably, my friend, that I feel that your health touches my own!"

Without waiting for Cain's acquiescence, Qin Shihuangdi rose from his carved chair and circled the table.

"Let us see how the healing is progressing," cooed the emperor as he peeled back the new bandage with his left hand. His right hand went to the polished Jian sword at his belt. Glancing at Lijuan, he drummed his fingers on the sword's hilt. Cain noted that the concubine averted her eyes from the emperor's glance.

Cain realized he had to concoct an explanation immediately, and one that the emperor would find convincing.

"Your wound is completely healed, Philo! Will you kindly tell me how this is possible?"

Cain's eyes briefly darted about, falling on one of the emperor's many wall maps. His answer flashed to him as he recalled his charting trip to the eastern Chinese coast.

"Of course, Majesty. I did not deem it worthy of mention at the time, but on my trip to the Yellow Sea some months ago, I chanced upon some medicinal herbs said by the local residents to possess marvelous healing qualities. With these plants, I was able to create a single dose of elixir. This is what I used on the cheek wound last evening after we parted. I hesitated to inform you, though, until I verified the medicine's potency."

The emperor listened intently to Cain's tale. Then he relaxed his grip on the sword and returned to his seat.

"Well, it seems that your concoction is most effective!" he exclaimed. Knitting his brows together, he continued, "You are a very resourceful man, and not just in cartography, Philo of Alexandria. If you have created one healing dose of medicine from these herbs, I should imagine that you can produce more. My alchemists will be at your disposal. They have extensive experience."

"You may rely on my most obedient efforts, Majesty. But the herbs were not plentiful, and my supply is now exhausted."

The Emperor waved his hand dismissively. "That deficiency is easily remedied. You and I will travel east and procure a fresh supply of these herbs. We will not rest, Philo, until we have more of this miraculous medicine!"

☙❧

Their departure from Xi'an was set for three months after the royal wedding. During the Emperor's absence, Li Si would act as regent, directing the day-to-day administration from the capital and bearing royal seals that empowered him to raise troops. Perhaps not coincidentally, Kwok-se decided to return to the Silk Road for another diplomatic and commercial venture abroad.

Cain pondered his predicament. Not since his final audience with Ramesses had his ruses to hide his longevity secret placed him at such risk. He was about to embark on what amounted to a wild goose chase with an increasingly unstable man who was capable of mass slaughter on a whim. Cain could only imagine the fate that awaited him when the trip's inevitable failure became evident. Granted, the Chinese had learned to employ herbs for a wide variety of medicinal purposes, but he was unaware of any whose effects remotely resembled his own regenerative powers. All that came to mind was the fabled Tree of Life that once lay within the Garden of Eden his parents had told him about eons ago. Even assuming this tree had survived the flood, which he doubted, the search party was headed in the opposite direction.

On the day of his own departure, Kwok-se gave his friend a warm farewell embrace, but he could sense more discomfort on Cain's part than he anticipated.

"Why are you so ill at ease today, Philo? I should think you would be enthusiastic about your upcoming journey. After all, he who assists the emperor in his quest can anticipate a flood of blessings."

Cain sighed. "I suppose I would be excited if I held any expectation of success. But candidly, my friend, I simply do not know the whereabouts of any magical plants."

Kwok-se's tone became more serious. "Listen carefully to me. I have waited until today to tell you this. You and I both know that His Majesty is slowly being poisoned by Li Si. I suggest you needn't find any herbs bearing special curative powers. Instead, your goal for this venture should be to draw the emperor as far away from Li Si as you can. Then, at all costs, find some way to convince him to cease ingesting the mercury potions. If you succeed, he will begin to notice improved vitality very soon, which you can attribute to any herb you wish to offer him as a substitute."

Cain saw the wisdom of his friend's suggestion, but he also understood how deeply Li Si's hooks were already set in the emperor.

With Kwok-se's plan offering at least a glimmer of hope, Cain now confronted the problem of where to steer the royal party, which numbered sixty thousand. On his previous journey while making the great map, he had not explored eastern China extensively, but had rather confined himself to the coastal regions. His first instinct was to suggest that the expedition focus on Zhifu, the island the emperor had visited twice before during his reign. Perhaps he could convince Qin Shihuangdi that, despite the emperor's previous disappointments, the islanders might hold the secrets of immortality after all.

"You have my assent, Philo. The climate of Zhifu is most invigorating, even if many of the inhabitants there are imbeciles!"

So to Zhifu they headed, but progress was slow. The emperor grew more and more easily distracted en route, prying into regional and local affairs with what seemed like obsession. Cain often wondered whether Qin Shihuangdi even recalled why they had set out on this journey in the first place. The mercury doses, administered daily by his physicians, were obviously exacting an increasing toll on the monarch's health.

Yet it would be a grave mistake, Cain reminded himself, to underestimate this emperor—to say nothing of his cunning prime minister, Li Si.

❧

As their search continued, Qin Shihunagdi seemed to deteriorate noticeably by the day, so Cain's urgency to act on Kwok-se's suggestion intensified. He had been quietly collecting a mix of exotic-looking herbs and grinding them into fine powder. Now, on a bright morning some two months after they had departed Xi'an, Cain rushed into the emperor's quarters with his "good" news.

"Majesty!" he exclaimed breathlessly. "I beg your pardon for the unannounced intrusion, but I believe I have fulfilled our quest!"

"I welcome the bearer of such tidings under any circumstances, Philo. What have you found?"

"Again, forgive me, but I wanted to be certain of success before offering even a progress report. I have secured a quantity of a potent mixture of herbs from a group of healers I encountered from a remote area right here in Zhifu. They assure me the preparation has powers beyond the imagination. And indeed, these men all possess an appearance decades younger than their reported age."

Cain removed the lid from an ornately decorated box and handed it to the emperor.

"Ah, a most stimulating aroma! How is the preparation to be taken? I am anxious to begin."

"As a tea, twice per day. But there is a more important aspect to the prescribed use of the herbs. I hope you will take no offense in my having consulted with the chief among these healers concerning your particular regimen. He tells me that the mercury you are taking will counteract the efficacy of the tea."

The emperor studied the box in his hand, and drew from the folds of his robe a vial of mercury, which he held in the other hand speculatively. "Well then, I will take no chances. We will await the results of an evaluation of these claims by my physicians in Xi'an. I will order Xu Fu to dispatch a fleet messenger to carry a sample of your mixture back for their analysis."

Cain bowed low, ostensibly out of respect but also to conceal his exasperation. Softly, he replied, "As always, your wisdom is worthy of your eminence."

❧

Three weeks later, Cain was scarcely surprised when Prime Minister Li Si and the emperor's second son, Hu Hai, joined the imperial party, accompanied by Qin Shihuangdi's chief physician. In effect, the government of China had moved from Xi'an to a small island off the coast in the Bohai Sea. Cain speculated on Li Si's motivations for coming, but could conclude only that the cunning prime minister wanted to assure himself personally that Qin Shihuangdi was following the advice of the chief physician, who predictably prescribed a doubling of the emperor's daily intake of mercury.

Disconsolate over his failure to carry out Kwok-se's advice, and mindful of the sinister glances directed his way by Li Si, Cain began contemplating how he might escape.

CHAPTER 51

China, 210 BC

After the celebrations of the Year of the Tiger in the winter of 210 BC, Li Si recommended that the court remove from Zhifu Island to the Shaqiu commandery on the mainland.

"Communications are far easier there, Majesty, and you will be more comfortable at the prefecture palace," the older man counseled soothingly.

"Then give the order for departure, Li Si. We shall take counsel at Shaqiu how to proceed with our quest."

❦

At Shaqiu, their quarters were more spacious and the food was better, but the Emperor's condition continued to worsen. Late one afternoon in early September, Cain received a summons for a special dinner to be held in the coastal palace. He assumed that it would be a formal meal for the top officials at court. But when he arrived, there were no other carriages in the palace grounds.

"I have invited you here this evening, Philo, so that we may share our souls in private," the emperor declared unsteadily as Cain bowed low before the throne. "Come, let us sit for a cup of tea together."

As the steaming oolong was served, the emperor confided expansively, "I have received messages that the entire tomb complex is complete at last. In particular, your splendid globe has been installed in the mausoleum. You have not failed to note my appreciation." Cain recalled the large reward that had been bestowed on him by the palace before the departure from Xi'an.

"My congratulations, Majesty. Your project is unprecedented. Its fruition must fill you with happiness."

"Yes," the emperor concurred, his pleasure seemingly marred by a hint of irritation. "Many of my advisors, including Li Si, doubted that it was feasible. But you know," he said leaning forward and staring with a feverish expression right into Cain's eyes, "the design provides for every conceivable future contingency." The emperor's voice wavered and the left side of his face seemed immobilized. Cain wondered if he was now blind in that eye.

"What measures have you taken in that regard?" asked Cain softly.

"Tomb robbing is an ancient pursuit. I am sure you learned about it when you lived in Alexandria. The Egyptian pharaohs employed various methods to prevent it, but few of them succeeded."

Cain nodded thoughtfully, recalling Menes and Ramesses.

"I have installed subterranean gates equipped with crossbows," the emperor elaborated. "Anyone who dares to enter the mausoleum at those points will be skewered within a split second of opening the gates. The arrows, by the way, are ten feet long!" At this revelation, the emperor let out a crazed giggle, after which he regained his composure with some effort. "And then, of course, the thousands of my soldiers east of the mausoleum will fend off any vengeful spirits from those whom I have conquered in life. Finally, there will be no workers who survive to tell how the mausoleum was constructed. All of them have by now been interred on the site," he concluded with satisfaction and an eerie smile.

Cain blinked. He had known many tyrants, but this man seemed to have taken leave of his senses.

"Let us now enjoy our meal," the Emperor said as he rose from his throne. "Lijuan will sing and strum the lute for our entertainment as we dine. I trust you will find the delicacies to your liking."

As the two men moved to seat themselves at a more formal dining table, the doors of the room swung open and Cain's old acquaintance from Xi'an, attired in a shimmering robe of black satin embroidered with silver crescent moons, entered with a deep bow to the emperor. Seating herself discreetly on a couch near the dining table, she began to tune her instrument.

Dinner progressed through a series of ten courses, including delicacies such as bear's paw, shark's fin, sea cucumber, camel's hump, and monkey brains. Each heaping platter was accompanied by a different variety of grape wine, rice wine, or Chinese spirits. The more exotic the fare, the more animated the emperor became. Over the meal, he reverted to the subject of western military and technological achievements that had been his preoccupation.

After dinner, the emperor dismissed Lijuan. Before her departure, she bowed low not only to Qin Shihuangdi but also to Cain, as if to suggest that a second encounter might be part of the evening's program.

The emperor led Cain to an alcove, where a wall partition was ornamented by an enormous black lacquer screen showing mountains and delicate cranes etched in pink jade with wings and eyes of pure gold.

After they seated themselves and more spirits had been served, the emperor gazed at his guest. He poured the contents of another vial into his porcelain goblet and then inquired, "Now tell me, Philo. What are your latest plans to locate regenerative herbs? I appreciate your efforts on Zhifu Island, but we must obtain an elixir that is compatible with my current medication."

Later Cain reflected that he had always known this moment would come.

Sitting alone with the emperor, looking into his anxious, twitching face, Cain simply couldn't think of any more excuses.

"There are no such herbs, Majesty. Indeed, there were never any herbs."

"How could that be? Your cure was miraculous. Medical science held no explanation for it."

Cain locked eyes with the emperor. "I lied to you, Majesty."

CHAPTER 52

Ercolano: Present Day

J uan Carlos was hard at work on an alternative rescue plan. After deciphering 90 percent of the door code, he sat in front of his laptop, contemplating the Google Earth view of the site. Rummaging in his backpack for his Magellan handheld GPS unit, he entered the precise latitude and longitude coordinates of the chamber's huge bronze entryway. Checking his watch every five minutes or so, Juan Carlos hurried through some calculations.

The apex of the chamber's dome should have stood around eighty to ninety feet above ground, he figured from Silvio's photograph of the fresco. This was just about the height of the pyroclastic flow let loose by Vesuvius in AD 79. As near as he could make out, the chamber had been constructed in what was today a sparsely forested area slightly to the north of the Villa dei Papiri. With luck, perhaps he could find the top of the dome with a metal probing rod.

"But even then, could I possibly punch through the dome in time?" he muttered to himself. As he continued to worry about Amanda's plight, Juan Carlos could not resist the backward pull of memories…

❧

He first saw Amanda at Q's Billiard Club in West LA. It was mid-December seven years earlier, only a few days after he had led UCLA soccer to the conference championship, scoring two goals in a 3–2 victory. That game seemed a lifetime ago, but it still brought a smile to his face.

Tall, dressed in jeans and a light and dark blue sorority sweatshirt to fend off the sixty-degree Southern California "chill," Amanda arrived at Q's in a flurry of glossy blond hair and the expiring sigh of a European-style moped. Juan Carlos watched from a window table, with half a burger and a few stray nachos in suspended animation on his plate. His soccer buddies were quaffing beers and flirting with the girls, but for Juan Carlos the center of attention lay at the curb, twenty feet away. A vision in two shades of azure made her way to the entrance, having left her helmet on the back of the moped. He stared out the window and whistled under his breath, *"Muy caliente!"*

As usual on a Friday night, the bar was crowded, and she quickly disappeared in the ruckus. Gordon Miller, a tall, affable teammate, sauntered by the table.

"So who were you looking at, J. C.?"

"Pigeons, Gordo, just pigeons."

"I didn't know you Spanish guys were bird lovers," chided the slightly inebriated goalkeeper. "She's a Kappa, right?"

"I think so. Glad I noticed her before you did," he smiled back at his friend, who rolled his eyes and rejoined the other guys.

Juan Carlos nursed the remainder of his meal, with the whirls of blond hair dancing in his mind. Half an hour later, cheers split the air from the billiards area. He decided to investigate. Threading through the crowd, he discovered that the blond moped girl was not only his center of attention, she was everyone's. As he watched, she calculated all the angles under a gaudy red fixture that brilliantly illuminated the table in the center of the room. Then she executed a devastating six-ball run, only to end ingloriously when she scratched the cue ball.

Dozens of Kappa Kappa Gamma sorority sisters let out a sigh of agony. All wore the same two-tone sweatshirt as Amanda. As Juan Carlos filtered the buzz, he gathered that the crowd had assembled for the semifinals of an intersorority nine-ball tournament. The best-of-five match was tied at two games apiece, but with Amanda's scratch, only the nine ball remained. With the cue ball in hand, Kappa's chief rival, Alpha Delta Pi, was now going to win, barring a miracle.

On opposite sides of the table, the blond and her playing partner, a buxom, olive-skinned Kappa sister, exchanged a farewell.

"We almost had it, Laura. Hey, next time! I'm outta here. Big test day tomorrow. Have fun!"

And then she was gone. Juan Carlos gave chase through the crowd, still thinking of what he might say to her. But he was delayed by some fans who recognized the Bruins's top scorer. When he made it to the curb outside Q's, the moped was in full sputter. Just before it sped away, he noticed a Spanish flag decal on the rear fender.

Intrigued, he returned to the bar and sought out Laura, who recognized him instantly. After a brief bit of chitchat about the game, Juan Carlos cut to the chase.

"So, does your playing partner have a boyfriend?" he asked, smiling broadly.

"Are you kidding?" Laura countered. "She's a total bookworm who rarely gets out at night…"

❧

Juan Carlos arrived late for his morning Classics lecture. To his consternation, the only vacant seat he could spot from the rear of Lenart Auditorium was in the front row. His spirits improved, though, when he reached the aisle and sat down in a hurry, right next to the girl he'd first noticed at Q's a month before. Her long blond hair was up in a bun, and she wore reading glasses and no makeup. Amanda, he thought, somehow managed to look both sexy and studious at the same time.

"So what's up with that Spanish flag decal on your moped?" Juan Carlos murmured to Amanda in Spanish as he sat down next to her.

Her reply came fluently in his native tongue. "I like the Spanish flag," she said. "Actually, I like a lot of Spanish things," not bothering to look up from her laptop at the late arrival.

There was no time for Juan Carlos to ask another question, as just then the guest lecturer took the podium.

"Good morning, my name is Dr. Archibald Walker, and I am from the Getty Museum…"

The polished speaker launched into his presentation, "Technology and Ancient Artifacts," with a flamboyant prop: an impossibly thick scroll which was about four feet wide, supported by a richly stained and polished wooden dowel with ornate handles.

"As you are all doubtless aware," Walker's flowing baritone captivated the audience, "the Dead Sea Scrolls are one of the landmark discoveries of twentieth-century archaeology. The texts shed momentous light on a broad range of long-debated issues, including the dating of a stabilized Hebrew Bible and the relationships between early Christianity and Judaism."

"Do you think I could borrow a pen?" whispered Juan Carlos to Amanda, again in Spanish.

"Sure, I've got an extra one. Here you go." Keeping her attention on Walker, she reached into her backpack and handed over one of her ballpoints. Their exchange, however, did not escape the lecturer at the podium.

"If you two would like the microphone, I'd be only too happy to surrender it," Walker quipped dryly.

Acutely embarrassed, Amanda shook her head apologetically.

"I am only jesting," Dr. Walker said. "Actually, I recognize this young man in the front row from his teenage years. He is the grandson of an old friend of mine in the profession, Dr. Silvio Sforza, who now directs the Museo Archeologico Nazionale. Juan Carlos's job in archaeology is assured, unlike the rest of you!"

The audience tittered ambivalently. Obviously, Dr. Walker was ignorant of Juan Carlos's soccer prowess. Amanda finally took notice of her seatmate.

"Now, where was I?" Walker asked rhetorically. "Ah, yes, the Dead Sea Scrolls. If I could ask you two to render me a little assistance?" Once again, he gestured to Amanda and Juan Carlos and beckoned them toward the oversize scroll at the edge of the stage.

"These incredible manuscripts have come down to us in many shapes and sizes. Most of their fifteen thousand fragments are tiny. Several of them, however, are immense. The Temple Scroll, for example, measures nearly thirty feet in length. Recently, though, many scholars have come to believe that even this manuscript may be dwarfed by a granddaddy. Experts hazard the theory that a yet undiscovered scroll, measuring ninety-eight feet—a figure arrived at by extrapolation from text density data—contains the entire Pentateuch, or the first five books of the Hebrew Scriptures. What would such a monster scroll look like?"

Motioning for Amanda and Juan Carlos to take hold of the ornate dowel, Walker grasped the end of the lengthy, blank white sheet. "If you two would kindly unfurl this for me."

With little choice in the matter, both students proceeded down the aisle toward the rear of the auditorium with Walker's prop. It was their joint baptism in fieldwork, they joked later.

Holding up a smaller scroll, crowded with tiny characters, Dr. Walker continued the lecture.

"Try to get a mental picture of tiny inscriptions consuming the entirety of the scroll your two gracious classmates have revealed before you. I submit that the accomplishment of storing the volume of data these larger scrolls contained was, in that time, as revolutionary as the first supercomputers. And consider the task of backing up the data! I believe you may now begin to appreciate, in a fresh way, the magnitude of the scrolls' discovery…"

After the lecture, Dr. Walker summoned Amanda and Juan Carlos to the stage to thank them for their help. Juan Carlos greeted him respectfully, as befitted an old family friend.

"Last I spoke to Silvio he told me you were across town at USC?"

"I transferred last fall, sir. A more highly regarded classics department here," the young man replied.

"And a better soccer team," Amanda added loyally. She had finally put the pieces together. He was the chiseled midfielder who'd torn off his jersey to celebrate UCLA's win in the championship game that Amanda and her sorority friends had attended last month.

So this athlete was also, apparently, a budding classicist? Amanda's interest was piqued. Walker interrupted her train of thought by handing his business card to both of them. "As a token of my appreciation, I'd be delighted to give you a tour of the Getty Villa. Feel free to call anytime." The two expressed their own thanks and departed the stage.

"So when did you acquire your fondness for 'Spanish things'?" Juan Carlos asked playfully while they were strolling to the rack where her moped was parked.

"I lived there for a year when I was fifteen," she replied.

"Ever go to Italica near Seville?"

"My dad and I traipsed all around there. I loved the great amphitheater and all the other treasures of Roman history. The three emperors who were born in Italica certainly left quite an imprint."

"My grandfather Silvio took me there once. And also to Mérida, in Extremadura."

"To Mérida? Really? I'm jealous!" Amanda grinned at him. "The cosmological mosaic there must have been awesome! I've only seen pictures."

"Yes, and their theater is also pretty special," he replied.

The two chatted happily, playing an archaeological version of "Do you know?"

"When I was growing up," Amanda told him, "my dad would bring home artifacts from land sites being cleared for oil refineries all over the world. I started my own little museum."

"Does your dad still travel a lot?" he asked.

"Constantly. Right now, he's in Nigeria, near Port Harcourt. Not too many Greco-Roman sites nearby."

"You must miss him."

"It's okay. I do get a little blue sometimes. I'm glad I'm in Kappa. My sisters don't let those moods last very long," she said with a smile.

His eyes brightened. "May I see you again?"

"Are you sure you're not too busy?" Amanda responded in a teasing tone. "I understand you spent quite a while chatting up my friend Laura at Q's last month!"

"Now listen…" he started to protest.

"Don't worry. Laura told me all about your conversation. Actually, I have a couple hours now before my class in Greek language. Wanna go for a cappuccino?"

CHAPTER 53

China, 210 BC

"**P**eople never lie to me, Philo." The emperor glared menacingly at his guest.

Cain's voice trembled slightly as he began his confession. "Majesty, when you noticed my wound's rapid healing, your eyes did not fool you. Rather, I deceived you with my explanation. The cure's source lay neither in medical science nor in alchemy. It had deep roots in my own past."

"Then Kwok-se misinformed me? He presented you as a cartographer from the West!" the emperor thundered.

"And so I was when Kwok-se traveled to Alexandria. Your childhood friend did not lie to you. Indeed, I have been many things, in many places."

The emperor leaned forward, intrigued by Cain's admission. "What are you saying?"

"Long, long ago, my God cursed me for slaying one man—my brother."

Before Cain could continue, the emperor broke in.

"Is *that* all you are worried about? I have killed many members of my own family, and massacred millions of enemies besides! I have ordered scholars and tomb laborers buried alive. Why do you think I have built the terra-cotta army to defend me against their spirits? Unifying China has come at a price, my friend!"

"The curse of my God is different, Majesty," replied Cain. Making sure he had the emperor's full attention, he spoke words that had never been heard by another human. "God has condemned me to a life of immortality."

Qin Shihuangdi was incredulous. "*Condemned!* How can eternal life be anything but a blessing of untold value?"

"I have been alive, Majesty, for literally thousands of years. Long before the Great Pyramids of Egypt were built, I wandered the earth's continents. You know me as a cartographer, but I have had many professions: merchant, architect, astronomer, athlete, engineer, and epic bard. Once, I even ruled an empire almost as powerful as yours. But, whatever my station, life for me has been a continual struggle to come to terms with the curse. I have never discovered those terms."

"You are saying then, Philo, that you already possess the immortality I seek?"

"Yes, Majesty. And I am also saying that you must be cautious in your search, because success may be failure in disguise."

Cain was surprised at himself. He had actually tendered to the emperor the most accurate account of his life that he had ever given to any human being. Why had he done so? Certainly he was trapped, and the alcohol had loosened his tongue. But Cain also felt a strange sympathy toward this unique individual. Here was a ruler of virtually unlimited means investing himself in an ultimately futile quest. Perhaps, if the emperor's ambitions were redirected, the destiny of many people in this amazing civilization could be altered for the better.

Meanwhile, Qin Shihuangdi lay back in his cushioned seat, his head wobbling. His face was an unreadable mask.

Cain shuddered slightly, imagining the possible fates that now awaited him. With the horrors the emperor had just admitted to, an outcome far worse than death might well be waiting for him. Cain actually pondered the prospect of Qin Shihuangdi ordering that *he* be buried alive! And what if the emperor simply killed him on the spot—surely the terra-cotta soldiers would be no match for God's sevenfold vengeance.

After several seconds that seemed like minutes, the emperor straightened and stared vacantly at Cain, his eyes twitching convulsively. Then, he burst into an uncontrollable fit of laughter. Tears began streaming down his face as he tumbled to the floor in a cackling heap, eventually gasping for breath to the point of alarming Cain. At length, the emperor collected himself and rose to speak.

"I simply don't believe you, Philo! If anyone would have found the secret of immortality by now, it would have been *me*. You are the most entertaining after-dinner storyteller I have ever met! For that reason, if for no other, I could never bring myself to move against you. For the rest of *your* immortality, you will always have a golden passport from His Imperial Highness Qin Shihuangdi. I earnestly request your presence at the wedding of my third son!"

Still laughing hilariously, His Majesty clapped his hands and a servant appeared. "Tell my secretary to inscribe passports for our distinguished visitor at once!" As the man bowed and departed, the emperor replenished their spirits and raised his goblet. "To eternal life!" he exclaimed.

The next morning, Cain did not expect to see the emperor, considering their late-night festivities and the ruler's obviously precarious health. But neither did he expect to encounter Lijuan, who knocked softly on the door of the chamber Cain had been assigned in the Shaqiu palace.

"Another breakfast invitation?" Cain inquired, only half jokingly. Something in her face, however, stifled Cain's banter.

"The emperor is dead," she whispered once he had closed the door behind her.

Cain paused. How much did this most favored of the emperor's concubines know about what he had confessed to the supreme ruler only hours before?

"Were you with him when he died?"

"Yes, he sent for me two hours before sunrise. But almost as soon as I arrived at his chamber, he fell into a coma. I sat by his side until he stopped breathing."

If she was telling the truth, Cain calculated that his secret was safe.

"What will happen now, Lijuan?"

"Li Si has already issued strict orders to conceal the death. He says a civil war could break out if people learn of it. But I think his command is for another reason. He wants Hu Hai to gain the succession, not the older son Fusu, as the emperor wished."

"Why are you telling me all this?"

"You would have found out anyway. You are not foolish. But I have another reason."

"Which is?"

The beautiful young woman looked down. "When emperors die, they...take their concubines with them," she murmured, choking back a sob. "They will take his body back to Xi'an. Then Qin Shi-huangdi and I will be reunited for eternity in the mausoleum."

Cain felt a stab of pity. Although she had played a spy's role, she probably had no choice. There was no doubt now that he had to slip away before Li Si's attention fell on him. But there was no way he could take her along.

"To live, you must take risks," he advised as he took her hand tenderly. "Disguise yourself as an old widow. Then find a way to disappear from the palace into the crowds of Shaqiu or a neighboring town. Try to make a new life for yourself out here in the East. It will be hard for them to find you."

"But no man will want me ever again if I am old and wrinkled," she protested tearfully.

"You can shed the disguise and move on again after a year or two," he replied. "To live, you must also make sacrifices!" Lijuan bowed and quietly let herself out the door.

☙❧

Cain had been planning his own escape for some time. His strategy also hinged on disguise. His first goal was to get back to Xi'an, where he had left the sizable rewards the emperor had bestowed on him for his mapmaking services. It was imperative, moreover, to detach himself as soon as possible from the treacherous Li Si. He could not be absolutely sure of Lijuan's veracity, and in any case he had no desire to get caught up in a palace coup or a civil war.

So he decided to adapt the ploy he had used in Alexandria and become an elderly merchant. On the pretext that the necessary cosmetics were needed for an alchemical experiment, he had previously ordered their purchase in the main Shaqiu market. Since he was well known as the late emperor's herbal advisor, no suspicions were aroused among the palace staff.

The next day, in his new disguise, Cain proceeded to exit the palace. As he skirted the perimeter of the main courtyard, he encountered a strange sight within. Li Si was shouting orders to a small contingent of guards, who were laying the First Emperor's corpse on an ox cart. Then, in an apparent attempt to mask the stench of the body for the long trip to Xi'an, they loaded the cart with dead fish.

As he hurried outside to join a waiting merchant caravan, Cain muttered to himself, "Not quite the funeral procession the emperor would have envisioned."

CHAPTER 54

Kashgar, Along the Silk Road, 210–50 BC

"You will all die before sunrise, unless someone tells me where I can find Kwok-se of Xi'an and Philo of Alexandria. These criminals are wanted for the assassination of our First Emperor. We know they are hiding in this area!" Yang thundered.

Burly, with a long mustache and fine armor, Yang was the leader of hundreds of armed men that streamed into the marketplace already bustling with Silk Road merchants. Atop a regal horse that bore Li Si's coat of arms, Yang scanned the crowd, looking for anyone matching the description of the two fugitives. Every stall and booth was suddenly silent. He cued his men, who then tossed lumpy vegetable sacks into the center of the square. The bags burst open upon impact, and dozens of severed human heads rolled in all directions, their vacant eyes staring at the stunned onlookers. The spectators leaped back, shrieking in their native tongues.

The bounty hunters now had everyone's full attention.

From his vantage point in the front row of frightened merchants, Cain witnessed the gruesome display. He noticed many of the severed heads were crawling with maggots, but some had likely been killed that very day.

Cain was still in disguise as an elderly merchant, despite fleeing Xi'an more than six months earlier. He was staying in Kashgar at a popular inn on China's western border while he searched for his old friend Kwok-se. He was in the marketplace that afternoon buying Chinese herbs, spices, and other trade goods for the next leg of his journey. Kwok-se's trail had gone cold months ago. Apparently Cain was not the only one looking for his friend.

Yang dismounted, drew his blade, and moved toward a startled Cain. How had he recognized him?

Suddenly, Cain felt a cool burst of wind blasting through the marketplace from the distant mountain passes, bringing with it the first drops of an early spring rain. Looking up at the gathering storm clouds, the approaching leader seemed to have a second thought. He spun around on his heel and addressed the audience behind him.

"This is what happens to towns that harbor fugitives!" bellowed Yang as he dipped his Jian sword to the ground and lanced the eye socket of a severed head. He then held up a bulging bag of coins for all the people to see. "Our prime minister offers a reward of one hundred sovereigns for these two murderers. Or you can remain silent and join these tongues licking my boots." He threw the purse into the air, and the gold coins spilled into the midst of the severed heads.

Hearing no response, the leader twisted around. As his calloused hand reached for Cain's neck, a shadow flitted across his face and his fingers closed, at the last second, around an entirely different neck. He thrust the pleading Chinese vendor to his knees and prepared to strike. The wily soldier was about to offer the crowd a live demonstration to jog their memories.

His polished blade was poised to arc downward.

"These vagabonds," interjected Cain in fluent Chinese. "What do they look like? I may have seen one." He then caught the imperial tracker's wrist on its backstroke. Cain had quick reflexes for an old man, hopefully not too quick.

Yang strained against Cain's grip, utterly shocked by the meddlesome foreigner. The two locked eyes.

Yang's men readied spears to slay the disrespectful bystander.

"Hold!" Yang ordered. Strangely, he found himself impressed by the old merchant's courage.

Cain gradually relaxed his grip and feigned an innocent grin. It took only a split second, but why had he gotten involved? These men were ruthless. What did it matter to him if another old merchant was slain?

"On your knees, for now you take his place!" commanded the angered leader. With that, Cain was quickly pressed to the ground by other bounty hunters who had rushed forward.

He was at their mercy.

Fearing Yang would need to save face in front of his men, Cain prepared for the blow.

Meanwhile, several soldiers held up wanted posters made of the finest silk paper bearing the images of Cain and Kwok-se for the crowd to view. Obviously, Li Si had spared no expense for this mission. No doubt other supporters, friends and relatives of the First Emperor had already been rounded up as the prime minister consolidated his grip on power.

Cain glanced up and noticed the leader examining him in detail. Was his gray hair showing its dark roots? He regretted not wearing a hooded cloak. He could feel beads of perspiration mixed with rainwater dripping down his cheek—would it smudge his makeup and give him away? Seconds later, his hair was violently pulled upward. Cain yelped in pain as a clump of hair was ripped from his scalp.

Yang examined the silvery strands for a moment and then demanded, "Where did you see these fugitives?"

"I only saw one of them—this man," Cain replied, pointing a shaky finger toward the illustration of Kwok-se. "It was on the southern branch of the Silk Road just a couple weeks ago. He was staying east of here, in Hotan. He was badly wounded, I would guess from a fall off his horse. Judging from his shattered leg and other injuries, there is no doubt he is still there recovering!" Cain sensed he'd spun a credible tale.

"You may survive yet, brave one," Yang smirked as he motioned for his men to release the informer at his feet. Then in a blur, he thrust his weapon into the neck of the elderly man Cain had earlier saved. Yang held his stance for a few seconds before withdrawing his sword in a single motion.

"Not even a sound, old man!" he cruelly exclaimed while deftly wiping his crimson blade on the shoulder of his victim.

Cain gasped as his tunic absorbed the errant arterial spray.

"Let this be a warning to all who would lie about the whereabouts of these fugitives." Yang stared downward at Cain as he delivered his proclamation. "We know that Philo of Alexandria aided a royal concubine to wear a wig and pose as an old woman to escape her glorious fate in Qin Shihuangdi's tomb! But we found her anyway and buried her alive! Be on the lookout for these fugitives," he barked, gesturing toward the posters being tacked to the nearby posts. "Young Philo of Alexandria will himself be disguised as an elderly man."

A nervous buzz emanated from assembled traders as they heard Lijuan's morbid obituary. Then, in hopes of collecting the prime minister's generous bounty, a crowd gathered around the illustrations of Cain and Kwok-se.

The bounty hunters checked other elderly men in the crowd by pulling their hair, but finding no impostors or anyone resembling Philo, the imperial trackers swiftly departed for Hotan. Yang ordered a few men to stay behind in Kashgar and confine Cain to house arrest at his inn. He knew Yang would be back, and when he returned, Cain's only reward for his "cooperation" would be a sword.

After a restless sleep during which he worried about the fate of his friend, Cain awakened. He had no intention of lingering in Kashgar as Yang's prisoner, and something he'd seen that morning gave him an idea. Many of Yang's men, it appeared, had also been victims of their leader's brutality, and the guards here at the inn were no exception. Cain reckoned that the men, once outside of Yang's purview, might lack the discipline of professional soldiers.

To his delight, loud snores greeted Cain's ears as he tiptoed to his door, and he wasted no time. Slipping out his window in the dead of night, he stole a couple horses from a barn on the outskirts of town and rode swiftly to the west, swearing to remain far away from China until everyone living there was long dead.

While Yang may have possessed some expert trackers, Cain, of course, was a master fugitive. Plus, the previous morning's cloudburst had fortunately grown into a steady downpour, promptly covering his tracks.

Once he was well clear of Kashgar, Cain isolated himself in mountainous terrain far off the Silk Road. Relying on skills he'd last employed thousands of years earlier, he would live off the land until the passage of generations cleansed his past. The imperative of survival now trumped any commercial ambitions or desires for companionship. Cain only wished he could have found and warned his friend Kwok-se. Hopefully, he had ventured nowhere near Hotan.

—❧—

In 160 BC, Cain finally determined it was safe to end his solitary existence, and he returned to the Silk Road. With its steadily increasing traffic from all parts of the world, the Silk Road now reminded Cain of a picturesque version of Alexandria, elongated and rural, where mountains reared their majestic crests and time had slowed down.

As in the great Egyptian city, he met scores of intriguing travelers from every conceivable culture. He sharpened his multilingual abilities as well as his commercial talents. The Silk Road, many times longer than the Nile River, became his nomadic home, and he easily disappeared into its cosmopolitan fabric. Living in thriving towns along its southern and western span, Cain continued to marry and raise families, but he inevitably abandoned them all. With no permanent home, he buried his wealth in dozens of secret hiding spots along the famous trading route. As on the Nile many centuries before, he was constantly on the move, following the calling and curse of his immortality.

☞☜

Eventually arriving in Syria 150 years after leaving China, Cain deemed it a good place to try to commercialize a process he had first seen long ago in his great wandering—the fusion of intense heat and sand. Experimenting with blast furnaces, new tools, and different types of sand, he set up a glass factory and presciently retained an ownership interest in its output. The locals were expert craftsmen and responded well to his tutelage. With their distinctive shapes and hues, some of the blown-glass pitchers manufactured there were nearly crystal-clear, and they soon became wildly popular with Mediterranean traders. With the injection of colorful minerals and pigments, glassmaking now became an art form, and the price of the wares soared.

Just before dusk one evening, Cain entertained a group of Egyptian traders at his manufacturing plant. During contract negotiations over pitchers of beer, they delivered devastating news: the Great Library of Alexandria had burned to the ground during a war between Emperor Julius Caesar and a rival. The Romans were fighting for control of Alexandria when dozens of ships in the harbor were set ablaze, and flames aided by strong winds jumped ashore. The library caught fire and all of its contents were incinerated.

Two hundred years of accumulated knowledge was now a pile of ash and rubble.

After hearing the tragic story, Cain excused himself from the party and went out for a walk. He felt ill. For fifty years he had been a contributing scholar at the Great Library, and now all of his maps, detailed charts, and translations of ancient cultures were obliterated. He would never again be able to walk the halls of the Great Library and read the works of Homer, Aeschylus, Plato, or Archimedes. All of the irreplaceable knowledge contained in the medical school and astronomy labs was lost. It was a disaster.

Cain leaned against a tree and placed his head in his hands. He had planned to contribute to the Great Library again one day, but now that was impossible. Was there nothing humans could build that would last forever? The pyramids were still standing after more than two thousand years, but even their sealed treasures buried under millions of quarried stones were still vulnerable to industrious grave robbers and foreign conquerors. After all, the pyramids were sitting aboveground in plain sight.

It was then his concentration was interrupted by an accounting scribe who had dutifully followed him outside. He also had news to report.

"Sir, please excuse me for sneaking up on you," he said, noting Cain's startled look, "but as ordered, the small shipment of glass we sent to Babylon to test the market price has returned with full payment."

He handed Cain a papyrus scroll with the transaction numbers. Cain's moist eyes bulged when he unrolled it and saw the figures.

"What? This can't be right—it says the blown glass fetched more than its weight in gold!"

"Yes sir. The Persian royalty eagerly purchased almost all of it! Our men reported that the farther they traveled from here, the more kings and queens along the Silk Road would pay!"

A golden sun was just about to set, and the rays struck the interior of Cain's warehouses. He stared at the papyrus ledger in his hands and glanced back over his shoulder to see crates full of sparkling blown-glass products stacked high inside his plant. In anticipation of the arrival of Egyptian customers, he had increased production significantly. These merchants intended to purchase his entire product line, albeit at a substantial discount from the prices in Babylon.

Looking up at the half-moon overhead, Cain wondered what astronomical price the glass would fetch if he carted it all to Xi'an, the extreme eastern point of the Silk Road. Enough time had passed, and it was safe to go back there again. Furthermore, he had heard reports that the Han dynasty was very stable and experiencing a new age of remarkable prosperity.

Rolling up the scroll, and jovially slapping it on the back of his now promoted scribe, Cain made his decision. Later that evening, the surprised glass merchants from Alexandria were bitterly disappointed.

Their sole supplier, and the most valuable commodity in the world, were headed to China.

CHAPTER 55

Xi'an 49–2 BC

When he arrived back in Xi'an, Cain found the city changed considerably from his time there during the reign of the First Emperor. Back in those days, Xi'an had the flavor of an improvised capital. Now, more than a century into the Han dynasty, bureaucracy ruled. But Cain was no stranger to bureaucrats, having witnessed layers upon layers of Egyptian officialdom firsthand.

He discovered that Kwok-se's old estate was for sale. Perhaps for sentimental reasons, he paid an exorbitant price to the owners who had, in turn, purchased it from the last of his old friend's descendants. Lining the pockets of the estate agents in charge of the sale allowed him to avoid objections to his foreign origins.

"Now you can relax," he told himself. From the sale of blown glass to the imperial dynasty, Cain had more money than he would ever need, and Kwok-se's estate afforded complete privacy. At last, he could surrender the nomadic life without misgiving. The main veranda, the old venue for tea with Kwok-se, was his favorite spot. By day and by night, he passed many hours simply staring at the river, pondering things past, present, and to come.

Even in such idyllic surroundings, however, Cain never entered into a haven of true spiritual repose. Memories sometimes delighted him, but other times they gnawed at him. There was little purpose in his life, he felt. And Xi'an, despite its picturesque local color, served as a reminder of the most bizarre irony in his whole experience: the obsessive quest of the First Emperor for immortality, and the dismal culmination of that quest.

How could he achieve serenity? Could he ever see his fellow human beings, or himself, in even half a redemptive light? These gnawing questions brought him to the edge of despair. His existence just seemed to drag on.

⚬⚬⚬

One evening in 31 BC, while standing on the veranda gazing at the sky, Cain called aloud upon God.

"For what have you made me? What would you have me do?" The frost of his breath ascended toward the stars, but quickly dissipated, bringing to mind the grain sacrifice God had rejected in his youth. Characteristically, no answer was forthcoming.

However, several nights later in a dream, Cain was haunted by the grievous story of the Alexandrian Library in ruins. Yet, he awoke the next day with a fresh insight. He recalled how, after the death of Tanith, he had found comfort and a sense of value in his role as a bard, preserving history through oral tradition. Now, so many centuries later, how much more was he, and he alone, equipped to preserve and convey the great arc of human endeavor? By the time he finished breakfast, the aftermath of a bad dream had been transformed into a compelling obsession: Cain determined that he would use his flawless memory to recreate and archive as many of the Great Library's contents as possible

In a mere five years he had completed his transcriptions of the Homeric epics, as well as the plays of Aeschylus, including dramas authored by that master tragedian after Cain had left Athens for Persia. Having read them in the Great Library, he could recall them word for word. He also transcribed everything of Sophocles and

Euripides, as well as a number of other tragedians from the golden age of Greek drama.

He then moved on to history, philosophy, science, and mathematics, with special attention to the theorems and doctrines of Pythagoras. Cain considered that these would be especially valuable for posterity, since Pythagoras wrote very little and his teachings were known almost exclusively from oral tradition.

Cain did not confine himself to texts, however. There was much to be known from drawings and scale models. He busied himself with sketchings for a scale model of Noah's ark, and also with reproducing the drawings he had made in Egypt for Menes and Ramesses. Then he turned to maps and charts. Cartography, after all, had been one of his most beloved vocations, both in Alexandria and in China.

Twenty years later, in 2 BC, he had virtually completed the archive. Now, his challenge was how to preserve it. Mindful of the First Emperor's great mausoleum, he considered subterranean caves, but he rejected that idea because humidity levels underground would eventually ruin the texts, if not the other artifacts. What he needed was a damage-proof repository that would still preserve the texts.

While reviewing a detailed map of the Mediterranean coastlines, a solution for the site of his archive came to him. He recalled the volcanic mountain he had seen long ago to the south of Rome. He had heard that it was now called Vesuvius. The mountain lay within the territory of the Romans, who had become the masters of the Mediterranean and most of the western world. If he acquired land near this mountain to establish his museum, would it not turn out to be the safest location for his treasures? For, when the volcano eventually erupted again, the ash would seal everything indefinitely, affording Cain the opportunity to play another unique role—the arbiter of the moment in the future when all these treasures of history could be "discovered" and revealed to the world.

❧

Reflecting on his labors in retrospect, he realized that gradually, almost imperceptibly, the project had afforded him the serenity that seemed so elusive a quarter of a century before. He recalled his dream of the ruined library, and also the clear, chilly evening on the veranda when he had called upon God for a direction in his life.

Had God answered after all?

As he pondered the question, he came to realize that his archiving work had rooted him in the same place far longer than any previous era of his life after the flood, save for his stay in the prison at Babylon. Why this blessed relief from a lifetime of wandering? If these endeavors, however unwittingly, were gaining him favor with his Maker, could he somehow obtain a reprieve from his infernal existence?

Then, it hit him: he would offer all this excellent work to God. Perhaps the one who had rejected his original, ill-fated offering would now accept this archive of humanity's achievements as a substitute and remove his curse at last.

Cain lowered his head.

> *"Eternal One. You have made me a vagabond on this earth for eons. Until now, I have known no peace. Yet here I bow before you with the product of all I have learned and done during that time. If my very best work is acceptable in your sight, I give it now to you. Do with it as you will."*

Accustomed as he was to silence in response to his infrequent petitions, Cain nevertheless yearned for an intelligible answer.

The next night, as he was finalizing his constellation maps, he noticed a strange object in the heavens. Using his telescope to study the western sky, he was astonished to see a brand-new celestial body that shouldn't have been in the constellation Leo. It certainly hadn't been there the night before. On the brightness scale devised by his old friend Hipparchus in Alexandria, the star—or whatever it was— rivaled the planet Jupiter. Cain decided at once to observe the star carefully and to consult his Chinese astronomer friends.

It was now late fall, and the skies were usually clear. Night after night, he viewed the new star, which, if anything, was becoming brighter than ever. He rejected the idea that it was a comet. Comets moved in orbits, and this celestial body appeared to remain in the same position.

After several weeks of observations, he made up his mind. It was time to begin the journey west to the archive's ultimate home, but he would investigate the strange star along the way. By his calculations, it appeared to be in a stationary position directly over the eastern Mediterranean seaboard. Surely it was being observed by astronomers in that region. Longing to know more about the star, Cain decided to sell the estate, pack up his entire archive of historical treasures, and organize hundreds of camels and attendants into a caravan that would take him over four thousand miles to the city of Antioch.

CHAPTER 56

Antioch: 1 BC

Cain arrived in Antioch after an eight-month journey along the Silk Road, which by now was extremely familiar to him. Oddly, as he passed through Kashgar, the strange object in the night sky dimmed, and weeks later it disappeared altogether. This development did not diminish his curiosity, however, but rather increased it.

He determined that Antioch was the most suitable staging point for an investigation of the mysterious star. The city was now a great urban center. It had been originally patterned on the grid plan of Alexandria and lately adopted by the Romans as the hub of their operations in the East. In fact, as a center of culture and science, it was now said that Antioch had surpassed its rival city in Egypt. Situated on the west coast of Asia Minor bordering the northeastern Mediterranean Sea, Antioch was now a major trading port of the Roman Empire.

Making inquiries, Cain discovered that the most knowledgeable astronomer in Antioch was an elderly scientist with South Indian origins named Gayan. They met at his small observatory in a lush park on the eastern bank of the Orontes River. Gayan's smooth, nut-brown features contrasted vividly with the snow-white circlet of hair on his balding pate. He wore an Indian kurta pyjama of tan-colored combed cotton, garb that struck Cain as affording both convenience and elegance in a warm climate.

"Can you tell me of your observations of Leo over the past year or so?" asked Cain, who still retained the name of Philo that he had used since his time in Alexandria.

"Yes, there was something extremely notable there, sir," replied Gayan. "No one in Antioch was able to explain it. I even sent couriers with inquiries to Rome. From our perspective, the heavenly object appeared to be anchored stock-still for over five months in the southern sky. I should say about thirty-five degrees above the horizon."

"Have you ever seen anything like it?"

"Never. Nor have I found anything similar in my review of historical writings about celestial wonders, Philo. Lately, however, some strange tales have arisen here about this phenomenon. These rumors are not, I hasten to emphasize, within the domain of science."

"And what are these tales about the star, Shri Gayan?"

"You know that there has always been a sizable Jewish community here in Antioch, sir. Some of them have interpreted the unusually bright star in the constellation Leo as a sign from their God. In particular, they are telling stories about the birth of a miraculous child in the Roman tributary kingdom of Judaea to the south. They are saying that the star was a heavenly omen, signifying the arrival of their so-called Lion of Judah. The child is being hailed as the future Messiah, or Savior, at least by some. Their claim has received support from men learned in celestial phenomena. They say the appearance of the star fulfills several ancient prophecies concerning the birth of a Jewish king in Bethlehem. A number of these men have traveled there to investigate the matter themselves."

"Is there any report from these travelers?"

"Sir, they have not been heard from since their departure. However, the Judaean king, a man named Herod, seems to have taken the claim seriously, since he has ordered the killing of all male infants in the area, apparently to prevent any challenge to his rule."

Cain winced at this news, remembering his painful losses long ago in Egypt. Collecting himself, he inquired of the astronomer whether anyone could explain why the celestial portent had disappeared.

Gayan smiled wanly. "I have posed that very question. Without exception, it is greeted with silence. Unless, of course, you believe the Jewish rumors. In that case..." Gayan held up his palms and a smile crossed his face.

"...in that case, well—if this Savior has been born, the need for the star has passed."

Cain exchanged astronomical shoptalk with the Indian and then bid him farewell. There was evidently nothing more to be learned about the star—at least from the realm of science. The nexus between celestial bodies and beliefs in the divine was nothing new to him; the link was timeless.

But he did not regret his long journey. After another week in Antioch during which he gave no more thought to events in Judaea, he mustered his caravan and embarked for Rome with a fresh shipment of silk and blown glass. Plans for his fortified repository of human knowledge were uppermost in his mind.

CHAPTER 57

Rome, 1 BC–AD 12

"The Palatine is an especially desirable address, sir," advised the seasoned land broker as he and Cain entered the estate. The property overlooked the Tiber River on one side and the Circus Maximus, Rome's largest sporting arena, on the other. "Augustus himself lives in this neighborhood." The broker, tall and balding with aristocratic features, had an aura of faded gentry that had fallen on leaner times.

After three days of house hunting, Cain had made up his mind. In the long term, his principal residence would be on the Bay of Naples, in the shadow of the great volcano. But he needed a base in the capital as well. There was enough space in the Palatine residence to store his thousand-strong collection of detailed maps and scrolls until he built his final repository. Plus, the land offered ample room for future expansion. He asked the price.

"They want four million sesterces, but they will likely settle for three and a half," said Metellus.

"Tell them I offer three point two million," said Cain. "I am sure we can negotiate."

"Very good, sir. If they agree to three point four, will you accept a deal?"

"Yes, but there is one thing I want you to do for me first."

"At your service, sir," the agent replied.

"A legally binding contract requires full Roman citizenship. Alas, my origins abroad have excluded me from that status, at least until now."

Cain gave his name as Marcus Flavius Pictor. He had told Metellus that he had been raised in Alexandria, the son of a Roman father and an Egyptian mother.

"Sir, citizenship is legally available to you, at a price," Metellus pointed out.

"So I have heard. How can this be arranged?"

"There is no problem," Metellus waved his hand airily. "If you can come up with one million sesterces, I can have the papers drawn up within a couple of days. My cousin is one of the censors."

Cain smiled. He had been willing to bet that Metellus was well connected.

⸙

After spending the night at an inn on the neighboring Aventine Hill, Cain returned down the Tiber to Rome's port of Ostia, where the large merchant ship he had purchased in Antioch was moored. A message from Metellus soon arrived indicating that the seller had agreed to a price of three point four million. Metellus also reported favorable progress on the application for Roman citizenship, which would confer important privileges on him in the areas of law, marriage, contracts, and property ownership.

It was therefore the opportune moment to off-load the large quantities of silk and blown-glass products, placing them on smaller launches that could navigate the fifteen miles up the Tiber to Rome and its thriving markets. Cain would use a portion of the proceeds to buy the small estate on the Palatine. Then he would sail to the Bay of Naples to scout the area around Vesuvius, the mountain of fire, for the perfect site.

While he waited for the various transactions to be completed, he took in the sights and sounds of Rome. In the age of Augustus, the city bore little resemblance to the Rome he remembered from his visit two and a half centuries earlier. Now ruling most of the Western world, the Romans had, in their way, accomplished a feat as astonishing as the First Emperor's unification of China. At the center of this vibrant culture was Augustus Caesar. Like the First Emperor of China, Augustus also had to fight for his supremacy and knew the potency of political propaganda. But the similarities ended there, Cain reflected. The Chinese Empire, though barely known in the West, dwarfed the Roman Empire in scale, population, and military might. He wondered if the two superpowers would ever clash.

Several weeks after moving into his new residence on the Palatine Hill, he invited Metellus to dinner to show his appreciation.

"What do you know of the Bay of Naples, my friend?" Cain asked as they reclined on couches in the villa's dining room, where the servants offered heaping platters of tenderly roasted suckling pig and chicken.

"Many of my clients have houses there. In fact, it is not at all unusual for people of a certain status to own a town house here in Rome and a villa on the bay. Pompeii, Baiae, and Herculaneum are the favored spots. The medicinal springs at Baiae have made it a premier resort. Julius Caesar had a villa there."

"You have kept current with the estate scene in the area, then?" asked Cain.

"Oh my, yes. I go down to the Bay at least six times a year. Some of my cousins own properties there, and I am always welcome. Are you thinking of investing in another property, Marcus? Perhaps a refuge from the summer heat here in town?"

Not wanting to appear too eager, Cain demurred. "It's a possibility. How would you like company on your next visit there?"

"It would be both my pleasure and my privilege," the agent replied suavely.

❧

Thus it was that, a month later, the two booked passage on a sleek
new ferryboat from Ostia to Naples. The journey itself was a brief two-
day sail. Cain was astonished at the development along the shoreline.
Wealthy Romans had discovered this coastal playground in droves.
As they looked at various villas that were on the market, Cain was
amazed by the level of luxury. He even recognized some of the cameo
glass vases that his vendors had sold to high-end clients in Rome.

Everywhere around the idyllic, shimmering Bay of Naples was
evidence of the thirst of the Roman elite for the prestige and status
that Greek culture conferred. Only half jokingly, Metellus quoted
to Cain the maxim coined by Horace, one of the emperor's favorite
poets: "Captive Greece took captive her savage conqueror." Yet the
Romans, in Cain's view, had succeeded in forging commendably
original styles in art and architecture.

Despite the opulent standard of living, however, he saw nothing
that appealed to him so directly and immediately as the estate on
the Palatine in Rome. Instead, savoring the creative challenge of
engineering that had always motivated him, Cain determined to
design and build the villa and repository himself. He would put his
distinctive stamp on this gift for the ages.

"Let us look at tracts of raw land, Metellus," he said after a few
days. "Which of these towns is the most secluded, the most exclusive?"

"I would say Herculaneum, without a doubt," the agent replied.
"Only the most affluent can afford the land there. Herculaneum is
much less frequented than Pompeii."

"How close is it from the shoreline to Vesuvius?"

"Approximately seven kilometers, sir."

Cain gazed at the volcano in the distance, rubbing his chin.

"Let us look in Herculaneum, then, near the water."

On the third day of prospecting, Cain found what he was searching for: twenty acres on the shore, with excellent locations for docking and boat storage. The price was six million sesterces, but Metellus's knack for negotiating sliced the final sale price by ten percent. After arranging for a thorough survey, the visitors left, with Cain eager to return to Rome and begin drawing up the extensive plans for his summer villa and repository.

ᐧᐧᐧ

Having acquired the necessary real estate, Cain now needed to replenish his resources for the construction of the repository itself. And so, in AD 1, he decided on a foreign mission. He had used the signet ring bestowed on him by Ptolemy in Alexandria to claim the lands in Spain and North Africa that he had bargained for with the Roman aediles on his previous visit two and a half centuries earlier. Stating that he was the lawful heir, he claimed and in due order received his "ancestor's" property.

One of the benefits of the *Pax Romana*, or "Roman peace," was that the rule of law prevailed in previously unstable regions. He was reasonably confident that he would find his lands undisturbed.

Before he sailed from Ostia to New Carthage on Spain's southeast coast, Cain gathered a cadre of skilled engineers and a company of soldiers if protection against pirates or trespassers should prove necessary. He also took three hundred experienced mining slaves on board, and he arranged for the purchase of thousands more slaves to be brought in a trailing fleet of ships within the next few weeks.

Slavery had been so common in his world—in Enoch, Egypt, Greece, Babylon, and Xi'an, not to speak of here in Italy—that he didn't give the matter a second thought. Nevertheless, having witnessed firsthand the cruelty masters were capable of, he was determined to treat his slave laborers humanely, giving them better food than most masters did, seeing to their injuries, and strictly warning his staff of overseers against any brutal mistreatment.

As Cain witnessed, conditions were wretched enough in the deep-vein mines. Workers dressed in tunics with leather aprons labored in all-day shifts to locate and then hew the ore out from the silver-bearing seams, sometimes six hundred feet below ground. Space was so cramped in spots that men lay on their backs or their sides as they used their iron picks, chisels, wedges, and tongs. Some galleries extended over a mile. Boys scrambled through the tunnels to collect the ore. Notwithstanding numerous advances in technology, the problems of poor ventilation, lighting, and drainage remained pervasive. And there was always the danger of roof collapse in the mines.

Despite the challenges of deep-vein mining, Cain's operation in Spain had produced forty-five thousand pounds of high-grade silver by the end of the year. Leaving a trusted foreman in charge of his Spanish mines, he sailed to North Africa. Here his plan was to use the purest of white reef sand to manufacture expensive blown-glass products for the market in Rome. At Carthage, he set up a large factory and supervised a team of skilled craftsmen, teaching them how to add ingredients to the glass in precise proportions to make it absolutely clear. Vases, glasses, and pitchers were soon being churned out of the factory at a rate of hundreds of pieces per day. Cain's entrepreneurial genius, combined with his eye for detail, resulted in glass products fit for a king.

With this factory up and running, Cain established a routine. Every year during the six-month sailing season, he traveled the western Mediterranean in his cargo ship, supervising his operations in Spain and North Africa and arranging new trade contacts. He lived in Rome for the other six months, making occasional visits to Herculaneum as he worked on the plans for the villa and repository he would build there.

One evening, while seated on the deck of his ship under a blanket of stars, Cain reflected on his commercial successes of late. He was no stranger to prosperity, but the pace in his accumulation of wealth since he'd dedicated the archival project to God was truly amazing. He hoped this was no coincidence and that his efforts would finally find favor with the Almighty and achieve the lifting of his curse.

CHAPTER 58

Rome: AD 12–29

ain could easily see the Circus Maximus from his estate on the Palatine Hill. More than that, he could hear the roar of the crowds rising up in chorus from the arena, so he determined to attend a chariot race to see what the excitement was all about.

He was instantly glad he'd decided to visit.

For pageantry and spine-tingling competition, the chariot races held in this Roman version of a hippodrome topped the Olympic Games in Greece. The dimensions of the track were unparalleled: two thousand feet long and nearly four hundred feet wide, with three tiers of spectator seats. From dawn to dusk for over one hundred days a year, up to a quarter of a million spectators from every rung on the social ladder in Rome cheered wildly for their favorite teams. These belonged to four different leagues called "factions": the Reds, the Whites, the Blues, and the Greens.

Immersed as he was in his mining, manufacturing, and building projects, Cain knew he could not compete in person as a chariot driver. Vicarious participation, however, was a viable option. Because he had recently signed a contract to sell his Spanish mines to the Roman state for the lump sum of two billion sesterces, Cain knew that he could comfortable hire and maintain a racing team, even as he completed his compound at Herculaneum in the style he envisioned.

So it was that Cain bought a stake in the Greens, a faction which had fallen on hard times. Its winning percentage had dropped precipitously, along with the value of the franchise. Cain sent for two dozen of his fittest mining slaves with an eye toward retraining them as chariot racers and turning around the fortunes of the Greens.

⌘

One afternoon, he persuaded Metellus to accompany him to the races. Naturally, the broker also declared himself a partisan of the Greens. As they sat in their shaded box, Cain looked out at the *spina*, the elongated structure in the middle of the track. Situated near the spina's center was the obelisk Augustus had pilfered from Egypt—the same obelisk, Cain noted to himself with a dash of pride, that he had quarried and transported down the Nile some twelve hundred years before.

In short order, Cain and Metellus were greeted by a tremendous roar from the stands, as two of the three Green chariots in the fourteenth race of the day converged on the *meta*, or turning post, for the seventh and final lap. In a split second, their plunging horses and rumbling wheels forced a Blue chariot driver, who enjoyed a slight lead, to edge too close to the large gilded column. His chariot overturned, and a third Green driver shot out to the finish. The Blue charioteer fortunately succeeded, at the very last second, in cutting the leather reins twisted around his waist, and he scurried across the track to safety, narrowly avoiding being run over.

"Splendid teamwork!" shouted Metellus, as a wave of sixty thousand green-clad spectators flailed their arms and roared in triumph at the rare victory for their faction.

Cain was hooked. Two weeks later, he upped his stake in the Greens to a majority share. He also held a conversation with Scorpus, one of the mining slaves Cain had brought with him to Rome. An especially brave lad of perhaps eighteen, he had played a key role in rescuing some of his comrades during a cave-in a few years earlier. The youth had singlehandedly descended over a hundred feet, tethered to a narrow lifeline, and tunneled through the rubble with his bare hands to reach his fellow workers in time before they suffocated.

"If you will train to become my main driver, Scorpus, I will promise you your freedom one day. You are strong, brave, and you have excellent reflexes. I believe you can do it."

The young man's eyes shone.

"It would be an honor, master!"

"Then I will hire you a first-rate trainer," said Cain. "On your thousandth win, you will be a free man. With up to thirty races a day, and with your skill and perseverance, that happy occasion may come soon."

Far from being a passive owner of the Greens, Cain invested heavily in the franchise. He bought a stable of Arabian racehorses, had several dozen lightweight four-horse chariots made, and arranged for the use of a practice track on the outskirts of Rome. He knew it would take time to turn the fortunes of the Greens, but the foundation for future success had now been laid.

His most important project, however, remained the development of his seaside villa. Having reviewed the finished blueprints many times over, Cain had estimated that the villa and repository would require fifteen years to build. By AD 19, the project was halfway done. Two thousand slaves had leveled the twenty-acre property, and hundreds of skilled craftsmen worked the cement, brick, and marble used in construction. The villa would provide fifteen thousand square feet of living space, while the repository would account for an additional eleven thousand.

As the buildings took shape, Cain gave careful consideration to the furnishings. In the villa, he decided for reasons of social assimilation that he would install the conventional Roman appointments: brightly colored frescoes on mythological themes, marble statuary of Greco-Roman deities, fountains, mosaic floors, and ornamental glassware. But the repository, as a more private retreat, would be different. Pagan religious themes would be absent there, and the décor would emphasize science, philosophy, literature, and the arts, just as at the Great Library of Alexandria.

Special security measures would be devised to safeguard the museum's contents. A custom-made bronze door with a unique locking mechanism would be installed. A concrete dome of revolutionary design would be constructed to cap the rotunda-shaped space, with metal bars embedded in the concrete to maximize its strength and durability. In the dome there would be an oculus, or roof opening, that could open and shut, allowing Cain's telescope a view of the heavens. The entire structure would rest on a huge foundation of salt crystals and other drying agents, thus ensuring excess humidity would not damage the treasures within. In the event that an unexpected rainstorm occurred with the oculus open, Cain designed a large drainage tunnel in the floor that emptied into a seaside culvert.

While Cain knew that nothing lasted forever—with the possible exception of his own life—he was determined that his repository would withstand the ravages of time.

❧

Monthly inspection trips to Herculaneum kept Cain occupied, but he tried to schedule them so they would not displace too much time from his other passion, the races. By now, he had become acquainted with many of the principal backers of the factions, who regularly invited him to their sumptuous banquets.

Cain had no time for romance in the midst of his frantic building and racing projects, yet nonetheless love found him. One evening in

AD 20, at a party held to celebrate the advent of the midwinter Lupercalia festival, one of the major backers of the Greens introduced Cain to a young woman named Julia. The daughter of a distinguished aristocratic senator, she impressed Cain with her wide-ranging knowledge of history and architecture. Cain asked Julia if she would accompany him to the races the next day, and she gladly accepted the invitation. Julia's passion for racing nearly equaled his own, although he had to get over the fact that she was a die-hard fan of the Blue faction.

They were married three months later. Julia's rather snobbish father seemed lukewarm about the match, since he suspected that Cain was secretly active in commerce, but the young man's ability to provide for his daughter and his social connections, both in Rome and Herculaneum, were beyond question.

In AD 21, to the aging senator's delight, the couple's union was blessed by a son. Cain chose the name Quintus, defying the Roman custom for naming the firstborn after the father. He did not want his son to bear the name Marcus, which after all was one of his myriad deceptions.

However, the parents' joy swiftly turned to concern when it became apparent that the infant was sickly. At first the doctors had no diagnosis, but by the time Quintus was three years old they identified his ailment as some form of lung disease. Cain thought sadly of the deaths of Jacuna and Nefran back in Egypt. Would another son soon be taken from him before his time?

Yet Quintus was a fighter. Although he became increasingly frail as he grew older, his spirit remained strong and determined. Cain could see, by the time Quintus was six, that the child was phenomenally intelligent. That year, father started taking son to the races. The crowd's enthusiasm was infectious, and Quintus jumped up and down with excitement at every race won by the Greens. The boy was a special fan of Scorpus, who had begun a consistent streak of wins several years before.

❧

In AD 27, while Cain was away on business, he received a message that Julia had fallen gravely ill from an infection due to an abscessed tooth. He cut his trading mission short to come to his wife's side, but by the time he returned to Rome she had passed away. Himself no stranger to grief, Cain knew that Quintus would be shattered by the loss, so he suspended all his trading activities and remained at the house on the Palatine for most of the next two years. He limited himself to only brief inspection trips to Herculaneum, where his villa was nearing completion.

Father and son became inseparable companions. Cain taught Quintus the game of senet, and in seemingly no time he found himself on the losing side, and no longer deliberately. Quintus enjoyed their sailing trips to Herculaneum, but he was always glad to return to Rome and the Circus.

By the time Quintus was almost eight years old, the boy's health had not appreciably improved, but his spirits had recuperated from the blow of his mother's premature death. Although Cain wondered periodically how long the boy could hold out in the long term, he felt he could leave Quintus in Rome for an abbreviated business trip.

Cain had twin objectives. The first was to inspect his sprawling glass factory in Carthage, Rome's erstwhile enemy. The sea journey to North Africa could be accomplished in about three days' sailing. His second goal was exploratory. He wanted to see the beautiful new harbor built by King Herod the Great at Caesarea Maritima on the coast of Judaea. Constructed of concrete, it was supposedly the largest artificial harbor in the Mediterranean. Cain had heard of it when he was in Antioch, but he had never seen it. The new port at Caesarea had turned Judaea, previously a Roman backwater, into an important trading post. Cain expected to sell a load of his fine glassware there, and perhaps also to purchase additional Silk Road goods as finishing touches for the estate in Herculaneum.

Bidding Quintus an affectionate farewell, he set sail early in the spring, promising his son that he would return by midsummer. He would have taken the boy with him, but the child's poor health precluded a journey over the open sea.

"Keep track of the horses for me, Quintus," Cain told him on the dock as the launch that would bear him down the Tiber prepared to depart.

"Don't worry, Father," the boy replied. "The Greens always win when I'm at the Circus!"

He gave his son a farewell hug, and then gazed steadily, waving his right arm, as the boy on the dock grew smaller and smaller in the distance.

CHAPTER 59

Judaea: AD 29

"Perfect sailing conditions, sir," declared Captain Felix with satisfaction. "We should be sighting land later this afternoon."

As a moderate southwesterly filled the sails of Cain's newly outfitted cargo vessel, the captain exclaimed further, "And the navigational instrument is outstanding! If you market that device, it will revolutionize travel in the Mediterranean."

The truth of Felix's words became clear soon after the lookout sighted the Judaean coast. Recognizing the lighthouse that marked the harbor of Sebastos, as well as the huge promontory palace built by Herod, Felix said, "Caesarea is dead ahead, sir."

Cain nodded and went below to change into fresh clothes. He was looking forward to seeing the harbor—indeed, it was one of the major reasons that Caesarea was on their itinerary. Business had gone well in Carthage, with progress at his glass factory exceeding expectations. Now, his vessel was laden with a shipment of fancy glassware—bottles, beakers, bowls, even ornamental candlesticks and chandeliers—which he would have no difficulty in selling to the traders who thronged Caesarea.

The harbor did not disappoint him. Captain Felix, whom Cain had hired largely because of his extensive experience in the eastern Mediterranean, explained how King Herod had built it over forty years ago.

"The secret was pozzolana, apparently—a special sort of soil," said Felix. "He imported tons of it from Pozzuoli in Italy." Cain knew the Italian port well, since it was close to Naples and was a major trading post for glass products.

"When the water and the fine, lightweight dirt mix with lime, it produces a durable mortar that actually solidifies under water," Felix continued. "Herod was finally able to devise a method for laying the wooden forms for the concrete, allowing him to build the two enormous breakwaters you see here, sir. The southern mole is almost one-third of a mile long. The harbor can hold as many as three hundred ships at a time."

Cain whistled his acknowledgment. He had designed and contributed to many audacious building schemes himself, but even he was impressed, especially with Herod's residence. A master of self-aggrandizement, Herod had ensured that his palace here was one of the largest in the western world. At the same time, he was careful to construct a magnificent temple dedicated to his Roman patron, the emperor Augustus, for whose title of "Caesar" the city was named.

While his commercial team busied themselves with eliciting bids for the glassware shipment, Cain and Felix, accompanied by half a dozen porters, went from shop to shop to evaluate buying opportunities. In addition to large quantities of top-quality silk, Cain purchased a variety of decorative items, including a stunning collection of agate tableware and several dozen decorative rock crystals, as well as a lampstand of free-blown glass.

After a weeklong stay, Cain spent his final afternoon in Caesarea walking alone through the city while his ship was being fully loaded. As he entered a public square close to the forum, an unusual sight greeted him. All around the square's perimeter, tables and chairs had been set up for what seemed to be a board game tournament. Umbrellas and awnings shaded the players, all of them men, from the late afternoon sun. As a longtime devotee of senet, Cain couldn't resist the temptation to linger, and perhaps pick up an attractive board as a gift for Quintus.

A sprinkling of spectators were following the progress of various matches, and Cain spent quite some time as an onlooker at a table where an especially animated game of senet was unfolding. Then, about an hour before sunset, he strolled over to the eastern wall on one side of the square. Just as he was passing a stall, he happened to notice a young man, perhaps eighteen or so, sitting in front of a board made of a beautiful mineral rock he had never seen before. The youth had evidently just arrived, and had yet to match himself up with another player. Cain was not surprised when the young man stood up, smiled at him, and beckoned him to enter the stall.

Cain inspected the beautiful gaming board closely. It was jet black with bright flecks of red and gold. The pieces were rectangular ceramic tiles with finger-size indentations in the center. Some of the tiles had intricate shapes of animals fired into them, and others simply had numbers.

"What stone is this board made of?" Cain asked the young man.

"I do not know, sir. It belongs to my father. My name is Abaddon. Will you sit down and have a game with me?"

Cain could see that the board was designed for senet, one of his favorites. Yet he hesitated. The sun was now dipping close to the horizon, and he needed to return to the port to ensure his ship was ready for departure early the following morning.

"I have a lot of money to wager," the youth declared proudly as he drew several silver pieces from the leather pouch attached to his belt. "You see these, sir? There are thirty pieces in all. My father sent me here to buy tools for the farm, but I have decided to gamble instead. The farm equipment can wait."

The youth's odd mixture of inducement and insolence puzzled Cain for a moment. Then he made up his mind to teach this adolescent a few things about gambling and respecting one's parents.

"I accept your invitation," Cain said firmly.

As he was about to pull back a chair to seat himself, the young man spoke again.

"Before we start, sir, would you kindly draw the netting so that the insects won't bother us?"

The boy glanced around as Cain pulled the netting closed. Like many of the stalls, this one was equipped with a semi-opaque screen used to shade the occupants and keep out bugs around sunset. The screen also enhanced merchants' privacy during sensitive commercial transactions, since passersby could not identify the individuals inside at a glance.

"Let me explain the rules," said Abaddon after Cain had drawn up his chair to the wooden table. Next to the board, Cain placed the beautiful bottle of mosaic blown glass he had brought along, full of drinking water for a hot day in early summer.

"But I know the rules of senet well," he objected.

"This is a modified form of the game, sir. I just want to be certain that you understand the differences between my game and the more familiar version."

Cain shrugged his shoulders. As his opponent laid out the tiles, forty for each player, the youth offered an overview of how each player could move his pieces and when a player was permitted to "take" one of the opponent's tiles. These rules diverged, in fact, from any version of the game familiar to Cain. But he had accepted the challenge, and as a gamer he was a quick study.

"From where do you come?" asked the young man, as the two of them began play in earnest.

"I am from Rome. I am here on a trading mission."

"Ah, Rome!" exclaimed Abaddon with a sigh. "I should love to travel there one day!"

"If you gamble your family's money away, you will find travel difficult," Cain dryly admonished with a meaningful gaze at his opponent.

"Money can always be had," the youth parried. A brief silence ensued, as tiles were taken on both sides.

Furrowing his brow, Abaddon asked, "And where do you go to now? Will you stay some time in Judaea?"

"No, my business here is concluded. I sail for Rome tomorrow, assuming fair winds."

"You have enjoyed your visit to Judaea? You will return one day?"

"Perhaps," Cain answered vaguely.

"Do you believe that the emperor Tiberius should control this country? There is a lot of dissatisfaction among the Jews here."

"I make it a point to steer clear of politics," Cain replied. The young man was certainly plying him with questions. "Look, let us focus on our game," he added.

During the ensuing silence, Cain took stock of the remaining tiles on the board. He was not doing nearly as well as he had expected. He had only seventeen tiles in play, to his opponent's twenty-two. If the young man stalemated him and he lost every tile but one, the game would be over and Cain would have to pay up on the wager. Perhaps his opponent's bravado that he could readily acquire money was justified, after all.

Cain lost a further three pieces on a single turn. Just as he was growing even more frustrated at the possibility of being defeated by a farm boy, the screen of netting was suddenly pulled back, and the last rays of the setting sun poured into the stall. With eyes glowing from the fiery sunset, Abaddon glared at an unannounced visitor who had dared to interrupt the game.

Cain, who had sat with his back to the stall's opening on the square, turned around to face the newcomer. He looked to be about thirty or so. With longish hair and a short, dark beard, he carried himself with dignity and grace. Cain noticed he had the hands of a craftsman. He was dressed in a simple, russet-brown tunic.

Abruptly, the young gamer addressed Cain. "I shall be back. I must go urinate." He quickly rose from his seat and then rushed by the visitor, disappearing out of the stall.

"Welcome to Judaea," said the man hospitably in Aramaic. "I can see by your clothing that you are not a native here."

"That is true," Cain responded in fluent Aramaic as he stood to greet the man.

"You are from Rome, then? Few Romans speak our language so well," the visitor replied.

"Thank you for your kind words, stranger. I have learned quite a few languages on my journeys."

Cain could see that the man was uncomfortable in the late afternoon heat, with perspiration beading his forehead. "Please allow me to offer you some water," he said, gesturing to the blown-glass bottle.

"I would be grateful for a drink," replied the visitor. Lifting the bottle to his lips, he swallowed deeply. Then, pausing to admire its dazzling swirls of blue and white, he said, "What wonderful workmanship! Where did you get this fine bottle, my friend?"

"I made it. Or, rather, my factory made it."

"And where is the factory that produces such beauty, if I may ask?"

"In Carthage. I established the facility some years ago," Cain said proudly. "Its output can now be found all over the world."

"How did you arrive at the notion of creating such a piece?"

"Well...it was a long time ago. While on a lengthy journey, I watched a bolt of lightning strike sand on a beach and turn it to glass," Cain explained. "That's when I conceived the idea of making glass one day. The designs have grown steadily more elaborate."

The visitor nodded but said nothing. Cain broke the pause in their conversation by inviting him to sit down.

"Will you care to stay and chat until my opponent returns?"

"You are most courteous. May I ask your name?"

"I am called Marcus Flavius Pictor. I grew up in Alexandria but now live in Rome. Here, take this chair." He drew up the seat his opponent had occupied from the opposite side of the table.

The visitor sat down but then raised his left hand in a quizzical gesture. Cain could see that a small black thorn was embedded in the man's index finger. The thorn had apparently been on the arm of the chair, although how the youth had avoided impaling his own finger on it escaped Cain. The wound must have been painful, since the thorn was stuck deeply into the stranger's fingertip, yet he gave only a brief wince. Then, he smiled and even chuckled softly as he removed the thorn and flicked it away.

Not wishing to embarrass his new acquaintance, Cain asked him about his business in Caesarea.

"What has brought you to Judaea's capital?"

"My father has a carpenter's shop two days journey to the northeast, in Galilee. He sent me here to deliver the chairs and tables for the game board gathering. I have been walking the square all day to make sure my customers are satisfied."

"Well, the table in this stall is extremely sturdy, and the chairs are level and don't squeak. If this furniture came from your workshop, you are to be congratulated."

"You are very kind, Marcus. May I ask in turn why you have come to Caesarea, all the way from Rome?"

"I wanted to see the new harbor," Cain replied. "I have been in the merchant shipping business for quite some time now, but never before in Caesarea. It looks like it could become a very prosperous market for me. Also, I am building a large house near Rome, on the Bay of Naples. It is almost complete, in fact, so I have been shopping for some house furnishings here."

"That is a coincidence. I too shall be building a large house soon," the visitor said.

"Well, on a carpenter's wage you will have to control expenses carefully!" Cain joked.

The stranger laughed and nodded.

Changing the subject, Cain gestured to the board and inquired if the visitor was familiar with the game.

"Oh, yes, I know it very well," he answered with a smile. "Let me see, now. Your opponent seems to be ahead."

Cain resisted the temptation to request any advice. The carpenter pointed to a tile bearing the image of a green snake near the center of the board.

"The serpent has had you trapped far too long, my friend." Placing his left index finger on the tile, he slid it toward Cain and added, "You must be set free." The carpenter removed his finger from the game piece. A drop of blood had collected upon the snake image within the tile's indentation.

Noticing the stranger was still bleeding, Cain reached in his tunic and offered him a piece of silk cloth.

"No thank you," the man demurred. "I am sure it could be much worse. But look—I have marred this game piece. I hope its owner won't be too upset." Rising from his chair, he continued, "Thank you for the water. As for your opponent, he will not be returning to this table." The stranger smiled warmly and turned toward the entrance of the tent.

"Are you leaving now?" Cain asked. "I have not even learned your name."

The visitor turned to face Cain and smiled. "I am called Jesus of Nazareth," came his reply, and then he strode out to the square and disappeared into the crowd.

Cain was perplexed. Why had this carpenter departed so abruptly? He stared vacantly at the town square, where board games continued even in the twilight. He glimpsed his young opponent, seated at a table about twenty-five feet away. Abaddon had apparently begun a new match with another gamer. He called to him several times but the young man ignored him completely.

Annoyed by the disrespect, Cain glanced back at the leather pouch on the table. Reasoning that the money should be considered forfeit, he attached the pouch to his belt, exited the stall, and strode purposefully toward the harbor. Upon reaching the port, he boarded his ship.

"No shopping today?" asked Felix upon greeting his empty-handed master.

"Actually, I passed the time in the square playing senet." Cain tossed the leather pouch to Felix. "Here, put this in the ship's treasury. Nothing too exciting. Only thirty pieces of silver."

Felix smiled. "Just the same, I'm glad that you and I play the game for fun." He turned and went below decks. Absently tossing the pouch from hand to hand, it struck him that the bag seemed a bit bulky for the sum Cain had mentioned. But with many more preparations to be made before tomorrow's sailing for Rome, he simply deposited the pouch in the strongbox, intending to verify the contents later.

CHAPTER 60

Ercolano: Present Day

uc Renard's helicopter touched down in Ercolano on the stroke of noon. A black Mercedes stretch limo conveyed the travelers and their bodyguards from the helipad to the dig site, barely half a mile away. Alerted by one of his team, Silvio hastened up the makeshift staircase to street level, together with Juan Carlos.

"Benvenuti, Signori," Silvio welcomed the visitors courteously. Archibald Walker made the introductions.

"Silvio, this is Mr. Luc Renard, one of our most munificent benefactors at the Getty. Mr. Renard, let me present my colleague Dr. Silvio Sforza. Oh, and this is Mr. Rudolph Schmidt, one of California's most eminent attorneys."

After handshakes all around, the normally diplomatic Walker, who had fortified himself from a pocket flask in the airport terminal restroom at Naples, plunged onward. Turning to Silvio, he said, somewhat indelicately, "Now, my old friend, you really must explain to us why you permitted Amanda James to enter the chamber so prematurely."

Silvio sidestepped the question. "We'll cover all that in a few minutes. The main thing now is to get Amanda *out* of the chamber." Gesturing to Juan Carlos, he explained, "We've been working on a digital recording to trace Amanda's steps in solving the word puzzle for the combination lock. We're almost there."

Silvio paused and looked dramatically at Walker, making sure he had the man's full attention. "But Juan Carlos needs your help. I believe you can likely fit through the crack and come to her aid. Please let him explain our progress to you. I'll keep Mr. Renard and Mr. Schmidt company up here."

Gratified at what he interpreted as Silvio's invitation to play a key role, Walker nodded. Excusing himself, he accompanied Juan Carlos down the stairway to an area enclosed by a privacy tarp.

After Walker and Juan Carlos had distanced themselves from the group, Silvio turned to Luc Renard. It was now the archaeologist's turn to ask direct questions.

"Mr. Renard, we have only just met. But I can't refrain from asking you about the mineral claim that you have evidently filed in conjunction with your purchase contract."

Luc waved his hand casually. "Oh, the mineral claim? That's standard procedure. My company always files such claims when I acquire property.

"It's only prudent. Don't take it seriously," Schmidt added.

"Well, I must inform both of you that in Ercolano such claims are taken very seriously," Silvio parried. "Let me pursue another point with you, however. When exactly do you anticipate that the title to the property will be transferred from your company to the Getty?"

Luc Renard was on the verge of replying when a helicopter with the Vatican's yellow-and-white flag and official insignia of two crossed keys flew low overhead. Abandoning his quest for information, Silvio suggested that Luc and the lawyer should join Walker and Juan Carlos to check on their progress. But Luc, concerned about the arrival of the Vatican helicopter, demurred.

"As the prospective owner of the property, I shall join you in greeting these unexpected visitors, Dr. Sforza."

A few minutes later, Silvio warmly greeted Cardinal Ravatti and Monsignor Notombo at their car and then made introductions. He informed Luc that Cardinal Ravatti was well versed in archaeology.

"You say you represent the Pontifical Commission for Sacred Archaeology," Luc said to the monsignor after the exchange of pleasantries. "What interest, may I ask, does the Vatican have in *my* excavation, Monsignor?" Silvio privately noted Luc's choice of pronoun, as well as the magnate's proprietary tone of voice.

"It is what you might call a routine procedure, Mr. Renard," Notombo replied suavely. "The Vatican is always represented when the excavation of any catacomb commences. Or the excavation of any site that *might* be a catacomb," he added.

"But you are a day early," Luc politely pointed out. "The site is closed until tomorrow. There are no excavations in progress today. It's Sunday, as you gentlemen are well aware."

Cardinal Ravatti intervened in a gravelly tone. "Well, Mr. Renard, you may become the owner of the land tomorrow, but you seem to be overlooking a more pressing matter—the safety of Dr. Amanda James."

Although he maintained a poker mask, Luc Renard was disconcerted. By somehow involving the Vatican, Silvio seemed to have outmaneuvered him, at least for the moment. He would have to proceed carefully.

"Ah, yes, Dr. James," Rudolph Schmidt hastily interjected. "We are effecting a rescue as we speak. But when she is safely out of the chamber, the entrance will be closed. There is certainly a difference, gentlemen, between a rescue and an excavation," he reminded the clerics.

Cardinal Ravatti was not accustomed to being trumped, and certainly not by an American attorney. Here on the doorstep of the Incogniti, he made his intentions clear.

"We agree that Dr. James's safety should be the top priority," Ravatti said. "But if she reports a catacomb or the presence of Christian remains, the Vatican will immediately assume oversight of this excavation in keeping with long-standing Italian and international laws. And regardless of the particulars of her initial report, we already have probable cause to conduct our own inspection." He glanced meaningfully at Renard and Schmidt. "*If* we find nothing of interest to the Vatican, gentlemen, the site is yours. But until then..."

"It is truly a pity that you are unaware of all the forces in play here," Renard interrupted. He moved fractionally closer toward Ravatti, seeming to ignore the presence of Notombo and Schmidt. "Your claims to legality notwithstanding, you will not be the one who dictates the fate of this excavation."

Cardinal Ravatti's eyes widened slightly in surprise as the brash billionaire dug the verbal knife in deeper. "The property *will* be donated to the Getty, so that whatever I find within will benefit the public. I did not acquire this land so that the Vatican could hijack it and sit on the discovery for fifty years."

Luc Renard spun on his heels and stalked toward the excavation, with Schmidt trailing after him like a puppy. After several paces, Renard called out to Ravatti over his shoulder. "When we meet again, *Cardinal*, it will be in a court of law."

CHAPTER 61

Rome and Judaea, AD 29–33

"All paid up?" Cain asked Felix after the captain had returned from the port administration office. He was eager to see his son, so from Caesarea they had made directly for Ostia, without bothering to break the journey in Naples in order to unload the items purchased for his villa in Herculaneum.

Felix reached into the leather bag he carried and handed Cain the receipt for payment of the port fees. He also withdrew a small leather pouch and gave it to his master.

"Everything is in order, sir. But while I was verifying the accounts and the funds in the treasury, I discovered something curious."

Cain opened the pouch with the silver coins that had been forfeited by his opponent at the tile game. Among the coins was the ceramic tile with the green snake, still stained with the blood from Jesus's finger.

"Very strange," thought Cain, as he closed the pouch and attached it to his belt. How could the tile have gotten in there? He was sure he had last seen it on Abaddon's game board.

"No matter, Felix. Have all the merchandise delivered to the estate. We'll decide there which goods we want to ship to Herculaneum."

The captain saluted, and Cain disembarked to board his smaller launch for the brief journey up the Tiber to central Rome.

Because word of his safe arrival had been dispatched from the ship, he had expected that Quintus would meet him at some distance from the estate on the Palatine. He longed to scoop the boy up in his arms as his son greeted him joyfully.

But there was no sign of Quintus near the entrance to the estate. It was only as he strode into the atrium that Cain glimpsed the boy, now confined to a wooden wheelchair. The disease that had weakened his legs, though, had not dulled the child's eyes. As a house servant guided the chair across the terrazzo floor, Cain reached out and took Quintus in his arms, hugging him fiercely.

"Father! It is really you!" Quintus cried. "I've dreamed about this day for so long!"

Suppressing a twinge of guilt for his extended absence, Cain kissed his son on the forehead.

"I, too, have dreamed of you, my son. I can't wait to cheer for the Greens together!"

The boy clapped his hands in anticipation. "There are races at the Circus tomorrow, Father! Can we go?"

"Why not? Of course we can go! We will leave for the Circus early and stay as long as you want."

"The new horse Fulgur will be running his first race. He's as good as his name, fast as lightning. I helped train him!" said the boy proudly.

"You're a trainer now, little man?" Cain smiled.

"Well, Scorpus allows me to help him sometimes. But he does most of the training, I have to admit."

"I see," Cain said. "He is our best charioteer. You can learn much from him." The proud father was pleased that Scorpus had, perhaps unwittingly, served as a big brother to his son.

"Let us have our meal now," he said, turning to the house servant. "The sea air has given me quite an appetite. What's on the menu?"

"Today we are preparing Corsican mullet with asparagus sauce, quail's eggs, and celery, sir," the man replied. "And for wine?"

"The Falernian, by all means." He then dismissed the servant with instructions to send for the local barber. Handing him the leather pouch that contained the silver pieces and the mysterious senet tile, he told him to secure it in the estate's strongbox. He then placed Quintus in the wheelchair and took hold of the seat back. "Let's go into the garden, son, and I'll show you what I brought you for your birthday," he said as he wheeled him forward. Quintus, who had turned eight while Cain was away in Judaea, clapped his hands again in pleasure.

They sat near the tall cypress trees flanking the western end of the peristyle. The sun was high now, but the trees provided ample shade, and the gently splashing fountains helped relieve the heavy, humid air of Rome in late summer. Cain reached into one of the bags that the launch's crew had delivered to the estate and withdrew a large package.

"There you are, son. Happy belated birthday!"

Unwrapping the package hastily, Quintus ran his hand smoothly over its contents: four highly polished agate horses pulling a *quadriga*, or racing chariot, made of the purest silver. All the figures had been fashioned meticulously to scale.

"Oh, Father, how beautiful they are!" he exclaimed.

"I should have gotten you two of these sculptures. Then you'd have one horse for each of your eight years."

"I'll put this one right next to my bed." The boy declared firmly. "That way it will be the last thing I see at night and the first when I wake up in the morning."

"I'm glad you like it. They are made in Sicily, but I came upon it in Judaea at a place called Caesarea."

"That's the provincial capital isn't it?"

"Why, yes, but how did you know?"

"I love geography! And Tisias is a good tutor, although he is strict." Tisias was one of the Greek freedmen whom Cain had hired as tutors for his son during his absence.

When the barber arrived, Cain drew his chair closer to a nearby fountain. During his haircut and shave, he plied Quintus with questions about his studies. Clearly, the boy was highly motivated. He had mastered Euclidean geometry theorems that would have challenged students twice his age, and he had memorized several entire orations of Cicero. The father beamed with pride as Quintus gave a rousing performance worthy of the renowned Roman orator, complete with dramatic arm gestures from the wheelchair.

"At this rate, you will be Rome's leading advocate when you grow up!" he complimented his son.

They ate in the garden. After lunch, Cain wheeled Quintus from the peristyle indoors to the child's bedroom. When his son had chosen a suitable spot for the agate sculpture, Cain was about to leave him for his afternoon nap when Quintus said, "I'm awfully worried, Father."

Cain's stomach tightened. He thought of the cypress trees in the garden, trees that were often linked with death and planted in cemeteries.

"What troubles you?"

"I worry about you after I am gone. I don't want you to be so lonely."

Tears came to the father's eyes. "He knows he may die soon," Cain thought, "but he's worried about *me*." With his back still to the boy, he attempted to redirect the pathway of their conversation.

"You are not going anywhere, son, except to the Circus Maximus tomorrow morning."

"Yes, I know. But tell me, Father. What actually happens when someone dies?"

Cain recalled one of their conversations after Julia passed away. He turned and faced his son. "You remember what we said about your mother?" he asked Quintus. "Death is a part of life. It's hard to understand, but death is a happy state, where a person is free of troubles. And many people think that, after we die, we are reunited with all those whom we have loved and who have gone before us."

"Then I will see Mother again? If I'll be with her, I am not afraid of death," Quintus declared.

"Yes, but you have many years to go before that, little man. Now lie down and get your rest. We have a big day tomorrow."

As he withdrew to the atrium, Cain marveled at his son's courage. The prospect that his son's life would be all too brief stood in stark contrast to his own longevity, and his ambivalence about it.

While Quintus slept during the late afternoon, Cain sent for the doctor who headed the team attending on his son.

"What is your prognosis, Junius?" he asked the physician, a trim fifty-year-old with close-cropped, slightly graying hair.

"The boy's physical condition has deteriorated significantly since you left, sir," the doctor answered. "It is possible that other organs besides the lungs have been affected. For two months now, his legs have not been able to support him. But his mind is vibrant. If anything, his interest in his studies has intensified."

"And how do you think he will be six months from now?"

"His disease consumes bodily strength," the doctor replied. "But the link between emotions—mind and spirit—and physical health should never be underestimated. Your son has tremendous willpower, sir. All I can say for sure is that his condition is chronic, not critical."

Safeguarding his son's happiness now became the guiding force of Cain's existence. The doctor's remark about Quintus's emotional state lingered in his mind. He decided to do everything possible to give the boy a full and satisfying life, whatever its duration.

Father and son haunted the Circus and the stables, with Quintus taking more and more of an interest in the mechanics and nuances of horse training. Cain gave the boy Xenophon's manual on horsemanship, written in Greek nearly four centuries before. Quintus absorbed every detail, amazing his father with observations on everything from how to break a colt to such esoteric issues as whether a colt should be fed with his halter on or off.

As the months slipped by, Cain received regular reports from Carthage concerning his blown-glass factory and from Herculaneum about his villa and repository. He limited his visits to Herculaneum, since without a hippodrome, Quintus found the place boring. When he felt his presence there was required, however, he left his son in the charge of Scorpus, whose relationship with the boy was now that of a mentor. Quintus accompanied the chariot driver to the horse sales and delighted in helping select new stallions for the Greens.

One day, at Cain's prompting, Scorpus arranged for Quintus to take his own chariot ride—this time in one of the larger, ceremonial chariots used for the great processions of owners and drivers that were arranged two or three times every season. With the track clear of other chariots in the early morning, Scorpus glanced at Cain, who nodded approvingly. Scorpus then handed the reins to the boy.

"Go ahead, Quintus, urge them into a trot," the driver said as Cain beamed.

Delighted, Quintus snapped the reins gently and the chariot accelerated. As they rounded the second turn, the boy exclaimed, "Just wait, Scorpus. In a few years I will challenge *you* to a race!"

Clapping his driver on the shoulder, Cain chimed in jovially, "You had better keep your skills sharp for that day!" Inwardly, however, he painfully contemplated the very different future his son faced.

ᘓᘏ᙭ᘔ

Because Quintus's condition seemed stable, Cain was able to travel on business each year. But here again he strove to make the trips as brief as possible, in order to maximize the time he could spend with his son. In AD 32, construction delays with the observatory in Herculaneum forced him to rearrange his schedule. The metal gears for the device that opened the oculus in the dome were not manufactured as specified. Cain, therefore, postponed his scheduled departure and endeavored to rectify the problems while the sailing season slipped by.

Then, late that autumn, when Quintus was going on twelve, Cain received a message from Carthage. As a result of a small civil uprising, there had been some light damage to the factory's warehouses. Although a sailing voyage could be highly problematic at this time of year, Felix had extraordinary seamanship abilities. Cain determined that he would set out from Rome near the end of November, sail to Carthage, perhaps to Tyre, and then return to Judaea for a brief visit.

He needed to be back in Rome for the chariot festival parade in the beginning of March the following year. This, the most important of the periodic processions, was a huge gathering, where the owners and leading drivers of all the factions would appear with much pomp and circumstance in the Circus Maximus. Because he was the majority shareholder in the Greens, now the winningest faction, Cain's attendance was expected. However, the desire to return to his son's side was far more compelling.

"When I come back, we will start looking for a horse," he told Quintus. "Not a sculpture this time, son, but a real horse. The stallion will be your very own. For your twelfth birthday."

Quintus's eyes sparkled. "Oh, Father, I will take such good care of him!"

"And what will you name him?"

His son's lack of hesitation suggested he had pondered the matter for some time.

"I will name him Crescens, for under my care he will grow strong!"

May the name be a good omen, thought Cain, as he hugged his boy.

CHAPTER 62

The Mediterranean, AD 33

"It's good to be back on board the *Nostos!*" Cain exclaimed to Felix, as the captain directed their departure from Ostia on an overcast morning with shifting, gusty winds. The Greek name of Cain's cargo ship meant "journey home."

"The weather may be chancy, sir. But your knowledge of these waters is unsurpassed."

"You sell yourself short, Captain. I have always felt safe in your hands."

Cain thought of his farewell with Quintus. Every time he left Rome, he had mixed feelings. He longed to take the boy with him, but Quintus's health might not withstand a long sea voyage. It was far safer for him to remain in Rome, where the doctors could keep a close watch on his condition and the kindly Scorpus could offer strong moral support.

Heavy seas on the voyage to Carthage delayed them a bit. But after supervising warehouse repairs there and loading a fresh shipment of blown glass, they made Caesarea in fifteen days, a fast run aided by moderate seas and steady southwesterly winds in sunny weather. It took Cain only a few days to transact his business, so he decided in favor of moving on to Tyre, where he hoped to purchase a large quantity of Tyrian purple dye and a consignment of salted freshwater fish from the Sea of Galilee. Both were highly desirable commodities that would fetch high prices in Rome. The dye was unique, and the fish were coveted as a culinary delicacy.

As the *Nostos* approached Tyre, Cain couldn't help but think once again of Tanith. Few people in his life had touched his heart the way she had. From the harbor, he glimpsed the balcony of the old estate that she and her sea-captain father Ahiram had once owned atop the hill. Time had weathered the stone, but it had not erased Cain's bittersweet memories. He had lost her so soon after she found him.

"Oh, God," he entreated silently, "please don't take my Quintus as well."

Curiously, the bazaar in Tyre had not changed much. This market was still one of the focal points of Mediterranean trade, the way it had been in the days of Ramesses and Moses. Although the sailing season was over, the bazaar still bristled with activity, with merchants concluding deals for overland trade ventures to destinations such as Petra, Antioch, and points east on the Silk Road. Cain had no trouble locating what he wanted.

Onshore winds meant that the visitors would have to remain in Tyre for at least a few days until offshore breezes favored departure. While Cain negotiated for the Tyrian dye consignment, Felix purchased supplies for the return voyage. He also identified a group of fishermen who had arrived in Tyre from a town named Capernaum, on the northern shore of the Sea of Galilee. Having agreed with them on a price for a large consignment of freshwater fish, Felix plunged back into the bazaar to meet Cain.

"The vendors are two sets of brothers, sir. They are Jews from Galilee. I sampled the fish, and they are delicious."

"Are they quoting a fair price?"

"I have negotiated that with them already. I am sure you will be pleased."

"Well done, Felix. How soon can the fish be loaded on the *Nostos?*"

"It can be done immediately, sir. The fishermen are standing by at the dock. But I have one more matter to attend to before we leave—the new canvas awning you requested. I will search for it now and join you at the port in an hour or so. Would you mind paying the Galileans in my absence?"

"No, of course not. But don't be too long. If the winds shift, we must leave as soon as possible."

"I understand, sir. The fishermen have a treasurer named Judas. He's the one wearing a yellow tunic."

Nodding, Cain made his way back to the port. His 160-foot cargo ship was anchored parallel to the dock, and his crew was working amidships with the group of itinerant Galilean fisherman to load the fish on board. He had never seen these fishermen before, but standing near the *Nostos* was an onlooker whom Cain recognized at once: the carpenter who had interrupted his tile game three years before in Caesarea and to whom he had offered water. The man was exchanging casual chat with the Galileans.

"Jesus of Nazareth!" exclaimed Cain. "What are you doing here?"

Jesus took Cain's hand. "Marcus Flavius Pictor, you have returned. How glad I am to see you!"

"Let us converse together in the stern of my ship. Come," Cain urged Jesus toward the aft gangplank, bemused that the carpenter had a memory almost as acute as his own.

When the two men had boarded, Cain guided Jesus to a sheltered spot under the awning.

"You know the visiting fishermen, then?" asked Cain.

"Certainly. They are all my friends. Do you see the two men on the left in the light blue tunics?" Jesus pointed to the workers amidships. "Those are Peter and Andrew. They are brothers. And, closer to us on the right are James and John. They are also brothers. The one in the middle, in the yellow tunic, is Judas."

"But when we met in Caesarea, you were a carpenter," said Cain. "Have you adopted a new profession?"

"Yes, you might say that," said Jesus with a grin. "These fishermen are a great help to me. But tell me, Marcus, about that house you said you were building. Have you completed it yet?"

"Well, no. I had expected to be finished by now, but some of the materials I ordered for the repository on the estate were not delivered up to standard."

"I am sorry to hear that. What will your repository be used for?"

Cain felt curiously disarmed in Jesus's presence. He saw no reason not to be candid.

"Well, part of it will serve as an observatory, but its main purpose is an archive. I have spent much of my spare time recently amassing a collection of great historical works. I am seeing to it that they are preserved for posterity."

Jesus did not probe the matter but said only, "You are to be commended, Marcus."

Shifting the focus, Cain asked, "In Caesarea, you mentioned that you would also be building a large house soon. Have you started yet?"

"Yes, indeed. It is almost finished."

"Well," said Cain, "I am always on the lookout for experienced carpenters. If you will travel to Herculaneum, I have the ideal next job for you. I recall very well the chairs and tables you built in Caesarea. They were top-quality furniture. I'd be proud to have such items in my villa."

"That is gracious of you to say," Jesus replied with a chuckle.

"Your work for me could become quite popular among the wealthy in Herculaneum. They demand nothing but the finest craftsmanship and materials."

"Believe it or not, Marcus, I actually do my best work with common components. Thank you for your offer, but I presently have important work to do here in Judaea. Still, I would be delighted to accept a future invitation from you."

"What is this important work you speak of, if I may ask?"

"My friends and I have traveled from Galilee to Tyre on a mission. Why not come and hear me speak about it to a gathering later this afternoon?"

Cain hesitated. He thought about staying, but during their conversation the wind had changed, and the ship's flapping pennants showed that an offshore breeze had finally arrived. He realized that a window for departure was opening, but it might be of short duration, and he had to be back in Rome in time for the chariot festival.

"I, too, must decline for now, Jesus. We have been waiting on the wind for three days now. This time of year, with such unpredictable weather, we have to sail when we can. I am eager to get back to Rome."

"Yes, of course," Jesus said. "You have a family there?"

"My wife died young," Cain told him. "But I was blessed with a son. Yet his health is poor. Every day is a struggle for him. The doctors say he has a chronic lung condition. Watching his body waste away, I would give up everything—my land, my houses, my ship, all my belongings—if only he could recover. He loves horses..." Cain's voice trailed off awkwardly, as tears welled in his eyes.

"I understand the deep love you have for your son," Jesus said, gripping Cain's shoulder warmly.

The offshore breeze freshened, and Cain could see that all the fish had now been loaded. Collecting himself, he strode across the deck and delivered a pouch of money into the waiting hands of Judas before returning to where Jesus stood.

"You are ready to sail, then?" Jesus asked.

Cain looked amidships and saw that Felix had arrived and the crew had begun trimming the sails.

"Yes. But I hope we will meet again."

"Nothing is impossible, Marcus. Have a safe voyage home." Jesus stepped from the ship's stern back onto the dock, then turned around to face Cain.

"Travel quickly," he said. "For your son's good health has returned."

His words were almost lost in the welter of shouts and commands as the bowline was cast off and the ship glided forward. Cain waved his hand in farewell.

❦

Cain had budgeted enough time for brief stops in Antioch and Athens. In Antioch, he would acquire more Silk Road merchandise and perhaps sell some of his Tyrian dye; while in Athens he would pick up the new telescope he had commissioned for his observatory. He would also see, for the first time, the renowned Parthenon, built on the Acropolis about thirty years after he had left the city for Persia. Many people had praised it as the world's most magnificent structure.

On the first leg, about two hundred miles northward from Tyre to Antioch, Cain and Felix chatted over lunch, savoring some of the salted fish they had purchased. They were seated in the stern, under the fine new canvas awning.

"By the way, who was that fellow you were talking with here on the ship when we were getting ready to cast off?" asked Felix.

"Funny that you should mention it. He's an interesting man from Galilee I met originally in Caesarea three years ago at the senet tournament. He knows all those men who sold us this fish."

"What was he doing in Tyre?"

"Well, that's the mystery of it. He had been a carpenter, and a very good one. But now he says he's on some important mission with those fishermen. He wanted me to come hear him talk. I couldn't quite figure it out."

"What's his name?"

"Jesus of Nazareth."

Felix blinked and set down his fork. "That was Jesus of *Nazareth?* Sir, when I was in the Hebrew section of the market buying the canvas, this name was on everyone's lips. Rumors were buzzing about how this man had supposedly healed a woman's daughter. The girl was said to be tormented by a demon. Jesus praised the mother's great faith and granted her request. Aside from the miraculous cure, many people were pointing out that this woman was not even Jewish. Jesus has apparently attracted a very considerable number of followers."

Now it was Cain's turn to be taken aback. What had Jesus said about Quintus's health just before their departure? His answer to his captain was decisive.

"Felix, we must find out more about this man Jesus. Do you remember Demetrius in Antioch?"

"Yes, of course, sir. He is one of your most trusted cohorts in trade."

"Demetrius owes me a large sum from our last transaction. When we arrive in Antioch, tell him I will forgive the entire amount if he will agree to go immediately to Galilee. He should interview people there, especially the fishermen, to find out everything he can about Jesus. Then, arrange to put Demetrius on a fast transport ship so that he can reach Rome before we do. I want to hear his report as soon as we arrive."

"Yes, sir. I will see to it."

As the prow of his ship smoothly cleft the turquoise sea, half of Cain's heart questioned his decision to decline Jesus's invitation in Tyre.

The other half strained with impatience to see Quintus.

CHAPTER 63

Circus Maximus, Rome: March, AD 33

hen Cain reached Rome, the chariot festival was already beginning. As he crested the Palatine Hill, he could hear the roars of an overflow crowd at the Circus below. They were keyed up to cheer on their faction at the parade and at the races that followed, in which the charioteers would compete for the winter season championship. There was no time to stop at his estate on the way, and Cain knew that the house servants would have wheeled Quintus to a trackside seat earlier that morning. The boy would never miss an event such as this one. He wondered if his son, under the guidance of Scorpus, had begun to scout horses for the birthday present Cain had promised him.

Gaining entrance to the arena was difficult because of the jostling crowds. As he approached the dirt track, Cain glimpsed the lineup of ceremonial chariots. Recognizing him, an official gestured urgently.

"Hurry right to your chariot, sir. Middle of the seventh row. Scorpus is waiting for you."

Thanking the man, Cain strode directly to the chariot, whose four horses were restively pawing the ground.

"I thank the gods you made it, sir," Scorpus hollered to his master, passing him a green vest. When Cain had donned it, Scorpus wrapped the horses' leather reins around his master's waist in a special parade custom that symbolized the close bond between the faction owners and their charioteers. During the actual races, it was the drivers who were girdled by the leather straps. Scorpus, clad in an emerald-green tunic, leaned over toward Cain with a smile.

"We have a terrific surprise in store for you, sir!" he shouted.

"What is it, Scorpus?" Cain yelled back, but his words were drowned by the chants and cheers of a quarter of a million spectators.

After the blast of a trumpet fanfare, the heavily adorned chariot, drawn by four coal-black Arabian stallions, slowly began to move. Twenty-eight rows—each one eight chariots abreast—would process around the track for two ceremonial laps. Each faction was represented by fifty-six chariots, with horses, drivers, and owners sporting the faction's colors. With nearly nine hundred horses processing at a majestic gait, the ceremony would take the better part of an hour.

Cain and Scorpus rounded the first turning post and headed back, waving to the crowd. Adoring spectators in the front rows of the arena were throwing thousands of flowers onto the track so that the horses could make their way over a dazzling carpet of colorful, sweet-smelling petals. The crowd's energy reverberated through Cain's body, creating a rush of adrenalin. All eyes were focused on the owners and their charioteers. They were the stars of the greatest spectacle in Rome.

Halfway down the track, the lead horses slowed. As Cain peered ahead, he saw why. An unusually large flock of hooded vultures had settled on the track about fifty feet ahead of the front row of chariots. The remaining rows bunched up, then ground to a complete halt, with the horses stubbornly resisting their drivers' attempts to urge them forward. Glancing behind him for a moment, Cain could see that the stallions were nervous, flicking their ears and beating the ground with their hooves.

Cain looked forward once more. Suddenly, he spotted the reason for this dangerous interruption of the parade. The vultures had not appeared by chance. A young spectator in the front row of the stands had somehow eluded the arena officials and was tossing chunks of bloody meat from a large bag onto the track.

It was Abaddon.

Cain immediately recognized his youthful opponent in the tile game that Jesus had interrupted in Judaea four years before. The spectators surrounding him seemed oblivious to his actions. What was he doing in Rome, sabotaging the parade at the Circus Maximus?

Cain felt Scorpus's hand on his shoulder. "Look there, sir," said Scorpus as the murmuring crowd tried to fathom the scene. Cain traced his charioteer's pointing finger to a position in the stands not far from where Abaddon stood. There, in the front row, was Quintus. But something was missing. There was no wheelchair. His precious son was jumping up and down and shouting to Cain, "Look at me, father!" Quintus had been healed!

Cain's mind whirled. For an instant his attention flicked toward Abaddon, and he found the youth's eyes locked on his own. The gamer was dressed in a scintillating black robe with red and gold flecks. The sunlight around him seemed to morph into shadow as he stared icily. Then Cain heard words that chilled him even more.

"Now you die!"

As if by command, the entire flock of vultures took flight and headed directly for the stalled procession. Their moving shadow overspread the horses and chariots. The thousand-pound Arabians, spooked by the shadow, began to bolt down the track at a full gallop. With the turning post ever closer, the riders and owners struggled helplessly to guide their steeds to make the sharp corner.

Realizing that a crash and a pileup were inevitable, Scorpus quickly reached for the knife in his belt and, at the very last second, managed to cut the leather straps encircling his master's waist. Most of the chariots in the front rows had failed to negotiate the turn, and Cain's plunging stallions, in total panic, charged headlong into the wreckage just as Scorpus's knife severed the last bond. The crowd's screams swelled with the anguished cries of men and horses, whose bodies jumbled together in a writhing mass.

Cain's chariot plunged into the chaos and overturned, taking Scorpus with it. Cain, thrown to the track, could feel the pounding stampede of hundreds of hooves striking the earth. Then those hooves dug into his body, fracturing his limbs, and lacerating an eye. The wheels of several chariots ran over him, severing three of his fingers and almost amputating his left foot. His back felt broken.

Just before losing consciousness, Cain glimpsed the heavy metal axle of a chariot hurtling toward him like a spear. There was no escape. The young tile player was right—he was finally going to die.

Suddenly, a golden, luminous figure of a woman with wings appeared in front of him. The creature swatted the chariot axle aside with a casual flick of her left hand, while with her right hand she deflected a stumbling horse that was mere feet from falling directly on top of Cain. The axle gone, the shimmering being ran her hand gently across his bloodied face.

Cain blinked in disbelief. When he opened his eyes, the figure had vanished.

He was surrounded by horrifying carnage. Dozens of men and horses had been killed on the track, in full view of the terrified spectators. The injured resembled the casualties on a battlefield, and their tortured screams filled the air. Cain called out for Scorpus but could not discern his voice in the melee, nor could he even turn his head to locate him. Cain hazily saw an emergency team approach him. His last thought was that his life had somehow been exchanged for Quintus's restoration.

In the comfort of that notion, Cain slipped into darkness.

CHAPTER 64

The Palatine: March, AD 33

"Please, sir, drink," begged Helvia, a young slave girl who cautiously touched a glass of syrupy brown liquid to her patient's lips. "The doctor says you need this before we begin."

Cain had just regained consciousness. Instinctively twisting his head to the side, he refused the foul-smelling mixture. Out of the corner of his good eye, he saw something glowing.

"No, leave me alone," whimpered a half-dead Cain. "I will heal by myself."

Circus Maximus track slaves had rushed his broken body on a stretcher to his estate on the Palatine hill, covering the short distance in minutes. Cain lay on his large kitchen table, his body a pulverized wreck.

"Brave man, but he's delirious," said Junius, the house physician. "Now," he ordered Helvia, "pinch his nose and pour it down his throat!"

The tourniquets on Cain's arms and legs were failing. Having treated many Roman soldiers after battle, the doctor knew his wealthy patient would surely bleed out if he did not act fast.

Helvia poured the opium concentrate into her master's mouth and then held his jaw shut until he swallowed. Next, she jammed a leather bit between Cain's shattered teeth, causing him to gag and gasp for air.

"That brew will help you soon," she assured him. "Now, please bite down, master."

The physician withdrew a red-hot branding iron from the oven as Helvia's strong arms locked Cain's bloodied head tightly against her bosom. Other nervous house slaves firmly secured their master's limbs. Cain tried hard to free himself, but to no avail. He could barely breathe through his fractured nose.

"Sir, you must stop struggling," urged the doctor. "You'll only make this worse." A slave himself, Junius wondered what punishment would befall him after the excruciating pain he was about to inflict on his master.

Junius placed a wet cloth over Cain's good eye to prevent him from witnessing the gruesome procedure. "This is going to hurt, master," cautioned the doctor. Knowing he could delay no longer, he pressed the glowing iron onto Cain's hemorrhaging shoulder.

Cain felt his flesh being seared, and the stench almost made him vomit. Again and again the doctor cauterized veins and arteries in areas formerly occupied by fingers and toes. Cain's muffled screams could be heard by the entire household staff. Curiously, when Junius moved to the wounds in Cain's legs and feet, the screaming stopped. The doctor surmised that his patient had lost feeling in his legs due to a broken back.

Finally, the narcotic took effect. While Cain was unconscious, Junius amputated a small portion of his mangled left foot. He then sewed nearly a thousand stitches in Cain's skin. Cain resembled a human jigsaw puzzle before they wrapped him tightly in linen bandages from head to toe.

Having done all he could, Junius considered the likely extent of Cain's internal injuries. "His life," the doctor sadly proclaimed, "is probably over."

❧

But of course, it wasn't.

For several days, Cain lay in a darkened room, slipping in and out of consciousness. At one point, he heard Junius murmur discreetly that he could not survive his horrific wounds. Groggy from the pain medicine, he listened to Helvia reassure a sobbing Quintus that his father would indeed survive.

After his staff had finally stopped drugging him, Cain gradually became lucid. He had never sustained such severe injuries. According to Junius, nearly every bone in his body was broken. Yet, Cain knew he had always regenerated in the past.

On the third day, he felt the return of sensation to his lower body and with it, a dull throbbing in his left foot. Even his appetite began to return. Daring to hope, he felt his willpower surging.

He ordered the servants to bring his son to him. As Quintus entered the room, Cain could not believe that his son was now walking, with no need of a wheelchair.

Cain weakly extended a wavering hand toward his son as Quintus swiftly approached his bedside.

"Father, I knew you would make it! How are you feeling?" Quintas asked, lightly grasping the remaining two exposed fingers of his father's right hand. Unseen by his son, under thick bandages, the nubs of Cain's severed fingers were swiftly regenerating.

"Better each day," Cain managed with a faint smile before changing the subject. "But look at you! How is this possible, my son? When did you recover your health?"

"It happened toward the end of January, Father, while you were away on your voyage. I woke up from my afternoon nap, and Helvia was about to place me in my wheelchair. Instead, I stood on my own, and then I simply walked by myself into the atrium!"

Junius broke in.

"He ran all over the house and garden that very afternoon, sir. This was no gradual remission. The boy's health was completely restored. Neither I nor any of my colleagues can explain such a transformation in a case of this kind."

"Some of the servants," Quintus joined in, "have been speaking of a sign from the gods, Father.

"Tell me, Doctor," asked Cain, his heart hammering in his chest, "did this happen on the twenty-fifth of January?"

"I believe it did," replied the startled doctor after a moment's reflection. "But how could you..."

Cain closed his eyes. It was the day he had departed from Tyre. The very same day on which Jesus had pronounced Quintus cured.

Turning to his son, he said softly, "My boy, this is not a sign from the gods. It is a gift from Judaea."

The puzzled look on Quintus's face gave way to eyes that were suddenly sad.

"Father, you know that Scorpus was killed in the crash?" Quintus's voice trembled.

Cain winced. "A great and loving heart, my son. We will all miss him terribly."

"But Father, what about his sons?" Quintus implored. "I don't know if I could survive without you."

Cain marveled at Quintus's character. "We will make sure all three of his boys are well cared for," he replied. "Perhaps you can begin teaching the oldest brother to help care for the horses and maintain the chariots."

"Thank you, Father. I will do that."

"I know you will be a great friend to him." Cain reassured his son.

Just then, Felix arrived, having been summoned by one of Cain's messengers. The sea captain had been boarding at the estate ever since the Circus disaster, out of loyal concern for his employer and in case Cain should need his services.

"How are you feeling today, sir?" Felix inquired.

"The pain is subsiding, but I can still barely move. Tell me, did Demetrius arrive safely in Rome?"

"Indeed yes, sir. After you left Ostia for the Circus, I made inquiries and located him. I knew you would want his report."

"Have him brought to the estate by lunchtime today."

"Very well, sir. I will see to it."

Cain's head slipped back onto the pillow. It was time to gather his strength. But he gave the servants strict orders to wake him when his visitor arrived.

☙❧

Demetrius reached the estate shortly after noon. Cain drew himself up in the bed, his eagerness outstripping the pain in his limbs. He was still wrapped from head to toe in splints and bandages, and a patch covered his wounded eye.

"Welcome to Rome, my friend. I trust you had a productive stay in Judaea?"

Accustomed to Cain's businesslike manner, Demetrius wasted no time in small talk over the Circus crash. Instead, he immediately provided the information his friend had so urgently requested.

"I arrived at the beginning of February and interviewed at least two dozen people in Galilee. They ranged from humble fishermen to merchants, wealthy landowners, and religious leaders. Their reports about this Jesus were both stunning and controversial," Demetrius said. "On the one hand, he was hailed by many as a miracle worker. In Judaea, Marcus, lame men have walked, the blind have recovered their sight, and lepers have been cleansed. Children suffering from deadly illnesses have been healed. One person even told me that Jesus actually raised a man named Lazarus from the dead!"

Jesus's last words to Cain on the docks of Tyre rang in his ears once again. "What else have you learned, Demetrius?"

"Well, sir, Jesus is not universally praised. Many Jews, especially in Galilee, regard him as a great moral teacher, but there is also substantial opposition to him. A number of my informants indicated that he claims to be the Son of God and the promised Messiah. These statements have provoked great anxiety among the local religious authorities, and even greater apprehension in the temple leadership in Jerusalem. Jesus has roundly criticized the Pharisees there as religious hypocrites. There are reports that they are plotting against Jesus, although their specific plans are unclear."

"How long did you remain in Judaea, Demetrius?"

"I was there nearly two weeks. I left on February 15, arriving here the day before you did. But we had no chance to meet, due to your accident..." Demetrius cast his eyes downward.

"It was no accident," Cain said darkly. "But no matter, Demetrius. Thank you for your efforts. I must rest now, but please have lunch in the garden with my son. The servants will attend you."

As he rested his head back on the pillow, Cain pondered the astonishing events of the past few years. Demetrius's report now allowed him to unravel many mysteries: the healing of his son, his miraculous rescue at the Circus, and the true identity of Jesus. Without a doubt, mused Cain, the reported claims about Jesus were true; no one but the Son of God could do what he had done.

As he took this in, more troubling realizations became clear. Abaddon must be the master of spirits, and he had set up the tile game in Caesarea in a vain attempt to keep him from meeting Jesus. It was he who had thrown the meat on the track at the Circus, attempting to kill Cain after he learned what Jesus had done for Quintus. The master of spirits had gone to great lengths, it seemed, to keep him away from Jesus of Nazareth.

Cain now understood his course. He must return to Judaea immediately. His third journey there would afford him a chance to thank Jesus and perhaps receive the answers to the riddle of his life. Even in his agony, even with virtually every bone in his body still broken, he would go to Judaea.

It was the Ides of March, the beginning of the sailing season. He could make the journey in two or three weeks if the winds were favorable. That afternoon, he sent again for Felix and disclosed his plans. The servants would lay his battered body on a stretcher and transport him from the estate to the Tiber River launch at sunset. A healthy Quintus could now accompany him as his cabin boy on the voyage.

"Will the *Nostos* be ready to weigh anchor tomorrow at sunrise, Captain?"

"You have my word on it, sir."

CHAPTER 65

The *Nostos*, AD 33

Cain's body regenerated rapidly. During the sea journey, therefore, he remained secluded in his stateroom, so as not to draw undue attention to the stark changes in his physical condition. Quintus tended to his father's needs. Himself the beneficiary of a sudden, unexplained cure, the boy was very curious about his father's swift recovery.

No longer able to evade Quintus's incessant questions, Cain decided to hold a candid discussion with the son he loved. So, before their meal was served one evening, he sat the boy down.

"Your tutors at home often speak of the gods, Quintus?"

"They frequently teach religion, Father. Especially when we read the myths and legends. I know about many of the gods and goddesses, both Roman and Greek," the boy said proudly.

"In Judaea, where we are going, the people known as Hebrews worship only one God, not many," Cain pointed out.

"He must not be much of a god. We Romans are only the latest of many to have conquered them."

"What if I told you that it was the son of the Hebrew God who healed you? And that he is healing me as well?"

Quintus looked puzzled. "How do you know this?"

"I have met him twice in Judaea, but I did not know who he was then. He said his name was Jesus. The last time I saw him, this man proclaimed to me that your health had been restored, and when I returned to you, I learned that you had been healed that very day!"

"A man? I don't understand," Quintus said.

"Nor do I. For some reason I cannot fathom, the Hebrew God sent his son into the world as a human being."

The boy looked at his father in awe. "Will we meet him when we get to Judaea, father?"

"I *must* meet him, for I need more than just physical healing, Quintus. Before you were born, I committed many evils. Now, I will seek out Jesus and ask for my *soul* to be cured."

"Father, you are not evil. You have always been kind to me. Years ago, many of the children in the neighborhood said you would abandon me in the forest to be eaten by wolves as I grew sicker. It is the Roman way to get rid of the weak, but I always had faith that you would not do that. I know you would *never* abandon someone you love."

Cain stared at his son, speechless. "If only he knew..." he thought.

After an awkward silence, he managed, "All I can tell you, son, is that the older one gets, the sicker one's soul can become. I believe only Jesus can help me."

Quintus nodded and said, "If he healed me, Father, he will heal you without fail."

Cain reached for his son, who melted into his father's embrace.

CHAPTER 66

Jerusalem, April, AD 33

The amphora dropped to the deck and shattered with a crash. The crew member who had been holding it scarcely seemed to notice the broken shards of pottery around his feet, so intently was he staring at Cain.

It was the morning of Friday, April 3, and the *Nostos* had just docked in Caesarea. With no time to offer an explanation for his full and miraculous recovery to his stunned crew, Cain issued crisp orders for two transport chariots to be brought from the ship's hold and hitched to teams of horses. He directed two of his Roman guards to accompany him, telling Quintus to remain on the *Nostos* and await him there. Although he was disappointed, Quintus abided by his father's decision.

Cain first rode to the port's administrative offices to question the Roman officials there about Jesus of Nazareth. One officer replied that he had heard from traveling Jews that Jesus had gone to Jerusalem, where he was stirring up trouble. Cain did not pause to express his irritation but rather hastened back to his chariot. Ordering his guards to follow closely, he set out for Jerusalem with his horses at a sustainable canter. It was shortly after the third hour, or nine o'clock in the morning. He had sixty miles to ride. If there were no mishaps, he could make Jerusalem by midafternoon.

Around the sixth hour, with the sun almost directly overhead, dark clouds rapidly appeared in what had been a clear sky all morning. Overspreading the sun, they heralded a storm. A strong southeast wind kicked up, and rain first spattered, then drenched, the road's dust. All the way to Jerusalem, the storm mounted in intensity, until the guards trailing Cain could barely see his chariot in front of them. Lightning and thunder seemed to be vying to rip apart the sky. By two o'clock in the afternoon, it was nearly as dark as night.

As his chariot rumbled through the outskirts of the city, he made out a familiar figure who apparently had sought refuge from the storm under a large olive tree. It was Judas, the treasurer he'd paid for the fish they'd purchased from Jesus's followers. Cain abruptly reined in the horses, and his chariot came to a halt. He did not pause for salutations.

"Where can I find your master, Judas?"

With disheveled hair, sallow cheeks, and reddened eyes, the man glanced away momentarily and then muttered, "They have taken him to Golgotha."

Golgotha. The place of the skull. Cain knew it to be a small hill outside the city walls.

"Why are you not with Jesus, then?"

"All the disciples have fled," the man replied chokingly. "But I, especially, am not worthy to be in his presence."

"What do you mean?" Cain asked with mounting urgency.

"I betrayed him to the Pharisees and scribes. They arrested him and brought him to the high priest. And all for thirty pieces of silver." Judas bowed his head in shame.

The silver coins the devil had left behind in Caesarea flashed across Cain's mind.

"What are they doing with Jesus?" he demanded angrily.

"They are crucifying him," Judas gasped out. "Oh, Master!" he exclaimed, breaking down in sobs of despair. "I am unfit to live!"

Cain regarded Judas coldly. Disgust and resentment welled up in him. Grabbing a length of rope from the floor of his chariot, he flung it at Judas's feet.

"Do with this as you must," he spat out at the man, as he spurred his horses onward toward the site of Jesus's crucifixion.

The streets began to narrow, and Cain's progress was blocked by crowds of people fleeing the violent storm. Lightning bolts forked across the sky from horizon to horizon, and claps of thunder sounded ever louder. Then, the ground began shaking violently, and people scattered in every direction. It was just after the ninth hour, and pitch dark between the lightning flashes.

When Cain finally reached Golgotha, he saw three crosses in silhouette against the inky sky. They presented a horrifying spectacle. In the center was Jesus, beaten and bloodied almost beyond recognition. Staring at him through tears, Cain could see he was too late.

The man who had healed his son was dead.

On his head had been placed a crown of thorns. Above, the words of a mocking inscription read:

THIS IS JESUS
THE KING OF THE JEWS

On either side of the cross in the center, two other men were in the last throes of their agony, crying out in the storm's fury. As Cain watched, Roman soldiers approached each cross, armed with hammers. With savage blows, they broke the two men's legs to hasten their deaths by asphyxiation. The dead weight of their bodies would cause their lungs to collapse.

Cain fell to his knees in front of the central cross. Almost everyone had fled the scene. Only a few onlookers remained, including a group of sobbing women, somewhat more distant, who repeatedly called on

Jesus by name. Cain felt himself overwhelmed by despair. His final chance to speak with Jesus was gone. Tears furrowed his cheeks.

As he wept, he watched the soldiers take Jesus's body down from the cross. Their commander, a centurion, supervised the dolorous task. When the soldiers had finished, the earth shook once more, prompting the centurion to declare, "Truly, this man was the Son of God!"

"But you *crucified* him," Cain muttered.

He thought again of the crown on Jesus's head. Thorns had served as a ghastly emblem in his own life, linking him to the Son of God's final agony on this dreadful day. The devil had scattered the thorns in the wheat field long ago, setting the stage for Cain's fateful attack on Abel. Now the devil had caused Jesus to be betrayed to his enemies, who tortured him with thorns before putting him to death.

Cain now saw how the master of spirits had tormented him through his whole life, driving a wedge between him and God through temptations, trickery, and even an attempt on his life at the Circus. Why would God have rescued Cain but then fail to save his own son from the devil's treachery?

Cain returned despondently to his chariot. Without a word to the guards, he retraced his way through Jerusalem and then took the long, muddy road back, not just to the harbor of Caesarea, but to his interminable life still saddled with guilt.

CHAPTER 67

The *Nostos*: AD 33

t was almost sunset when Quintus knocked on the door of his father's stateroom. Cain had remained secluded in his cabin for four days, with strict orders to be left alone. All Quintus knew was that his father had returned late at night from Jerusalem. He learned from the guards that his father was moody and seemed depressed, but they said nothing about Jesus except that he had died on a cross. Quintus could scarcely imagine such an execution, especially one carried out against a man whom his father had described with such reverence.

After the ship had been restocked with extra provisions, they set sail early on Saturday morning, despite high winds and storm clouds on the horizon. The *Nostos* was on a direct course for Herculaneum. The challenge for Captain Felix and his crew this evening was to navigate the narrow, hazardous strait between Sicily and North Africa before they made their northward turn toward Rome. Submerged reefs in the strait had claimed many a ship.

"Come in," Cain called in a weary voice.

"Father, our supper will be ready soon," said Quintus hesitantly. "May we talk together?"

"Yes, son. Sit down here at the table." To distract himself, Cain was poring over a large chart of the North African coastline.

Quintus could sense that his father, normally so upbeat and encouraging, was still brooding over the events in Jerusalem. He didn't know how to begin, so he asked directly, "Father, what happened in Jerusalem?"

Cain stared at the boy sorrowfully, "They crucified Jesus, Quintus."

"How could he die, Father? You said he was the Son of God!"

"I don't know, son. He healed you, and many others, but why he could not save himself is a mystery."

"Were you able to see Jesus before he died?"

"No, I was too late," he said bitterly.

Cain rose from his chair and crossed to the bed, where he reclined with his head propped up on the pillows. He motioned for Quintus to remain in his seat. A simple supper of hot fish soup and bread was brought to the cabin.

"Take some food, Quintus. I am not hungry,"

While the boy ate, his father described the storm that had delayed him on his chariot ride to Jerusalem.

"If it were not for that storm," he said sourly, "I might have reached Jesus in time."

"Did you see any of his followers?"

"None that I recognized," Cain replied, suppressing any mention of Judas, whom he regarded as a traitor, scarcely a follower.

"That's odd," remarked the child. "I would think Jesus's friends would stand by him if he were in trouble."

The boy speaks truer than he knows, thought Cain.

Quintus had finished his meal. His father did not seem especially inclined to talk further about Jerusalem.

"Where are we headed, Father?"

"We are going straight to Herculaneum."

"Oh," the boy said with a disappointed frown. "I thought we were headed for Rome. The new racing season will be starting next week."

"I'm sorry, Quintus," Cain said absently. "But I have important work in Herculaneum. Now, if you are finished with supper, please return to your cabin and get ready for bed. I haven't slept in three nights."

As his father waved his hand in dismissal, Quintus rose from his seat and quietly departed.

With a sigh, Cain rolled onto his side and curled up, facing the bulkhead. After a short while, he finally fell into a much needed sleep.

☙❧

Once again, the crosses stood at Golgotha, grotesquely silhouetted against a lurid purple sky. Cain, at the foot of the cross in the center, stared up at the pierced body of Jesus, flanked by the two thieves. A sudden lightning strike blinded him, and he shut his eyes in pain. When he opened them again, the scene had changed. He himself, writhing in agony, had been crucified. Across from him, he saw Abel, his head lolling in death. Jesus, in the center, was also dead.

"Too late!" Cain shouted to the darkness. "Too late!"

"*Yes, too late,*" a metallic-sounding voice echoed in Cain's dream. "*I've told you all along that God would abandon you forever. Why, look at what just happened in Jerusalem. God has forsaken his very own son! He is a faithless God, yet you stubbornly wish he will somehow accept you. You have no hope of an afterlife with God. Your only chance is with me. God has forsaken you, too, just as King David said in olden times.*"

Cain recognized the phrase as one of the psalms sung by the Hebrew translators in Alexandria. "You are not above quoting the Scriptures for your purposes, evil one?"

His dream visitor gave vent to a gurgling laugh. "*The Scriptures delight me, Cain! They provide a matchless record of human folly. Illusions without number can be found in them. But I am not here to debate you.*"

"Why, then, have you come?"

"*You disobeyed me. That is why I punished you at the Circus in Rome. But then I restored you to full health, so that you would come to know my power. I could have healed Quintus, if only you had asked me and shown homage.*"

Cain noticed that the spirit failed to mention the winged being who had rescued him from the chariot axle. "It never occurred to me to ask you," he muttered.

"*More's the pity, because I am stronger than God. I helped the wretched humans put God's son to death. I entered into Judas and turned him. No one can contend with my power.*"

"Quintus was healed, and not by you, spirit! Jesus declared it to me. You cannot deny that fact!" For the first time in their encounter, Cain raised his voice.

"*Let us not argue,*" the spirit replied soothingly. "*Instead, let us set our sights calmly on the future. The eternal future. God is just playing with you, my friend. He trifles with you the way a mongoose toys with a snake. Yes, your son was healed. But don't be deceived. Both you and Quintus will be destroyed when God seeks retribution for the slaying of Jesus. The end of the world is at hand, Cain, but this time there will be no ark. There will be total annihilation from an angry God. But just as you found rescue on a ship with Noah, now your own ship can be your salvation.*"

Cain's curiosity stirred. "What do you mean by that, spirit?"

"*The Nostos opens the door for your suffering to end on your own terms! Go on deck, walk to the bow, and throw yourself overboard. The tremendous pressure of the bow wave will end your misery instantly, and the sweet haven of my outstretched arms will receive you. You will find peace there!*"

Cain knew that the crusted layers of sharp barnacles on the ship's hull would result in one of the most painful deaths imaginable. The agony of his flesh being torn apart as he rolled under his ship would equal or exceed what he had suffered at the Circus. Yet his mind wavered as the spirit left him.

Perhaps that was exactly the sort of death he deserved.

⟐

After a few nightmarish hours during which he was neither awake nor asleep, but almost delirious, Cain gasped for air. Covered in a cold sweat, and clad only in breeches, he stumbled from his stateroom and exited from the midship companionway to the deck. The *Nostos* was racing downwind, driven by gale-force gusts. Captain Felix and the eight oarsmen struggling to steer the ship did not even notice him, as they were focused intently on keeping the ship positioned down the face of the mountainous ocean swells. If the *Nostos* slipped sideways, she would broach and quite possibly capsize.

As Cain traversed the heaving deck toward the bow, occasional lightning bolts lit up the pitch-black sky. Towering above his head and hissing in his ears was a phosphorescent green bow wave. When he reached the front of the ship, the master of spirits whispered in his ear. *"The moment is now! Abandon your vain hopes and enter eternity with me!"*

Cain stared forward, anticipating the next surge. Adorning the prow of his ship was a beautiful sculpture depicting a mermaid with dolphins. As his gaze fell upon it, the figures were transformed and melded into the entangling figure of a sea serpent twisting back toward the ship and staring directly at Cain with large, fiery eyes. It was as if the devil had sought a front-row seat to watch the first man ever born commit suicide.

Distracted and unnerved, Cain had to struggle to maintain his footing on the pitching deck. A bolt of lightning blinded him temporarily, just as he heard the sound of multiple thuds on the deck. When the ship rolled suddenly, he slipped and fell flat on his stomach. Stretching out his hands to break the fall, he skidded forward on a slippery substance. A loose nail sticking up from the deck pierced the palm of his right hand. Then he realized what had happened.

Large squid leaping from the bow wave had landed on deck. Their oily bodies had combined with the ship's roll to cause his fall.

Lying prone, Cain saw the feet of a man between him and the bow. Looking upward, he gasped as he recognized Jesus of Nazareth standing over him, dressed in a white cloak and barefoot. Jesus's face and head were pristine. There was no trace of the wounds he had endured from scourging and the crown of thorns.

"That is not the way," Jesus said tenderly as he extended both his hands to help Cain to his feet. He noticed that Jesus's hands and feet, in contrast to his face, still bore the imprint of the nails used to pin him to the cross. Stunned, and struggling to regain his composure, Cain stared at the man he'd seen crucified less than a week before. The two stood together very near the ship's prow. Although the storm continued unabated, Cain was somehow able to maintain his footing on the pitching deck and clearly hear Jesus's words above the crashing of the waves. Even Jesus's cloak draped loosely, unruffled by the wind.

Jesus turned slightly and placed his hand on the head of the wooden sea-serpent figure. A dark, powdery dust spewed from the sculpture and blew out to sea as the master of spirits was evicted, and the prow resumed its original shape of a mermaid surrounded by dolphins. Then the dust gathered itself into a tight cloud, reversed course, and flew against the prevailing wind toward the stern. Cain's attention, however, remained riveted on Jesus, and so he failed to see the particles strike the crew manning the steering oars, including Captain Felix. The ship immediately lurched as the sailors altered its course by about thirty degrees. Jesus then turned back and faced his audience of one with a smile.

"Wha...what are you doing here aboard my ship?" Cain stammered.

"I came to see you, Cain."

Cain flinched. It was the first time anyone since Tanith had addressed him by his given name.

"I thought you were dead. I saw you on the cross!"

"Yes, I was dead. But now I am alive again."

"How is this possible?"

"You made your own inquiries through Demetrius and came to believe I was the Son of God. You have lived in my creation longer than any other human being. Do you not believe that with God all things are possible?"

"I suppose I do now," he acquiesced after a moment's reflection.

"And so you understand that my Father has raised me from the dead," Jesus continued.

Nodding less than confidently, Cain asked, "So, why have you come to see me?"

"I wish to continue our conversation," Jesus said in a reassuring tone.

"Will this remain between us, or will your Father come to know about it, too?"

"If you have seen me you have also seen my Father. I and my Father are one."

Cain paused. Although he could scarcely grasp the full implications, there was only one conclusion he could draw from Jesus's statement. He was standing in the presence of God.

"Let me ask *you* something," said Jesus gently. "Why were you in such a rush to find me in Jerusalem?"

"I wanted to thank you for healing Quintus. But, most of all, I needed to talk about my cursed life," he added.

"The moment was not right then. I was busy laying the cornerstone for that house I am building. But now, please tell me what has troubled you."

After catching his breath, Cain plunged in. "Your cure of Quintus was a miracle, but *my* daily regeneration has been a curse. I merely asked you for protection against those who might slay me, and I ended up fated to linger on and on through these thousands of years."

"My child, what you saw as a curse, I meant as a blessing. Have you considered that I marked you not only for protection, but also to give you the time you needed to journey home to me?"

Cain pondered Jesus's answer to the great question of his life. It seemed as though Jesus was suggesting that all along, it was in his own hands to return to God, yet he continued to wander away. He was instantly filled with remorse, and countless confusing thoughts about his past flooded his mind, but at length Cain could only permit himself to respond, "I'm sorry it took me so long."

"Cain, though you may be the oldest, you are by no means my only wayward son," Jesus said warmly. "Now, tell me. Do you have any other regrets?"

Sensing where the conversation was headed, but still hesitant, Cain responded, "Well, I cannot believe I actually offered *you* a carpentry job!"

Jesus chuckled. "I was flattered, but I meant now that you know who I really am."

"Of course," Cain glanced downward. "About Abel. I am truly sorry for what I did that day."

"I am glad to hear that, but you must understand that your sin did not consist just in Abel's killing," Jesus said pointedly. "It actually began the moment you yielded to anger with your brother. I warned you that such rage is fertile soil in which the devil cultivates all sorts of evil in your life."

Cain hung his head as Jesus continued. "Consider his work against you from the beginning. He stirred your anger first against your brother, then me. From that day forward, he twisted your thinking to keep you away from me. But his attempts to convince you that I was angry and had abandoned you were all lies. I have nothing but love for you, Cain."

"But how can you love *me*? I am guilty of hundreds of sins."

Jesus raised an eyebrow and cleared his throat.

Realizing the foolishness of his comment, Cain admitted, "Okay, so many that I have lost count. My guilt and regret are bottomless."

Jesus smiled. "I created you, and all of humanity, out of love. I desire nothing from people other than to be in loving relationship with them. Yes, you sin. Out of anger, out of fear, out of selfishness. And then the devil declares that you are unworthy. But this is false, because my love for you is not based on how you act or feel. It is the essence of who I am. This is why I came into the world!"

"So why did you allow them to kill you?"

"My death was planned from the beginning. I took all the sins of humankind upon myself, and I bore the punishment of death so that people would not have to bear it themselves. And I have risen from the dead to give all who come to me the gift of eternal life."

"The *gift* of eternal life?" Cain exclaimed incredulously. "I have tasted this bitter fate. For me, death would be more welcome."

Jesus replied, "I know that you, of all people, are tired of living, but I am not talking about the life of your flesh. I am talking about the life of your spirit, your soul. If your soul dies, you and I will be separated for eternity. I love you too much to have that happen, which is why I died in your place."

Cain reflected on these words and realized anew the depth of the master of spirits' lies to him.

Jesus continued, "You said you would welcome death, as though your life has been only a burden. Have you not had times of great joy?"

"Yes, of course. I particularly remember my happiness with Tanith long ago. Our love made me constantly content."

"Yet you had so little back then," Jesus reminded him.

"You mean our simple circumstances? As I think about that time, it was then that I felt more freedom than at any other point in my life."

"When else have you been happy, Cain?"

Cain thought for a moment. "When I was working on the reconstruction of the Library of Alexandria. During that time, I felt a freedom from my curse of wandering, and after making an offering of
my efforts to you, for the first time ever, I thought I was gaining your
favor." Cain hesitated and then continued more solemnly. "I know
that in the time of Abel my offering of surplus wheat was contemptible,
but I hope that this second gift of my best labor is acceptable."

"I respect your offering very much. As you began to surmise in
China, this is one of the special purposes for which I created you. But
let me explain something else. You will truly return to me only if you
offer your whole heart. You have named your ship *Nostos* well. Once
you make your journey home, you will be in my house forever."

"How do I do this?" Cain asked.

"Understand that it is your sin that separates us. Accept my gift
of forgiveness for all your sins. And in your heart, try living every day
for me instead of for yourself."

"Thank you for your gift, Lord. I am certainly ready now for a different way of life."

As Jesus embraced him, Cain implored, "Can I share my story
with others?"

"Leave that to me," Jesus reassured him. "Your story will be told
at the right time. I promise."

"Jesus, I also want to know if Abel is in your house," pressed Cain.

"Yes, he is, and you need have no fear of the day when you see
your brother. Despite your brilliance, Cain, not even you can understand the full measure of heaven. It is a place of eternal joy and peace.
Abel knows this peace now. And you too, one day, will live at peace
with him and all who are there."

"Is Tanith there?"

"Concerning Tanith, you may rest assured that I am a righteous
judge."

As Jesus spoke these words, predawn light began to illuminate the ship's surroundings. Cain glanced for a moment over the prow and registered a terrifying sight. Sailing before a scudding wind at nearly twenty knots, the *Nostos* was on a direct collision course with a partially submerged reef from which the roar of crashing waves could already be heard. Jesus, glancing at the crew, cried in a loud voice, "Come out!" Behind Cain, the demons immediately departed from the sailors and flowed into the group of squid on the deck. The sea animals writhed and lurched spasmodically.

As the bow of the *Nostos* dug into another huge wave, water soaked both Cain and Jesus and flushed the large squids overboard through the drainage holes on the side of the deck's railing. Cain momentarily took his eyes off Jesus and looked astern to see what was happening. Captain Felix, no longer possessed by a demon, saw the reef ahead and shouted orders at his crewmen. Cain felt the ship swerve sharply under his feet as the crew managed to skirt the deadly reef just in time. His surge of relief merged gratefully with the receding sounds of the pounding surf as his ship left the obstacle behind. He looked back toward Jesus but found he had vanished. On the starboard side, a blinding sunrise flooded the water with light. The storm had abated, and the sea was calming.

Cain ran back to the stern. "Did you see that?" he breathlessly asked Felix.

"Yes sir, I did. Thank the gods for the sunrise, sir, or we would have run right into that submerged reef. I shall mark it on our chart. The strong winds brought us to the hazardous area sooner than I could have anticipated. I apologize for my inattention, sir."

Of all the crew members within earshot, Cain inquired, "Did anyone see me up at the bow?" Greeted with silence, he realized that his conversation with Jesus had been entirely private.

Cain pressed the captain's hand to reassure the man of his confidence in him. "Yes, indeed, Felix. Thank God!"

As he drew his own hand away, Felix saw the blood and pointed
to it. Cain looked down at the palm of his right hand where the nail
on the deck had pierced it. He realized that, despite a new day's dawn,
the minor injury to his hand had not healed.

"Shall I summon the ship's doctor, sir?" Felix asked.

"Yes, Felix. It appears that I need him."

The captain was puzzled to see the broad smile on his master's face.

Cain drew in a huge breath of fresh morning air, and he was
filled with excitement over the events of the last few minutes. Before
Felix went below, Cain wrapped his arms about his loyal ship captain
and shouted to the wind, *"Nostos! Nostos!"*

CHAPTER 68

Herculaneum, AD 64

On a brilliant summer day, Cain found himself in one of his favorite spots in all Herculaneum: the fruit and vegetable garden that adjoined his villa. Even the mid-July heat could not temper his enthusiasm for planting, irrigating, pruning, and all the other activities which, over time, had converted his garden into a peaceful retreat. On practically every day of the growing season, he worked alongside the gardeners and servants who helped him tend the plants, eagerly soliciting their ideas on ways to make the garden more bountiful.

On this particular morning, he was helping his head kitchen chef, a portly woman in her fifties. They were sorting the fruits of the latest harvest.

"Let us put all the unblemished fruit in that box, and also the finest grain," Cain said.

"Will those be for the party, sir?" The chef referred to the sixtieth-birthday celebration that was planned that evening for Felix, his longtime sea captain.

"No, Helvia. You know we always have plenty for our needs. We will be loading all this food on the wagons headed for Pompeii. The drivers will distribute it to the poor and the hungry."

The chef shook her head as he glanced away. Although she had been through this routine with him for many decades now, her professional pride always bristled at having to prepare meals with anything but the highest quality ingredients.

Cain left her and strolled to the arboretum, where the shrubs and trees surrounding the oblong pool were in full flower. He glanced at his own reflection in the water. With flowing, salt-and-pepper hair, he had grown visibly older, but his chest and stomach, although hefting a few extra pounds, were still in outstanding shape. He doubted, however, that Felix shared any of his own relief at the passage of the years.

That evening, the party was in full tilt when Helvia's husband approached Cain. The man was in charge of the villa's boathouses, maintaining a number of vessels for recreational use on the Bay of Naples.

"Sir, may I speak with you in private?" asked Secundus quietly.

Cain enjoyed a relatively informal relationship with all his servants, founded on mutual respect. He knew that Secundus would interrupt the festivities only for an important reason, so he gestured to the *tablinum*, his office on one side of the atrium, and the two men stepped into the small room, opulently appointed with colorful frescoes.

"Sir, I regret the intrusion, but I felt you should be informed immediately. A Roman fishing vessel reached port this evening in Herculaneum. One of my cousins serves on the ship's crew. Just now he sent me an urgent message from the villa boathouses."

"What was this message?" Cain asked. Secundus's anxiety was palpable.

"All of Rome is on fire, sir! A great conflagration has swept through the city for the past two days. Before he left Rome, my cousin heard that someone had started the fire in the wooden shops around the Circus Maximus. But strong winds spread the flames so that they quickly ran the length of the Circus and then rose to the hills. Only four of the fourteen regions of the city have escaped damage!"

"The blaze has reached the Palatine, then?" Cain asked urgently.

"Yes, sir. It is said that even Nero's own palace has been destroyed."

"Where is the emperor? Is he in Rome?"

"That is not known, sir. Some say he is connected to the fire. Others swear he was not in Rome when it started, but rather in Antium."

Cain was familiar with Nero's luxurious villa at Antium, thirty-five miles south of Rome, having visited there several times for ceremonial occasions at the emperor's invitation.

Nero's whereabouts were not his chief concern, however. As he listened to Secundus, he realized that if the fire had reached the Palatine, his own estate might be threatened. And, most important of all, his son might lie in harm's way. Quintus had lived in Rome since coming of age, and Cain had given him an estate, adjacent to his own, as a wedding gift twenty years earlier. For more than a decade now, his entrepreneurial son had run a thriving business, supplying Arabian horses to all the Circus Maximus chariot-racing factions.

Cain decided to sail to Rome as soon as possible, but he would wait until the celebration was over that evening to inform Felix. Instead, he summoned the first officer and ordered him to ready the *Nostos* for a voyage to Rome the following morning.

CHAPTER 69

The Palatine, Rome, AD 64

On the Palatine hill overlooking central Rome, the devastation was heartbreaking. By some miracle, Cain's estate had largely survived the blaze, with only a few outlying buildings reduced to ruins. Most of the other residences in Rome's most exclusive neighborhood, however, had been gutted by the fire.

Including his son's.

Cain, Captain Felix, and the ship's crew sorted through the charred remains of what had been Quintus's dwelling. Grotesquely delicate, foul-smelling wisps of smoke still swirled above the rubble. A sickening feeling gripped Cain as he dug deeper into the blackened ruins of his son's home.

He led the team to the area that had been the family's sleeping quarters. The stench was overwhelming, and the search party pressed moistened cloths to their faces. In what had been Quintus's bedroom, they found four skeletons huddled together. An engraved iron arm bracelet on one of the charred bodies confirmed Cain's worst fears. Quintus had worn it since he was a teenager.

Cain watched through soggy eyes as his crewmen gently placed the remains of his family on wagons for the return journey to the Tiber and then to the harbor at Ostia. Anger such as he had not experienced since ancient times swirled in him as he burned to avenge the death of his beloved Quintus. But against whom could he direct his rage?

As the crewmen's mournful task continued, Cain stepped outside the smoldering remains for a breath of fresh air. A well-dressed, pudgy-faced young man on a white horse promptly accosted him.

"Don't worry, my dear Marcus. I will find the ones responsible for this crime. They may hide, but they will never escape!" exclaimed the horseback rider.

Cain recognized Nero, whom he had known from the emperor's childhood as a racing fan at the Circus Maximus. The emperor was widely reported to roam the city without an escort at all hours of the day and night.

"Nero, the fire has claimed my son and his family. All are dead!" Cain tearfully cried aloud. "Who would do this?"

As the emperor formulated his response, Cain remembered the rumor circulating about Nero's involvement in the fire, and his hand found its way to the hilt of his sword.

"Your loss will be a gain to the state," replied Nero grimly, without a hint of condolence. "The Christians have done this, Marcus. For their pains, they will be exterminated. The slime from Judaea must not be allowed to spread. They are barbarians, pure and simple. Cannibals! Do you know that they eat the body and blood of their so-called Messiah? Any missing child in Rome is said to have been sacrificed by these lunatics!"

Cain was crushed. Within minutes, he had to endure the loss of his loved ones and then the blasphemy of this arrogant despot. Fortunately, Nero was too caught up in his tirade to notice Cain gently easing his sword back into its scabbard after hearing his explanation. Nero never knew how close he was to tasting Cain's sword.

"I will hunt them down, Marcus," continued Nero. "Every last Christian in Rome and the provinces. They will provide us with novel, dare I say delicious, entertainments! And not only in the arena as meals for wild beasts. I have already put some of them into thorn baskets and made them human torches to serve as street lighting. You will see. Have patience, you will see!"

With a roar of maniacal laughter and a crack of the whip, the emperor wheeled his mount and galloped away toward the Circus Maximus.

Cain could not wait to get underway from Ostia back to Herculaneum, but the scene at the port was chaotic. The Great Fire of Rome had been brought under control after nearly six days. What was not controlled, however, was the Roman populace, many of whom were both homeless and hungry. The grain supply to the city had been disrupted, and tens of thousands of angry residents had streamed into Ostia to board any ship they could. Desperate refugees clogged the docks, begging, screaming, and shoving for space aboard departing ships. Small children were being thrown into the arms of crewmen as a tool for their parents to board behind them.

Cain ordered his crew to take as many citizens as the *Nostos* could safely handle. However, his ship couldn't possibly accept the hundreds who clamored on the dock, and the crew, with swords drawn, was forced to form a human cordon guarding the gangway from being swamped by panicked refugees. Cain asked Felix to summon all the available cargo vessels in his fleet as quickly as possible to take on additional passengers.

"How much shall we charge them for their passage, sir?" asked Felix.

"We will not collect any money. Life will be hard enough for them when they reach Naples."

That evening, the *Nostos* set sail. As Cain strode the deck mourning the loss of Quintus and his family, the tearful laments of many of his passengers reminded him that they, too, had lost loved ones in the fire. He wondered as well how many Christians would fall as scapegoats into Nero's slanderous net of vengeance. He highly doubted that the emerging Christian movement would resort to setting the city ablaze and thereby attract the hatred of its other citizens. After all, they too enjoyed Rome's protective embrace.

Late that evening, as he sat at the ship's stern sipping a beaker of Chinese tea, Cain heard a strange, rustling noise coming from a stack of wooden cargo boxes piled on the starboard side. The crew had directed all the refugees to remain amidships, so Cain supposed that the rustling sound was the work of an animal—perhaps one of the ship's cats.

Then a pair of large blue eyes peered at him through the cracks between the boxes. He reckoned that one of his young crewmen had burrowed amidst the cargo, most likely to sleep off a drinking binge. Cain reached over the top row of boxes to grab the ne'er-do-well, but promptly withdrew his hand. Whatever it was had bitten him!

His assailant stood up—neither a cat nor a crewman, but a tall, beautiful, red-haired woman presented herself to his gaze. She was perhaps in her early thirties. Her tawny locks rippled down to the small of her back, and her wet, ragged clothing was stained dark with soot.

"You need not try to rip the hair from my head! I am only fetching a ride out of Rome on this ship, good sir!"

Cain was astonished at her directness, but met it with his own. "You mean you are stealing a ride on *my* ship, good lady!" he rejoined. "How did you get aboard past my guards?"

"Very simply," the woman replied casually. "I swam from the dock to the far side and crawled up one of your dangling anchor lines. Your guards had told me the ship was full, but I needed to get away from Rome."

Cain stared at the young woman for a few moments. Then he asked sympathetically, "You lost your home in the fire?"

The woman looked down, her hands trembling. "Not only my home, sir. My family is missing as well. The first night of the fire, I awoke to the acrid smell of smoke. The house was burning. I grabbed whatever clothes I could and ran for my life."

"There is no word about your family since that night?" he inquired gently.

"There was pandemonium in the city. I learned that my husband was found dead. He was a military officer. I pray that my sister made it out in time, but I shall probably never know. Meanwhile, I have led the life of a beggar these past few days. I have lost everything." She broke down in sobs.

His heart went out to her. But he didn't tell her about Quintus. Somehow the moment wasn't right.

"I admire your tenacity in getting aboard my ship," he told her. "We are sailing to Herculaneum, and you are welcome to travel with us," Cain said, holding her trembling hands. "Try to calm down now. The worst is over. I will have my crew help you to clean up and then get you some food."

The woman looked up into his eyes. "Thank you for your generosity, kind sir," she said. "My name is Rina."

"And mine is Marcus," Cain said to her softly. "Welcome to the *Nostos*."

Two hours later, they met again at the ship's stern, while the *Nostos* was making good time before a moderate northwest wind. At this rate, they would be home the following day about noon. A thorough cleaning and a new robe had transformed the stowaway. Whatever her origins, her long red hair and blue eyes were thoroughly distinctive. Cain decided he would ask her tomorrow about her family roots. In the meantime, they bid each other goodnight. Rina slept on deck under a tarpaulin, while he retired to his stateroom directly below. As he settled into his comfortable bed, he could hear her crying herself to sleep.

❧⸎❧

The following day dawned cloudy, and the wind had dropped during the night. With this change in the weather, they would not arrive until sunset. Cain felt compassion for all the refugees abroad, but he sympathized especially with Rina.

"Your Latin is accented, but I can't place it," he told her as they sat near the spot where they had first met. "Have you always lived in Rome?"

"Oh, no," she smiled. "My husband was in the army and we lived wherever he was stationed abroad. His most recent posting was in Britannia. We were there for five years."

"I remember the white, chalky cliffs in southeastern Britannia from a visit long ago," Cain said. "Many Romans find the country cold and damp, but I thought the landscapes were beautiful."

"You lived in Britannia, too?" Rina asked.

"No, I was just a merchant traveler. I went there before the Roman invasion of twenty years ago."

"Yes, before the Romans," she echoed with a faraway look in her aquamarine eyes.

Rina told him she had been born in northwestern Gaul. Like her husband, her father had also been a military officer. She had never stayed in one town long enough to call it home. Cain thought she handled her rootlessness, though, with a certain charm and elegance.

"When we arrive in Herculaneum," he said on an impulse, "you must make your home at my villa, at least on a temporary basis. I think you will find it comfortable," he assured her.

Rina hesitated. "I have heard from the crew that you are in mourning as well," she said. "You have my sympathy for your loss, and surely you would prefer to be alone in the coming days?"

"I appreciate your condolences. Please accept mine as well," Cain replied. He reflected for a moment and then continued, "Actually, Rina, I should very much enjoy your company."

And that is the way they left the matter, as the *Nostos* coasted the region of Campania, heading for the Bay of Naples.

⚬⚬⚬

Two days after their arrival, Cain buried Quintus, his wife, and their two children in a simple ceremony. After he said an emotional farewell prayer, he noticed that Rina, who was present at the side of the burial plot, was looking on dry-eyed, presumably because she was so drained by her own loss.

Over the next few weeks, they frequently walked the estate together, commiserating over their losses, and learning more about one another. Rina, it turned out, was given to firm opinions, especially on the topic of slavery.

"The idea that one person should belong to another as property is inhuman!" she exclaimed one day on their walk.

Privately, Cain agreed, but he decided to plumb the depth of Rina's conviction.

"Throughout history, slavery has been the rule, not the exception," he pointed out. "Why should the Romans be any different from all other civilizations that we know of? Look at Egypt and Persia. Even the Greeks, for all their democratic talk, had slaves."

"You speak of the past, but we should be living now in an age of greater enlightenment," she countered.

Cain thought sourly of Nero but refrained from interrupting her.

"You must know that some of the Stoic philosophers, Marcus, have begun to question the ethics of slavery. You are familiar with Musonius Rufus? He teaches care for the soul and love for one's neighbor. And he believes that slaves ought to be treated as equal to free men."

No Roman woman he had ever met had either considered slavery as a debatable custom or had invoked the philosophy of Stoicism.

Cain noted that Rina was unusually well educated. And she was audacious. Anyone in Rome who called for the freeing of slaves could be accused of inciting them to rebellion. He decided to meet her frankness with a candor of his own.

"I have allowed my slaves here at the villa to purchase their freedom," he told her. "They have all become paid servants, and all have chosen to remain on the property in my employ."

"Really? Perhaps you could you use an extra employee."

"What do you mean?"

"I can't just stay here under your roof without earning my keep," she told him. "I've spent much of my time here admiring the magnificent stable where you keep your prize parade stallions. Many in my family were great riders and trainers, and I have a good deal of experience myself. I would like to help train and groom the horses."

Cain grinned. "Do you have your eye on a permanent position?" he asked teasingly.

"Oh, no," she arched her eyebrows in mock surprise. "Just for a few months. Then I'll be moving along."

Those few months soon became many more. Cain found himself absorbed as he watched her exercising the horses with unusual skill and grace, but their relationship soon transcended the equestrian domain. More and more, they enjoyed each other's company. When he told stories about his travels at the dinner table, Rina embarked on those journeys vicariously, as if she were there. Her anti-slavery diatribes had evolved into more expansive critiques of Rome's subjugation of its conquered peoples. Not fully forthcoming with his own views on the subject, Cain nevertheless rejoiced in her idealism. They discovered many mutual interests besides their passion for horses.

A year after the Great Fire, at the annual birthday party for Felix, they danced to the music of the best musicians in Naples. Although Cain was several decades her senior, Rina admired his vigor and youthful spirit, while he thought that she surpassed all the Roman women he had ever met. Aside from her stunning beauty, she was highly intelligent and poised. Rina had quickly gained favor with everyone on his staff, not least Felix, who had signaled his encouragement numerous times during the past year.

Freed from the misgivings that haunted all of his past relationships, Cain found himself falling quickly and easily in love.

The two were married at the villa later that summer. Cain had wanted to invite his extensive circle of friends from Herculaneum and Rome. However, Rina insisted on a small but elaborate ceremony. They decided to defer a wedding trip until the beginning of the next sailing season.

⌾⤙⤙⌾

In midautumn, however, a travel opportunity presented itself.

"Rome beckons, my love," Cain told her as they finished breakfast. "The other owners of the Greens have been requesting a meeting for months, and I don't believe I can put them off any longer."

"Yes, I suppose I have been keeping you too much to myself," Rina admitted, eyeing him playfully across the table.

"Besides," Cain said, "your introduction to my friends there is overdue, and reconstruction of the Palatine estate is now complete. I can't wait to show you the new buildings. We set sail tomorrow."

Rina hesitated, briefly looking out at the stunning view of the bay of Naples. Then, recapturing her husband's gaze, she told him, "But you are forgetting, my darling. The prize mare you gave me on our wedding day is ready to foal. Believe me, I am anxious to join your social circle in Rome, but I really must attend the birth." Matching the look of disappointment on her husband's face, she added, "I promise to accompany you on your next trip."

Unable to contend with his wife's logic, Cain instead rose and led his new bride to their bedchamber upstairs.

"Then, if we must be apart for these two long weeks, let us be certain we will both remember *this* day fondly!"

CHAPTER 70

Rome, AD 65

"That was my final chariot festival parade. After that, I let you fellows have all the fun!" Cain jested with the other wealthy owners of the Green faction. His associates still marveled at the way he had survived the appalling crash at the Circus three decades prior. Although Cain had visibly aged, his vigorous looks and obviously impressive fitness provoked envy in his large circle of friends and business contacts in Rome.

"And then you went off on that crazy voyage to Judaea still bleeding from your injuries. You were so young and foolish," chided Lacerta, the gray-haired champion of the Circus who had won his freedom from slavery nearly thirty years ago. "Marcus, you never did say why you went on that trip," he added.

"No, I didn't," smiled Cain. "But I found what I was looking for!"

He had never shared with anyone his encounter with Jesus. After all, how could he possibly explain the transformation of his life from immortal to mortal? Happily for him, the other owners in the room knew better than to question Cain further on private matters, as one did not become one of Rome's wealthiest citizens without having secrets.

On the final day of their meetings, Cain suggested that the group adjourn to the newly opened Neronian Baths near the Campus Martius. This sumptuous facility had become one of the city's most popular destinations for the relaxation of both rich and poor during the past few years. They arrived at the Baths shortly after noon. Cain had definite views on the sequence of pools he favored: first the lukewarm water, then the hot, and then the cold for a final plunge. His associates, though, all favored starting with the cold and then ramping up the temperature, finally basking in the hot-air sauna. So the group split apart for several hours, pledging to reconvene in the sauna toward the end of the visit.

As he entered the *tepidarium* for his warm bath, Cain admired the ornamentation. Elaborately decorated recesses along the marble walls served as storage lockers for the visitors' garments. The floor of the main chamber featured a gaudy medley of mosaics, while the ceiling was intricately arched and decorated with garden scenes in red and blue stucco. He sent a servant for a large flagon of beer and a plate of dried olives. After a relaxing soak, he sat down next to two middle-aged gentlemen who were engaged in an animated conversation. From their scars, Cain guessed that they were career soldiers.

"Paulinus was right to show them no mercy, Fronto," rumbled one of the men to his friend. "His successor was a patsy."

"I completely agree, Gallus," replied Fronto, nodding his head vigorously. "But the war was so *unnecessary* to begin with. To think that thousands of Romans were killed by these savages before the revolt against us could be tamed. And all because of the greed and stupidity of one man, that idiot Catus Decianus."

"He should never have been appointed procurator by the imperial administration. Donkeys have more sense," concurred Gallus.

The men broke off their talk to greet Cain, introducing themselves as legionary commanders, the equivalent of generals, on leave from Britannia.

"We were just speaking of the revolt that began five years ago," explained Gallus. "My colleague feels strongly it should never have happened."

Cain smiled encouragingly. "What provoked the Britons to rebel?" he asked. "Were they not treated well?"

Fronto waved his hand dismissively. "If the emperor's agent had listened to reason, seventy thousand Romans would still be alive today and three of the largest towns in the province would still be standing," he growled. "You have heard of King Prasutagus?" he asked Cain.

Recognizing the name of the former tribal king of the Iceni in southeast Britannia, Cain quizzed the general. "He made a treaty with us, didn't he?" His curiosity was motivated, at least in part, by what Rina had told him of life in Britannia.

"Correct, sir. And you are looking at the man who negotiated that treaty. Before he died, Prasutagus bequeathed his kingdom jointly to Rome and to his daughters. Afterward, though, things started to go wrong when his greedy widow, Queen Boudica, claimed the royal lands of the Iceni for herself. Still, we might have kept the peace if Catus, our procurator, had behaved sensibly. Instead, he enraged local opinion by having Boudica publicly flogged. And, if you please, he arranged for her teenage daughters to be violated in front of the people."

"What a fool. I had no idea!" exclaimed Cain. "The Iceni must have been outraged."

"That, sir, is an understatement!" Fronto replied. "Catus gave the Iceni a rallying cry. Boudica had no difficulty raising an army three times bigger than Rome's. With the governor and most of our troops miles away on the other side of Britannia, we were caught shorthanded. Governor Paulinus returned in the very nick of time to put down the revolt. But not until Boudica had burned London to the ground."

"What happened to Boudica after her defeat?" Cain inquired.

"It's generally thought she took poison to avoid capture. Like Cleopatra in Egypt, you know."

Gallus now joined in. "Foreign queens have been a millstone around the neck of Rome, my friend," he said darkly to Cain.

"But Boudica is dead, presumably," Cain answered. "And order is now restored in Britannia, is it not?"

"We have kept the peace, at a price," agreed Gallus. "But the evil of that red-haired witch lives on. Her younger sister, a stunning princess named Rhiannon, helped Fronto here negotiate the inheritance treaty by serving as his interpreter. After the revolt was suppressed, I took Rhiannon captive and sent her as a slave to my house here in Rome. Interpreters are not supposed to have red hair down to the waist and turquoise eyes," he remarked, a bit wistfully.

"A feisty sort," commented Fronto with a chuckle. "As I recall, you couldn't control her, Gallus. Especially in bed!"

Gallus poked his colleague sharply in the ribs. Then, lowering his voice, he leaned over to Cain. "As you doubtless know, sir, the emperor continues to blame the Christians for the Great Fire," he imparted. "But the truth lies elsewhere, my friend."

Cain had heard a number of conspiracy theories about the previous year's disaster—including several that attributed arson to Nero himself and his capricious whims. It had even been whispered that the emperor had sung and played his lyre from a private stage as he watched Rome burn. And rumor also had it that he burned the city only to clear construction space for his new palace, the fabulous Golden House.

"What do you believe happened, commander?" Cain asked Gallus.

"I know for a certainty that Rhiannon started the fire," he replied. "She was seen torching the shops at the Circus Maximus on the first night."

Fronto nodded his head. "Tell him how you had your house slaves tortured," he urged.

Gallus waved him off. "They confirmed the whole story. That

witch was just waiting for a series of dry, windy days to take her revenge on Rome. She is a murderer!" he hissed.

"Calm yourself, Gallus," said Fronto. "The arsonist will be found. After her capture, she will surely be crucified."

"I'll hammer in the nails myself!" exclaimed Gallus. "I lost more than just my house in that cursed fire," he added. The strong soldier suddenly looked vulnerable, perhaps haunted by the memory of family members who had perished in the fire.

Cain shivered in the lukewarm water, his mind racing as he considered the resemblance between Rina and the description of the arsonist. Had he married the very woman whose wanton act of revenge had caused widespread ruin—not to mention the deaths of his beloved son Quintus, his daughter-in-law, and his grandchildren? The details in these soldiers' narrative were disturbing, at the very least. He decided to probe further.

"Gentlemen, I spend most of my time now in Herculaneum. But my circle of contacts in Rome is still wide. Besides the hair and eye color, does this Rhiannon have any other distinguishing features or characteristics? I ask you only in case I ever see her and would have the chance to report her to the authorities."

"Yes, she does," declared Gallus. "She is unusually tall for a woman, and she speaks Latin with the trace of a foreign accent." The general paused for a moment, then added, "Oh, she also has a small beauty mark on her right cheek."

Cain's stomach sank. He had always regarded Rina's distinctive blemish as an adornment. It had taken only a moment's revelation to transform it into an odious malignancy.

Thanking the generals for their fellowship, he hastily left the tepidarium. Eschewing even short plunges in the hot and cold pools, he dispatched his servant to find his fellow team owners and inform them that a sudden message from his villa in Herculaneum required his prompt departure.

＠⋇＠

Aboard the river launch en route back to Ostia, a seething Cain stared down at the placid waters of the Tiber, angry not only at Rina but also at his own gullibility. He was not sure what he would do when he arrived back home in Herculaneum.

CHAPTER 71

Herculaneum, AD 65

F or three days, Cain kept his own counsel. When Rina asked him how his business had gone in Rome, he replied in generalities, omitting all mention of his visit to the Neronian Baths and his conversation with Legion Commanders Fronto and Gallus. But the sight of the beauty mark constantly unnerved him. He would have to bring her deception to an end, he decided.

"Let's take a long horseback ride," urged Cain one day after lunch. "We can explore the beach at Oplontis. You may find some appealing seashells there for your collection."

Rina happily agreed. "And the sea air will do you good after your trip to Rome," she said. "It will brush out the cobwebs," she added jokingly.

Cain ordered two of his favorite parade stallions to be readied. At the front gate of the villa before the couple left the grounds, two of his guards approached on horseback to accompany the riding party, as was customary. Although the towns along the Bay of Naples were the playgrounds of affluent aristocrats, they also attracted kidnappers and thieves. Protection against bandits was a routine, and prudent, precaution. The guards were surprised, therefore, when Cain dismissed them, only asking to be handed a *gladius*, a short sword sheathed in a leather scabbard.

They rode for two hours, covering the twelve miles south to Stabiae, and then doubling back toward Oplontis, which lay seven miles from Herculaneum. Rina did most of the talking, telling Cain excitedly about the new foal, a beautiful white Arabian. Near Oplon-tis, at Cain's suggestion, they branched off the main road and took a trail through thick underbrush down to a sandy beach. Gentle waves lapped the shoreline, which stretched for miles in each direction. Typical for this time of year, there was not a vessel in sight. Cain could see that, by land and by sea, they were entirely alone.

Dismounting, they sauntered barefoot along the surf line, looking for unusual shells as they held the reins of their horses.

"I have some other news to share with you," Rina told him. "Nothing about horses, though," she added mysteriously.

When Cain didn't look up, she could tell he was preoccupied. Ever since his return from Rome, he had been uncharacteristically withdrawn, almost guarded in his speech.

At length, he took his eyes off the sand. Drawing in the reins slightly, he looked at her and said, "Something troubles me, Rina."

"Yes, what is it, my husband?"

"What was the real reason you declined to join me in Rome? After all, we have plenty of servants who could have tended to the foal."

A shadow crossed Rina's eyes. "The city holds bad memories for me."

"Yes, I know that. Yet I find it strange that you didn't even ask me to inquire about your sister. You might have cherished some hope of tracking her down, or at least of knowing her fate for certain."

"I did not want to be a burden to you, my love. Besides, the Roman way of life has taught us all to endure the loss of loved ones with resilience, whether the cause is warfare or disease or accident. Was it not so for you with the loss of Quintus?"

The two stopped walking and stood stock-still. Cain stared at Rina, marveling inwardly at her ability to lie with such conviction.

"Ah, yes, about Quintus," he replied. "On the day of his burial, I could not help but notice that you remained dry-eyed, Rina. You shed not one tear, although your husband, and probably your sister, died only a few days before."

Rina searched for words to answer him. Finally, after a long pause, Cain spat out, "There were no lost loved ones, were there, *Princess Rhiannon?*"

Rina's expression could not conceal her shock. He knew her true name! In panic, she let go of her horse's reins and dropped to her knees, sobbing uncontrollably.

"Tears will not rescue you now, the way they did on board the *Nostos*," he said grimly, staring down at her.

Cain collected the reins of her horse. With his left hand, he intertwined them with those of his own mount. With his right hand, he slowly drew the sword from his belt and raised it high over his head. Rina looked up and locked eyes with her husband.

"I know all that you have done!" Cain shouted. "It is now time for the *truth!*"

Rina could manage no response other than a terrified gasp at the sight of the blade poised to strike her down. Cain dropped the circled reins to the ground. Grasping the hilt with both hands, he let loose an anguished scream as he plunged his sword downward.

CHAPTER 72

Ercolano: Present Day

D r. Archibald Walker and Juan Carlos stood behind the tarp next to the narrow crack in the wall. Their heads together, the two painstakingly reviewed the digital recording of Amanda's voice.

"The static at that particular point is maddening," Juan Carlos told Walker. "I'm sure the noise covers her identification of the missing pictogram."

The young Spaniard showed Walker the chart he had made, listing the matches between the five key words in the proverb and the images of the hourglass, the sword, the Chinese "truth" character, and the serpent.

"We have identified all the matches except one," Juan Carlos added. "And we know the proper sequence." Looking at Walker's thin, wiry frame, he asked, "Do you think you can fit through the crack, Doctor?"

Walker didn't hesitate, replying, "Amanda isn't the only agile member of our profession, my boy! If Goldilocks could do it, I can do it."

Juan Carlos, forcing himself to ignore this patronizing remark, tried to refocus Walker. "Remember that there are twenty-one unidentified pictograms in all. The one we need is the image that can be plausibly associated with the word *story*. Take the chart with you, Doctor. You'll also want this." Juan Carlos handed him a thin flashlight with a powerful halogen beam.

Walker folded the notepad sheet and put it in his pocket.

"If you can open the door, please be careful, Dr. Walker. There may be poison gas inside." He choked back emotion as he thought of Amanda.

"That's already occurred to me, young man," Walker rejoined wryly. "Remember that Silvio and I were clambering around ancient ruins when you were in diapers."

Rolling his eyes, Juan Carlos simply replied, "Sure. Buona fortuna, Archie."

Walker's spine stiffened as he briefly glared at Juan Carlos. "My name is Archibald," came his rebuke as he wriggled through the thin crack into the narrow, twisting corridor that led to the entrance doors. Switching on his flashlight, he noticed that the ground was broken by dozens of fissures. After the corridor curved to the right, Walker's light picked up the remains of the robot, smashed by a heavy piece of debris. A bit of steam rose from a vent in the ground. Feeling slightly claustrophobic, he reached for his hip flask, but found to his consternation that his last bit of liquid courage was gone. He continued gingerly along the remaining twenty-five feet of the narrow corridor and was relieved to find himself in a more spacious opening before the doors of the chamber.

He approached the right-hand bronze door. "How strange," he thought. The portals were similar to the ones Luc Renard had installed at Villa Colosseum in Point Dume.

Scanning the pictograms, Walker narrowed down the suitable matches for the word *story* to three choices. After two failed attempts to open the door, he concluded the papyrus roll must be the missing pictogram. As he began to press the symbols on the door in what he knew was the correct sequence, his pulse quickened and his eyes widened with anticipation.

Before pressing on the raised scroll, he stepped back from the doors and savored the moment. Not only would he, Archibald Walker, receive most of the credit for this site's historic discovery, he would also be hailed as a hero, teach Silvio a lesson, and impress Luc Renard—all with one touch of a button!

CHAPTER 73

On the Beach Near Herculaneum, AD 65

Falling to his knees, Cain trembled as he released the hilt of his weapon. Then he collapsed on the ground in racking sobs. "Oh, Quintus, forgive me, my son!" he wept.

"No, Marcus. It is *I* who need *your* forgiveness," Rina pleaded, sobbing. "The deaths of Quintus and his family resulted from my setting fire to Rome. You cannot know the depth of my guilt and regret for the harm I have caused."

Cain stared at her once more. With his calm returning for the first time in days, he stood up, took her hands, and raised her to her feet. Then he took his beautiful wife in his arms.

Rina, still weeping, tried to wriggle free from his embracing gesture of forgiveness. Yet he would not release her. Taking her head in his hands, he forced her to look at him, rather than the blade of his sword that now held the horses' reins fast in the sand.

She returned his gaze with pleading eyes. "I always feared you would find out one day," she told him, "but I was afraid to ever tell you the truth. I thought I would lose you. How could you not have killed me for what I did? It is the Roman way."

Cain placed his fingers gently on her lips. "I have come to know the evil that anger brings. To take revenge on you would serve no purpose—I am not your judge."

"But I have deceived you since the day we met!"

Reflecting on his own countless deceptions, Cain declared, "We must let go of the past, Rina." Embracing her tightly, he whispered, "I love you."

"Oh, Marcus, I never thought in a thousand years I would fall in love with a Roman man after they slaughtered my people," Rina confessed to him. "But I do love you as well, with all my heart."

Leaving the horses, the two strolled together in silence, each mulling the extraordinary series of events leading up to this fateful encounter. As the sun angled lower, they turned and faced the shimmering sea. Finally, they began a slow walk back to the horses. As the sun set, Rina tugged gently at Cain's hand and he turned to face her once more.

"My life has been saddled with tremendous guilt over the fiery deaths of so many innocent people," Rina said in a low voice. "I only meant for my brutal master to die. Sometimes I cannot breathe, the burden is so great. And at night, lying next to you, I see the terrified faces and hear the cries of Rome's citizens in my nightmares."

Cain held his wife close, pressing his chest against hers. He knew her memories would not fade easily, if ever.

Rina continued, "Lately, though, I've been having another set of dreams. A soothing voice talks to me. It encourages me to continue my revenge and set fire to all things Roman. Then, it torments me over and over with an incomprehensible saying."

An eerie feeling came over Cain.

"What does this voice say to you?"

Rina replied, "The voice just keeps repeating, *'Neither death nor time can turn a story's truth to dust.'*"

Cain was stunned. The devil was no longer targeting him, but now both Rina and his life's work were in jeopardy. He made a mental note to change the sequence of the combination code on the doors to his observatory. Then, he tried to reassure his wife, saying simply,

"I used to hear a voice just like that in my dreams. I was finally able to silence it by listening to the advice of someone I met not long ago."

"Who was this person?" Rina asked him eagerly.

"He was a carpenter from Judaea..."

CHAPTER 74

Herculaneum, AD 65–78

"Have you ever cut the umbilical cord, sir?" the midwife asked Cain.

An intriguing question to ask of the first person ever to have one, he mused.

"Yes, I have, but never for a girl," he proudly answered.

"Well, you must be prepared. Because there are two girls, sir!"

Cain was elated—he was the father of twin daughters!

He and Rina named them Callista and Alexandria. Over the next few years, the twins became the jewels in the crown of their marriage. As a parent, Rina turned out to be practical and strict, while Cain, to his own surprise, proved malleable. The couple found that the joys of raising the twins only deepened their own relationship. Cain could not recall such happiness since his days long ago with Tanith on the outskirts of Athens.

Cain and Rina agreed that the girls would be educated by Greek tutors, and once the children had reached the age of six, they entered into a rigorous routine of classes at the villa. Such a regime was unconventional, since education for girls in Rome at the time was haphazard, at best. Nevertheless, the parents were not to be deterred. Astronomy, mathematics, history, and languages were core subjects for the girls' curriculum, and Cain himself often outlined the lesson plans for their tutorials. When the twins were going on seven, the family also began frequenting the open-air theater at Herculaneum.

It was here that they first met their neighbors, Drusus Octavius Balbus and his wife, Tullia. Drusus was one of Herculaneum's most generous benefactors, having contributed the funds for a major new extension of the local public baths. Tullia was a talented painter. After lunch at the villa one day, she suggested that it would be an honor if Cain would permit her to paint a mural of his observatory, the domed building on the grounds to the south of the villa, for display in the dining room of her house. Well aware that estate painting was an established genre of Roman art, he accorded Tullia permission.

Over the next few months, Tullia enjoyed the run of the villa for her mural project. Her husband sometimes accompanied her, especially when Rina had scheduled one of the monthly wine-tasting parties. Although Cain never allowed guests to enter the observatory, Drusus seemed inordinately curious about the building his wife was painting.

"Is there a special material on your ceiling in there?" he asked Cain at one wine tasting. "I can see something sparkling from my estate when the dome is open."

"Only a field of stars painted on the inside of the dome, with an inset of glass crystals," he responded, hoping that Drusus would drop the subject.

"*That's* what made it look like diamonds, then!" Drusus remarked knowledgeably.

"I'll show it to you one day," Cain reassured him. "There's just a bit of additional work to do," he fibbed.

⚭

In AD 78, when the girls were nearing thirteen, Cain decided it was time to show them the observatory. He was still in excellent health, but thoughts of the repository's future had begun to occupy his mind.

He wanted to formulate secure plans for the transmission of his legacy. When the project was initiated over a century ago, he thought he would remain immortal, but clearly his time of natural death was now approaching. Also, Cain and Rina had agreed that it was time to move the girls' religious education beyond the instruction in mythology they'd received from their tutors, and what better way to start than with a visit to the repository.

Therefore, on an afternoon in early fall, Rina and the twins stood at the observatory entrance as Cain entered the code into the combination lock. After the bronze doors clicked open, the group entered the dry interior. He activated the dome mechanism, admitting rays of sunlight into the museum. Then he stepped on a floor section, inscribed with a diagram of a fish, triggering the counterweights that closed the great bronze doors.

The children were astonished at the scope of the collection. The huge circular room measured over 370 feet in circumference, with the domed ceiling ninety feet above the floor, sparkling with precious gemstones the size of small walnuts rather than the glass crystals he had mentioned to Drusus. In the center of the room stood a large telescope and a metal wheel that turned a gearing apparatus linked to the dome. Savoring his role, Cain guided them clockwise around his treasure trove of sculptures, paintings, marble reliefs, maps, and manuscripts.

The parents had discussed this moment in advance. They both wanted to ensure that the twins would be able to make the transition from the Greco-Roman heritage they had absorbed in their tutorials to the mysteries of ancient times and also to the teachings of contemporary Christianity.

"Now, girls," Cain began as he led them to a life-size sculpture of a man and a woman depicted in a loving embrace. "These are your grandparents on my side of the family."

"And what was our grandmother's name?" asked Alexandria.

Cain glanced at Rina for a moment, but he found that her attention had been distracted by another display.

"Her name was Eve," he proudly replied.

"Father, she is beautiful," Callista chimed in. "But, did the sculptor complete this work?"

"What do you mean?"

"Well, her navel seems to be missing."

Cain paused the conversation, ostensibly studying the work as if to take his first notice of this omission. Then he turned back to Callista and said, "No, my dear daughter. The artist knew exactly what he was doing when he formed Eve." He smiled slightly at the quizzical look that remained on Callista's face as he led them to the next displays.

There were scale models of the Kingdom of Enoch, Noah's ark, the Egyptian pyramids, the tomb of the First Emperor of China, and the Alexandrian Library. At each exhibit, the twins drew in an audible breath.

Callista pointed to another group of items at one end of the room. "What are those, Father?"

Cain led the girls through the artifacts. There was a collection of wooden ship models, a variety of blown-glass creations, and a bronze rendering of a device with the wings of a bird. There was a small working facsimile of the mechanical grain reaper, carved in silver. There were also two golden tablets with symbols in an eastern language the girls did not recognize.

Noting Alexandria's interest in the tablets, Cain explained, "Those were given to me by a powerful ruler who lived in China long ago. He was obsessed with finding immortality."

"Did he find it?" asked Callista while twirling her pigtails.

"Not exactly, young lady," he said after a slight reflection. "But he did accomplish a great deal while he was alive. When we have more time, I will tell you his story."

Alexandria drew their attention to the mathematical formulas carved on the lower walls. "Where did these come from?" she asked.

"Many of these formulas are the discoveries of Greek mathematicians and scientists," Cain explained. "Look here, Alexandria," he gestured to one of the diagrams. "You know this theorem very well. It is the Pythagorean formula for the dimensions of right triangles."

As they sauntered along the outer edge of the repository inspecting the collection, the girls gazed upward to the enormous Circus Maximus mural.

"Father," asked Callista, impatiently tugging on Cain's toga, "who is that strange looking boy in the crowd near Quintas? He's wearing a dark cloak and is standing in a shadow when everybody else is bathed in direct sunlight. He looks so...mean, like a demon."

Cain studied the scene for a few seconds, reliving it in his mind. "He's mean, yes, and also quite fiendish. He was part of my life for a time. Perhaps over supper tonight you shall learn more about all the wonderful things preserved in this repository."

He motioned his family onward.

A few steps to the right, and they stood in front of a large cross. The girls shrank back as they viewed the agony of the condemned man's figure, which had been sculpted in white marble and painted with startling realism.

"Is that the crucifixion of the gladiator Spartacus on the Appian way?" asked Callista.

"No, his name is Jesus. He was the Prince of Peace, not a warrior."

"Oh, we've heard of Jesus," said Alexandria.

Callista chimed in, "Yes, we've been told stories about him almost every time we go to Pompeii. There's this man in the square who won't stop talking about him."

"Pompeii?" Rina exclaimed. "What have you two been doing in such a shabby neighborhood?"

Feeling a bit sheepish, Alexandria explained, "Mother, Helvia likes to take us to the *macellum* there. She's always complaining about the high prices in the local food market. We thought you knew."

Cain stared at the girls in wide-eyed amazement. Apparently, their introduction to Christianity had already begun. He smiled at Rina, hoping to calm her obvious concerns over the girls' safety, and then interjected, "Well, dear daughters, I am happy you have learned of Jesus already. Your mother and I have much more to share about him. But for now, let's see the rest of the observatory while we still have light."

Rina nodded and motioned them to the manuscript collection, located opposite the main entrance to the observatory. She wanted the twins to appreciate the complex system of labels that identified scrolls from so many different cultures: Egypt, Greece, Persia, China, and Rome.

In the center of the collection was a special case with an ornate wax seal. Within were a series of papyrus scrolls that told, in complete detail, the story of Cain's life.

"This case may never be opened," he told them. "Promise me that you will protect these scrolls above all others when I am gone!"

Cain's emotion was unmistakable, and Rina and the girls pledged their assurance. After they turned away from the final exhibit, Cain walked to the perimeter of the rotunda and pulled a bronze lever, and the thick, heavy bronze doors of his museum swung open to welcome the warm rays of the setting sun.

Rina promptly excused herself and strode swiftly in the direction of the kitchen.

"Where's mother going in such a hurry?" Callista asked her father.

Their answer came instead from Rina in the distance. *"Helvia!"*

CHAPTER 75

Herculaneum, AD 79

As August drew to a close, Naples and all the towns around the bay were in an especially jovial mood. Holiday crowds streamed in to Herculaneum and Pompeii to celebrate the annual feast day of Vulcan, the Roman god of fire, and also to commemorate the birthday of the emperor Augustus, who had been deified after his death sixty-five years before. Drusus and Tullia had invited Cain and Rina to a special holiday luncheon.

The two couples sat on the marble terrace of Drusus's villa overlooking the sea as servants discreetly placed glasses of wine and platters of fruits and cheese on the hardwood table. The conversation turned to the earth tremors that had become steadily more frequent and powerful in the region over the past four days.

"These little shakes are nothing compared to the earthquake seventeen years ago. You remember *that* one, don't you, Marcus?" asked Drusus.

"Indeed, yes," Cain nodded. "I hear that the damage over in Pompeii is still being repaired."

Just then, as if the elements had taken umbrage at their chat, a sharp thunderclap exploded from a cloudless blue sky. The roaring blast was unlike anything they had ever heard—except for Cain. The couples leaped to their feet and looked in the direction of Mount Vesuvius in time to see the summit of the volcano exploding high into the air.

"Vulcan must desire to leave his underground forge and join us personally for this feast!" joked Drusus. But Cain, who had witnessed the volcano's devastating power long ago, knew better.

"This is no joke, Drusus."

"You really think there is cause for alarm, Marcus?" asked Tullia. "We just started lunch."

"Tullia, we must evacuate Herculaneum as soon as we can," Cain answered decisively. "And that means on the water. By land will be too dangerous." Turning to Drusus, he added in deadly earnest, "Ready your boats in the harbor without delay, and put as much distance between yourself and Vesuvius as you can, or you will surely die."

As Cain and Rina hurried back to their villa, they could see that an enormous cloud was stretching upward from the volcano. Most of the cloud was white, but other portions of it were stained with dark, ashy patches.

"This is just the beginning," shouted Cain as the guards at the front gate saluted him smartly. "Quickly, Marcellus!" he said to one of the younger gatemen. "Run to the boathouses. Tell Captain Felix to prepare the *Nostos* and have Secundus ready all of the smaller boats." Glancing at the sun, he added, "It is now almost the ninth hour. Tell them we must leave as soon as possible"

The young guard nodded and sprinted off in the direction of the beach. As they entered the villa, Cain turned to Rina.

"Believe me, the volcano is lethal. The ash cloud will collapse, and then an avalanche will follow. All of Herculaneum and Pompeii will be covered in a deep layer of molten rock."

"Should we take shelter in the observatory?" Rina asked with alarm.

"No. Our only chance is to get out. Please tell Helvia to organize the staff. Everyone must be on board the *Nostos* before darkness falls. The cloud will soon blot out the sun."

An hour later, Secundus appeared from the boathouses to report that all the vessels had been readied. He added that buildings in the town of Herculaneum had started to crumble from intensifying ground tremors.

"Spread the word to anyone you see on the beach, Secundus," Cain told him. "People need to leave at once. You know the capacity of our vessels. Take on as many evacuees as you can."

"Many of them still refuse to leave, sir," said Secundus. "They do not believe they are in danger."

"Make them believe if you possibly can," Cain ordered. "Otherwise, they will perish."

As the sun's light waned, Cain led his family and staff from the villa to the boathouses. Ash had started to fall, thinly at first and then in heavier densities. When the shoreline came into view, Cain could not suppress an exclamation of astonishment at the patches of pumice rock already floating in the water. On Vesuvius, to the east, sheets of flame were lighting up parts of the mountain. He noticed that several of his sailors had tied pillows to their heads, as a protection against dust and small fragments of lightweight stones that showered down from the sky. A ghastly, sulfuric odor had filled the air.

Already, 250 people were aboard the *Nostos*, but Captain Felix assured him there would still be room for family and staff. Felix gestured to the rowboat that would take them out to the flagship, anchored in the bay. Rina boarded first, followed by the twins. But as Cain stepped into the rowboat, he heard Drusus calling out to him from his own sailboat nearby.

"Marcus, I've been trying to find you. You left the roof of your observatory open!"

Cain shook his head. He clearly remembered shutting the dome and the oculus. It was the first thing he did once the evacuation was underway.

"Are you certain, Drusus?" he shouted.

"Yes. I could see the circular opening as we were leaving our villa."

Turning to Rina and the twins, he said, "I have to go back to the observatory. Felix, I won't be long, but there is no time to wait for me here. The rain of pumice is getting heavier every minute. And even this light onshore wind will impede the *Nostos* with its present load. Getting the ship safely out of the harbor will be difficult if you don't leave immediately."

"But what about you, sir?" the Captain implored.

"Is there another rowboat available?"

"Yes, sir, just as you ordered. It's in the boathouse, with a crew of four oarsmen standing by."

"Fine. Leave now for safer waters. You should go at least thirty kilometers from here."

"I suggest we dock in Misenum, then," said Felix. "Hopefully, Fleet Admiral Pliny will lend us assistance."

"Good plan," Cain said. "He is a personal friend of mine. I will take the smaller vessel and meet you there as soon as I can."

He turned to Rina and the girls. "My loves, I have no choice. If the oculus remains open, my life's work will be ruined. Please don't worry. I'll follow you and we will all meet in Misenum."

"I can go with you and help—we can let the twins sail with Felix," Rina offered.

"No, there will be plenty of time for me to get away safely. You go with Felix. I need you to look after the girls and help calm the frightened passengers."

"Father, please hurry—we're scared!" cried Callista and Alexandria in unison.

He kissed his wife good-bye, hugged his teenage daughters, and stepped ashore. Felix ordered the oarsmen to stroke, and the small boat began to move out into the bay, ferrying them swiftly to the safety of the *Nostos*.

It took Cain longer than he had expected to get back to the observatory. The grounds of his unguarded villa were crisscrossed by refugees, whose shrill laments and cries of alarm could be heard through the inky blackness of the artificial nightfall. Many of the town's panicked residents were finally seeking the shortest route across his property to the beach. They shouted out in the darkness for their relatives. Some of them called on the gods, while others shrieked that the gods had forsaken them and were bringing the world to an end. The scene was only rendered eerier by lightning flashes, as the volcanic eruption created its own localized weather system. Using a torch to see, Cain had to wade through ankle-deep ash and pumice stones as he crossed the villa's courtyard.

Finally reaching the observatory, he quickly punched in the code and opened the thick bronze doors. Once inside, he stepped on the floor section shaped like a fish, and the portals slowly swung shut behind him. Drusus was right—the oculus was wide open, and pumice and ash were accumulating on the floor. Cain looked around the enormous circular space, intermittently illuminated by the lightning. He used his torch to ignite a few of the freestanding candles against the wall to provide a dim but steady source of light. Then he extinguished the torch.

Should he take anything at all with him? he wondered. The fortified chamber was constructed to secure all the contents that would tell his story to future generations, but Cain decided there was one treasure that he could, and would, salvage.

Opening a small lacquered box, he withdrew the game tile stained by the blood of Jesus during their first meeting a half century ago. Unlooping the sturdy silver chain he had attached to the tile, he hung it around his neck.

Then he turned his attention to the metal wheel in the middle of the observatory, directly below the small opening in the center of the dome. This was the mechanism that controlled the gears that would close the oculus and seal the dome. As he turned the wheel, he could feel the ground vibrating beneath his feet and could hear a low rumbling noise getting louder by the second. As he recalled from his great wandering, this signaled the worst. Pyroclastic flow, a super-heated mixture of mud and ash, was racing down the slopes of Vesuvius toward Herculaneum.

Cain now knew he would not make it out alive.

"*Stop!*" boomed a metallic voice in the darkness. A flash of lightning through the oculus briefly illuminated Abaddon. Cain immediately apprehended the purpose of the devil's visit. Ever the opportunist, he sought the destruction of the observatory's contents by Vesuvius's fiery discharge. Cain ignored the order and urgently continued his task.

"*Oh, isn't that just like you, Cain? Abandoning your wife and children in this crisis to tend to your narcissistic little collection,*" the devil hissed. "*But for naught, you fool. It all burns tonight. You will do as I command! Otherwise, I will ensure that your slave woman of a wife is captured by the Romans and executed for her crime!*"

Cain paused momentarily at these last words, but then daunt-lessly resumed his effort at the wheel. The oculus was slowly closing, with only a narrow sliver of sky remaining.

"*Let go of that wheel, damn you!*" shouted the master of spirits, as he forcibly restrained both of Cain's arms with supernatural strength. Another lightning flash forked down through the oculus, illuminat-ing the antagonists for a second. The light caught the silver of the chain around Cain's neck and highlighted the tile.

"*And give me back my game piece, accursed one!*" roared the devil. But as he grabbed the tile with his left hand, he was instantly para-lyzed, looking up at Cain with his mouth agape in shock. His right hand remained fixed on Cain's arm, but it no longer impeded his progress. Cain spun the wheel in one final revolution and then heard the counterweights kicking in. The oculus would shut on its own now.

Before it was fully closed, however, the initial wave of Vesuvius's pyroclastic mud splashed over the observatory. Cain glanced upward as the small, shrinking gap in the oculus admitted a narrow column of searing death that hurtled down toward him and the devil.

Only an instant remained before they were both frozen in time by the lethal incursion. Yet, in that brief moment, Cain's perception expanded in proportion to his unique lifespan, and he was blessed by a series of wondrous assurances. The devil's perennial assaults on his destiny had been divinely thwarted. His repository of history and, more poignantly, his own story, would be preserved and one day revealed, as Jesus had promised. For the first time ever, his loved ones would survive him. And, at long last, he would rest in peace in the presence of his Maker.

With elation that only he could experience, Cain looked his ancient enemy in the eye—and smiled.

Then the dome sealed everything.

CHAPTER 76

Ercolano: Present Day

Amanda James stared at the two ash-covered figures frozen in front of her. A ghostly silence engulfed the chamber. In contrast to the shattering roar of the volcano's ancient eruption, the stillness jolted her back to the here and now as her vision drew to a close.

"Incredible," she murmured, looking at the tile dangling from the neck of the powerful wrestler she now knew to be Cain. Drawing a deep breath, she checked her watch. It was a few minutes past noon—millennia had been compressed into a mere three hours!

Amanda carefully removed the chain from around Cain's neck, noticing some exposed portions of bone on his skeletal frame that was otherwise coated by hardened mud and ash. Next, she nervously extracted the tile from the devil's grasp. As she did so, his right arm and shoulder disintegrated into coarse powder, revealing a grotesque, hollow shell. In the cool dry air of the cavernous repository, she now understood that only one of these two beings had truly perished here.

The other was still on the loose.

Examining the ceramic gaming tile in the halogen beam of her headlamp, Amanda saw the green serpent depicted on it, partially obscured by a small, dark blot that she knew was the blood of Jesus.

It hadn't been a hallucination!

Since the vision had ended at the instant of Cain's death, she found herself wondering whether Rina had survived on that terrifying night. Abruptly, a stark image from one of the towering blood-draped murals on the walls of Luc

Renard's villa flashed through her mind. It was the vivid portrayal of a tall, red-haired woman about to be devoured by lions in the Roman Colosseum. Amanda was shaken as she recognized the striking female in the painting. Rina looked about ten years older than she remembered her. Had the devil made good on his threat to take revenge and have Rina killed as a wanted criminal, or was she swept up with other Christians and barbarically sacrificed for the pleasure of Rome's cheering mob? Amanda guessed she would never know the real reason behind Rina's execution.

Even more perplexing was the fact that Cain's wife was completely unknown to history. How then, could Renard have possibly commissioned a painting that celebrated her death? Further reflection on the tabloid billionaire did nothing to quell her rising alarm. She recalled his extravagant party at Villa Colosseum. The suave host had vigorously attempted to lure her to Japan instead of Italy. Renard's job offer had seemed so flattering last Thursday evening, but now Amanda suspected it was a deliberate attempt to prevent her from making this discovery. What else to make of the near miss on the highway the moment she'd rebuffed him? Or the man at the airport in Rome—the limousine driver holding a placard with her name on it? Or the car that chased them on the drive to Ercolano?

Luc's real aim in this bizarre set of circumstances crystalized in Amanda's consciousness. The devil was working overtime to thwart Cain's most cherished wish: that his story be told one day.

Shuddering, Amanda knew there could be only one conclusion regarding Luc...

Zzzzzt. Her headlamp flickered and died.

Amanda fought to keep sudden panic at bay. In the haunting quiet she could almost hear the blinking of her eyelids while she adjusted to the inky blackness.

"Relax," she told herself, "it's just the batteries." Feeling her way toward the curvature of the rotunda, she pulled out the fancy lighter Juan Carlos had given her in case of an emergency.

"Thank you, Johnny!" she whispered, flicking the cap open with a loud *ping* that resonated through the chamber. As she lit several candles, a warm

glow began to brighten the observatory. Wavering shadows of the marble statues and other artifacts sprang to life along the soaring, circular wall.

Although she was skittish, her professional curiosity returned. Amanda
tried to resist, but she couldn't help but imagine how this stunning archaeological and religious discovery would propel Silvio's team and the Getty to
the world stage. After all, Silvio was right—this find would indeed rival the
unearthing of the Dead Sea Scrolls!

Dr. James moved slowly, lighting more candles as she mentally catalogued
the objects she examined. All the exhibits matched her vision exactly. With
half the room lit, she glanced upward to the ceiling. Sure enough, sparkling
diamonds and other gemstones the size of golf balls were embedded in the
dome to depict the constellations of the Milky Way galaxy. A shimmering full
moon, with the iridescence of mother-of-pearl, glinted benignly down at her.
Anchored next to the ash-covered bodies, a large, complex looking ancient
telescope bore witness to its owner's interest in the heavens. The British
Museum in London would marvel at this collection of antiquities!

Yet those same stuffy curators would be stunned by the physical proof of
Cain's existence, Amanda thought.

She moved toward the rosewood cabinet containing the scrolls that
chronicled Cain's life story. She grabbed a small pick out of her backpack.
"Professional standards be damned," she thought, given the magnitude of
what had just happened. She would break the seal and stuff the protective
metal tubes into her knapsack and head out. Surely, Silvio would understand.

As she was about to chip away the thick wax on the cabinet door, she felt
a low rumbling vibration, and suddenly the chamber lurched violently back and
forth, almost knocking her off her feet. Dozens of splintering cracks rocketed
up the interior wall as the observatory shook. Several of the sparkling diamonds embedded in the ceiling fell to the floor, one grazing a minor cut in her
forearm. She dropped the pickax and covered her unprotected head. Nearby,
two cabinets containing colorful glass specimens broke free of their wall
anchors and toppled with an earsplitting crash.

After almost a full minute, the stone floor ceased undulating like a giant slab of gelatin. Irregularly shaped fissures in the walls high above continued to spit out dust-laden chunks of plaster and broken concrete. The gargantuan structure was groaning under its own weight. Fearing the entire chamber might collapse, Amanda sprinted toward the iron lever Cain used to open the bronze portals and pulled downward with all her might. She had to get out!

"Come on, come on—work..." she nervously whispered while beads of perspiration spotted the front and back of her T-shirt.

She heard a distant grinding sound, and the twin bronze doors of the observatory slowly ratcheted open toward her.

"Yes!" She pumped her fist, knowing she would make it out alive.

Amanda slipped through the entryway and reignited the lighter to guide her way back through the winding crack. She could hardly wait to breathe fresh air and share the amazing news concerning the artifacts inside the chamber with Silvio and the team. Perhaps she could even figure out a way to explain the fantastic vision to Johnny!

But in the flickering darkness, her excited state of relief rapidly yielded to alarm.

Her path was blocked.

Outside the bronze portals, the earthquake had squeezed together the already narrow rock passage to just a few inches. Worse, grotesquely protruding from the crack was a lifeless human arm, crushed at the shoulder.

"Johnny!" she shrieked in horror. But something from within the nightmarish sight caught her eye. There, on a finger that was too small to belong to Juan Carlos's hand, a familiar signet ring reflected the lighter's flame with a purplish gleam.

"My God...Dr. Walker!" There was no mistaking his ring. She had seen it time and again as he pontificated to her from behind his desk at the Getty. What was he doing here? She fought down the bile rising in her throat, her trembling hands dropping the lighter to the floor as she backed away from the terrifying scene.

After a minute, Amanda managed to bring her breathing under control as she struggled to comprehend Walker's demise. In the silent gloom, she heard it.

The striking of a match.

Amanda wheeled around and gasped at the sight of the white-haired, diminutive figure of the muralist, Giovanni Genoa. He stood near the mud-splattered telescope in the center of the observatory. His courteous smile was belied by the unflinching gaze that he riveted on the ceramic tile still firmly clasped in her hand.

Giovanni Genoa's grin broadened as he set a wooden match to a candle wick in front of him, illuminating his wizened features.

"Buon giorno, Signorina James!" he greeted. "It is so enchanting to see you again. And to find you here, of all places, in this cabinet of curiosities!" He gently blew out the match and a swirl of smoke jetted across the chamber, whorling against the life-size crucifix hanging on the wall.

"Bull's-eye," he spat.

Ignoring his twisted humor and the feigned sincerity, Amanda noticed that throughout the salutation, his attention darted between her eyes and the tile. Despite the thumping in her chest that seemingly reverberated throughout the chamber, she summoned her courage and took a small step toward him. Sure enough, he moved an equal distance away from her. Emboldened, she slowly proceeded toward the artist, initiating a tense promenade as they traced a gradual circle around the ash-covered corpses under the oculus.

This was no guardian angel sent to rescue her—just the opposite.

"What are you doing here, Signor Genoa?" she demanded, hoping her tone exuded confidence.

"I might inquire the same of you, signorina, but for your obvious professional interests." Gesturing around the periphery, he added, "What splendid marvels were created in those ancient times! They are beyond our wildest imaginings. I know you must be thrilled to see these exhibits. They would be so important to the Getty Museum. And speaking of the Getty, you see that Dr.

Walker has once again been seeking the limelight you deserve, although this time apparently without much success."

"How dare you! He must have been trying to rescue me from this place," she retorted. "I'm indebted to him."

"His death is most unfortunate. May I point out, however, that it opens the way to fresh possibilities?" Genoa's voice was softly persuasive.

Propelling the painter backward with each step, Amanda frowned. "What do you mean?"

"Why, you are Dr. Walker's most obvious and qualified successor!" gushed the muralist as he duplicated her casual gait. "If the Getty were a more equitable institution, you would have been promoted long ago. Now the way to a higher-ranking position has been cleared for you."

"I would never seek to profit from his tragic death!"

"No one would make such an accusation, my dear young lady," oozed the pained words of the diminutive man. "We all have to make our way in the world. That celebrity television career in Japan wasn't right for you, Dr. James. I apologize for underestimating your ambitions, but I can now arrange an even greater future for you at the Getty; a future that makes full use of your obvious talents…but first, you must do me a small favor."

"And what is that, Signor Genoa?"

"Actually, I would ask your cooperation in two matters. First, you must agree never to divulge certain items in this collection. Then, return that tile in your hand to its rightful owner. It is of no real historical importance to you or the Getty. If you agree, I will escort you to safety and see to it that you obtain your rightful place at the Getty."

She looked down at the ceramic token in her hand. "And what if I refuse?"

"Come, now," Genoa wheedled. "What is a tiny piece of clay in comparison with your future?"

Amanda held the tile up and studied it. "We both know this is far more than a piece of clay. If I do what you ask, you will either kill me or leave me to rot in this chamber."

"That is a most uncharitable remark, signorina. I come here to assist you, and you treat an old man so discourteously." Genoa furrowed his brow. "Strange, though, that you have not inquired how I arrived in this godforsaken place. Perhaps you were expecting someone else, no?"

"Perhaps I was, but you're no mere painter, and you're certainly no saint. Shall we just drop the pretense, Satan?"

"Marvelous deduction, young lady." The painter looked at the likeness of the cloaked youth portrayed in the shadows of the mural overhead. "You are indeed a master puzzle solver and deserve cathedrals full of praise! No doubt you cobbled together the clues to my existence from the walls of this repository of lies," surmised the devil as he stretched both hands toward the Circus Maximus mural. "But no matter, for I am here to present you with options. I always try to help, never to kill or injure anyone!"

"That's a lie!" she burst out, gesturing to Cain's corpse in the room's center. "I saw you try to kill him at the chariot festival in Rome. I know this as a fact!"

The devil arched his bushy eyebrows, taken aback by the accuracy of Amanda's declaration. "How could you possibly know *that?*" His eyes earnestly scanned the candlelit chamber, and he noticed that the rosewood cabinet containing Cain's life story still bore an unbroken wax seal.

"Now tell me, exactly what have you *seen*, young lady?" the devil purred inquisitively.

Realizing her mistake, and clutching the tile even tighter, Amanda dropped her guard and boldly declared, "Well, this pendant may have been yours, but Jesus's blood transformed it. When I touched it, I received a vision of Cain's entire life!"

"How intriguing! So now you understand how I deal with an uncooperative murderer. However, I always reward my followers. Take Luc Renard, for example. Riches suited him just fine, but I am well aware of your professional ambitions. I would have no difficulty arranging for you to become the Getty Museum's curator of antiquities after a few short years in Walker's post."

Pausing to gauge her interest, the devil added for good measure, "And what if that lovely face and body of yours could remain youthful for decades to come? I have that power..."

"You take me for a fool?" she interrupted hotly. "You claimed responsibility for Cain's youthfulness and regeneration, but it was just another of your countless lies."

"Amanda, please, if I may be so bold, life is all about getting your fair share, being happy here on Earth, and making it last. Quite frankly, I don't see that happening with you. Open that locket you're wearing, and whom will we find?"

Amanda considered her mother's faded picture inside the locket.

The devil continued, "Nothing but the past, my dear. You've been a lonely workaholic ever since God robbed you of your parents. Is that how you want to spend your prime years?"

Irritated, Amanda countered sharply, "Maybe not, but I wouldn't be thrilled to hang out with you and your followers. Besides, I have people who care about me."

"Yes, I know you fancy that impetuous young Spaniard out there. You may find out presently how foolish it is to place your hopes in him. Your only real hope lies with me, not some washed-up soccer star."

Amanda shook her head. "There's no way I'll trust anything you say. I will not give you this tile."

The devil sighed. "If you wish to complicate matters, we shall do it your way. In time, you will learn to trust me. For the time being, however, to make you feel more comfortable, you may be the keeper of my tile."

His voice then deepened and boomed across the chamber. "But you must remain silent about your vision."

"You seem awfully insecure about Cain," Amanda countered with a touch of confidence. "I do suppose the story of his extraordinary life and redemption would prove somewhat disruptive in your realm of hopelessness."

As their slow circular procession continued in the semidarkness, Amanda felt an irregular surface beneath her feet. Glancing down, she recognized that she had stepped on the grated drain Cain had installed in the floor to catch rainwater. Would it afford her a means of escape?

She stopped strolling toward the devil, who in turn halted. Amanda was now convinced.

She held all the power, and it was right in her hands.

Facing the devil, she smiled broadly and declared, "I'm afraid I'll have to pass on your offers, signore. The excavation team knows I'm down here. It's only a matter of time before they rescue me."

The charming expression abruptly departed from Giovanni Genoa's face. The devil gestured up to the ceiling of the observatory and sternly intoned, "Very well. Behold the dome above. Let me show you what your creator has in store for you."

Amanda caught her breath as she glanced upward just in time to see a vivid portrayal of Mount Vesuvius erupting. The scene unfolded like an IMAX movie on the inner surface of the dome. Unlike two thousand years ago, however, the explosive power of the volcano was unleashed solely toward Ercolano.

The devil took his time letting the scene unfold before he continued. "As you can plainly see, Amanda, the tremor that crushed Dr. Walker was more than just a quake. It is an omen of your death. In just a few minutes, Vesuvius will bury the town of Ercolano once again. Your creator is toying with you, my dear. He gives you a vision of hope, only to trap you alone in this chamber to be entombed forever."

On the curvature of the dome overhead, Amanda could now see a tide of pumice and ash emerging from the mountain's belching summit.

"You have much to live for, young lady," he said, almost in a fatherly tone. "A very promising future in your profession waits. And think about Juan Carlos. God is going to let him die as well, if I don't intervene. Your human companions will not rescue you in time. Only I can do that for you now!"

"How do I know what you are showing me isn't just a conjuring trick?" Amanda asked, her voice cracking slightly.

"How do you know that Vesuvius is not erupting? Can you afford to take that chance? After all, Walker is surely dead—from an act of God, no less!"

Amanda was speechless, so the devil pounced again.

"I am compassionate, Amanda! I truly feel for the human beings on this earth. My gaze is always fixed on the future, not on the past."

"What sort of future do I have pledging my soul to you?" she sputtered.

The devil's voice softened further. "There is no need for melodrama. I have not done business that way since the Middle Ages. Our agreement will be simple. I will convey you out of the chamber to safety. In exchange for my aid, you will take your rightful place at the Getty and secure my tile under protective glass so that it can be seen, but not touched. And, of course, you will tell no one of your vision. It will be our secret."

Amanda gazed at the priceless exhibits in the observatory, a look that was not lost on the devil.

"I will even arrange for you to take custody of most of the artifacts in this chamber," he added.

"I've already made it clear that I am not willing to negotiate," rebuffed Amanda, but with a tone that revealed more reservation than confidence.

The devil sensed an opening. "All right—cooperate, and I will also save Juan Carlos. After all, he had no idea what he was getting into here, did he? And think of the nights that await you in his loving embrace!"

As Amanda's hesitation continued, he added grandly, "Remember what I told you at Villa Colosseum. Those days in Rome must have been a great time to be alive, if you were not the sacrifice. Would you be God's sacrifice now? Should Juan Carlos become the innocent victim of your heroics?"

Amanda's anxiety mounted as she saw the avalanche of lava barreling down the mountain slope, smashing through the outskirts of Ercolano. Her chance of escape was practically zero if Vesuvius had erupted. Even the observatory's drain, which might connect to a seaside culvert, would probably be impassable. There was nothing on earth that could spare Juan Carlos from the pyroclastic swath, and she would never be able to tell Cain's story to anyone from the grave.

Her mind clouded with doubt. If she allowed the devil to save her, perhaps she could later figure out a way to work around this deal. Or was this the devil's way of getting his evil talons into her, like the orphan back in Chicago?

"It gets even more gruesome. Listen!" the muralist proclaimed with a hint of glee.

She could now hear the deafening sound of the death wave crushing hundreds of structures. She saw crowds of men, women, and children running down the streets, screaming in terror before the superheated volcanic flow enveloped them.

"You evil little troll! You delight in human suffering. I hate you!" Amanda retorted, wiping back tears for the victims of Vesuvius's wrath.

"Don't hate me. I didn't cause the volcano to erupt. Hate the God who is responsible for this slaughter."

Amanda closed her eyes. Precious seconds passed as the devil silenced the noise of the approaching avalanche. The only sound that could now be heard was the tapping of his well-worn Bruno Magli loafer against the stone floor as he awaited the young archaeologist's next move.

Just then, a loud squeak echoed through the chamber. The devil's neck twitched slightly as he scanned for the sound's origin.

Amanda did not notice the devil's surprise because her attention was diverted to an odd motion in front of her. Layers of mud began to flake off the mummified body of Cain. The metal wheel in his hands jerked slightly in one direction and then the other.

Was he coming back to life? Would Cain be her rescuer?

"Cat got your tongue?" the devil asked sweetly, trying to seem as if he was still in control despite this strange development.

Amanda gulped.

The devil continued, fresh confidence filling his voice as he pointed his index finger upward to the dome.

"Because you defy me, young lady, the oculus will now open, and you risk the same fate as that coward buried next to you. In a few seconds, boiling lava will spiral down into this chamber, bringing you, and all these knickknacks, to a fiery doom!" The devil punctuated his prediction with a demented howl of laughter.

The wheel stopped and started, and then began to turn steadily in one direction. Flashbacks from her vision flooded her mind. Amanda had witnessed Cain's heroic end, and now she questioned how she would face her own death.

"This is your last chance," the devil declared. "Agree to my terms and I will stop the wheel before the counterweights open the oculus fully. I can still save you, and your lover Johnny. But know this: I will slay Juan Carlos in a most unfair manner if you renege on our deal."

Amanda desperately considered her options. Was the devil lying, or was this really her last chance? Or was this all a test of faith? She stared once again at the dome as the annihilation of the city continued to play out overhead.

The devil spoke a final time. "As you can see, my dear, Vesuvius has no more patience for this amusing chitchat. Nor, at this particular moment, do I. Make your decision."

"Now!"

Amalfi Coast, Italy
Seven Hours Later

Speeding along the elevated highway above the picturesque Amalfi coastline, the Alfa Romeo 8C Spider negotiated the last few hairpin curves on the SS163 before reaching the small resort town of Praiano. Sunday evening traffic was almost nonexistent.

"We just blew right by the hotel!" Juan Carlos shouted over the roar of the wind and the four hundred horses thundering under the hood.

Downshifting the silky-smooth transmission, Amanda braked hard and swung the red convertible into a sharp U-turn, bringing the Spider to a dead stop in front of the Tramanto d'Oro. A quaint but upscale hotel, it was popular with high-end travelers from all over the world.

"Take good care of this bambino," she said with a broad grin, tossing the keys high in the air toward the wide-eyed valet attendants, who tried to outjump each other for the chance to park the exotic roadster.

Stepping out of the passenger side, Juan Carlos could smell the brake pads still sizzling from their seventy-kilometer sprint along one of Italy's windiest highways. Offering his arm to Amanda, who was shaking out and straightening her windblown hair, he exclaimed, "Chica mia! That was some driving!"

"Gracias, Señor, for letting me pilot your rocket ship," she replied. "After what we've been through today, I sure needed a release."

"You've come a long way from that motor scooter," he joked.

Taking his arm, she added, "Sorry I wasn't very talkative on the drive down here. I had a lot on my mind."

"I understand," he said, before looking at his watch. "Hey, there's plenty of time to catch the sunset before dinner. Let's make our way to the balcony."

As the two glided through the bright but understated lobby, Amanda brought them to a pause in front of a glass enclosure showcasing three Renaissance-era ship models.

"Johnny, just imagine the adventures those sailors must have had," she mused, her thoughts filled with vivid memories of the *Nostos* and its high sea adventures.

Eyeballing the Spanish galleons, Juan Carlos replied, "I think you'll prefer the menu here to the fish sauce and dried bread served up on those old-world sailing ships."

Amanda laughed, "You're right, and thanks for suggesting our little get-away. This place is great!"

"You haven't seen anything yet. Wait till we get outside."

Reaching the terrace, with its spectacular panorama of the coastline, they sat down next to each other at a table alongside the wrought iron railing. Other well-dressed couples were scattered about the patio enjoying the last rays of the crimson sun as it dropped toward the horizon.

"You weren't kidding!" Amanda exclaimed. She took in a deep breath of fresh sea air and glanced down toward the crashing waves some hundred meters below.

"Now you know why I wanted us to get out of Ercolano," Juan Carlos said. "The whole town smelled like sulfur from those fumaroles on Vesuvius."

Amanda just nodded, wondering if that was all he had in mind in proposing this particular destination.

Greeted promptly by a waiter, Juan Carlos ordered two glasses of Brunello di Montalcino. Quietly, they took in the breathtaking views along the peninsula and toward the sailboats and megayachts that were wending to and from the island of Capri in the distance. Amanda remembered Cain sailing by this beautiful little paradise many times, as it marked the final approach to Herculaneum from Carthage and Judaea.

While they waited for their drinks, she twirled the ends of her blond hair around her index finger and stared at the sea, lost in thought. Why her? Amanda felt so spiritually ill-equipped for what just happened. She hadn't set foot in a church in seven years, and her knowledge of the Bible came almost solely from her profession. Now, however, she wasn't the same person who went through those bronze portals to the past—or was she? Shifting her gaze back to Johnny, she wondered if she could ever tell him about her vision.

Then a wild thought crossed her mind—*the tile was in her purse!*

Juan Carlos broke the silence. With a gleam in his eye, he reached into his jacket pocket and produced two small cigars.

"Time to make good on your promise from last night," he said. "You deciphered the combination lock on the chamber doors in no time. I say we celebrate your success."

The look in Amanda's eyes did not match her pearly smile as she accepted the *Romeo y Julieta* Petit Princess from him.

"After what happened to Dr. Walker today, it doesn't feel right to be celebrating…"

"I understand," he sighed as their wine arrived. Amanda noticed the waiter's lapel badge bore the name Farzad, along with his hometown of Tehran. After a swirl and a perfunctory taste, Juan Carlos nodded his head to signify his acceptance of the vintage. Once the wine was poured, he raised his glass. "A simple toast, then, to honor his life. To Dr. Archibald Walker." The couple clinked their glasses in silent remembrance of the Getty's mercurial department head.

Drawing up her courage, but then pausing for a second, Amanda reached into her purse and retrieved a small object. Holding it tightly in her hand, she extended it toward Juan Carlos.

"I have something very important to give you," she said mysteriously, and then she opened her palm.

"Ah—my favorite lighter! Thanks for taking care of it."

"Well, to be honest, I dropped it in the observatory. I remembered it when you lowered the rope through the oculus to pull me out. Hopefully there's no damage."

"Not a scratch," Juan Carlos smiled as he *pinged* the lid open. Amanda leaned toward him and cupped his hand gently as the flame caught the tip of her cigar.

"Whew!" she said with a wrinkle of her nose after puffing the slender corona to life. "I haven't done this since college."

"Chica mia, I brought you a mild one. You'll be just fine."

Their hands drifted together across the table, and the two leaned back and savored the beauty of the Amalfi Coast as the sun's rays gilded the Tyrrhenian Sea.

Amanda's thoughts once again drifted to the tile. Although tempted, she couldn't take the chance of showing Johnny the ancient pendant. Besides, without Cain's personal scrolls, no rational person would believe the story of her vision. She needed more time to work out a plan.

"...and that is how Cardinal Ravatti ended up at the site," Juan Carlos said. He had just finished retelling some of the day's events and turned to see her reaction.

There was none. She hadn't heard a word.

"Amanda?"

She stirred. "Oh yes, the sunset." Amanda yawned while she stretched her arms and arched her back ever so slightly. Curling her long fingers around her wine glass, she took a sip and politely gestured toward the west.

"Hey, Johnny. Maybe there will be a green flash this evening. It sure looks clear enough."

"Uh—a green what?" he queried, now thoroughly confused.

"It's astonishing! The top of the sun gains a phosphorescent crown of green light just as it dips below the horizon—but only for a few seconds."

"That would be great," he replied gracefully. "I've never seen one."

"Really? I've seen hundreds of..."

Amanda stopped herself midsentence, realizing she was confusing scenes from the vision with her real-life experiences.

Juan Carlos gave her a curious look, and then he chuckled, "Sometimes I can't tell whether you're joking or being serious!"

She gave him a coy smile, deciding to change the subject.

"Tell me something, Johnny. How did you find the top of the dome?"

"It wasn't much of a problem. We had the GPS coordinates from the robot's last position in the crack, so I was able to extrapolate from that point to the approximate center of the underground chamber."

"Wait—to do that you had to know the exact size and shape of the chamber!"

"You're right, and I did! It turns out that Silvio had a picture of a first-century fresco that he found in a nearby dig site a few years ago. It showed a Roman couple standing in front of the doors of the circular observatory. From their height, I could estimate the relative dimensions of the overall structure."

Amanda's eyes widened a fraction as she sipped her wine.

"I'd love to see that picture sometime," she said matter-of-factly.

"Sure, I'll ask Silvio to show it to you. Anyway, when the earthquake hit, I moved as fast as I could. My handheld GPS unit guided me pretty close to the apex of the dome. What I didn't expect was that Carmelo had gotten there ahead of me!"

"What was he doing there?"

"He told me that Silvio sent him in case Walker couldn't open the doors. I was relieved to see that he had already cleared away most of the soil covering the top of the dome. By the time I arrived, there was only a thin layer to scrape off. Imagine that—the height of the observatory was just about equal to the avalanche Vesuvius put out two thousand years ago!"

Lost in reflection about how little the scene outside the observatory resembled the devil's fantastic picture show on the dome, Amanda simply smiled in acknowledgment.

Juan Carlos continued, "Carmelo had a pry bar and was pushing as hard as he could on the ridge of one of the interlocking plates that formed the oculus, but they barely budged. I looked around and found a service hole that directly accessed the gears for the mechanism. We leaned into the pry bar, slamming it back and forth until finally the whole oculus just spiraled open on its own. Whoever built that observatory must have been some engineer!"

If only he knew, Amanda thought. The magnificently designed repository and its contents were the product of one of the greatest artists and engineers of all time.

Then she chimed in. "From down below it was the scariest thing. In the dim candlelight, it looked as if the corpse were coming to life and turning the wheel that opened the oculus!"

"Amazing how the mind plays tricks on you," Juan Carlos offered, hoping to quell Amanda's obvious concern.

Nodding her head and taking a deep breath, she asked, "What do you think will happen now with the observatory?"

"Well, I spoke with Silvio earlier before we left this evening. He was still with the *Polizia di Stato* having to justify the excavation beneath private property. He thinks the whole thing will turn into a huge fight between Renard Enterprises and the local property owner. Apparently, the owner became aware of the discovery and is trying to stop escrow from closing. Either way, whoever wins that round is still going to have to deal with Cardinal Ravatti and the Pontifical Commission. Silvio thinks it could be years before anyone is allowed to excavate."

"That would be terrible," blurted Amanda. She had not counted on that news.

Just then, as the sun dipped below the horizon, the sea breeze picked up. Amanda, who was wearing only a light dress, caught the eye of Farzad and motioned to the attentive waiter. She politely requested that he bring one of the hotel's propane heaters over to their table, and he left quickly to comply.

Juan Carlos looked at her with furrowed eyebrows. "What did you just say to the waiter?"

"Didn't you hear me? I'm getting a little chilled, so I asked him to wheel over a heater." She took a tiny puff on her cigar as she finished her explanation.

"In *Persian?*"

Amanda caught her breath and almost gagged on the smoke she'd accidentally inhaled. Stifling the urge to cough, she realized she had just spoken fluently in a foreign language she'd never studied—at least until that morning! At a loss to explain, she hoped her momentary discomfort would divert Johnny's attention.

Perplexed, but ever the gentleman, Juan Carlos rose from his chair and removed his jacket, placing it gently over her shoulders. Amanda stood up, and as they embraced she melted into his chest. Gradually, she regained her composure.

"I'm sorry," she said, "but I'm not exactly myself. It's been a long day."

"It's okay, chica mia. You were alone in the dark for a long time. Anyone would be shaken up."

She squeezed Juan Carlos even harder, longing to share with him all she had been through. What he had just said echoed in her mind: *"Alone in the dark."* Regardless of what her future held, Amanda knew one thing.

There was no way she was going to face it by herself.

Drawing back slightly from her rescuer, Amanda offered him her lips. Juan Carlos's response told her everything she needed to know. After a passionate kiss, she took both of his hands in hers and looked deeply into his eyes.

"Johnny, I'm still puzzled about what happened to me this morning. But I know one thing for sure: I must get back into that chamber!"

❧

Meanwhile, in Rome, two men were climbing up a dark stairwell.

"Five stories and no elevator!" grumbled Luc Renard, as he and his bodyguard began the final flight of stairs in the dank, decaying apartment building. It was located just off of the Via della Conciliazione, the main artery leading from the Tiber River to St. Peter's Square.

"May I offer some assistance, sir?" the bodyguard inquired as he saw Renard clutch his side in pain. Both men were perspiring profusely, even though sunset was imminent.

"Don't worry, Enzo. I'll make it on my own. This isn't my first visit here, you know."

Gaining the top floor, the two men approached a lone door halfway down the hall. At Luc's tap on the brass knocker, there was no initial response except for the slight whirring sound of a security camera, which focused on the dark-suited visitors from a niche in the ceiling. Then, with a slight click, the door opened of its own accord.

Luc checked his watch. "Wait for me here, Enzo. No other visitors—and make sure the jet is ready to depart for Mumbai at 9 p.m. sharp."

"Will do, sir."

"By the way, tell them to be certain we have enough rupees on board so we're not delayed by Indian customs."

As Enzo nodded and stood guard beside the doorway, Luc stepped forward into the foyer of Giovanni Genoa's studio.

Peeling off his gold-skinned sunglasses, he paused briefly to admire the Renaissance period paintings in the foyer. They could have been originals, he knew, but Genoa's uncanny skills did not rule out the possibility that the works were ingenious forgeries. Shrugging his shoulders, Luc entered the main studio.

As he recalled, this was an enormous space—in fact, the artist's workplace occupied most of the building's top floor. True to Renaissance practice, a number of Genoa's acolytes were hard at work on a dozen or so easels, putting the finishing touches on the master's latest works. The young men and women were all in their twenties and early thirties.

"What an unexpected pleasure, Luc!" exclaimed the white-haired artist. With a clap of his hands, he dismissed his apprentices, who bowed respectfully in farewell. In short order, Renard and Genoa were alone.

"And what occupies you today, Giovanni?" inquired Luc as he approached the muralist's own easel. The devil was midway through a romantic scene of a young man and woman kissing on a terrace overlooking the sea. Luc noticed that the painter had adopted an unusual perspective: the point of view of a barn owl, perched high on a tree branch and eyeing the young lovers. Had more details been painted in, Luc might have recognized the couple as Amanda and Juan Carlos and the seashore as the Amalfi Coast.

"You are in need of refreshment, Luc?" the host grinned as he gestured toward a decanter on a nearby marble-topped table.

"No, I don't care for wine this evening," Luc replied, wiping a silk handkerchief over his sweating brows. He was still catching his breath from the climb up the stairs. "Tell me, Giovanni, with all the modern buildings in Rome at your disposal, why did you choose one without an elevator?"

The painter, swirling away with his brush on the canvas, absentmindedly replied, "Well, I never use the stairs, you know."

Rolling his eyes, Renard glanced out the window down at the street. In the gathering dusk, he could make out a steady procession of people walking purposefully down the Via della Conciliazione toward St. Peter's Square.

"That's quite a crowd gathering at the Vatican," he remarked. "Is there some special occasion tonight?"

"Nothing special in my opinion," Genoa's tone turned sour. "But for the followers of 'His Holiness,' a real treat. They are gathering for a candlelight vigil, at which the 'Supreme Pontiff' will address the hordes of faithful on the theme of wars and famine in Africa. His speech will follow up on his papal encyclical letter, another of those boring manifestos that the 'Vicar of Christ' feels compelled to issue from time to time."

He spat out the pope's traditional titles with venomous sarcasm.

"He will blame the work of the devil for these evils," the rant continued. "He will appeal to his followers for..."

Having heard several such tirades before from the painter, Luc interrupted him midsentence.

"I have to leave shortly for India," he declared, oblivious of the devil's look of astonishment at the interruption. "Listen, we both know I have you to thank for helping me build my business empire."

Genoa slowly twirled his mustache, knowing full well that Renard had not climbed five flights of stairs to talk about gratitude.

Luc continued, "In return, I've done all you asked, complied with everything since we first met in Chicago. Now, I want something that money can't buy. I want you to keep your promise."

"My promise?" the artist repeated the word with an air of surprise.

"Exactly. You gave me your word you would heal my scars. That orphanage fire was nearly thirty years ago, but the scars remain. The best medical care in the world cannot heal them. Skin grafts, stem cell regeneration, cosmetic surgery—all have failed. Even the experts I visited in Tokyo can't help me."

"What are a few scars? At least you're alive," the devil replied flippantly.

"The scar tissue restricts my mobility, and sometimes the wounds crack open and bleed when I exert myself. See for yourself."

Luc removed his blazer and unbuttoned his slightly bloodstained shirt to reveal a grotesquely lacerated stomach. Despite his general appearance of fitness, he was hardly the picture of health for a man just turning forty.

"I suppose clothes really do make the man," chuckled Genoa, who then feigned concern. "I had no idea of such lasting effects. You must be in considerable pain."

"Yes, but I don't have to be. You have often held out the prospect of a complete cure. I have done everything in my power to safeguard your interests in Ercolano. Now, I ask that you keep your side of the bargain. Please, heal these scars!" Luc's voice thinned perceptibly. His tone was no longer that of a chief executive, but of a supplicant.

"*Pace, pace, caro Luciano,*" murmured the devil. "I will help you when the time is right. But things did not go so well in Ercolano, did they, my friend? All the items in the buried chamber were not, in fact, secured. I was compelled to pay a personal visit to that young woman from the Getty, Amanda James, and reveal my true identity—a revelation that I care to make only in the most extreme circumstances."

"Keeping your identity a secret is not my concern," replied Luc dismissively. "Perhaps you're simply stalling because you don't really have the power to heal me."

Giovanni Genoa reddened with rage. His mouth twitched and his arms whipped the air.

"You insolent urchin! *E tu, ragazzo damnato,* Luc Renard. Perhaps you need a little reminder of the basis for our relationship!"

In an instant, the artist transformed himself. He was no longer the elderly painter, but a tall, athletic man in his early thirties. Luc was looking once more at the fireman who had carried him from the burning orphanage.

"You must never forget," his antagonist continued, as the fireman's physical form slowly morphed back into the stooped figure of the artist, "that you not only owe me your life, but your livelihood and freedom as well. What would become of Renard Enterprises and its founder if I revealed your little secret?"

Luc turned aside momentarily, recalling how the events of that day had changed the course of his life so drastically. He'd never intended to start the fire that burned down the orphanage. He'd been spray-painting graffiti in the basement when the water heater ignited the fumes from the can. It wasn't his fault the janitor had left his oily cleaning rags nearby. Then, weeks later, the hospital visit from his rescuer, who turned out to be no fireman at all. Indeed, the devil was very forthcoming that day, revealing his role in causing the horrifying consequences of Luc's prank. Thus, a twelve-year-old was blackmailed into a bargain that would ultimately enrich and yet enslave him.

"No, I have not forgotten," he replied softly.

"Fine. Now that your memory is refreshed, may I share with you my generosity?" Genoa's voice sweetened as quickly as a chameleon changes color. "You will be cured in short order, but first you must retrieve for me what Amanda James stole from the observatory."

"Did she take the diamonds?"

"Oh, no," said Giovanni with a smile. "Those are for you to keep! In fact, you will have no problem retaining any of the chamber's contents. I will ensure that the Italian judges and attorneys will cooperate, as a result of some compromising circumstances that will befall them. And don't worry about Cardinal Ravatti or Dr. Sforza. I will deal with them personally."

"So what did Amanda take from the chamber?"

"She pilfered a small, ancient pendant, which I will describe to you very specifically. She may not admit to having it in her possession, but she does.

You will either have to steal it from her or charm her out of it, but find a way. When you bring the pendant to me, I will cure your scars permanently."

Luc looked puzzled. "Do you really need me for this? If you appeared to her in the chamber, why didn't you take it from her then?"

The devil broke eye contact with his protégé and gazed out of the westernmost window of his studio, where the apex of the Egyptian obelisk in St. Peter's Square was just visible in the dusk. Clearing his throat, he discharged some opaque mucus into a spittoon. At length, he replied to Luc's question.

"I think it is only fitting that the patient himself should procure the instrument of his healing."

Luc's eyebrows rose as the devil continued.

"I fashioned the pendant long ago. It is a small ceramic tile bearing the image of a serpent. A trace of my own dried blood is smeared onto it, imbuing it with wondrous powers. The tile can fully heal any human malady."

"So I'll be cured the moment I touch this tile?" Luc asked eagerly.

"It's more complicated than that. Actually, you must take great caution *not* to touch the tile with your bare hands. The pendant is so powerful that it will induce delirium—or even death. You must bring it to me so I can safely invoke its effects for you."

Giovanni took a step toward Luc and lowered his voice slightly. "And you should know, since Amanda has touched it, she is almost certain to be suffering from severe delusions. Do not trust what she says about the tile, or anything else."

Silence filled the air for a few moments. Then Luc nodded. "Fine—the pendant in exchange for my cure. But I expect you to uphold your side of the bargain immediately, once I bring you the tile."

"*Va bene, Luca,*" smiled the devil. "Now let's get a breath of air." He gestured toward the rooftop balcony. The ornate doors swung open and the two strolled into the night.

From several blocks away, they could hear the singing in St. Peter's Square, which was now fully illuminated for the Pope's scheduled speech.

"Do their songs bother you?" Luc asked the older man.

"Not in the least, my friend! Their praise of folly simply shows that my work on Earth is never done."

Luc surveyed the scene in silence. His mind was already far from this balcony in Rome. Giovanni had not directly answered his question. Why, he pondered, would the devil not simply repossess the tile from Amanda? Surely the tile's creator would be immune to its negative effects. Perhaps the object had other powers that Genoa was concealing from him. If the devil didn't want Luc to know about them, they must be worth having.

As he gazed out at The Eternal City, Luc Renard promised himself those powers would soon be his.

We invite you to comment about the novel on the book's website:
www.waywardsonnovel.com

TOM POLLACK (C), **JIM ALVES** (L) and **JOHN LOFTUS** (R) are longtime friends, all with professional backgrounds in the investment business. When Tom shared his original idea for *Wayward Son*, Jim and John eagerly jumped on board to assist in crafting the novel. The three reside with their families in Orange County, California.